Waiting for the End of the World

BOOKS BY MADISON SMARTT BELL
The Washington Square Ensemble
Waiting for the End of the World

Waiting for the

End of the World

Madison Smartt Bell

Ticknor & Fields · New York · 1985

For Harmon,

who cooks so hard,
and asks so little credit.

[signature]

Library of Congress Cataloging in Publication Data

Bell, Madison Smartt.
Waiting for the end of the world.

I. Title.
PS3552.E517W35   1985   813'.54   85-2743
ISBN 0-89919-377-3

Printed in the United States of America

V   10   9   8   7   6   5   4   3   2   1

The author is grateful for permission to quote from
the following works:
The Velvet Horn by Andrew Lytle, copyright 1983 Andrew Lytle.
Reprinted by permission of the University of the South.
The Conference of the Birds by Farid ud-Din Attar. Translated
from the French by C. S. Nott, © 1954. Reprinted with
permission of Shambhala Publications, Inc., P.O. Box 308,
Back Bay Annex, Boston, MA 02116.
Beneath the Underdog by Charles Mingus. Copyright © 1971 by
Charles Mingus and Nel King. Reprinted by permission
of Viking Penguin Inc.
Russian Fairy Tales, collected by Aleksandr Afanes'ev, translated
by Norbert Guterman. Copyright 1945 Pantheon Books,
copyright renewed 1973 Random House, Inc. Reprinted by
permission of Pantheon Books, a Division of Random House, Inc.
The Satanic Bible by Amton Szandor LaVey. Copyright © 1969
by Anton Szandor LaVey. Reprinted with permission
of Avon Books, New York.
Soledad Brother: The Prison Letters of George Jackson by George
Jackson. Copyright © 1970 by World Entertainers Ltd. Reprinted
by permission of Bantam Books, Inc. All rights reserved.
Under the Volcano by Malcolm Lowry. Copyright © 1947 by
Malcolm Lowry. Copyright © renewed 1975 by Margerie Lowry.
Reprinted by permission of Harper & Row, Publishers, Inc.
"Song of Renunciation" from *Swan's Island* by Elizabeth Spires.
Copyright © 1982, 1985 by Elizabeth Spires. Reprinted by
permission of Holt, Rinehart and Winston, publishers.

For Beth

Alex Roshuk
Margaret Roshuk
Nina Roshuk
A. T. Roshuk
Neil Cartan
&
Peter Taub

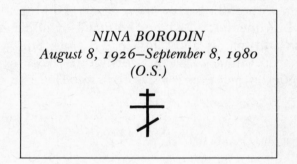

NINA BORODIN
August 8, 1926–September 8, 1980
(O.S.)

Acknowledgments

My thanks to Chip Bloodgood, Tom McGonigle, Nina Ro-shuk, Peter Donald, and the Saint Nicholas Russian Ortho-dox Cathedral, for research assistance crucial to the writing of this book. To the MacDowell Artists' Colony, Chris Barnes in particular, for creating the oasis of time in which much of it was written. To Rick Feist and Mekki Schmidt, who lived patiently with endless typewriter noise. To Meg Blackstone, Deborah Schneider, and Jane Gelfman, for unflagging moral support and lots of good advice. To Cork Smith, who has always been willing to let me work out my own destruction, or salvation, whichever it may prove to be.

Contents

I'm about to let God kill me just so I can meet him.

Fats Navarro according
to Charles Mingus,
Beneath the Underdog

Prologue

July 1982

Bad Weather in Virginia

AT QUARTER TO EIGHT *on a Tuesday morning, a highway patrol car appeared on the vast desert surface of Interstate 81, about ten miles out of Roanoke and southbound for that city. It was hot for the early hour, the air motionless, the sky oppressive. A red-tailed hawk angled over the highway and tilted toward the patrol car in a movement of the most fleeting interest. Profiting from the vagaries of the weather, the hawk rode a thermal straight up into the sky as if on an elevator.*

Inside the car the air conditioning had been turned all the way up by Laurie Henderson, the driver. Henderson was twenty years of age and had quit the AVF after the minimum tour of duty because it was not sufficiently spic-and-span for his taste and because of the oft-arising circumstance in which niggers told him what to do, sometimes making fun of his name in the bargain. Henderson had been initiated into the highway patrol some three weeks previously, and today was resplendent in the tightest possible uniform, high spit-shined boots, silvered sunglasses and a Smokey-the-Bear hat with a metal band, the ends of which hooked outward like the horns of the devil. A rabbit's foot attached to Henderson's key ring swayed near the barrel of a very short shotgun, which rode in a holster between the two seats.

In the passenger seat was Billy Morris, older and heavier than Henderson and far less trim. At fifty-three, Morris ordinarily drove a desk, and his ambition was largely confined to the possibility of early retirement. He now rode shotgun with Henderson because superiors had judged that the latter might benefit from the restraint of a more mature mind. Henderson had joined the highway patrol in the happy expectation that no one there would tell him what to do, but he got along well enough with Morris, who had the sense to leave his name alone.

"Slow down some, boy," Morris said now. "We gots to set a good example to the people of the Commonwealth of Virginia."

Henderson moved his toe on the gas pedal, causing the speedometer to drop from seventy-seven to seventy-five.

"Pappy, I'm hongry," Henderson said. "Pappy, I want me a great big breakfast."

"You on duty, boy."

"It's a Truckstops of America right here at this Cloverdale exit."

"I wouldn't eat there if I was you."

"Now why is that?"

"I know a man that works there and he packs his lunch."

Henderson twitched the wheel and the car plunged down the exit ramp.

"Hey," Morris said.

"I got to get me something," said Henderson. "It's a Burger King just down the road from that truckstop."

He slowed the car and turned on US 117 and the TOA began to slide by the right-hand windows of the car.

"Just a minute," Morris said. "Pull in here."

"I thought you said they don't make nothing fit to eat."

"Pull in. Next to that truck there."

Morris got out of the patrol car and walked to the back of a sixteen-foot chopped van. On its rear doors were a large diamond reading DANGER and a small one reading NRC. The doors were closed with a heavy padlock, above which dangled a numbered tin seal.

"The sonofabitch is sealed anyway," Morris said. He slapped his holster and marched quickly toward the truckstop's door, Henderson following.

The TOA was divided in two sections — a truckers' express line, which was busy, and a tourists' area, which was quiet. Morris took the truckers in at a glance and moved toward the counter in the tourist section, where two people sat: a dumpy man with an adjustable cap on, and a middle-sized kid in his late twenties with dark hair, two stools away from the other. The dark-haired kid sat very still, his left thumb hooked over the edge of the coffee cup before him, the other hand resting at a belt loop, both hands, Henderson noticed, laced with fine white scars. Morris passed him by and sat down next to the older man. He lifted the cap from this man's head and replaced it backwards. The cap was made of blue plastic mesh and had a patch at the front of it which said BAMA FEEDS.

"It's a hot one, ain't it?" Morris said. "Packy?"

"Why, Billy Morris," said the man in the cap. "On the road again."

Morris lifted a glass of iced tea from the counter in front of this Packy and held it to his nose. "Now ain't you hot in this here jacket," he said.

"Cold in here with that air conditioner," Packy said, as Morris's hand chopped toward the jacket's side pocket, met something smooth and hard, went into the pocket, and came out with a pintsize paper sack.

"Now, listen," Morris said. "I want you to go and get on that truck and drive it to where it's supposed to go. I know the route and I am going to follow you and if you stop between here and the state line I will be damn sure you lose your license at the very least."

"I ordered already," Packy said.

"Go."

Packy rose from his stool and abruptly left the building. Morris stood up too, the bottle hooked between his knuckles at its neck. The dark-haired kid was somehow also gone. The two patrolmen turned to leave as a stained and weary waitress arrived with a platter of bacon and eggs.

"Hey," the waitress said. "Somebody got to pay for this."

"Oh hell," Morris said. "I guess I do." He turned to Henderson.

"I guess you got your breakfast."

"Me eat after him?"

"You can see he ain't tetched it."

Twenty minutes later Billy Morris rose from a half-finished cup of coffee to pay the check. He had watched with quiet wonder as Laurie Henderson ate his way through Packy's breakfast and followed it with three plate-sized blueberry pancakes. Walking back to the car, Morris considered and rejected the possibility of tightening his own belt by as much as one notch. He slid into the passenger seat and deposited Packy's bottle in the rear as Henderson started the car.

"That wasn't so bad like you said it would be," Henderson said.

"Sure you got enough, now?"

"Hold me to lunch, I reckon."

"I don't see how you can do it."

"Do what?"

"Eat that way and not get fat."

"I don't eat bread."

"Now what do you think pancakes are?" Morris shook his head and looked out the window.

"Where to?" Henderson said.

"Back north. We gone follow that sonofabitch Packy and make sure he does the right thing."

"Oh yeah. What was all that anyway?" said Henderson.

"That was Packy, and Packy is what's wrong with the unions. Or maybe not. But they ought to be able to find him something to do beside drive them bombs."

"Bombs?"

"Well, it ain't supposed to be. But just a little piece of what's on that truck would make you a nice little bomb."

"That a fact?"

"It is. That is also why he ain't supposed to stop that truck for nothing or nobody, and he ain't supposed to drink while he drives it neither."

Henderson grunted and slid down in his seat. The car ate up several miles of highway with no exchange of words inside of it.

"Though he ain't such a bad feller, old Packy," Morris eventually said. *"Just a bit too sociable for that job if you ask me. He likes to stop and have a couple. And I wouldn't quite put it past him to pick up a hitchhiker."*

"Ah well," Henderson said, in tones of no particular interest. A bend appeared in the road and Henderson straightened it out by slopping across both lanes, almost scraping the concrete divider.

"Watch that," Morris said. *"Hey."* His attention was drawn to a passing patch of blue on the right shoulder. Henderson turned toward him.

"We got to go back," Morris said. *"I want to check on something."*

Henderson increased speed slightly, then stabbed the brake and cut the wheel hard left. The car rose over the divider, reversed directions in midair and landed without significant loss of momentum.

"Where you want it?" Henderson said to Morris, who was holding his hat down with one hand.

"*I want it stopped, and let me tell you something, the next time you try such a jackass trick as that I'm gone take a gun and kill you.*"

Henderson shrugged and let the car coast to a stop on the shoulder. Morris got out, crossed behind the rear of the car, and walked to the median. From the smell of the air the weather seemed more definitely inclined toward rain. A short, cold burst of wind lifted the blue cap from the far side of the roadbed and carried it toward where Morris was standing. When Henderson reached him he had it in his hand and was inspecting the patch.

Morris crossed the next two lanes and peered over the west embankment. Twenty feet down its slope Packy lay facedown with one arm twisted in an unnatural fashion around a scrubby bush; he was not moving, and the grass was discolored along the path of his apparent slide.

"*Christ Almighty,*" Henderson said, as he stepped onto the shoulder and caught this view.

"*Yeah,*" Morris said. "*Okay, cowboy, get down there and see how dead he is.*"

He glanced at the cap in his hand and let it fall. He watched the uneasy progress of Henderson down the embankment. Henderson took Packy by the left shoulder and lifted him partly up. Packy's underside was very bloody and there was a wide and seemingly deep gash in his rib cage.

"*Pretty dead,*" Henderson said.

"*Better not move him then,*" said Morris. Henderson rose and arched his back and stared at the fingers of the hand that had touched Packy's dead shoulder. *How's that million-dollar breakfast riding,* Morris thought, but kept this to himself.

"*Goddamn,*" Morris said. "*He ought to had his gun on him. Laurie, check in the back of his belt and see if you don't find a Browning.*"

Henderson turned up the back of Packy's coat.

"*Empty holster,*" he said.

"*Yeah,*" Morris said. "*That's a fine place to hide one, all right. Except you can't get at it if you're sitting down.*"

He turned a little away from the ditch and looked toward the eastern sky, which was empurpled and veined with silent lightning here and there.

"*What we gone do?*" Henderson called to him.

"I'd say a prayer if you know one," Morris said.

Grown suddenly cold, he hugged himself at the elbows and turned round and round, hoping to see the truck somewhere. He thought first speculatively and then with firm intention of the pint he had dropped in the back of the car. The truck was absolutely nowhere to be seen, was gone in the thickening air.

Part I

The Unicorn

I shall live in this world.
I shall live in this world
But not love it.

Elizabeth Spires,
"Song of Renunciation"

1

Bedford Avenue

RECENT RAIN shimmered on the sidewalk, on Broadway, Brooklyn, in early morning and before the heat. From the doorway of a tenement at the corner of Berry Street issued a boy astride a plastic horse with blue head, yellow saddle, and black wheels. Horse and rider fumbled down the stairway to the street with a tin wagon clattering behind, the wagon rust-flecked and frozen-wheeled and hitched with a cluster of old twine which passed from its handle through a jagged hole in the hindquarters of the horse. At the foot of the stairs the boy paused and then swung the horse toward Broadway. House keys were pinned to the plastic pommel of his saddle, for the boy lacked a whole pocket in the pair of shorts which was all he wore.

The rider moved east on Broadway, propelling his horse with bare feet, his feet distinguishing by instinct between the glittering of fresh raindrops and the sheen of the triangles of broken glass which littered the sidewalk. The wagon, its rear wheels not turning, scraped over the concrete. Behind this caravan a wild dog pack appeared, led by a dissolute German shepherd with a lame front leg. The pack made a formal pass at the door of the Broadway Diner, where a large man in white appeared like a cuckoo out of a clock, slinging dishwater. The lead dog avoided the splash with casual ease and moved the pack along Broadway. The dogs loped past the boy without one head turning to inspect him. The boy followed them more slowly, passing down the block and out of sight.

Within the half hour he was returning home, horse moving briskly, wagon loaded with prizes from the street: a square of mirror, barely chipped; four tapered dowels from an abandoned bedstead; a Superball, still live. On the north side of Broadway, Larkin was sitting in the doorway of his building, his first cup of coffee cradled in his hands, watching sunrise diffuse light along the street. He saw the boy guide his horse down Bedford Avenue and turn the corner, making good time. Larkin yawned and, opening his eyes again, he noticed that the boy had begun to miss beats with one leg, his left. The boy crossed his leg over his saddle and scrutinized the sole of his foot, went on, flinched, and stopped again. Glass in the foot, Larkin thought, wiping his eyes once more. The boy abandoned his horse and went at a queer fast limp toward the Berry Street tenement, already setting up a howl for mother.

Larkin's newly cleared eyes focused on the keys pinned to the plastic horse. Mentally he debated his policy of noninterference, then set his coffee on the doorsill and crossed the street. He took the horse by its plastic ear and went awkwardly stooping after the boy. Around the corner he could see him being received by a bag-shaped woman in a pink print dress.

Larkin stopped and straightened up and indicated the horse with its disregarded cargo. The woman spoke to him in Spanish, revealing snaggle teeth and no meaning he could discern.

"The keys," Larkin said.

The woman spoke again more rapidly, jerking one hand. The other held the boy tightly by his upper arm. Larkin had no Spanish.

"No habla," Larkin said. "No se habla." He bent and shook the key ring against the horse, making noise. The woman made a fast move for the keys and Larkin went away. Back on Bedford Avenue a small, unlucky-looking mouse was contemplating his coffee from a distance of inches, and Larkin flushed it into the street. He wondered if the boy would be whipped or comforted or both; so early in the morning, Larkin thought, and the world has already found room to accommodate this one small catastrophe known to me.

Some days later the boy was seen again in the street by Larkin, who guessed him age five or six. The boy appeared in high spirits and was indeed able to smash Larkin's third-floor window with the found Superball, thus making Larkin's own floor a hazard. Larkin returned the ball without resentment, though he was too afflicted with lassitude to sweep. He drew an imaginary semicircle around the broken glass and began spending more time on the roof.

Rooftop, Larkin studied the changing shades and values of the air. He lay faceup, four stories removed from the immediate swelter of the street, his horizon bounded on all sides only by the atmosphere. These were the last wasted days of August, and the sky more often than not was clear. Larkin lay for unnumbered hours, regarding its deep blue transparency.

Motionless and almost unblinking, Larkin cushioned his head on his hands. His knuckles and heels sank gently into the heat-softened tar of the roof, but his mind was parted from such sensations. Empty air spread over him in colors modulated by the passage of the sun. In the earliest hours of morning this air was flooded with mist which rose from the river three blocks distant. Sunrise brought spears of yellow light arching from the east, puncturing the mist and evaporating it. With absolute concentration, Larkin believed that he could see the individual particles of suspended water destroyed by the power of the light, and he could feel this process also in the dew drops on his face and hands which were the last to go. When all the mist was burned away, Larkin's vision was rejoined with the upper air.

With full day the sun curved to the south, out of Larkin's line of direct sight. The sky's color deepened across turquoise into richer blues, while Larkin stayed transfixed beneath it, imitating the thorough stillness which was all that he could see. Time measured itself by no seen motion but only in some few sounds which came in series to his ears: a raised voice or loud radio, a muted backfire from the street, the susurrus of trains coming down over the Williamsburg Bridge behind his building. The appearance of a bird or a drift of clouds irritated Larkin, who wanted only to watch the air perpetually blending into itself — condensation, evaporation, events without beginning or end. In the absence of any other visual fixture the dots coursing across his own eyeballs were sometimes capable of distracting him. On reasonable grounds he suspected the air itself to be subtly poisoned and he waited for some clear sign of this fact to appear.

At evening the sun was crushed against the western horizon and all its light appeared stained with blood. Larkin renewed contact with his body and rose smoothly to his feet. The sun was jammed into the Manhattan skyline as if caught in a row of broken teeth, and to Larkin the earth appeared to be tilted. He looked south to see the roofs and higher walls of Brooklyn flaring sharply into orange, then shifted his glance to the river, now dappled with misleading rose-colored light. Down on the Manhattan and Brooklyn bridges the lamps were snapping alight like beads dropping onto a string. After a long full day of nothing, here was too much something. Larkin placed his hands over his eyes and caused it all to disappear into a quiet and furry darkness.

Apart from a little necessary eating, this was an average day for Larkin, in August 1982.

Wrapped in his well-practiced solitude, Larkin went into the street. He walked quickly south on Bedford Avenue with his eyes bent on the surface of the pavement. The asphalt was embedded with many a lost or discarded thing. Larkin zigzagged across the street, stalking a pattern of bottle caps like a bored crow, moving from one minute coincidence to the next. Because there had been a cold snap he wore a long dull-colored raincoat which guttered around his ankles in the persistent wind.

Four-story row houses lined the street on either side. Laundry wreathed the fire escapes of the few buildings that were not empty and sealed, but there were no faces at the windows, which were closed against the unseasonable cold. Larkin crossed the next street and turned left. He paused for a moment to inspect a black skull-and-crossbones drawn on a tenement wall. The legend beneath it was familiar to him: IF YOU DONT LIVE HERE DONT HANG OUT. Larkin was not tempted to linger.

He went east on Division Street and crossed a star-shaped intersection to reach a sizeable concrete triangle designated by a signboard as LOUISE SOBEL PARK. Sacred to the memory of Louise Sobel were three or four wasted trees and up to twenty concrete benches crowded together at nonsensical angles. Larkin sat down on one of these, first scraping away a pile of sacks and bottles with the side of his shoe. On the bench nearest him lay a wino snoring irregularly, with a knit hat pulled down to his upper lip.

Turning away, Larkin frisked his raincoat pockets for cigarettes or money and found neither. He removed his seat to another bench at the southeast vertex of Louise Sobel Park, from which Lee Avenue angled off at forty-five degrees into the territory of the mad Jews. Farther down, black-coated, shawled, and bearded figures floated through the limbo of their mystic world. This was someone else's dream. Larkin knew their rituals only from the changes in their movements on the street. He moved again, to a bench beneath a leafless sapling whose stunted limbs were festooned with bicycle tires.

Larkin rested the nape of his neck on the bench's top rail and stared into the meager heart of the bicycle tree. He credited Louise Sobel, whoever she may have been, with some sense of either humor or perversity. The park was paved up to the very bark of the trees and its surface was harder than the sidewalk or the street. But only in Louise Sobel Park could a tree, that incomparable work of God, grow bicycle tires all over itself.

A spatter of cold rain ended Larkin's rapture in the wonders of the world. He went quickly down Havemeyer Street with his head tucked into the collar of his coat. On South

Eighth Street he entered a bodega and traded a subway token he had found in his watch pocket for five Marlboros and
three dimes. He returned to Bedford Avenue with his hands
clasped before him, sheltering the cigarettes from the rain.

In the cool of an evening Larkin walked north on Berry Street.
His feet took impressions from the sidewalk through the thin
soles of his shoes. He passed a school and a storm fence hung
over with vines and doubled over to Wythe Avenue. Here
the Esquire Shoe Polish factory raised a sheer gray wall stories above the other buildings on the block. Larkin walked
through the factory's doorless entrance and picked up a short
length of pipe he had hidden in a ruin of plaster the last time
he had been in that place.

The stairs of the vacated Esquire factory rose through the
middle of the building, flanked on either side by enormous
high-ceilinged lofts. Little was left in these spaces except for
the dank-smelling air. On a series of previous visits Larkin
had combed every floor for any worthwhile bits of machinery
that might still be drifting around in the dimness, but all that
remained was not only bolted down but in most cases welded
too. Larkin kept to the stairwell, mounting toward the roof.
The empty chambers returned a twofold echo to his steps,
and at every landing he stopped to let it die, listening.

Despite the pipe he always carried, he had never found the
least stirring of human life inside the place. The only signs
of other prowlers were a few piles of cans so ancient with rust
that their labels could no longer be discerned. Larkin moved
at his ease in the factory now, lugging his pipe and pausing
to listen from habit alone.

The roof of the Esquire factory was wide, much cluttered
with assorted rubble, and surfaced with thick bubbly asphalt.
Moving toward the eastern balustrade, Larkin gave some attention to where he put his feet, since there were holes in the
roof where one might lose a leg. He leaned against the re-
taining wall and lit a cigarette, hands cupped against the wind
which came down hard from the shelterless sky. The flat roofs
of Brooklyn spread out far below him, beyond all plausible

geometry. The horizon was broken by two checkered water towers, flanked by the night's first stars and the dim figure of a crescent moon.

Larkin moved around the edge of the roof and skirted the stairwell. The wind had enough bite to chill his face. To the south he could see a long line of bridges; on the nearest a subway crawled like a bright centipede. He skipped to the next windbreak, the hutch over the elevator shaft. The elevator was long out of service and its cables hung motionless to the ground floor. Larkin lit a match and dropped it down the shaft, watching its decline into the dark. Then he moved away from the shaft housing and went to the western wall.

Far across the river the towers of Manhattan rose behind a dull brown line of project houses fronting on the water. The city skyline was backlit and tinged with red and gold by the retreating light of the sun. Larkin stood exposed to the wind, which plastered his ears to the side of his head. He stared at the enchanted city, which he well knew to be unreachable. More elusive than a simple mirage, it did not only recede before him but hid behind him and on either side, whenever he tried to enter it. However, this was reality, one of fifty-seven different kinds of decoration, according to the Hindus. Larkin was an apostle of half a dozen strange religions and believed them all. A careless sound behind him made him turn.

He raised his hands above the wall and the wind brought a shower of sparks from his cigarette, distractingly pretty in the deepening darkness, in which Larkin could see several thick shadows moving his way. He flicked the cigarette laterally along the wall and sidled in the opposite direction. The shadows wore leather vests with knee-length fringes, which Larkin remembered as the colors of a gang he'd never seen north of Division Street before, not that it mattered now.

He had no confidence in the pipe against such numbers. Larkin slipped softly toward the elevator shaft and when he had reached it he went behind the housing, dropped to his knees and crawled. He could hear a hiss of voices but it came no nearer. The shadows had moved away from the stairwell. When Larkin reached it, it was empty, and he left the building unhindered.

Toward the end of the month there was constant wind. It stood up from the river like a live thing, stretching out urgently to the east. This wind was air with a purpose. It crossed the vacant space intervening between the river and Larkin's roof to nag at his hair and clothing where he lay. Briefly disturbed by this change in his state, Larkin learned to conceive of himself as a stick or stone impervious to such harrying along its edges. Still the wind succeeded in altering things; it hurried Larkin's tranquil sky ahead of it.

He himself remained still while the wind hastened all around him. The sky in these days was fractured by motion; unfamiliar aircraft scored lines on its surface which were irregularly crossed by pigeons and the odd gull lost from the sea. Larkin was ill at ease in the new conditions. The air itself was shattered and seemed on the point of departure and in the flurry of its motion it could no longer capture light; fragmentary color rushed through it and was gone. Larkin wished for the wind to arrest itself for his inspection, but it afforded no visible figure to his eye.

At twilight Larkin moved west on South Fourth Street, in the long shadow of the ramp to the bridge. His shoulders brushed the huge stones of the ramp whenever he veered to avoid obstructions on the sidewalk. Ahead of him the wall defined a long and dreary prospect toward the river. The street was empty where he walked, though the wall returned echoes from busier zones to the north.

At Driggs Street the stone ramp soared away into a steel elevation, and Larkin turned left into the space where the wall had been, meaning to go back up to Broadway. A crackle of hot Spanish stopped him in the shadows under the bridge; he was about to blunder into a quarrel. There in the bright opening where the pedestrian walkway rose toward the light, a woman and a man were arguing. The girl (Larkin guessed her under twenty) was doing all the talking. She snapped her head from side to side in the vigor of her discourse; rich black hair hissed around her head; her long-nailed fingers sliced at the air. She left the man with some fast and final denunciation and marched directly at Larkin, who by instinct crowded closer to the wall. The girl shot a glance his way that might have cracked the stones behind him, then stalked away toward the river.

Larkin followed her with a glance of admiration, for she was most certainly beautiful, tall and long-legged and taut with her anger. She passed him, balanced with a perfect grace on the impossible high heels that the chiquitas of the neighborhood loved to wear, and didn't miss a single step as she slammed her way across Fourth Street.

Larkin held one eye on the other man until he undid himself from whatever she'd said and shrugged off up to Broadway. Then Larkin put his head back into Fourth Street, but the girl had vanished. Desultorily, he followed the path she had taken, dragging his fingers along the storm fence that here replaced the stones. At the end of the next block there was a wrecked truck behind the fence, and Larkin stopped to examine the stuffed animal that crouched on its hood. The species of this creature was uncertain. Its eyes had been thumbed out, it had no recognizable shape, and its only clear feature was its fangs, with the lips drawn back around them in a snarl. That the beast had eaten the beauty seemed unlikely, but Larkin couldn't have said for sure.

Huddled in his raincoat, Larkin daily walked the frontiers he conceived as his: Broadway east to Marcy Avenue, Marcy north to Grand, Grand west to Kent Avenue and the waterfront, Kent east to Havemeyer Street — a route shaped in an ingrown spiral which would finally bring him home. On Bedford Avenue a pathway of blue hyphens had been painted down the street, as guidance to whom or what Larkin didn't know, and wouldn't cross his borders to find out. From his rooftop the blue dashes seemed a perforation, as if the whole botched neighborhood was prepared to be torn off and discarded by some almighty hand, a power discontent with its imperfection. Which fancy, Larkin knew, was an unhealthy symptom; he knew the paths of paranoia as well as he knew the streets.

But Larkin had no use for walking on a line; his walks curled through the neighborhood like the slow process of decay. Buildings crumbled before and behind him; sometimes rumor gave out that lives had been lost too. Returning to his own corner, Larkin could stand and see the shimmering towers of the World Trade Center framed by the crumpled buildings farther down the block, the bright towers not just across the river but clearly in some other, hallucinatory world.

It was soothing to Larkin to watch the structure of Williamsburg, Brooklyn, sliding off the angle of the world. Down by the stacks of the shipyards, corrosive East River water lapped at the shoreline, gaining slow fractions of inches. Larkin stood with his hands clutching chain-link fence, pressing himself into the river wind. It was twilight; through the diamond links he could see the dim shape of a freighter hulking in black water. A snarl of razor ribbon crawled along the fence's top, protecting the boat from human predators, though not, Larkin thought, from other, subtler threats. All borders were most surely breaking down: the ship's hull dissolving slowly in the water, faces of buildings parting under the force of the acid air, even the pavement splintered by the roots of the ubiquitous and indestructible heaven tree. Larkin could no longer tell where the world left off and he began. His thoughts were ready to dance away and leave his fingers tangled in the fence. He reclined his cheek against the cool chain links and recalled a roasted pig's head, seen leering through a window down on Broadway, no more obviously an object than an image on the glass or on the eye.

August succeeded by September, the weather continued cold and rainy. Larkin poked his nose out on the roof and saw a spiral of smoke somewhere to the north, lit weirdly from below as it probed through the fog toward the night sky. He made a quick run down to Driggs Street and began climbing the walkway to the bridge. The light drizzle had evidently discouraged other pedestrians and Larkin had the ascending corridor to himself. He went rapidly up the grade. Clearing the top of the walls around the ramp, he could look back south onto the roof of his own building, could see the occasional umbrella mushrooming down his street. Where the bridge turned from stone to steel, the walkway turned a corner away from the tracks and here Larkin moved up a gentler slope.

He climbed a few yards more to the bridge's first tower, where a little stone tollbooth perched at the edge of the walk. This turret was locked and washed over with graffiti, but the balcony wrapping around it was open. Larkin edged cautiously around each corner, wary of anyone who might have got there first, but the balcony was empty. From the north side of the turret he spotted the fire, a warehouse near the edge of Greenpoint, two blocks off the river. The building was burning at both ends and the middle, in the high style of Williamsburg arson. Far away to the north Larkin saw a fire truck angling back and forth, getting no closer to the fire, the thin shriek of its siren climbing toward him like a voice in a half-remembered nightmare.

Returning along Broadway, Larkin stopped near the smoked-cheese factory, having noticed two amorphous figures just before him, one stooping over the other, which lay prone on the sidewalk. It was the girl from the bridge, that other time. One of her heels had slipped out of its incredible shoe and the shoe was trailing her foot by its toe. The girl lay face down with her hair pooling in the triangle of her arms.

The man rose from his bent position and looked about himself. Larkin was not sure he recognized the man, was not at all sure what he was doing, what was going on. Larkin faded closer to the wall. The man's glance rotated through him without reaction. Larkin folded his arms, gripped his elbows hard. As he had long suspected, he had become invisible.

The man took the girl by her shoulders and lifted her to

some semblance of a standing posture. When he released her she revolved bonelessly around her twisted shoe, her hair hanging inert across her face, and collapsed to the sidewalk again. Nothing broke her fall. She did not make a sound, other than slightly husky breathing. The man raised his hands palms up and twisted his head a quarter turn toward Larkin, as though he might be looking at him out of the side of his left ear. The girl rested on the narrow edges of her arms, breathing audibly.

"Get up," the man said. "Get up, bitch, everybody looking at you."

Restored to human substance by these words, Larkin took one noisy step forward. The man scooped the girl up with an angry motion and carried her, over his shoulder, across the street. There he slung her body through the side door of a battered Econoline van. The carapace of a Volkswagen had been welded to the top of this van, like a gun turret. The van itself was rusty red and the turret was a hideous green, so that the whole ensemble resembled an infected wound. The man jumped into the driver's seat, ground the engine alive, and roared down Broadway. The van tilted around a corner onto Kent Avenue; Larkin heard it howling through silence toward the Navy Yard.

He drifted over to Kent Avenue himself, but turned the other way on reaching the corner. Walking on the west side of the street, he passed under the blank fortressed warehouses and the high steel gates that closed off the waterfront. At Grand Street there was a break in the fortifications and Larkin went over a gravelled surface into a park of sorts, where a few scattered benches and picnic tables tilted hopelessly toward the dark river. He passed the benches by and climbed a pile of large boulders that rose from the East River water. On the highest stone he stood erect, his feet curved to its surface through the bottoms of his shoes.

There was not the slightest hint of a breeze. A fearful reek of dead fish steamed up between the gaps in the stones below Larkin's position, where the poisonous eddies of the river turned endlessly upon themselves in the darkness. The bass line from some sort of dance music was coming across the flat black surface of the river from the south. Larkin turned toward the bridge, where the arc lights were bleeding down softly into the glossy water.

The music came nearer and turned treble and clear. The party boat emerged from the hood of the bridge and found the center of the river. Larkin could see stick figures jerking back and forth against a glow of fluorescent light as the boat drew even with him. He recalled a disaster story he had once read or heard. A gallon wine jug had come crashing down into one of these boats, most likely from the bridge but purely out of nowhere as far as the passengers were concerned. The bottle shattered on the boat's railing and bloomed accelerating needles of glass into a group of foreign tourists idling there. Their faces were burst open and their blood arched into the reflections of the river; it was daylight at the time. One, if Larkin remembered right, had lost an eye. They had, of course, no warning. It was only the devil, just telling them hello. Larkin, who had briefly closed his eyes around this image, opened them again. The boat he was watching now proceeded upriver without incident, out of earshot, out of sight.

On the chill morning of another day, Larkin walked aimlessly down Broadway, pausing at the window of the Flor di Oro Restaurant and Bakery at the corner of Havemeyer. A devil's brew of pork and plantain bubbled behind the steamy window of the restaurant, adjacent to a five-tier wedding cake which had gone unclaimed for an age. The cake was crumbling like tired concrete and the figure of the bride had fallen down a gully to the third layer, where she lay facedown in a crust of icing. The black-suited groom turned slightly askew on top of the cake; he appeared to be looking for something. Beyond, a single customer sat at the counter scooping up a plate of rice and beans.

Larkin was hungry, but too listless to eat. He drifted away from the Flor di Oro and walked to the north, passing under the tubular hull of the Brooklyn-Queens Expressway, with cars droning over it, going elsewhere. Near the base of the bridge he entered a small park and stood between two cement pavilions with their rafters collapsing and their roofs torn away. Human feces appeared here and there among the more ordinary litter that covered the concrete surface on which Larkin walked. In the center of the park was a large equestrian bronze of Washington, turned a nacreous green by the weather. The horse's head drooped slightly, while Washington himself stared levelly through the trestles of the expressway toward the half-ruined buildings beyond. A chiselled inscription on the pedestal, VALLEY FORGE, was barely legible beneath layers of spray-painted gang slogans, foreign as Arabic. A flight of pigeons whirled elliptically around Washington's cockade.

Larkin vaulted to the top of the pedestal, balancing himself against the horse's cold metal flank. On one blank wall of the short block opposite the park three painted figures were frozen in some mortal struggle; one flourished a large sword above the others. Larkin rang the bronze with his knuckles and the birds deserted Washington's hat to fly to the dome of the building on the corner, a bank that had been converted to a church. The tripled crooked cross of Russian Orthodoxy had been affixed to the top of the dome, and the sight of this token gave Larkin a queer itching discomfort of mind. He heard the opening door of the neighboring spice factory, around the corner and out of his sight, and the chill air was suddenly shot through with cinnamon and clove, as sweet or sweeter than the smell which the faithful claim must emanate from the remains of a dead saint.

An hour past nightfall Larkin hovered in the door letting onto his fire escape, it being too cold for the roof. Bedford Avenue ran across Broadway and past it to the south, a dark closed corridor, while above it the overcast sky reflected the sullen glow of the city. At the horizon's edge the lamps of cars beetled across the Brooklyn Bridge, silent in their distance. Nearer, down to Larkin's right, a jungle drumbeat pounded from the doors of the Vista del Mar, where the solvent youth of the neighborhood were beginning to gather.

Larkin watched vague figures passing through isolated cones of street light along Broadway. Car doors banged up and down the street, and an occasional clear phrase floated up to him, disconnected from its sense and context. Two teen-aged boys closed in on the doors of the Berry Street tenement, wielding indelible markers. Larkin saw hieroglyphs growing on the glass, outlined sharply by the light of the hallway behind.

He watched; a stranger appeared from around the corner, short and squat with a smooth oval trunk that reminded Larkin of a turtle's shell, devoid of hips or neck. The human turtle eddied up behind the shadows on the steps and waited very quietly for them to finish. The boys turned, one of them began to form a mocking phrase, and the stranger's arm flicked out idly at waist height. The one who had been speaking bowed to his toes, his insult lost in a sudden expiration of breath, and the stranger's arm stabbed toward the other, who jumped sideways off the steps. A little cloud of brick dust puffed from the wall, and Larkin could now see that the stranger held a length of broomstick at the end of his stubby arm, a weighted club, he would guess, from the effect. The escaped boy darted east toward the sheltering dark, and the stranger turned back to the other, raising him to an upright position with a clout from the back of his empty hand. He then gave the broomstick a military twirl, laid it to rest in his armpit, and disappeared around the corner from where he had first come. The beaten boy's legs melted under him; he slipped from the steps and curled beside the trash cans on the sidewalk. Cursing himself for an interfering fool, Larkin ran down his stairs, wondering if the boy were not already beyond salvage. But by the time he reached the street the second one had returned and was raising the other to his feet. Larkin watched the pair drag painfully away from the hallway's circle of light, then crossed Broadway diagonally to the tenement steps. A dwindling trail of vermilion dots marked the boys' progress toward wherever they were bound. The turtlish man came back around the corner and favored Larkin with a bright and placid smile. He mounted the steps and began to scrub at the graffiti with a rag and kerosene.

New blood.

*

Between Saturday night and Sunday morning, Larkin flung himself back and forth between the walls of his room. There was a queer itch at the top of his head, which seemed an omen of some catastrophe. Larkin smelled smoke, fire, trouble. At last he snatched his shoes and keys and headed for the street, hoping to walk off his restlessness.

Outside there was next to nothing going on. The bartender was locking the doors of the Vista del Mar, and on the stoop of the club a few late customers were finishing their last joints of the evening. Larkin tasted trails of their smoke as he passed them, bound north. At the corner of Third a few street savages stood immobile before a trash-can fire. Larkin passed them on the far side of the street and went on to Grand, where he stopped at the corner. To the west a patrol car was stopped in front of the door of the Warsaw Bakery. Two heavy-jacketed cops leaned on the car, talking in low voices, steam rising from their lidded coffee cups.

Larkin walked west to Berry Street, turned again, and headed home. A wave of exhaustion went entirely through him, dampening his anxious desire to scratch the inside of his head. If he could preserve this fatigue until he reached his bed, Larkin believed that perhaps he might sleep. Though his feet dragged like bricks, Larkin forced himself to hurry. He walked head downward, observing almost nothing at all.

At Broadway Larkin threw himself around the corner, hastening toward Bedford Avenue and sleep. A couple standing very quietly beside the stairs of the Berry Street tenement drew just the slightest flicker of his interest. He reached his door, unlocked it, let his eyes close as he trudged up the stairs. The door to his room closed behind him of its own weight and Larkin dropped his keys on the floor.

The rattle of the keys abraded all of Larkin's senses and woke him up completely. His head lit up again with the same groundless foreboding. Larkin gnashed his teeth with frustration and combed his mind for the source, which he found surprisingly quickly. The girl standing in the pair by the tenement was the one from the bridge and the collapse on

Broadway, that same dark endangered beauty. The couple had been much too silent, much too still. It was this, their nothing-going-on, that Larkin suddenly distrusted. As the thought struck him, the street outside erupted into screams. Larkin plunged down his stairs and hit the pavement at a dead run.

Across the street the girl rolled on her back, tumbled across the hood of a parked car. Her arms were flung back over her head, drawing up her blouse to expose her diaphragm, which contracted at a machine-gun rate. Her mouth was thrown so far open that her jaws appeared to be unhinged; her tongue thrust upward like a sword. The screaming was continuous, high and pure.

There were two men near her now and as Larkin reached the group one of them put his hand on her, not too roughly, on her arm. The girl sprang immediately up, clawing blindly before her, and propelled the two men into the middle of the street. There seemed to be words entangled in her screaming now, but Larkin couldn't make them out. The power and clarity of the screams did not diminish for an instant.

Larkin moved into the street and placed himself between the girl and the two men, facing the girl. Her eyes were open but she did not seem to notice him. She screamed on, not at Larkin but around him, with all the intensity of possession. Larkin assumed a boxer's stance, with his fists held tight to his face to protect himself from scratches. The girl continued to yowl like a tortured cat.

Larkin looked over her head, toward the entrance of the tenement. An elderly man dashed out of the glass doors. For no reason at all Larkin noticed that he was very flashily dressed. The old man had on patent leather shoes and the points of his mustache were waxed. He stopped beside the girl and began to chatter to her in hysterical Spanish. One of the men behind Larkin swung over his shoulder and hit the old man in the cheek.

Larkin extended his fists like scoops, enclosing the old man and the girl. Walking forward, he began to herd them toward the tenement's doorway. The old man's eyes locked onto Larkin's for an instant.

"Look," he said, very slowly and distinctly. "Behind you. There is a gun."

Larkin jerked his head involuntarily around. Behind him the gangrenous Econoline van was parked at the corner; he had not noticed it before. There was indeed something like a gun barrel slanting out of the turret on top. Without marking the positions of the two men, Larkin turned back to the old man and girl and went on maneuvering them toward the door. A sensitive spot manifested itself between the tendons of his neck, right at the base of his skull, where he imagined the bullet would enter. The old man and the girl back-pedalled up the stairs. Larkin followed them through the door and stood facing them in the tiny hallway, with his arms still stuck out before him like the cowcatcher on a train. Noticing this, he dropped his hands and slumped into the buzzer plate, exhaling for the first time in a while.

The girl had stopped screaming somewhere along the way. She stood with her back to Larkin, engaging the old man in an urgent but apparently calm conversation. The old man looked over her shoulder, giving Larkin a glance of the purest good will. He offered no more English, however. Larkin left the hallway and walked out onto the sidewalk. The two men were standing quietly by the van, but Larkin did not look at them. He went across the street with his shoulders sagging, climbed the stairs, picked up his keys from the floor, and locked himself in. His sense of impending disaster seemed wholly defused. Larkin strolled easily to his window and stood looking back down on Broadway.

The two men still rested by the open side door of the van. Both had lit cigarettes and they were passing a tall can of beer between them. Larkin watched them dully for perhaps fifteen minutes, not giving them much thought. Then the door of the tenement popped open, and Larkin caught a burst of reflection from its glass. The girl walked out and crossed the street, her high heels clicking loudly on the pavement. Her head was bowed in evident hopelessness; Larkin couldn't see her face. The two men shifted to receive her. One climbed behind the wheel of the van. The other drew her into the side door, gripping her wrists tightly, holding her hands close together, in front of her.

Larkin whirled away from the window and crouched, facing the wall. He snapped both his fists out hard and fast at the wall, first the right and then the left. Perfect punches: his knuckles barely grazed the paint bubbles on the surface of the brick. Larkin held his position. A single cord of tension ran through his shoulders, down his spine to the slight bow of his legs. The shadows of his own hands reached toward him from the wall.

Larkin felt perilously close to the borderline. Only when the slowly accruing pain of his stance became unbearable did he permit himself to relax. He drew his hands slowly away from the wall and flexed his fingers outward, staring at the tracery of white scars that crisscrossed all over the backs of his hands, like the seams of poorly made gloves. In the faint light leaking in from the window, he perused the fine web of scars as though it were a hieroglyph which might after long and detailed study surrender some kind of meaning. At last he let his hands drop to his hips.

"Oh Hell," Larkin said aloud. The words bounced strangely in the air of the empty room. "I've been wasting my time." He took an aimless turn around the room and pitched himself at a mattress on the floor. For a moment he lay on his face, then he rolled wearily onto his back, not troubling to cover himself. Sleep would most probably refuse him this night, as on so many others. Larkin lay with his eyes open and bent on the ceiling, probing his internal darkness, negotiating another evil city of the mind.

2
Larkin

CLARENCE DMITRI LARKIN was born on April 1, 1954, in
Bellevue Hospital, New York City. The precise date of his
birth, like the name he received, was briefly a matter of con-
troversy. Mrs. Larkin, who chose "Clarence" for its pronounced English flavor, lived in fear of American supersti-
tion and insisted that the child's birth be reckoned from March
31, when she began labor, instead of the moment after midnight when the boy was delivered. Mr. Larkin, who wasted
much argument to the effect that his son was likely to be no
less miserable as a "Clare" than as a "Mitya," did not object
to fathering an April fool, a term which in any case was
meaningless to him.

Infant Larkin, pronounced normal and healthy by all authorities at Bellevue, was removed from that institution to
the domicile of his parents in Stuyvesant Town, at the east
end of 14th Street, in the island of Manhattan. A large and
placid baby, Larkin cried seldom, was lenient on the point of
small-hour feedings. Periodic excursions along 14th Street,
in a stroller propelled by his mother, seemed a matter of
complete indifference to him. Larkin learned to walk and
talk on schedule, though he didn't have a lot to say for himself. He showed no disposition to blunder off the small balcony of the apartment which the Larkins occupied on the
eighteenth floor of their Stuyvesant Town tower — a two-
bedroom unit identical to the hundreds of others that surrounded it vertically and horizontally. Baby Larkin gave no
trouble.

Indeed the preschool Larkin was so quiet and docile that his
father appropriated a corner of the second bedroom to do

the work that he brought home. Larkin senior was an actuary who worked hard. Sitting at a folding card table, Mr. Larkin produced volumes of disposable statistics, calculating accurately by hand, resharpening his pencil until it reached the little tin ring at the end. Larkin the younger lay silent in his small caged bed, his hands disposed at random at his sides, his large black eyes fixed steadily on nothing.

Elsewhere in the apartment: a kitchenette, another bedroom, the living room, ruled by a sullen black cat. The glass doors to the balcony were usually shut, it being either too hot or too cold to open them. Mrs. Larkin prowled the enclosed space in pink, furry slippers, preparing popular foods of Eastern Europe and watching TV, while her husband, closeted with their first son, made money. Over the black-and-white television set, a framed photograph of Lenin hung cockeyed on the greenish wall. This photograph was never a topic of discussion.

Mrs. Larkin having announced a second pregnancy, her husband compiled some personal statistics and removed his growing family to a bungalow in New Jersey. A portion of the extra space thus obtained was given over to a respectable upright piano. Clarence Larkin, four years old, began piano lessons. He sat the obligatory hour per day, with his feet dangling well above the piano's pedals, playing "Twinkle, Twinkle," "Lightly Row," and the simpler sections of Bartók's *Mikrokosmos*. Mrs. Larkin, heavy with pregnancy, hummed along before her kitchen window, looking out onto a featureless patch of lawn. She began to dream of Carnegie Hall recitals: her son bowing easily over huge bouquets sent by anonymous admirers; money, glory, fame, and pride. Mr. Larkin purchased a cowhide briefcase and commuted daily to New York by rail. The black cat expired and was not replaced; Mrs. Larkin didn't entirely trust it around children. Somewhere in a closet, the implacable visage of Lenin glared into the corners of an unpacked box.

A second son was duly born, Thomas Feofil Larkin. The family grew familiar with prosperity. Larkin senior took semiannual exams and had his salary raised accordingly. Thomas and Clarence were introduced to the wonders of private education. A superior piano was acquired for the Larkin sons, likewise a more accomplished teacher.

Clarence Dmitri Larkin reached adolescence and survived the period without extraordinary incident. As he had been a quiet child, he became a quiet teen-ager, not given to car wrecking or staying out very late at night. Once in a while he discreetly smoked a little dope. He had friends of the appropriate sort, number, and gender, none of them very close. He never beat up his little brother.

Clarence Larkin was an adequate student, only a little better than average. Each day after school he came home and played the piano with the deadly accuracy of a machine. The recitals had already begun to take place, though with less pomp and circumstance or grandeur of locale than envisioned by Mrs. Larkin. Encouraged to a degree by his teacher and much more so by his mother, Larkin began to cross the river to Juilliard during his last two years of high school. Larkin's piano tutor privately believed that Thomas Larkin was much more likely to have a career than his elder brother. Clarence Larkin struck him as the sort that burned out early.

To all appearances, Mr. and Mrs. Larkin lived entirely within the glassine American present, like insects trapped in a paperweight. They never spoke of wherever they had come from. They practiced no religion, though they did observe the holidays recognized in a major way by the state. Only the diminishing thickness of their accents betrayed that they had perhaps not sprung from the central New Jersey soil like healthy, nourishing vegetables.

Clarence Larkin graduated from high school at the appropriate moment and entered the Juilliard School of Music in the fall of 1972. Each day he rode a commuter train beside his father, the one carrying a briefcase of scores and the other a case of mathematics. Clarence Larkin hammered on at the piano, a full-time musician now. However, the vortical forces of the city began to bend his direction slightly, without completely drawing him in. Larkin began drifting downtown, past Bellevue through the devil's market of 14th Street and over to Stuyvesant Town, home of his dimly recalled childhood and entirely unremembered birth. Something in this landscape, Larkin felt, was asking to be unearthed, examined, and perhaps preserved.

With winnings from a minor music competition, Larkin bought his first camera. He cruised 14th Street with the Nikon extended from his face like a prehensile eye. Larkin crammed everything he could into the Japanese rectangle; his first pictures were not selective at all. He felted the windows of his New Jersey bathroom and developed miles of film, while his mother, beyond the blacked-out door, worried and complained about the smell.

The sound of the piano was less often heard in the Larkins' suburban bungalow. By the end of 1973 Larkin had defected from Juilliard to the Rhode Island School of Design, moving from one artistic group to another only slightly less claustrophobic and paranoid. Larkin's mother never got over it; his father was indifferent, as to most things, and his brother rose to pre-eminence as the family's musical star.

For three years Larkin travelled between his school and various rattrap Providence apartments. For two years he dutifully learned the conventions of commercial photography. During his last year, however, something queer began to happen to his prints. Larkin's pictures grew confused, developed unpredictable layers, seemed to reflect a great uncertainty of mind. Larkin lost favor with his professors and graduated with no honors attached to his degree.

In the course of his sojourn in Providence, Larkin divested himself of his first two names and became just unmodified "Larkin," a name which was in any event a radical simplification of something longer and less pronounceable, that transformation having most probably occurred at Ellis Island, somewhere in the unacknowledged past.

*

If anyone had questioned him on the matter, which no one did, Larkin would have divulged just this much information about his personal history, but not more.

The Larkin of 1982 stood five-foot-ten. His weight varied between 145 and 155 pounds. His arms, quite large and powerful, were a little long for his height, and his legs, correspondingly, were a little short. His torso was thick and nearly circular, like the bole of a tree. His features were rounded and rather soft. His eyes were almost black and slightly almond shaped, giving his face a noticeable Oriental cast. Larkin's hair was black and he kept it cut close against the smooth oval of his skull. On occasion he wore glasses with clear plastic rims. As a rule he favored loose clothing. He possessed a natural ability to move from place to place without making the least sound. His appearance and demeanor produced a somewhat misleading impression of enormous inner calm.

Concerning his ancestry and family history, Larkin sometimes told the following story:

"My grandfather was a member of the minor aristocracy and owned a small parcel of land in the Ukraine, not far from the city of Kiev. Because of his social position, my grandfather became a deacon of the church. He was rather more devout than would have been ordinary for a young man of his day, and yet at the same time he was quite hot tempered.

"A little before the dawn of a cold winter day, my grandfather went to church for some reason known only to himself and accidentally came upon a thief who was engaged in stealing the collection box and some of the altar plate. Witnessing this crime, my grandfather fell into a violent passion. Alerting the thief of his presence with a loud shout, he rushed toward the altar. The thief was startled and uncertain whether to defend himself or flee. Before he could reach a decision, my grandfather, completely overcome with his own rage, seized the heavy cross from the altar and struck the thief on the head with it. The thief fell instantly dead, profaning the sanctuary with a copious flow of blood from his wound.

"My grandfather, then twenty-four years of age, was convicted of manslaughter, a charge which he did not attempt to defend, though he might successfully have done so, and subsequent to his trial he served a ten-year sentence in Siberia. A decade later he returned to the Ukraine, weathered by considerable suffering, though he was still a young man and his health was unbroken. There was no particular stain upon his character; on the contrary, most of the local community was in sympathy with his impulsive action of ten years before. But my grandfather's mind was uneasy and his conscience knew no rest; he could forgive himself for the murder, but not for carrying it out with a cross. Eventually he took his trouble to a holy *starets* in Kiev. After his conversation with the *starets,* my grandfather concluded to expiate his crime by voluntary and permanent exile from Holy Mother Russia. He relinquished the whole of his property to a younger brother and embarked on a ship for America."

This story which Larkin told of his grandfather was in no way true.

3
Larkin's Dream

"Come and see."

Midway through the night Larkin departed from the prison of his body and rose into the center of the air. He was himself and yet not quite so. He hovered in the deep sky on six long wings hinged to the middle of his spine. He possessed the paws and talons of a cat and a large leonine head. A serpent's tail stretched out behind him on the hard wind blowing from the west. This beast that was and was not Larkin again admonished him to see.

The veil of seeming was torn loose from the world and

nothing remained but void. The river and the Brooklyn shore became a single emptiness through which the griffin-Larkin soared without progress, moving neither forward nor backward. The griffin gestured westward with its forefoot and Larkin saw —

The buildings of the city were instantly alive with fire. The city's unitary structure went transparent as a crystal honeycomb, within which Larkin could separately perceive eight million luminescent souls. Larkin floated on a powerful blast of wind, in the midst of an odor of lotus and honey. With a human and gentle voice the griffin urged him again and again to regard the spectacle. The amazing, unbearable light coming from the city bound all his senses to itself. The vision was forceful as the sudden return of memory.

The griffin's voice combined with the wind and Larkin was shocked back to ordinary consciousness. He found himself dangerously near to the low balustrade of his roof. Larkin felt undone, overcome by the bereavement of the rudely awakened sleepwalker. Looking across the river, he saw that the city remained untransformed. A foul-smelling breeze from the river dried the few tears he seemed to have cried in his dream.

4

The State of the Earth
According to the New York Post

ON AUGUST 2, 1982, the front page of the popular tabloid concerned itself largely with President Reagan's Middle East policy. A box in the lower lefthand corner promised an investigation into WHO KILLED MARILYN MONROE.

Inside the paper, Brezhnev criticized Reagan, implying that the American president was responsible for the Israeli sack of Beirut. Reagan, who claimed that he was doing everything within his power to stop the conflict, repudiated the charge.

Queen Noor al-Hussein of Jordan (formerly Elizabeth Halaby, of American birth and a Princeton graduate) announced her intention to spend the month of August in Bridgehampton. An attempted coup was suppressed in Kenya. In Belfast, the first specimen of a new variety of pipe bomb exploded, injuring one British soldier. George Carpoczi, Jr., asserted that a coroner's inquest into the death of Marilyn Monroe was long overdue. Rita Jenrette, ex-wife of a discredited US senator, was quoted as saying to social columnist Earl Wilson, in an irritated tone, "I am not free with sex."

On August 3, the *Post* continued its daily practice of advertising the lottery it sponsored with photographs of lightly clad young women. The captions generally featured a pun. Wins in five figures were reported to be common. The name of the game was Wingo.

Boxer Gerry Cooney, the defeated Great White Hope, appeared at Xenon with "Deb of the Year" Cornelia Guest. The unidentified corpse of a young blond woman was found in the river near the 69th Street pier in Bay Ridge. Her arms and neck were bound with electrical wire. The precise cause of her death was not immediately certain.

In the Bronx, teen-aged Jose Agosto was hit with two fire bombs while out jogging. "I don't know why anyone would do this," the youth's mother stated. "He was such a handsome boy." The sixteen-year-old actress-model Brooke Shields purchased a town house on East 62nd Street for $1.8 million, "plus change."

President Reagan visited the US "Corn Belt" and praised the farmers there. In Beirut, the war continued. The appearance of a twelve-foot shark forced the temporary closing of a Far Rockaway beach. The mystery of Marilyn's death remained unsolved.

The August 4 edition of the *New York Post* carried the following headline: REAGAN TELLS ARAFAT TO GET OUT. The un-

known slayer of the woman found in Bay Ridge was christened "The Night Stalker" and was credited with four more
victims. The corpse of a Wall Street executive was found in
Jersey City. Friends and colleagues found his presence there
mystifying and his death entirely inexplicable. An ancient ar-
tifact found in Mexico was said to resemble the space-crea-
ture movie puppet E.T.

On August 7, police broke up a large and lucrative call-girl
operation on Long Island. The prostitution ring was reported to have catered to "Hollywood celebrities," among
others. Juvenile actress Natassia Kinski stated that she did
not regret having posed in the nude, in the company of a
large python, for fashion photographer Richard Avedon. The
noted transsexual tennis player Renée Richards opened an
ophthalmology clinic in the East 30s, Manhattan. In New Jersey, the death penalty was reinstated by the legislature. No
explanation was found for the crash of a Boeing 727 which
had taken place during the previous week. The crash had
demolished an entire block of houses in a New Orleans sub-
urb, killing a total of 154 people.

On August 14, the *Post* reported the arrest of Charles Mayo,
a surgeon, for conspiracy to murder his wife, a pathologist.
Israeli officials threatened to "resume the saturation bomb-
ing of Beirut" if the PLO refused to withdraw from that city.
In New York, James Capozzi slashed a welfare worker with
a razor because he was upset about a reduction of his benefits. Marie Osmond's wedding dress, which had been reported stolen, was located at a dry cleaner's.

On August 16, John Hinckley wrote a letter to the editors of
High Society magazine from the mental institution to which
he had been confined subsequent to his attempt to assassi-
nate President Reagan. Hinckley's letter requested prints of
nude photos of his inamorata Jodie Foster, which the magazine reputedly had in its possession. A three-hundred-pound
suspect was apprehended in the rape and murder of a thirty-
year-old businesswoman on the Upper East Side. At Ken-

nedy Airport, an officer who was assisting in the deportation of a Dominican citizen was killed by his charge, whose whereabouts remained unknown. An eighteen-year-old girl, who had been accidentally shot in the brain by a nail gun that was in use on the opposite side of a Sheetrock wall from her, remained in critical condition. A policewoman was suspended from the force as a reprimand for her disrobed appearance in *Beaver* magazine.

The *Post* headline for August 21 read as follows: FONDA LEAVES NOTHING TO JANE, PETER. In Florida that day, a student was severely bitten in the arm by a nine-foot alligator. Soraya Kashoggi, the ex-wife of Sheik and sometimes arms-dealer Adnan Kashoggi, continued to negotiate for a larger alimony settlement. A three-card monte dealer was stabbed to death by business associates on the corner of 42nd Street and Sixth Avenue, Manhattan. In Miami, a retired professor of accounting used a shotgun to kill eight employees of Bob's Welding and Machine Service, because he felt that they had failed to repair his lawnmower properly.

In the Bronx, on August 23, a nineteen-year-old boy shot and killed his fifteen-year-old girlfriend during the course of an argument with her. Karen Baldwin, the newly selected Miss Universe, declined to discuss premarital sex. Toxic fluid was found to be leaking from a truck abandoned on the corner of West 32nd Street and 11th Avenue. Vicki Morgan produced love letters signed by Alfred Bloomingdale in support of her "palimony" suit against the department-store tycoon.

WIDOW SLAIN IN HAMMER ATTACK, read the headline of the August 28 edition of the paper. In New Jersey that day, a swarm of bees invaded an apartment complex, causing twenty-seven people to be hospitalized with stings.

On September 30, two preteen muggers attempted to rob an elderly Bronx woman, but were thwarted by a neighbor's dog. In the course of their lengthy divorce trial, socialites Roxanne and Peter Pulitzer each testified that he or she suspected the other of plotting to murder him or her. Policeman Arthur Kunan identified one Samuel Brown as the man who fired on him during the holdup of a Brinks van on October 20, 1981, during which incident two officers were killed. In Massachusetts, four young girls dislocated their jaws while screaming at a concert given by teen idol Rick Springfield; the four required emergency dental attention. Five hundred Queens residents marched on a Jamaica police precinct in protest of the recent unsolved murder of a seventeen-year-old local coed. Copies of Webster's New Collegiate Dictionary were removed from the Carlsbad, New Mexico, school system, because they contained definitions of "obscene" words. Three airmen stranded in the Canadian Rockies were rescued after their position was detected by a Soviet satellite. Morgan Fairchild, star of the popular TV series "Flamingo Road," stated as follows: "I'm not as dumb as I look."

In Crown Heights, Brooklyn, an elderly woman burst into flames while returning home from her day's shopping. Her body was entirely consumed, including the bones; only a residue of slightly oily ash remained. Several eyewitnesses firmly stated that the immolation took a matter of seconds, definitely well under a minute. There was no apparent cause. Police and fire department personnel soon arrived at the scene, and subsequently a bomb squad and an antiterrorist unit were called in as well. None of these services could provide a precise explanation for the event. Experts were puzzled by the fact that while the complete destruction of the woman's skeleton indicated a temperature in excess of four thousand degrees Fahrenheit, portions of her clothing and the contents of her shopping bags remained intact. The woman was reported to be a member of the large Orthodox Jewish community in Crown Heights, and was admired and respected by all who knew her. Her name was withheld. Using a pair of black-handled kitchen scissors, Larkin clipped this article neatly out of the paper and placed it in a cream-colored manila folder which contained other, similar material. On the outside of the folder had been printed the letters SHC.

5
Larkin at Home

THE FOLDER labelled SHC lay with one of its corners abutting on the edge of a large work table placed near the southern end of the loft where Larkin lived, in a building near the corner of Bedford Avenue and Broadway, Brooklyn. On the same table were a stack of test prints, some boxes of slides, and an illustrated manual on techniques of clinical photography. On a second table of similar size, adjacent to the first and to the east of it, was a jumble of different grades of paper. Some of the sheets had drawings on them, or partially resolved photographic images. Most were blank. Also on the second table was a middle-sized radio with the back torn off of it. The radio worked, and was turned to WPIX, which played, in the phrase of the hour's disc jockey, "Nothing but love songs." Behind these tables, on the south wall of the loft, were three windows overlooking Broadway from a height of three stories. At the southwest corner was a small door with reinforced glass panes, which gave access to the fire escape.

To the northeast of the first work table there was a long cylindrical wood burning stove. The cylinder stood horizontally on short legs and was approximately three feet long and two feet in diameter. The stove was completely wound round with iron tubing, whose purpose was to diffuse heat outward from it. However, because Larkin never kept a fire burning continuously for very long, the stove did not produce much heat.

The stove was supported by a platform about four inches high, which was surfaced with ceramic tile. Just to the north of this platform was the mattress on the floor where Larkin slept. Crumpled on the surface of the mattress were several rather grimy blankets. The mattress was pushed against the outer wall of the sizeable darkroom Larkin had built for himself. This darkroom was trapezoidal in form and contained all of the usual appurtenances. It had a wooden door with a curtain of black felt behind it.

Through a light-sealed slot in the darkroom wall, a length of plastic tubing ran to the kitchen sink, which stood at the northernmost end of the loft, under two small sash windows. These windows afforded a view of a shaftlike vacant lot, enclosed by other buildings on all sides. A couple of clotheslines were strung between the buildings, under several tall and healthy specimens of the heaven tree. The big fan-shaped leaves of these trees reached as high as the lower sill of Larkin's windows.

There were no fixtures in the kitchen area other than the sink and a full-size refrigerator. Larkin did his minimal cooking with a toaster oven and a double-burner hot plate, which were placed on the kitchen table, before a single straight-backed chair. The exit door of the loft was directly west of the kitchen area. The bathroom was in a closet just off the landing outside. A narrow flight of stairs led straight to the roof.

The central area of the loft, which was generously large, remained entirely vacant. All of Larkin's furniture was disposed against the walls. On the wall south of the exit door, just opposite the darkroom compartment, was a square gray filing cabinet, which stood about waist high and measured roughly four feet by four feet. The drawers of the cabinet were very shallow. This cabinet contained the whole of the work which Larkin had completed in more productive times. On the handles of its drawers, untroubled dust had reached the height of a quarter inch.

Larkin's current work-in-progress was displayed more or less at eye level along the length of wall between the file cabinet and the southwest corner of the loft. This work consisted of a series of prints on pieces of paper averaging about two feet square. The prints featured a combination of photographic and lithographic techniques. All of them involved the human form either as a whole or in part. Across the wall of prints, the body of man was in some sense dissected. Doors opened everywhere in the anatomy, revealing various activities going on inside: men appeared on scaffoldings; some-where a battle was going on; people were having a drink, or making love. Animals and insects peered out curiously from breasts or brains. Each of the prints was extraordinarily dense with such imagery. Most had been heavily drawn over with oil pastel. Many had scraps of paper or magazine photos glued to them here and there. Some had sheets of translucent plastic attached to them, enhancing the layered effect. The prints exuded a sense of unease; none appeared finished or satisfactory. None had satisfied Larkin.

Another long work table was positioned directly in front of the wall of prints. On this table lay an incomplete picture, with several grease pencils scattered across its surface. This print depicted the outline of a human head in three-quarter profile. One of its eye sockets was filled with an antique clock face which lacked hands. The other held a dark and liquid human eye, though the eyelids around it were of greenish snakeskin. Through a section in the area of the cheek and temple, one could observe a group of men who were engaged in building some structure which lacked a foundation.

Just to the north of this print, on the same table, stood a plain black dial telephone, which was connected through a Panasonic Easaphone answering machine. The answering machine was not turned on. Past the edge of this table Larkin stood with his foot on the sill of the fire escape door, one hand grasping the door frame. The door itself was opened to an angle of seventy degrees. The telephone began to ring. Larkin did not answer it.

6
Larkin Goes to Bellevue

AT LENGTH responding to some call or other, Larkin packed a bag with a camera and lenses. He picked up a compact Lowell light kit and left the loft. The two floors below him were occupied by die cutters; Larkin nodded at them from their landings as he went down. He pushed open the heavy metal door and was in the street. Behind him the door closed itself by means of a counterweight which hung from a cable and pulley.

At Marcy Avenue Larkin climbed the staircase to the El train and went through the turnstile. He walked down toward the east end of the wooden platform and looked toward the bend in the tracks, but there was no train yet in sight. Where the platform crossed over the expressway one plank was smoldering a little. Larkin returned to wait in the area near the token booth. On the far side of the tracks a copper molding dangled from a tall stripped building, swaying and moaning to itself. More people appeared on the platform, which began to vibrate under the weight of the approaching train.

Larkin took a seat in a rear car. The train tilted around the curve that approached the bridge, gathering speed for the upward grade. As the train ascended its windows were blanketed with a dull fog. Larkin could just barely see the girder rushing by the window opposite him. On the far side of the bridge the train dropped into the utter darkness of its tunnel. Larkin rode three stops and got out at Canal Street. He pushed his way through a crowd of Chinese and caught the uptown 6.

Six stops. Larkin climbed out of the subway at 28th and Park and started toward the river. At the end of the street he had taken he came into a wide dreary brick esplanade, terraced by slow degrees down toward First Avenue. Men and women in loose white lab coats wandered aimlessly over the bricks. There were benches where they might have sat down had they chosen, but it had rained a little and the seats were damp. Larkin passed among them and crossed First Avenue, bound for the side entrance of Bellevue.

Inside the lobby, visitors in varying states of anxiety clustered around a horseshoe-shaped information desk, where nurses checked files and sometimes gave out passes. A group of uniformed guards prevented unauthorized persons from entering the two yellow hallways at either side of the desk. Elsewhere in the lobby there were numbers of people draped on ranks of leatherette armchairs. Larkin sat down on one of these.

On a vinyl couch across from him a massive black woman sat motionless, expressionless. A small boy was with her and her hand clamped his arm like a manacle. Away behind this pair, groups of people in descending stages of decrepitude or despair sat equally still, blending finally into the dull colors of the lobby. Only the black child moved, twisting into every position his trapped arm allowed.

Six or seven, Larkin idly guessed, doesn't look sick. Visitors, maybe. The child's bright eyes were on him now and Larkin looked away toward the secret interior of the hospital, from which a man was now approaching him. This person wore a lab coat buttoned to the neck and a photo-ID card which stated among other things that his name was Dr. Anton Leveaux.

"Anton," Larkin said. They shook hands and moved together toward the outer door.

"Our man is already across the street," Leveaux said. A photocell spread the glass doors for them and they were on the sidewalk. "An odd one," Leveaux said conversationally. "Facial tumors, not malignant. He's up for surgery later in the week."

Larkin shifted the strap of his camera bag and made no remark. He and the doctor gained First Avenue and walked a block uptown to another building. Inside they made several turns on a long corridor, arriving finally at a small examination room where the patient waited.

"Larkin," Leveaux offered, "our photographer."

The patient did not reply. Larkin opened the Lowell kit and began quickly to set up lights and position them. He then unpacked his 35-mm Nikon and fixed it to an aluminum tripod he had brought. Leveaux had seated himself on a straight chair in the corner. Larkin crouched behind his camera. He looked at the patient, who sat on a black revolving stool, through the viewfinder.

The patient was a white male whose age could not easily be guessed, owing to the curious deformity of his face. A tuberous growth or growths had obscured his features, indeed usurped them. He had no discernible nose and his mouth was a mere recessed shadow, like a hole dug among the roots of a tree. His eyes looked out over a roll of tissue the approximate shape and color of a Chinese eggplant. His expression was impossible to read. Larkin pulled focus, took a shot, then another and another, bracketing exposures.

"Could you give me a profile?" Larkin said. The patient rotated on his stool. Larkin took three pictures, moved closer, took three more.

"All right," he said. "Left profile?" The man obediently swung round 180 degrees. Larkin, camera to his eye, appeared to freeze. The moment which passed was far too long for focusing, and in any case he had not touched his lens.

"Larkin," Leveaux said, to no reaction. He called the name louder. Larkin started and the camera snapped. The sick man, responding to instruction, turned to present a new facet of his disfigurement.

Larkin sat at a desk in Dr. Leveaux's cramped office, unwinding film from his camera. Leveaux had propped himself on a low bookshelf on the wall. He had removed his lab coat and stood surprisingly colorful in a red checked shirt, with polychromatic pen caps sticking out of its pocket. He watched Larkin drop film in a can, make a note of the session in a worn date book.

"Contact sheets for you in a couple of days," Larkin said, looking up. "Unless you need it sooner."

"No," Leveaux said. "That's good."

"What will you do for him?" Larkin said.

"Well. We begin by cutting away the growths. Or as much as we can. Some organs are, um, involved. I'll want you for another session, by the way, when that phase is done."

"Then what?" Larkin said.

"We start the reconstruction. Or construction. With him there's not a lot to go on. We're basically building straight from the bone."

"Will he look like Robert Redford?" Larkin said, without a trace of humor in his tone.

"Doubtful. But we like to think he'll look more human than he does at present. He's got mental problems too. He's been like that from childhood. Family not too helpful, thought he was cursed by God."

"More human," Larkin said. He reached for a standard pay form and began to fill it out.

"I can pay you early if you need it," Leveaux said. Larkin folded his date book away into a pocket.

"The usual's okay," Larkin said. Leveaux removed a blue Bic pen from his pocket and began to twist it around and around in his fingers.

"Larkin," he said. He looked at the pen and put it away. "Have you been taking the Dilantin?"

"I've been okay," Larkin said. His hand crawled backward along the edge of the desk and hid itself beneath it. Leveaux put the cap of a green Bic in his teeth and pulled the pen away from it.

"If there's a money problem you can get it through the clinic. All you have to do is tell me."

"It's all right," Larkin said.

Leveaux found the cap with the point of the pen and fished it out of his mouth.

"When you have a grand mal seizure, you won't think it's all right," he said.

"It's okay, Anton," Larkin said. "There isn't any problem."

7
Doctor Anton Leveaux

ANTON LEVEAUX was born in 1953 in Québec Province, Canada. Three years later his family moved to the United States, settling in an area near Boston. Anton Leveaux became a US citizen. Son of bilingual parents, he retained a good knowledge of French. Leveaux held an undergraduate degree from Yale University and was a graduate of the Vanderbilt Medical School. In the fall of 1982, Leveaux had been a surgical resident at Bellevue for a little over one year. He hoped to return to Boston and set up a practice as a plastic surgeon when his residency was complete.

Dr. Leveaux had met Larkin early in 1981 after reading his résumé, which was on file at the hospital. The résumé stated that Larkin had some ability as a clinical photographer. Leveaux, a fairly ambitious young doctor, was interested in assembling an illustrated book on certain surgical procedures in which he specialized. He persuaded hospital administrators to allot funds to hire a photographer, arguing that the material which would be obtained had potential publicity value. Larkin had worked with Leveaux on a free-lance basis for roughly fifteen months. Leveaux had told him about the planned book and the two had written a profit-sharing agreement to cover its eventual publication.

A memo attached to the résumé informed Leveaux that Larkin had been admitted to Bellevue in the fall of 1979, suffering from acute alcoholism and severe lacerations of both hands. His wounds were duly repaired and he went through detoxification. Afterward he entered a Bellevue mental ward and remained there as a voluntary inpatient for eight months.

Though Larkin had sometimes been violent during the initial phase of his treatment, and exhibited pronounced self-destructive tendencies, he was not considered psychotic. He seemed to respond well to a therapy program which did not involve the use of drugs, and had signed for his own release in the fall of 1980. Larkin had participated in outpatient therapy for a couple of months after his discharge and had then abandoned it. His condition was judged to be stable. It was not known whether he had resumed drinking or not.

The memo further stated that Larkin had been tentatively diagnosed as an epileptic during his term at Bellevue. He had no grand mal seizures while in the hospital, and his medical records prior to 1979 gave evidence of none. However, he seemed occasionally prone to petit mal seizures — lapses of interior consciousness which lasted a minute or two on the average, and could very well pass unnoticed by anyone. It was thought that Larkin had been unaware of this condition prior to his entry into the hospital. The petit mal seizures were successfully controlled with a small regulatory dose of Dilantin, the drug normally used in such cases. On his departure Larkin had been given a prescription for Dilantin; whether he used it or not was unknown. His epilepsy was thought to be unrelated to the personality disorder which had initially caused him to enter the hospital.

Dr. Leveaux knew of Larkin's presumed epilepsy, but it had not affected his performance in even a minor way before the session with the facial-deformity patient. Though Leveaux was not especially familiar with epilepsy, he was reasonably certain that Larkin had suffered a petit mal seizure during that session. His concern for Larkin's medical well-being was more professional than personal. The two were not intimate. Leveaux thought Larkin a very cold fish, but he was a good photographer.

8

Larkin Gets Cats

A CONCRETE-COLORED CAT appeared before Larkin's street doorway, mewling in a low monotone. Larkin noted its presence one cold morning, on his way to the bodega for coffee. A few minutes later he came back with a twelve-ounce bag of Bustelo; the cat was still there. Larkin invited the cat upstairs and scrambled it an egg. The cat ate willingly but did not seem particularly pleased. It continued to mewl as though in response to some dull pain. Larkin shredded newspaper into a shallow cardboard box, thinking, So. Now I have this cat.

The cat remained but did not get any happier. Larkin bought cat food in seven flavors; though the cat ate with interest, its mood did not improve. It mewled steadily and sadly, pausing only to eat or sleep. Larkin attempted to cheer up the cat by naming it with ridiculous names, finally settling on Dwango the Magnificent. But to all appearances the cat was not amused.

A week or ten days after Dwango's arrival a second cat turned up on Larkin's doorstep, a tiger-striped kitten this time. The kitten was silent, but it pushed urgently against Larkin's ankles when he tried to go in the door. "Ah," said Larkin, "the word is out. There's a fool on Bedford Avenue who takes in strays. Beat it, little cat." The kitten poked its head in the crack of the closing door. Larkin took it upstairs.

On close examination it turned out that the tiger-striped kitten was crippled, injured in the second joint of its right hind leg. The kitten moved jerkily, thumping the bad leg like a club on the floor. Larkin massaged the stiff joint between his thumb and forefinger, and felt what seemed to be solid bone, no sign that the leg had ever been flexible. He called Anton Leveaux and described the injury over the phone. Leveaux mumbled about calcification and suggested that the kitten was not worth treating. Larkin stopped worrying; the kitten could maneuver to its own evident satisfaction, and seemed better humored than Dwango, despite its troubles. Larkin did not give this kitten a name.

9

Larkin and Sybil

LARKIN DRUNK; his head rolled on his round shoulders like a pool ball lost on the floor. He had a full glass of Irish whisky in front of him, which he was having trouble finding with his hand. He doubted he had the money to pay for it anyway.

"Do you think we should break up for good," Sybil said, not phrasing it as a question. Larkin made a gesture expressive of indecision and helplessness. Sybil was a woman of medium build, rather pretty, an employed journalist, sitting on the edge of her chair. Larkin and Sybil had broken up for good four times previously — or was it five?

"No," Larkin said, "I don't know."

"You don't love me," Sybil said. "Why should we keep seeing each other?"

Her eyes were large, but not tearful. Larkin made a try for her hand, which she quickly removed from the table. He then located his drink somehow and raised it to his mouth.

"Cheers," Larkin said.

"We're not having any fun," Sybil said. "I don't want to be here. You don't want to be here."

They were sitting in a bar on West 72nd Street, in a small dark booth. The bartender was elderly and stooped, with false teeth and false geniality. Drinks were fairly cheap. On the wall opposite the bar, three old crones in shawls sang raucously; one played the piano more horribly than Larkin had ever heard anyone play the piano. The three crones reminded Larkin of the witches in *Macbeth,* although they were singing tunes from *South Pacific* rather than uttering incantations. Above the bar, two stuffed parrots nestled in a steel ring, their tail feathers brushing the bald spot in the bartender's head.

"I like it here," Larkin said.

It was true, he did like it there. It was three blocks from Sybil's apartment, where he had picked her up a few hours before. How are you, Larkin had said, have any adventures this week? No, not really. Sybil worked for a magazine, where nothing of particular interest had happened since Larkin had seen her a few days previously. An editor at this magazine, a lunch-time acquaintance of Sybil's, had finally decided to start seeing a psychiatrist. Otherwise, not much.

Larkin and Sybil waited in line to see a foreign movie. Standing in line, Larkin tried to recall some amusing event

from his life which he could tell Sybil about; he did not succeed in doing this. Larkin had had a drink before meeting
Sybil, or possibly a couple. During the movie Larkin did not
have a drink and after it his system was disturbed by the ebb
of alcohol from his blood stream. Leaving the theater, Larkin
closed his hand around Sybil's sweatered elbow and piloted
her into the bar, a place he liked. The drinks were cheap, the
parrots sympathetic, and the musical crones lent the place a
gruesome ambience which probably appealed to Larkin more
than to his companion.

"That's not really an argument," Sybil said. "You know what
I mean."

"I wasn't looking for an argument," Larkin said. "I'm tired."

"You're drunk, you mean. Clare, we're not doing each other
any good."

"Sure we are," Larkin said, without real confidence. He
finished his drink and rattled the glass toward the bartender.

"You ought to watch that, too. I don't want to see you in
the hospital again." Larkin looked guilty and said nothing.
Sybil was a light drinker, comparatively speaking.

"I don't think I can do it any more," Sybil said.

A fresh drink appeared at the back of Larkin's hand. He
turned his hand over, picked it up, and took a sip.

"I know I'm not being nice," Sybil said. "But you're not
stopping me."

"I don't know how." Larkin closed one eye, clutched his
glass. Sybil appeared to be at the end of a long dismal tunnel.
She wore a black cashmere sweater, with a hood that lay in
becoming folds around her shoulders. Her hair was swept
up and to one side, the ends of it just grazing the folds of the
sweater. Larkin wanted to rush through the tunnel, embrace
her, tell her something true. He had no idea how to accomplish this. He opened his eye.

"Three years. That's been a lot of blood under the bridge.
I do love you."

"All right. But it's a bad marriage."

Larkin could see from a crimp at the side of her mouth
that Sybil might cry, which he did not want to happen. By

now he knew she would leave anyway, and he didn't want to have to watch her leave in tears.

"All right," Larkin said. "I don't suppose I walk you home."

"You don't," Sybil said. She got up and moved around the table to touch Larkin on the forehead with a cool and friendly kiss. Larkin's hands went naturally to a familiar spot beside the small of her back. He pressed his face to Sybil's and held it there till he felt dampness on his cheek. Unfair, Larkin told himself, and let her go.

"You call me," Larkin said. "Otherwise I'll worry."

"I'll call," Sybil said. She made an abrupt turn and vanished in the shadows near the door.

Larkin hunched over the table, looking at reflections in the Formica. He finished his drink and started on Sybil's, an Irish coffee which she'd hardly touched. Caffeine alerted Larkin to his financial problem. But when he asked for the check he found that Sybil had paid it. Larkin was outraged by this. He wanted to chase Sybil up to 75th Street and force her to take money. But he didn't have any money, and the taste of coffee had clarified his mind to the point of understanding that a longer, messier scene with Sybil would be pointless. Larkin left the bar, looked at the subway station on its island in the middle of the street, and began walking down Broadway.

It appeared to be later than Larkin would have thought; there were not very many other people out on the street. Larkin was a strong and steady walker. He went through Times Square, Herald Square, Madison Square, Union Square, not faltering, following Broadway's diagonal to the southeast. Larkin had met Sybil at Bellevue when she was an outpatient and he was an inpatient ready for release. Sybil was probably right to say they had never been in love. However, they had found comfort in each other. Very likely the affair had outlived its usefulness. Sybil was entirely correct in assuming that Larkin could produce no strong argument to the contrary.

If I had been sober, Larkin thought. By the time he reached Houston Street his feet felt like bricks. If I had been sober, I wouldn't have had the nerve to say as much as I did. Sybil was possibly right about everything, though Larkin, looking from the outside in, tended to believe that whatever they were doing was worthwhile because they were doing it and had been for a long time. He turned on Spring Street and walked toward the Bowery.

But now, of course, they weren't doing it any more. Which would seem to close the case. A man in the Spring Street Lounge was putting an iron bar through the door handles, closing the place for the night. Larkin hurried past to the Bowery, where he crossed to Delancey and began to approach the bridge. He was tiring, but it would be too long a wait for a train. Then again, Larkin's dealings with Sybil had moved through the same cycle several times before. And a period of separation would give him more time for his own queer business.

He climbed the staircase and began to move up the long concrete walkway, his legs protesting the slope. Two parts of his mind that didn't ordinarily communicate suddenly made contact. The queer business was presumably drawing to a conclusion. When it was finished, the Sybilline cycle, familiar to Larkin as the hands on a clock, would be permanently arrested.

Larkin found it disagreeable to think that this particular clock could stop. The issue was too contradictory for his taste. He stood in the middle of the bridge, forcing his paradoxes back to their separate mental chambers, trying to concentrate on the dark shape of the city beyond the water, a vision which on this occasion failed him. From the perspective of loss, Larkin could better value Sybil, could plausibly claim that he had loved her. The city was mute and he was cold. Larkin couldn't seem to cry.

10
Larkin Visits the Sparrow

ANOTHER NIGHT. Larkin fed the cats, put out the lights, and left his building. He walked a block across Broadway and entered the Berry Street tenement. The stairwell was rich with the smell of cooking pork. At a door on the second floor Larkin knocked and was admitted.

"This is our house," the Sparrow said. "Let everyone who suffers come. And meet the competition." Larkin laughed. The door let into the kitchen, which was dark. Rusty pots stood jumbled on the stove. In the sink a broken tap gushed water into a wine bottle.

Larkin followed the Sparrow on a twisted path, threading between waist-high piles of newspaper, into an inner room lit by a faint amber bulb overhead. The room crawled with assorted debris. The Sparrow moved a mass of clothes and ashtrays from a section of couch to the floor and motioned to Larkin, who sat down. On the floor near his feet were a dozen or more empty Gordon's gin bottles, standing amid a tangle of cable. On the couch around Larkin, sundry accumulated papers reached to shoulder height. All the floor space was taken up with tall stacks of records; there were several hundred records in the little room.

The Sparrow picked his way to the corner where the turntable was and started something on it. Sound immediately swallowed the room. The Sparrow had redesigned his system by principles known only to himself. The amplifier stole electricity from the light bulb and the room grew dimmer. Mingus, Larkin thought it was. He let his eyes close till the cut was over.

The Sparrow was seated in a dull-green, high-backed armchair. He resembled less a man than a hanger with brown clothes on it. Long straight black hair framed his beaked and narrow face. He chain-smoked Camel Filters, tipping ash into a coffee can which stood on the windowsill near him, next to a broken ceramic head of a dog. The tone arm lifted from the record.

"So what's new?" the Sparrow said.

"Very little."

"Working?"

"The flower truck, two days a week. And photo at Bellevue. When they call me." The Sparrow dug into a pile of records and produced something by Eric Dolphy.

"And yourself?" Larkin said.

"Everything is very usual," said the Sparrow. He played another cut, a long one. Larkin smoked a cigarette.

"Karin called," the Sparrow said. His eyes flicked over Larkin's folded hands and then quickly away.

"Did she?"

"Said to say hello."

"Well. Do you happen to have a gin bottle with gin in it?"

"The refrigerator."

Larkin went into the kitchen. A small window above the sink looked out over a series of low roofs to the wall of a bank, where a red digital clock was pulsing. Larkin turned to the refrigerator and took out a quart of gin and a quart of tonic. The refrigerator was otherwise totally empty. He drank deeply from each bottle and carried them both to the Sparrow.

"I know what's new," Larkin said. "The cats."

"Cats?"

"These two cats showed up and I let them stay."

"How do they like it over there?"

"All right. I guess. But one of them yowls all the time. He never shuts up. I think I depress him. Pass me that bottle."

Larkin drank and lit a cigarette.

"I think this cat doesn't approve of the way I live my life," he said. The Sparrow's cheeks caved in around the cigarette he was smoking. Larkin drank tonic.

"I think maybe the cat is right," Larkin said. "Maybe he has a point."

Without comment the Sparrow got up to start another record. The music swelled and conversation ceased.

Larkin sat quietly, smoking one cigarette after another, drinking frequently from the gin bottle. After a couple of hours he got up and swayed into the kitchen. He brushed the wine bottle from under the faucet and let water play over his hands and wrists; the cold against his pulse helped a part of his wits return. From the sink he could see the Sparrow's birdlike face profiled against the light of the next room.

"Heard from Arkady?" the Sparrow said.

"Not recently," Larkin said. "I think he's in Jersey. The dacha. You need the number?" He sagged into the sink, his belt buckle clicking on the metal.

"I have the number," the Sparrow said. "It's nothing particular. I was just wondering."

Larkin raised his eyes to the window. The clock on the bank read quarter to twelve.

"I should go," Larkin said. "It's almost midnight."

"That clock is broken," the Sparrow said, without turning to look. "It's always almost midnight. Around here, anyway."

11
In the Flower Truck

LARKIN JOCKEYED a cream-colored Econoline van through heavy late afternoon traffic, working his way up Sixth Avenue toward Central Park. Loud ragged music crashed out of a radio in the black dashboard. Larkin drove fast and with considerable savagery.

He double-parked on 59th Street, got out and went to the back of the van. On the double doors were lettered the words AARDVARK FLORISTS, together with a telephone number. Aardvark was a small operation which profited from being listed early in the yellow pages under florists. In this way, Aardvark drew a lot of random calls.

Larkin opened the doors. On the floor of the van was a long flat box containing roses, his last delivery of the day, he hoped. He took the box under his arm, locked the van, and went down the sidewalk to the Hotel Navarro. A doorman in a red, gold-braided jacket blocked his way.

"Take it around to the back, sonny," the doorman said in robot tones. "Deliveries use the service entrance. Take it around to the back."

Without answering Larkin returned to the van and began to circle the block. He was caught behind a horse-drawn cab and had to go slowly. On 58th he double-parked again. The service door was not clearly marked and when Larkin finally found it it was locked. He pressed the buzzer and waited, five minutes, ten.

At last the door cracked open and a busboy clothed in soiled white reached out for the flowers.

"I'm supposed to deliver it direct to the party," Larkin said.

"Not here you're not," the busboy said. "House rules."

"Screw the house rules," Larkin said, halfheartedly. He shrugged and turned over the box. The busboy drew it inside and banged the door.

Larkin shifted the beeper which hung on his belt and reached into his pocket for a dime. On the next corner he found a phone booth and called the Aardvark office.

"Larkin," he said. "I'm in midtown. Anything else?"

"Not really."

"Clock me out, then," Larkin said, and hung up. Walking back to the van, he peered upward. The narrow strip of sky visible between the buildings was full of dark lumpy clouds. It was four-thirty or a little later. Larkin started the van and headed for FDR Drive, hoping to get out of town ahead of the rush-hour crunch.

Though the expressway was clear, there was a bottleneck on the Triboro Bridge. Larkin crawled by inches past the tollbooths and onto the roadway. The radio was playing a new song from Britain. In this song, a girl's voice told how she picked up a boy in a London rock club, how they left the club together, how she refused to take him to bed with her. Then the boy's voice took over the story, describing his anger and boredom, telling at last how he murdered the girl. The song concluded with loud screaming. It was rather effective, in its own dismal way. Larkin turned off the radio.

The thunderclouds had darkened the day and lightning was flashing over the river. The other drivers around Larkin struck him as nervous. He reached the far foot of the bridge as the storm broke. It was a heavy, lashing rain, flooding the windshield so that Larkin could hardly see. But he drove faster as the traffic thinned out, speeding deep into Queens toward Aardvark's lot, driving almost blind.

The rain had not abated when he pulled up at the lot. Getting out to unpadlock the chain-link gate, Larkin was instantly soaked to the bone. He parked the van in its slot inside the fence and chained the lot up again behind him. The rain had such force it seemed almost to bruise his skin. Larkin didn't bother to run to the subway.

12
Tommy

THE WEATHER had turned clear and bright. Larkin piloted the flower truck down a West Village street lined with ginkgo trees, their fan-shaped leaves yellowing in the cool of late October, some few already fallen. He parked the van at a curb beside a tiny park and walked down Hudson Street to deliver a bouquet of tulips. There he collected a tip and turned back, humming a little. As he approached the van, the beeper at his waist began to chirp. Larkin called the office from a phone booth in the park.

"Larkin," said the small voice cupped in his ear, "You've got an emergency phone call. A Dr. Leveaux. At Bellevue. Says for you to call back right away."

Larkin cleared the line and dialed the number he had been given. He asked for Leveaux and while waiting he could distantly hear the doctor's name being paged through the halls of the hospital. Leveaux was on the line in seconds.

"Where are you, Larkin?"

"The West Village." Leveaux muttered a few French curses and then recovered himself.

"How fast could you get here? With a camera?"

"Call it fifteen minutes. I've got a camera with me."

Leveaux breathed relief into the phone.

"Good, good. Just come straight to the photo room when you get over here. I'll be waiting there."

"Just a minute, Anton, what's the hurry?"

But the doctor had hung up. Larkin made good time to Bellevue and found a parking spot just off First Avenue. He walked quickly into the building, swinging his camera bag, and followed a stripe on the floor to the photo room. A uniformed policeman stood outside of it. Larkin knocked and Leveaux opened the door and urged him in.

"What have you got cops here for?" Larkin said.

"They brought the boy," Leveaux said softly. "It's a police case this time. Child abuse."

On the examination table a Hispanic boy lay facedown, his head turned toward the door, his dark eyes vacant of expression. The boy seemed around the age of ten, perhaps younger, and was extremely thin. A nurse worked over him with a liquid from a pan, trying to loosen his shirt, which seemed to adhere to his back somehow.

"Get set up, Larkin," said Leveaux. "We have to finish quickly. The police want to talk to him when we are done."

Larkin raised his tripod to maximum height so that he could take pictures from above. He climbed on a stool to focus. As Larkin looked through the view finder, the nurse succeeded in drawing the shirt away. Larkin reeled on his stool.

"Jesus Christ Almighty." He was nearly shouting. "What

happened to this kid?" The child's back was etched with a five-pointed star, an inverted pentangle with its three points aimed downward toward the boy's waist. At each point of the star was inscribed a character from some language Larkin didn't recognize. Every stroke of the design was an open wound, festering and blackened at the edges.

"Be quiet, Larkin," Leveaux said. "For the love of God. Just be quiet and take the pictures."

Larkin sat in Leveaux's office, both hands clutched on his camera bag. Leveaux was also seated, in a chair he had just dragged in from the hall. The doctor's forehead was sunk into his palm.

"I've seen horrible things," Leveaux mumbled after a time. "Every day I see horrible things."

"I know," Larkin said. "But most of them have a sort of accidental quality to them, don't they, Anton? But somebody did this. Somebody did this one on purpose."

"*Les diabolistes,*" Leveaux said.

"What?"

Leveaux raised his head. "Devil worshipers," he said. "There's a cult, over in the West 40s where they found him. He's not the first. They have a ritual to torture children, it seems."

Larkin leaned back. A slow, cold certainty spread over him from a dark spot in his mind that seemed older than himself. The pentangle and its lettering glowed in this black circle, unfamiliar no longer. Leveaux was still talking.

"The police have told me." Leveaux's English had become a trifle blurred, in a way Larkin couldn't recall hearing before. "There were two other children last year. With these symbols, as you have seen, cut and burned into their bodies."

"What happened to them?"

"On this one they have used a soldering iron," Leveaux said. "The policeman showed it to me, there was flesh still on the tip. Burnt flesh."

"Where are the other children, Anton?"

"Ah. They were dead when they were found. In that same

neighborhood . . ." Leveaux produced a very thin smile. "You might say this one is lucky."

"You might."

"But the pain must have been terrible. We gave him morphine . . . The wounds are four or five days old and shock only lasts for so long. And he was walking on the street with that thing on his back. A woman in a store saw him and called the police."

"Is there any family?"

"Ah, Larkin. That is maybe the very worst thing. They think perhaps it is his own father who did these things. Because they found the soldering iron there in the apartment where he lives."

"Tell me he's locked up, Anton."

"Unfortunately no. They cannot find him. And do you know, Larkin, he may take the child back? Because the police say there is not good proof. And the boy will not speak. He is afraid maybe, or who knows what mental damage there could be, perhaps he is an idiot by this time."

"Can't you keep him in the hospital?"

"For a few days, not more. The treatment is not so difficult and we always need beds. After a few days he must go. To his father or to Spofford, the police say."

"Spofford?"

"The juvenile center."

"Anton, that's a jail."

Leveaux flashed his palms outward. "There is nothing I can do, Larkin." Leveaux's face was twisting. "Nothing. I have no authority to interfere with police and courts. Maybe he will have told them something while we are sitting here. But if he will not speak . . . since they found him he has not said one word to anyone." Leveaux looked at his watch.

"*Merde,* I must go to the surgery. Larkin, do me one favor. The police may be finished with the boy now, go and tell the nurses they must move him to the ward."

"Check," Larkin said, getting up.

"And the pictures, the pictures by tomorrow, for the police."

"I'll do it all tonight," Larkin said. "Don't worry about the pictures."

Halfway down the hall Larkin was struck by an ugly thought. He stopped and turned; Leveaux was still in sight.

"Anton," he called. "Do you know what they call that neighborhood?" Leveaux stopped, perplexed.

"Hell's Kitchen," Larkin shouted. "How do you like *that?*"

The cop was gone from in front of the photo room. Larkin knocked and got no answer. He opened the door. The boy was crouched on the table, apparently ready to jump. When he saw Larkin, he relaxed into a sitting position. Larkin closed the door and leaned against it.

"They'll send you back," he said. "They're going to send you home. Do you want to go?"

But the child did not respond.

"If you would rather go with me," Larkin said carefully, "get down and stand on the floor."

The boy slipped from the table and reached to a chair for his shirt. Larkin noticed that his back had been coated with some sort of ointment. On a counter against the wall were tubes of antiseptic and other unguents; Larkin swept these hurriedly into his camera bag. He bolted down the empty hall to a supply closet, where he found and unfolded a wheelchair. There were lab coats hanging on a rack and Larkin put one of these on, adding a surgical mask as an afterthought, then rolled the chair back to the photo room.

"Let's go," Larkin said. "Quickly, now." The boy got into the wheelchair and Larkin pushed it toward the exit. He passed several hospital personnel in the hallway but no one challenged him. Larkin took the wheelchair down a ramp to the sidewalk and rolled it to the cross street where the van was parked. He swung the boy into the passenger seat and kicked the chair aside. Then he jumped into the van himself and drove to Williamsburg.

It was dusk when Larkin brought the child to Bedford Avenue. "This is where I live," he said, leading the boy up the stairs. "It's all right as far as it goes." He reached his landing, unlocked the door and brought the child inside. The stove had gone out and the loft was cold. Larkin built a new fire and lit it, talking disjointedly the while.

"Don't know if you're used to a wood stove but it'll be warm in a little while . . . you just have to keep it going . . . keep a good fire and it'll get hot in here . . ."

The boy stood still in the center of the loft, his eyes darting into the corners. Dwango came out of the kitchen and rubbed against his legs, mewling discontentedly just the same.

"That's Dwango . . . the cat that can't be satisfied . . . don't worry about him . . . he's got everything . . . and here's the kitten, he doesn't have a name." Larkin pointed to where the kitten slept on a folded towel near the stove.

"What's your name, anyway?" Larkin said. "Can you talk that much? Or would you? Can you tell me your name?"

Still the boy said nothing. He was hugging himself at the elbows and Larkin saw that he was shivering a little; he wore only the light shirt and the house was still cold.

"Here . . . get over there . . . sit by the stove . . ." The boy didn't move, so Larkin took his arm and led him to the fire. He brought a blanket and barely stopped himself from dropping it over the child, realizing how much it might hurt his back. Larkin set the blanket on the floor.

"Use this if you want it . . . ah. Food. There must be some food here . . ." Larkin scavenged the refrigerator, finding a half carton of milk and three yams, nothing more. But milk was reportedly good for children. Larkin poured off the remainder of the carton into a cup and brought it to the boy, who had seated himself cross-legged on the floor. He went back to the kitchen, rubbed the yams with oil, and put them into the toaster oven. As he did so his beeper went off.

"Oh," Larkin said. "The truck." He started toward the stove, changed his mind, and went up to the roof to get more wood. He brought down two loads and stacked them against the rear wall.

"Listen," Larkin said. "I have to go out for a couple of hours . . . there's sweet potatoes should be ready in one hour.

Keep the fire going, and better not answer the phone if it rings . . . can you handle that?"

The boy looked up; his lips parted but he did not speak.

"All right," Larkin said. "You don't have to talk. As long as you understand everything . . . Listen, I'm turning the oven off. If you know how to do it, turn it back on. I bet you know how to do it . . ." He shut off the oven and left.

Larkin circled the BQE to Queens and dropped off the van, avoiding the office. He rode back toward Brooklyn on a jammed rush-hour train, nervousness building in him. What if the boy understood nothing, was an idiot, as Leveaux had suggested? What if he somehow set the building on fire? Getting off at Marcy Avenue, Larkin realized that the boy might well speak nothing but Spanish, assuming he was rational at all. He hurried home, not optimistic.

Inside, the loft was warm, the fire thoroughly built up. The boy still squatted by the stove, but he appeared to be asleep. Larkin saw that the kitten had crawled up into his lap. He went into the kitchen and found a yam and a half, neatly sectioned, warming in the oven. Larkin salted the food and ate.

Back in the main room, the boy had opened his eyes. He was stroking the kitten with complete attention. Larkin indicated the mattress with his forefinger. "You sleep there. Whenever you're tired."

He took the camera bag into the darkroom and began to work on the film under the light of a red bulb. When the strip of negatives had dried he made a contact sheet and selected five for printing. Exhibits A through E, to be delivered to Leveaux in the morning. Larkin stood over his printer, watching the hard white light confirm the devil's imprint on the sensitive squares of paper. Here was evidence of something Leveaux and the police would not consider, proof for dim suspicions Larkin had for a long time entertained.

It was late when Larkin emerged from the darkroom, but the boy was still nodding by the stove. Larkin lifted him onto the mattress and stretched himself out by the stove. But the boy got up and lay on his side on the floor. Larkin moved the mattress nearer to the heat and placed the boy back on it. Again the boy got up, moving to the far side of the stove. Larkin gave in. He made a pallet for the child out of loose clothes covered with a sheet, and slept on the mattress himself.

In the morning Larkin rose early and took a train to Bellevue, arriving at an hour when he knew Leveaux would be off duty. He dropped the photos at the front desk, scrawling a note on the envelope which falsely stated that he would be out of town for several days. On the way back to Brooklyn he picked up a first aid manual which contained a section on burn treatment. Back in Williamsburg, he cruised the markets, filling his shoulder bag with more appealing foodstuffs than he had troubled to buy for quite some time.

It was another clear day and sunlight was rushing in the windows when Larkin returned to the loft. The boy had got up and evidently stoked the fire. Larkin saw that his shirt, which was stained with pus and blood, had again begun to stick to the burns.

"Can you get that off?" Larkin said. The boy leaned forward and tugged the shirt from his shoulders. The tearing sound it made as it came away from his back set Larkin's teeth on edge, though the child did not even murmur. At any rate the boy had proved that he understood English and was somewhat in his senses.

Larkin boiled water in the kitchen, scalded his own hands, and mixed a solution to wash the boy's back. He squatted on the floor, holding the first aid book open with his toe, and according to prescription cleaned the wounds and anointed them with the lotions he had stolen from the hospital. Throughout, the boy's face remained empty and he made no complaint.

Finished, Larkin picked up the shirt from the floor and shook it out. The pentangle appeared in perfect detail on the cloth; there was no getting away from the thing. Larkin turned on the answering machine to handle any callers. He took the shirt into the kitchen and put it on to boil, then went out to a secondhand store on Kent Avenue. Here he searched out a few changes of clothes in approximate small sizes, and also bought a short jacket with an imitation-fur lining. Back in the loft he spread these purchases on the floor in front of the boy.

"For you," he said. "But maybe you shouldn't wear a shirt for a few days. Till those burns heal. If you can stay warm enough by the stove." The boy did not react. Larkin knelt on the floor, facing him.

"Tell me something," Larkin said. "Tell me your name, at least."

There was a silent pause, during which a log fell in the stove.

"It's all right," Larkin said. "You can —" He stopped, on the point of saying that he could be trusted, that there would be no more torments here and perhaps not much more pain. But he did not fully believe this himself. Possibly the child already knew better, understood that the secret heart of the world held only agony and fear. It was not unlikely that any terror the boy might have would one day be fulfilled.

Larkin stood up. "You've got to have a name," he said. He hesitated. "I'm going to call you Tommy. If you don't like that, say so." Larkin went into the kitchen and made sandwiches.

For two weeks Larkin stopped answering the phone; he let the machine take messages but never listened to them. He stayed away from the hospital, though he continued to deliver flowers two days a week. He did rather more cooking than had been his custom, hoping to tempt Tommy, who did eat enough to put on a little weight.

Tommy could not exactly have been said to prosper, but appeared reasonably content. He got on well with both the cats; it even seemed to Larkin that Dwango whined less since Tommy had come. The child made small efforts to be helpful: banking the fires, washing dishes, sometimes baking potatoes or preparing a bean soup when Larkin was out on the truck. Larkin took him once to the roof, where he crouched low to the asphalt and refused to approach the edge. He gave no sign of wanting to leave the building, and Larkin thought it better that he did not. All Tommy's movements were quiet and orderly; Larkin grew to enjoy their community of silence.

It troubled Larkin that he had no strong painkillers. He knew the burns had to hurt, though Tommy never betrayed a trace of discomfort. Larkin gave him as much Tylenol as he considered safe, and treated the burns twice a day. As far as he could tell they were healing normally, from the edges in, slowly turning to ropey red scars. Larkin worried about this scarification, but he had no idea how to prevent it.

Twice daily Larkin ran his oiled fingers over the scorched pentangle, touching it as lightly as he could manage. The unknown characters claimed a constant place in his mind and Larkin found he could not stop thinking about them. But he thought it a poor plan to dwell too long on Tommy's back.

Hiding in his darkroom from the boy, Larkin made new prints from the negatives and examined the wounds in close detail. He copied the five characters in a circle on a piece of paper, leaving out the star. After nightfall he took the paper to the Sparrow, who had some expertise with hieroglyphs and code.

The Sparrow tilted the paper under a lamp.

"You must be slipping, Larkin," he said. "Go up to Lee Avenue and you'll see this stuff written all over the walls. It's Hebrew."

"All right," Larkin said. "Maybe I am slipping. What does it say, wise man?"

The Sparrow passed through a curtain into his bedroom and came out paging through a dictionary.

"Here we go," he said. "Leviathan."

"The old serpent," Larkin said, considering the matter aloud. "Will he speak soft words unto thee?"

Bent beneath the ceiling bulb, the Sparrow continued to thumb the dictionary. "Where'd you get this, anyway?"

Larkin had prepared no answer to this question. He lied and claimed he'd found the paper on the street.

Larkin listened to his message tape one morning when Tommy had gone to wash. The boy's wounds had healed enough so

that he could take a shower. There were several calls on the
tape from Leveaux. The first one briefly mentioned the child's
disappearance from the hospital and inquired if Larkin might
know anything about it. The next few threatened Larkin with
all sorts of mayhem from police, judges, social workers. The
most recent message was rather weary in tone and merely
requested that Larkin return the call. Larkin prepared himself for duplicity and dialed Bellevue.

"I've been out of town for a while," he said, when the doctor came to the phone. "I'm not sure if I understand all your
messages."

"Are you sure you're not sure?"

Larkin didn't answer this; he disliked telling outright lies.

"The boy vanished," Leveaux said, "if you didn't 'understand' that from the messages. And as far as anyone knows
you were the last one to see him before that happened. Tell
me one thing, Larkin, was he still in the photo room when
you went back?"

"He was there," Larkin said. "Maybe his father could have
taken him."

"He could have," Leveaux said. "But he didn't. He was seen
in the neighborhood last week, looking for the boy."

"Did the police pick him up, then?"

"No. He's gone too, now. The police have a man at his
apartment, but he hasn't been back there."

Larkin leaned back, put his feet on the table, looked at the
dust on his windows.

"That's really too bad," he said.

"Listen, Larkin. If you have that boy, you're out of your
mind. He's badly hurt and from the way he was acting, I'm
ninety percent sure he's autistic. He could hurt himself, kill
himself. He could hurt other people. Believe me, children
like that can do real damage. And you could be in quite a lot
of trouble. The boy needs help. Professional help. Larkin,
you're not a doctor."

"Help like they hand out at Spofford?" Larkin said. "Like
what he's been getting around the house at home?"

"Okay," said Leveaux. "I don't know if you're sane or not
and I really don't care. I'm not even going to ask you if you

took the boy. But the police have been all over me for two weeks and I'm getting very tired of that. If it ever occurs to them to ask for your name and address I'm going to give it to them."

"I have nothing to hide," Larkin said. "My life is an open book. If they come out here they'll only be bored. But one thing, Anton."

"What?"

"Call me if they are coming over. I'd like to clean up for them. The place is a mess. Would you do that?"

"I might. But don't count on it, Larkin. I'd suggest you clean up anyway. As you put it."

"Thanks, Anton," Larkin said. "Just let your conscience be your guide."

He hung up. Tommy had re-entered the room and was standing near the south windows, drying himself. Larkin gazed at him abstractedly; he was thinking chiefly of other things. Tommy's face was lit by a dusty shaft of sunlight and there was a faint hint of a smile somewhere about him. He turned his head through the sunbeam and Larkin saw something just below his hairline he'd never noticed before. Larkin reached stealthily for his glasses and put them on. In fine white scratches on Tommy's forehead were inscribed the numerals 666. Larkin suffered an icy sense of déjà vu. He could now see traces of other old scars on the boy's chest above the towel, but he felt no desire at all to inspect them more closely.

13
Larkin Answers the Telephone

A TUESDAY MORNING, Larkin stood dull eyed in the doorway to the street, warming his hands on a tin cup full of coffee. A brown two-door sedan nosed uncertainly down the street and drifted to a stop at the curb opposite. Inside it a man shuffled paper, then he got out of the car. This man wore a blue polyester suit, a wide striped tie, and rectangular steel-rimmed glasses. With his right elbow he clasped a vinyl briefcase to his side. He wandered across Broadway toward Larkin, reading something from a clipboard in his right hand. Reaching the sidewalk, he glanced up at Larkin from the clipboard.

"Is this thirty-two Broadway?"

"It is," Larkin said.

"Ah. Is there a, ah . . ." The stranger squinted at his clipboard. "A Clarence . . . D —, D — . . . a Clarence Larkin? Living here?"

Larkin looked down at the man's lowered head from the raised step of his entry. The stranger's hair was a frizzy blond and thinning in places. On the top sheet of the clipboard, Larkin could see the printed logo of New York's Department of Social Services.

"Nope," Larkin said. "This is a commercial building." He gestured to the window by the door, where the die cutters had put up their sign. The social worker looked up with a half smile.

"I knew it," he said. "The wrong address. Again."

"Secretaries," Larkin said, shaking his head.

"There's not any Larkin that *works* here, is there?"

"No Larkins anywhere around here at all that I know about," Larkin said.

"Well . . . thanks anyway. I couldn't use a phone here, could I?"

"Sorry," Larkin said. "Can't do it. Rules." He went inside and locked the door. Up above he could hear his telephone ringing. Larkin ran up the stairs to answer it.

When he picked up the receiver he said nothing, only waited. After a moment, Leveaux's voice spoke.

"Larkin? Are you there?"

"I'm here, all right," Larkin said.

"Well, look," Leveaux said. "The police are asking around about that boy again. It looks like one of our nurses took the story to the *Post*. About that, um, design, and the rest of it. I don't know if you would have seen it."

"No," Larkin said. "Sorry I missed it."

"It was two days ago," Leveaux said. "Well, since the story the police came back here again. This time they talked to the nurse, not me. She knows you were here that day, she was in there prepping the burns when you took the pictures. I think she gave them your name, Larkin."

"Sweet of her," Larkin said. "I always wanted to be in the *Post*. Do you think she gave the address?"

"I doubt she had it. But somebody from Social Services called and asked me for it. That was yesterday."

"Terrific," Larkin said. "Maybe they'll put me on welfare. How long before the address gets back around to the police, do you think?"

"What difference does it make? Larkin, you're missing the point."

"Did they ever find the father?"

"No. Not yet. Larkin, bring the boy back to the hospital. If you'll just do that, I can take care of it. I can keep you out of it altogether. Bring him back."

"What if I don't even have him?" Larkin said. "What if he really isn't here?"

Leveaux did not reply.

"Thanks for calling, Anton," Larkin said. "Don't worry if you have trouble reaching me for a little while. I might be out quite a bit."

Larkin hung up, reached across the table to the answering machine, and turned it on. Tommy roused himself from his pallet and went out to the bathroom on the landing. Larkin jumped out of his chair, lit a cigarette, and began pacing up and down the apartment, smoking in hard, fast drags. Tommy came back into the room and put more wood on the fire. Larkin got himself another cup of coffee and sat down, looking reflectively at the boy.

"Tommy," he said. The child rose from the stove and turned to face him.

"Where could you go if you weren't here? Is there anybody else you could sort of stay with for a while? Anybody at all?"

Tommy sat down abruptly on his pallet and turned three-quarters away from Larkin. He looked intently at one leg of the stove. The kitten arrived and Tommy knocked it away, returning his clenched hand to his lap.

"Okay," Larkin said. "It was only a question. Don't worry about it." On the table just behind his chair, the phone rang loudly and the answering machine clicked on. Larkin wheeled around and poised his finger over its switch.

"Message for Larkin." The voice emerged scratchily from the machine's speaker. "It's Charles. Can you come up and —" Larkin picked up the receiver and shut off the tape with his other hand.

"Sorry," he said. "I just walked in the door." The other voice continued after a barely perceptible pause.

"Can you come up here? It's about the camera supplies."

"When?"

"Tonight. Ten-thirty."

"I can't tonight," Larkin said. There was a hesitation at the other end of the line.

"It's fairly important." Another pause. "We need to discuss the scheduling."

"I can't help it," Larkin said. "I have to take care of some things before. It'll have to wait a couple of days."

"Are you sure you can't come for an hour tonight? One hour."

"I won't be in town," Larkin said. "I have to go out. I'll meet you day after tomorrow. Five o'clock."

"Here."

"Not good. It's . . . too far. Come to the other place, where we met before."

"Met when?"

"The first time."

"It would be better here."

"No," said Larkin. "Do it my way this one time."

The caller hung up without replying. Larkin pressed his ear to the phone, listening for any irregularity on the line, but he heard nothing.

Putting down the receiver, he got out of his chair and grabbed an empty laundry bag from the floor. He started toward the table where Tommy's few clothes were stacked beside the radio, but something near the windows caught his eye. A fine point of light hovered on the Sheetrock wall, lobbed there perhaps by some reflection from the street. The light flickered in an even pattern: there, not there; on, off, on. Larkin stopped in the middle of a step. The laundry bag trailed from his fingers. He stared at the light as though hypnotized. His jaw slackened and his eyes grew round.

Tommy turned around on his bed and saw Larkin frozen in the center of the room. When a minute had passed without Larkin moving, the boy went over and pushed him sharply in the small of the back. Larkin stumbled forward and then walked normally to a chair and fell into it. Slowly, deliberately, he massaged his eyes and temples. Then he raised his head and looked about the room. Larkin picked up Tommy's jacket and tossed it to the boy's neat catch.

"Okay, get ready," Larkin said. "We're taking a trip to the country."

14
Little Russia

AT THE PORT AUTHORITY Larkin and Tommy boarded a bus for New Jersey. Seated in the back of the carriage, Larkin leafed through a *Post* he had bought in the station, but the story about the search for the missing boy had not carried over. The trip took a couple of hours and Tommy dozed off in his seat.

When the bus stopped at the main station of a faceless Jersey town, Larkin woke the boy and they got off the bus. The wait for a connection was long and dreary. Larkin bought Tommy two candy bars and installed him in a molded plastic seat. He himself went around the block to a liquor store and bought a bottle of Chinese vodka, which he dropped into the shoulder bag he was carrying. Back in the bus station, Larkin walked up and down and smoked.

The second leg of the journey was shorter and there was no station at the end of it. Larkin and Tommy got out at a crossroads and the bus groaned slowly away from them. Across the road was a low barnlike structure, painted red, and behind it a wide lake. It seemed warmer than it had been in the city, and the sky was a charitable blue.

Larkin and Tommy crossed the road and stood in a gravelled parking lot before the red building. To their right, at the top of a small round hill, there was a white church with gilded onion domes, each topped with the Russian cross. A glittering mosaic figure of a crowned and bearded saint, two stories high, covered the facade. The saint raised one hand, in benediction or perhaps in warning; his face was distant and severe.

A small brown Shetland pony came around the curved wall of the church from the rear. Someone had tied a green garden hose around the pony's neck and the hose trailed several yards behind him. The pony came to the stairway which led up to the church and trotted down the grassy slope beside it. The copper screw at the end of the hose rang down the steps like a little bell. Reaching level ground, the pony stopped and sniffed, then went around the red building toward the lake.

Larkin looked back up at the church. At the head of the stairs, a lean wild-haired man had suddenly appeared. His mouth worked vigorously but no sound emerged from it. Indeed, it was eerily quiet all around.

"That's Evstifeyko," Larkin said, touching Tommy's shoulder. "The holy fool. He lives in a hut behind the church. He never goes more than fifty yards from the sanctuary, they say."

Evstifeyko turned away and ambled into the shadow of a clump of trees beside the church. Larkin handed Tommy the laundry bag which contained his clothes and together they began walking down the road.

After a quarter of a mile Larkin turned off to the left. Here there was a small house built in two mismatched sections. The right-hand part was painted a flaking yellow and the part to the left was bare wood. The ground was lower under the left section and a wooden ramp went up to its door.

"They say that other room floated here a year there was a flood," Larkin told Tommy. "Arkady's grandfather looked out one day and saw it sitting there . . . so he built a foundation under it. That's what they say."

The yard in front of the house was untended and tire tracks crossed it here and there. It was sheltered from the road by a low line of miscellaneous bushes. No car was in sight. Larkin went to the right-hand door and opened it with a key. He and the boy went inside.

The little house was divided into two rooms and there was a small enclosed porch off the back. Someone seemed to be in the process of reinsulating the walls. There were tools and bits of Sheetrock scattered on the kitchen floor. In the other room, three beds had been crowded together. Spread over the beds were a TV camera, a monitor, and a portable video deck.

Larkin stepped down into the porch and opened the back door. A long yard, edged with tall trees, stretched back to a thicket at its far end. The grass in the yard was overgrown and brambly. Disrepaired furniture and appliances scattered the yard, poking out of the tangles. In one place someone had scratched out a little garden.

"Well . . ." Larkin said to Tommy. "You can go out and look around. Just don't go too far from the house."

The boy went down the porch steps and wandered toward the end of the yard. Larkin went into the kitchen, found a pot in the sink, and started coffee. He took the vodka out of his bag and put it in the freezer, then went to stand in the open roadside door.

Presently a long tan car, patched with Bondo around its door handles, drove into the yard and stopped, and a large man got out of it. He was not fat so much as massive. Heavy black hair poured out of the round cap on his head, and there was a full square beard resting on his chest. Around his neck he wore a blood-red scarf with fringes. Larkin felt the surge of warm well-being which always came over him when he saw Arkady after an absence. He went down the steps and embraced the bearded man.

"It's good you've come," Arkady said. They went into the house. Arkady opened the refrigerator and began to put things into it from the paper bag he had brought: eggs, a box of mushrooms, a carton of milk. Larkin poured coffee into two cups. Arkady turned from the refrigerator, holding up the vodka.

"Look what our luck brought us."

"Yes," Larkin said. "I brought something else, too." They carried their cups to the porch and sat down at a circular table.

"You've been doing some work on the place," Larkin said.

"I think I'm going to spend the winter here. My father is angry again. I don't really want to go back to Brooklyn."

"That's bad."

"I don't know. I'd feel better if he weren't left alone. He's totally blind now, I think. But he seems to get angry whenever I go there now. Like me when I eat meat."

"How does he get around?"

"He gets around. Radar. He still goes to work, even. People in the neighborhood step out of his way."

"I saw Evstifeyko on the way in."

"Yes . . . have you seen the Sparrow?"

"Last week. He's about the same," Larkin said. "You know, the weather's very strange here. Almost like summer, and it's green. It's been much colder in the city."

"Yes. I still have some things in the garden, even . . . Maybe it's the end of the world, who knows?"

Larkin looked at him curiously, but Arkady's dark Tartar eyes revealed no special meaning.

"I've got a little boy with me," he said suddenly. "He's Spanish, I think, but he doesn't talk at all. His father is a devil worshiper, I heard, and he burned some hexes on his back with a soldering iron. I kidnapped him from Bellevue. The police are looking for him in New York."

"Why didn't you let them have him?"

"They want to restore him to the bosom of his family. Arkady, I was wondering if you could keep him here for a while. I think the police found out I have him, and I've got some other things to deal with right now anyway. He doesn't eat so much and he's very quiet. He can take care of himself fairly well. The burns are almost healed and I brought some ointment to put on them. I have some money I could give you, too."

"Where is he now?" Arkady said. Larkin pointed to the porch windows. Arkady got up to look out. Tommy was roving through the thicket, deep in the yard.

"Well. I'll keep him," Arkady said. "You can hang on to your money for now though. I don't need so much here."

"Thanks, Arkady."

"Don't worry about it. Let's go out and dig up some potatoes."

Arkady Zeraschev, born in 1956, had been raised between the Park Slope section of Brooklyn and a Russian immigrant community in New Jersey. His mother, a devout Orthodox Christian, had raised him firm in the faith and though the adult Arkady seldom went to church he had forgotten no part of its teachings. Like Larkin, he was conversant with a number of other doctrines as well.

When Arkady was nineteen, his mother left his father and settled permanently in New Jersey, living in what had formerly been the family's summer home. Arkady's younger sister moved with their mother; he himself remained with Fyodor Zeraschev, a civil servant, in the brownstone Fyodor owned in Park Slope. Eventually he quarreled with his father over his refusal to finish college and become an engineer. Arkady left the Brooklyn house and for more than a year lived mostly in the streets, staying with friends, visiting his mother sometimes, often staying nowhere at all. During this period he supported himself marginally with technical odd jobs.

Arkady possessed a godlike power over all machines. Equipment blossomed under his touch. Arkady became a film technician and thus made contact with Larkin and the Sparrow, the latter being a professional sound man. Arkady molded the three of them into a skeletal but self-sufficient crew, which could do work ordinarily requiring ten or more people. For a couple of years the group got along by providing cut-rate service to a variety of low-budget productions.

When his mother died in the fall of 1981, Arkady got out of commercial film. The Sparrow became a union sound man, and Larkin also quit the business. Arkady's sister had left New Jersey to become a nun after her mother's death. Arkady began dividing his time between New Jersey and the Brooklyn house of his father, with whom he was somewhat reconciled. He still did occasional film work, enough to meet expenses. But he intended to spend most of his time in Little Russia, to remain there long enough to meditate on his past and perhaps to devise a future. The story which Larkin falsely told of his own grandfather was true of Arkady's.

Nightfall. In the kitchen, Larkin washed potatoes and sliced mushrooms; Arkady chopped onions and minced garlic with a cleaver. Sitting in a chair against the wall, Tommy watched them work. The two cooked an enormous dish comprising potato, egg, and a wealth of spices. They carried three plates onto the porch and began to eat.

Arkady and Larkin ate hugely, incredibly. After a time Tommy withdrew from the table and watched them from a corner, his eyes widening. Larkin and Arkady ate steadily, without conversation, refilling their plates again and again till there was nothing left.

Arkady pushed his chair back and smiled. "We thank Thee, O Christ our God, that Thou sated us with Thy earthly good things. Do not deprive us also of Thy heavenly kingdom," he said. "And now, *let's drink the vodka.*"

Larkin took the plates into the kitchen and came back with the bottle, frosted now, and two tall tapered shot glasses. Arkady poured until vodka trembled at the brim of each glass.

"To Holy Mother Russia."

They touched their glasses and drained them. Larkin poured.

"To your mother, may she be singing with the angels in heaven even as we speak."

Arkady poured.

"To my little father. And to your parents and kin as well."

Larkin poured.

"To the desert saints."

Arkady poured.

"Health and happiness to the Sparrow."

Larkin poured.

"To the Apocalypse. And the heavenly kingdom too if there is one."

Arkady reached for the bottle and knocked it over. Nothing came out. The bottle was empty. Larkin attempted to stand up and crashed sideways onto the floor. He began to laugh hysterically, not trying to get up. Arkady also laughed, his laughter seeming to shake the walls and floors of the little house. Larkin laughed until tears flowed from his eyes. He rolled over on his back and began to talk, slowly, with long loose pauses between his words.

". . . I think we're acting like idiots, Arkady . . . but do you remember, Paul said it's better to be a fool for God than a wise man for all mankind . . . I think he said that but perhaps I may have remembered it wrong . . . my memory is not like it used to be . . . it was perfect once . . . I never lost one second from my life . . . yet I hated it . . . do you know, Arkady? . . . in the future men and women will be completely without memory of anything . . . already I've seen it . . . there are certain people even now who have developed to that state . . . I had great pride in my memory . . . now I labor at forgetting, learn to forget . . . I don't remember much at all now . . . but I still dream, more than before . . . I've been dreaming of the beasts in the Apocalypse . . . the holy beasts, not the others . . . but possibly it's all a fantasy, from some demon . . . I don't have the strength to be certain . . . for a long time I've known that the demons are real, material . . . they are not only ideas . . . just look at the boy . . . I call him Tommy, did I tell you? . . . he answers to it . . . but several demons visit me now . . . most often the one of despondency . . . a dull wretched little devil, without even a face, really . . . I suppose I shouldn't complain about the quality of my demons, though . . . when he comes I can't do anything at all . . . I've been trying to make pictures, new ones . . . inside the body . . . things that might be happening there . . . they frighten me and I can't finish them . . . I sit with my demons and don't move . . . for hours sometimes . . . time falls away from me and I don't know it's passing . . . Saint John wrote, there should be time no longer . . . I think we really are in the last days, Arkady . . . it's what my dreams seem to be saying . . . but maybe the dreams are demonic too . . . the desert fathers defeated their demons with continual prayer . . . prayer of the heart . . . Lord Jesus Christ, have mercy on me, a sinner . . . I have found my heart and entered it but it was a burning house . . . I think that many people are burning inside . . . did you know Arkady, that now they are beginning to literally burst into flames? . . . they burn and are gone in seconds . . . I've been keeping a file . . . spontaneous human combustion . . . almost no one has really noticed yet . . . the papers try to call it other things, other explanations . . . but there will be more . . . many more . . . I think if I could pray without ceasing, I would pray to burn."

"I think it would be a good idea if we drank some coffee," Arkady said. "What do you think about that?"

"All right . . . I doubt I could get up to make it, though."

"No," Arkady said, with deep seriousness. "It would probably be much easier for me. Since I'm already sitting in a chair, instead of lying on the floor like you are . . . I'll make the coffee." But for some time, Arkady did not move either.

Coffee was somehow produced at last and Larkin raised himself to the table to drink it. His eyes, like Arkady's, were red from the tears of laughter. The two did not speak. Tommy had been located in the bedroom, already asleep.

Larkin finished his coffee. "Can we go next door?" he said. "I'd like to go to the attic."

"I had to shut off the electricity over there," Arkady said. "I've been working on the wiring."

"Aren't there still some candles?"

"All right." Arkady got heavily up and led the way to the door. Outside it had grown somewhat cooler. Arkady went up the ramp to the other part of the house and fumbled with a padlock on its door. Larkin waited for him to enter before he chanced the ramp himself. Once inside he closed the door behind him.

The room he was in was completely dark. Larkin took a step and a pile of books tumbled and slithered around his feet, some of the thousands of tracts and lives of the saints that Arkady's mother and sister had kept. Larkin could hear Arkady moving away and he followed the sound into the next room, feeling his way along the wall. This room was also crowded with what seemed probably to be more books. Arkady's footsteps were mounting the stairs. Larkin groped to a stairway at the far end of the room and followed him up.

In the attic, Arkady was lighting candles, long white slender candles which stood in ranks at one end of the room. The roof was peaked, triangular, with wooden rafters. Behind and above the rows of candles hung several icons, painted by Arkady's sister. Arkady lit a square of charcoal which lay on a tile before the icons, and placed a chip of frankincense on top of it.

Larkin regarded the icons: hooded saints, a dark-eyed Madonna, the remote Byzantine Christ. A feather of sweet smoke rose from the tile.

"We should pray to the saints," Arkady muttered. After a few minutes, when the incense had been consumed, he snuffed out the candles and lit a tiny lamp which hung on a fine cord from the peak of the roof. Arkady touched the lamp and set it swinging from side to side. The lamp passed like a scythe between himself and Larkin; it did not give enough light for them to see each other clearly. In a low even tone, Arkady began to chant.

   . . . Svaty Bodge . . .
   . . . Svaty Krepky . . .
   . . . Svaty Besmetny . . .
   . . . Pomeeloy nas . . .

Larkin joined in the prayer, echoing Arkady's monotone, repeating it over and over to the rhythm of the swinging light.

. . . Svaty Bodge . . .
. . . Svaty Krepky . . .
. . . Svaty Besmetny . . .
. . . Pomeeloy nas . . .

The chant bored into Larkin, calmed him, soothed him, united with his pulse. Later, when Arkady had blown out the lamp and Larkin lay in the bedroom seeking sleep, the little light continued to swing across his mind, back and forth, regular as a metronome.

In the morning both their hands were trembling. Larkin got out of bed first and crawled into the kitchen to make coffee. A squirrel was sitting in the sink. Larkin shooed it out the open window where it had apparently come in. After a few minutes Arkady came into the kitchen. He rummaged in a cabinet and found a pint bottle with vodka in the bottom. Arkady took a drink and passed the bottle to Larkin wordlessly. Larkin took a drink. Somewhat more steadily, they carried their coffee to the porch.

"Are you hungry?" Arkady said.

Larkin laughed. "Not much."

"Neither am I."

"Listen, Arkady, I'm leaving you keys to my place in Brooklyn." Larkin pushed two loose keys across the table. "You can stay there if you need to be in the city. I won't be there for a while."

"Where are you going, then?"

"A little urban camping, maybe." Larkin paused. "I feel like I could use some time in the desert."

"Do you? Don't forget, they have demons in the desert too."

"I know," Larkin said. "Arkady, I'll be listening to my machine. If anything happens with the boy, or whatever. I'll get the message if you call."

"All right. Do you want anything done if I do go to Brooklyn?"

"I don't think so." Larkin drained his cup. "I guess I should say goodbye." He went into the bedroom. Tommy opened his eyes and sat up in bed.

"I'm going away . . . You're staying here for a while, with

Arkady," Larkin said. "It's all set up. You'll like it here, it's better than the city."

Arkady was standing in the bedroom doorway. Tommy looked over at him and smiled. Larkin put his hand on the boy's head for a moment, then removed it and went out of the house.

Outside the day was gray, the sky clouded, with a promise of rain. Larkin stood facing Arkady at the roadside.

"Well, I think he likes you," Larkin said. "He doesn't smile that much."

"It'll be fine," Arkady said. "If you want I can drive you to the bus station."

"No. I'd be better off alone, I think . . ."

"Larkin, did I ever tell you that story about the unicorn?"

"I don't think so."

"They say when Noah built the ark, the unicorn refused to get on it. Because he was proud and preferred solitude. The unicorn was a strong swimmer and he kept his nose out of the water for twenty days."

"And?"

"A little bird came along and perched on the unicorn's horn. The weight pushed his head under and he drowned. That's why there aren't any unicorns anymore."

"How much did the bird weigh?"

"Not much at all. Be careful, Larkin."

"Yes, Batiushka," Larkin said, in sudden irritation. "Did I ask for your advice?"

"No. Maybe you're just lucky."

"Maybe . . ." Larkin's anger left him again. "It was good to see you."

Larkin put down his bag and stepped forward. He and Arkady kissed each other on both cheeks. Larkin hefted his bag and began walking down the road, his hands in his pockets, the bag snug against his hip. Arkady watched him steadily receding. Larkin came to a bend in the road and disappeared.

Part II

The Cell

The revolutionary is a doomed man . . . He is an implacable enemy of this world, and if he continues to live in it,
that will only be in order to destroy it more effectively.

Sergey Nechayev,
Catechism of the Revolutionary

15
Riverside Drive

CHARLES MERCER STOOD at the wall phone, smoking steadily, listening and responding in soft dull tones. After hanging
up he made a note on a scratch pad hung beside the phone,
tore out the page, and took a seat on the porch. Mercer glanced
at the sheet, snapped it into a double fold, and tucked it into
his shirt pocket. He sagged back into the couch, a low soft
affair, and looked up at the moldings on the high ceiling.

"Well," Mercer said. "Looks like he's not coming tonight."
He turned to look at the man sitting next to him on the couch.
"He says he's busy, Simon."

"Busy?" Simon said. "How so?" Simon was long-boned and
exceedingly thin. He wore horn-rimmed glasses with slightly
oversize frames, which gave him a perpetual look of mild
surprise. His hair was dirty blond and thinning at the back.
A thick shock of it hung over his forehead. Simon was rather
more smartly dressed than the other people in the room,
wearing a soft blue crewneck sweater, pressed jeans, and a
dark sport jacket. His face was conventionally handsome, and
he might have been mistaken for a male model, were it not
for his skinniness and height. Mercer turned away from him
and stubbed out his cigarette in an ashtray on an end table
by the couch.

"He didn't really say," Mercer said. "I told him it was important. He still said he couldn't make it. Going out of town,
he said."

The room they were sitting in was large, airy, and quite

pleasant. There were two people in it besides Simon and Charles Mercer. In an armchair opposite the couch where they sat was a heavyset man in dark green coveralls. His hair was black, cut long and parted in the middle, and he wore a mustache which curved around the corners of his mouth. His name was David Hutton. Above him, on the cream-colored wall, hung a Warhol print of Chairman Mao.

"That's just beautiful," Hutton said. "I said the guy was unreliable. Didn't I? Ruben?"

The fourth man sat on a window seat in a large bay window which looked out over Riverside Park from a height of eight stories. His dark hair was cropped in a bowl pattern and he wore aviator glasses, half-tinted at the top. Ruben Carrera was his name. He sat sideways in the windowseat, cross-legged, half-turned away from the others in the room. In the park below a wind was blowing fitfully, turning up the leaves on the trees.

"I agree with David," Carrera said.

"He said he could meet the day after tomorrow," Mercer said.

"Well, then," Simon said. He removed a small leather date book from his inside pocket and opened it. "Today is . . . November second. Correct?"

No one bothered to confirm him.

"I don't see such a severe problem," Simon said. "We'll meet with Larkin on November fourth. Correct?" He looked at Mercer.

"You got it." Mercer was a small wiry man, with reddish curly hair and pale eyes. He bent to a leather jacket crumpled at his feet and took another cigarette out of its pocket. Lighting the cigarette, Mercer cupped his hands against a nonexistent wind. On each of his fingers, between the second joint and the knuckle, was a smooth shiny scar.

"Charles, you smoke too much," Simon said. "You shouldn't smoke at all. Some day —"

"I know, I know," Mercer said. "Comes the revolution, the capitalist imperialist cigarette companies will drown in an ocean of blood. Don't worry, Simon. I can roll my own. Grow it too if I have to."

"Did you set a time with Larkin?"

Mercer took the phone pad sheet out of his pocket and inspected it.

"Five o'clock."

"Well. Can we all be here?"

"It's not for here," Mercer said. "Too far for him, he told me."

"What the hell is that supposed to mean?" Hutton said. "He's been up here before."

"Where, then?" Simon said.

Mercer hesitated. "I'm not totally sure," he said at length.

"Oh Christ," Hutton said, shifting in his chair.

"Have a little patience, David," Mercer said. "He could have been worried about the phone. Or maybe there was somebody there when I called. We don't know any of that. Probably he was just being careful."

"Paranoid, you mean," Carrera said.

"In a certain context, paranoia can be a valuable quality," Simon said. "We do need to know where we're meeting him, though, don't we?"

"I think I know," Mercer said. "He told me, where we met the first time. I doubt that would mean your office, Simon, not if he doesn't want to come here. I think he means the first place he met me."

"And where would that be?" Simon said.

"That park off 23rd Street, by the Flatiron Building," Mercer said. "What do they call it?"

"Madison Square," Carrera said.

"That's that, then," Simon said. "Madison Square, November fourth, five o'clock." He marked the book and dropped it back into his jacket pocket.

"I don't like it," Hutton said. "I never have liked Larkin. He doesn't operate on schedule like the rest of us. He's always just a little bit weird. I don't see why we have to have him in."

"Don't you really, David?" Simon reached into his jacket again and drew a hat pin out of the lining. The hat pin was seven inches long and had an imitation pearl bead at the end of it. Simon began to clean his nails with the hat pin. Because of its awkward length, he held the pin immobile and moved the fingers of his other hand across its point. "Are you volunteering for his position, David?"

Hutton looked down at the oriental carpet underneath his thick shoes.

"David has a point," Carrera said. "I think Larkin is a complete lunatic. From what I've seen."

"Of course he's a lunatic," Simon said. "But he's our lunatic. We need one."

"If he's crazy, then he's unreliable," Hutton said. "Like I keep telling you. We want stable people. Do we want wackos?"

"For this particular project, we do," Simon said. He shifted the hat pin and began meticulously paring the nails of his right hand. "Trust me a little, David. I've studied Larkin and I can control him. I know how his mind works and I know what he'll do."

"But where does he stand?" Carrera said. "Is he in the cell or not in the cell or what? You've never been very clear about that, Simon. We don't know where he came from or anything. He hasn't shown a real commitment. That's what bothers me."

"Really, now?" Simon looked over the hat pin at Carrera and smiled with unpleasant rigidity. "It occurs to me that by the Mau Mau criterion, Larkin is more firmly committed than any of you."

Carrera reversed his position in the window seat, turning his other profile to the room. The left side of his face was strikingly different from the right, which was attractive in a sharp bony way. On the left side, Carrera's features were masked by a large burn, which resembled molten plastic, or perhaps a many-fingered hand. The scar extended over Carrera's left nostril, drew down the corner of his mouth, and vanished into his eye socket, under the dark glasses. In fact, Carrera was blind in the left eye.

"Yes," Simon said. "I think that we just might institute the Mau Mau method in this group. Now. That would reduce dissension, wouldn't it? Indeed it would. I'd like each one of you to carry out an action. On your own. By say, day after tomorrow, four o'clock. Have it done before we meet Larkin."

Carrera turned full face to the room and grinned. "Finally," he said. "It's only the group that's been holding me back."

"I'm so glad you're pleased," Simon said, concentrating on the hat pin and his nails.

"What, just like that?" Hutton was sputtering, half out of his chair. "In forty-eight hours? No planning? Simon, you're crazy too."

"Use your imagination," Simon said. "Remember, 'The urge to destroy is a creative urge.' "

"You say those quotation marks so nicely," Mercer said. "Do we get an arms issue for this at least?"

"Of course," Simon said. "David, you can go ahead with that."

"I won't be needing anything," Carrera said, still grinning.

"Well, I will," Mercer said.

"So that's all settled," Simon looked across at Hutton. "Correct?"

"Oh sure, Simon. Anything you say. Anything at all." Hutton subsided to the edge of his seat.

"Just for the sake of argument, Simon," Mercer said. "Do you get to play Mau Mau yourself?"

Simon whirled round, a blur of speed, the hat pin glittering in his right hand. The pin shot through a fold of Mercer's shirt and buried itself full-length in the cushion behind him. Mercer could feel the cold sliver of metal against his rib cage, but he remained outwardly unmoved. Simon withdrew the pin and turned back toward the room. The pin protruded from between his first and second fingers, an extension of his white-knuckled fist. Simon presented its point to the light.

"Don't you worry about me," he whispered. "None of you has to worry about me."

"Very impressive," Mercer said. "You punched a hole in my shirt. I don't have such a lot of shirts."

"I'll give you one of mine," Simon said tightly. "I don't want any more argument. I just want you all to bring me some heads."

16

The Arsenal

MERCER, CARRERA, and Hutton climbed into a dusky brown elevator cage and rode creakily down to the lobby of Simon's building. In the elevator Hutton rocked on the balls of his feet and several times cleared his throat as if to speak, though he never did. Carrera continued to grin, behind his glasses; Mercer was merely silent. Outside the building Carrera chopped one hand downward to indicate his farewell and walked quickly up the hill toward Broadway, leaving Hutton and Mercer standing on the sidewalk.

"My sweet Lord," Hutton said. "Now what?"

"Go out and kill somebody before four o'clock Thursday," Mercer said. "I guess."

Hutton wiped damp hair away from his forehead.

"Simon's gone crazy, I swear he has," he said. "I could use a drink, could you? We can walk over to the Dublin House."

"Come on, it's the middle of the day. I'd rather we go down to your place and look over the stuff."

"Just a beer, then."

"Ah," Mercer said. "Pick up some on the way if you have to have it."

Mercer and Hutton walked over to Broadway and took a downtown express. At 34th Street they changed for the local and rode to 28th. Hutton lived in a Chelsea highrise, between Seventh and Eighth avenues on 26th. On the way back up Seventh, Hutton ducked into a deli and bought a carton of Guinness.

Hutton's apartment was minute: a narrow living room and one bedroom. The kitchenette was on the short hall connecting the two. In the living room was a long black couch, a color TV with a cable connection, and a couple of dessicated house plants. The ceiling was so low that Hutton, a big man, seemed to hulk in the room. Mercer went to the couch and sat down on it. Hutton broke out two beers and took the rest to the refrigerator. He came back from the kitchen with a pint bottle of bourbon.

"Take a beer," Hutton said.

"Nah, too early."

"Keep me company."

"Okay." Mercer accepted a Guinness. Hutton took a shot from the pint and chased it with beer, then leaned back on the couch. The two faced their grayish reflections on the blank television screen.

"I don't believe this," Hutton said. "I really don't." He picked up the pint again.

"Give me that," Mercer said.

"Sure."

Without drinking, Mercer put the bottle on the floor on the far side of himself, where Hutton couldn't reach it.

"Better stay out of the whisky," Mercer said. "You get all screwed up, you're going to go out and do something stupid, and ha ha, we all go to jail. Don't do it."

Hutton tensed for a protest, then didn't deliver it. "Okay," he said. "I guess you're right."

Mercer lit a cigarette and flipped the dead match in the direction of one of the potted plants.

"Who were the goddamn Mau Maus anyway?" Hutton said.

"Bad boy, David. Don't let Simon find out you don't know, or you'll have to listen to a long boring lecture."

"Why don't you just tell me in a short boring lecture?"

"African guerrillas. You had to have one clean kill in advance to get into the Mau Maus, which I think is what Simon had in mind."

"Crazy," Hutton said.

"Look, I hate to bring this up, David, but if you and Ruben

hadn't bitched about Larkin, Simon never would have thought of this."

"Yeah. I guess."

"I mean, Simon is just being consistent. You've got to remember, Larkin already went down south and brought back the goodies. Leave out the ideology and that puts him way ahead of us, in the way Simon's talking about. Especially after you and Ruben make such a big point of the whole thing. Whose idea was that, anyway?"

"You know I've never really trusted Larkin."

"Sure, fine. Did Ruben tell you to bring it up today?"

"Well. He did say something."

"Ah, David. You've been had. Ruben's wanted to do his own action for months. Now he's happier than a hog in deep mud. He's going to go blow something up and love it, and you got to go shoot somebody you don't really want to shoot."

"Do you really think he could have doped out the whole thing beforehand?"

"Doesn't it sort of look like that?"

"Oh God."

"Well, maybe he'll blow his hands off or something," Mercer said. "Ruben's not all that great with detonators, supposedly. If he was, we really wouldn't need Larkin."

"Why couldn't he have just brought it up direct?"

"It's the way he is. Look, David, maybe I shouldn't have told you, but you ought not to let anybody jerk you around. Next time somebody asks you to do something, think what's going to happen before you do it. *You* dope it out beforehand. Right?"

"Goddammit. But Ruben really doesn't like Larkin either. I know that."

"Sure. I mean, maybe Ruben didn't plan today out straight from A to Z. But it all could have been kind of anticipated, you know?"

"I guess I do now."

"Hindsight is a wonderful thing."

"But you, Charlie, you really don't think Larkin is a little nuts?"

"He's got to be a lot nuts to do what he's going to do. But don't forget I brought him over in the first place. I think he's okay. Today is the first time I'd say he was ever shaky, and so far that's minor."

"We hope."

"Well there's nothing we can do about it right now. Forget it. Let's have a look at the hardware."

Hutton stood up and motioned to Mercer to help him move the couch. That done, he took a knife from his pocket, knelt, and began to chip plaster from a place about two feet up the wall. Hutton slipped the blade under a piece of paper tape and sliced laterally about six feet. Then he wedged the knife into the crack and pried. A section of plywood, which was hinged to the floor, folded out from the wall and disclosed a coffin-sized cavity.

"Nifty," Mercer said. "Build that yourself?"

"How do you close it back?"

"Just reglue the tape and spackle over it. Doesn't take long and it's not that easy to see."

"Especially when it's behind the couch."

"Yeah." Hutton was taking a number of long packages out of the compartment in the wall. Each was wound in a strip of oiled sheeting. Hutton began unwrapping them in the center of the floor.

"Hot stuff," Mercer said. "I don't see any shotguns, though."

"What do you want a shotgun for?"

"Well," Mercer said. "It's really hard to miss with one."

"You won't miss much with most of these. A machine gun is about like squirting a hose. All you have to do is watch where it's going."

Mercer picked up a Thompson and began sighting it around the room.

"Budda budda," he said. "Humphrey Bogart."

"I'd stay away from that one," Hutton said. "It's about the worst thing we got. Those old drum magazines will jam."

Mercer put the Thompson down and crouched over the other guns. Among the litter of greasy rags were two Sten submachine guns, an M-1 carbine, a Beretta 12, and a Skorpion, the latter two compact machine guns with folding stocks.

"You're better off with the Sten," Hutton said. Handling the guns had visibly cheered him. "Or one of these little mothers, they're easier to hide. What do you like?"

Mercer picked up the Skorpion.

"This looks okay," he said. With the stock folded over the barrel the gun was under a foot long. It was light and compact in Mercer's hand.

"Yeah, that's a nice little gun," Hutton said. "Let me show you how it works." Hutton took the Skorpion, demonstrated the loading and mimed firing, then drilled Mercer in these activities several times.

"Boom," Mercer said. "I like this thing."

"Yeah," Hutton said. "I suggest you use the butt if you have time to unfold it. It gives you a lot more effective range and helps keep it from jumping around."

"Sure," Mercer said.

"I'll give you two clips and sixty loose rounds," Hutton said. "You should be able to do plenty of damage with that. I'd appreciate it if you brought some back, we don't have unlimited ammo. On full auto it burns them up pretty quick."

"How quick?"

Hutton did a mental calculation.

"Let's say, fifteen rounds a second. That means you can empty a clip in a second and a half. Which you might want to remember."

"Sheesh," Mercer said. "Where'd Simon get these, do you know?"

"Through the International, so he said. They came down through the other cells. The Skorpion is Czech and it had to come from abroad. The Beretta too, probably. Maybe he could have picked the Stens up over here, but I doubt it."

"Does it all work all right, by the way?" Mercer said. "I've had some unhappy experiences in the past."

"No problem. Simon and I drove out to the Pine Barrens and test-fired everything. Even the Thompson was okay then, not that I'd want to count on it."

"I'll trust you," Mercer said.

"They're all really good guns," Hutton said. "One of the worst things about this whole stupid business is it endangers the guns."

"How's that?"

"Ballistics. Let somebody tie a bullet to one of these guns and you can say goodbye to your head. Really ought to junk them once they've been used. I bet you Simon never thought of that."

"Can't you fix them some way?"

"Yeah, but it's a real pain, and anyway we can't do it. You have to replace about five parts, none of which we got."

"Well. It won't matter much when the Times Square thing goes down."

"Sure, and he's risking that too. I still say this maneuver is insane." Hutton was again sinking into gloom.

"I don't like the rush part so much myself," Mercer said. "You can make too many mistakes if you're in a big hurry."

"Right. And I got to work tonight, tomorrow night too."

"What time you get off?"

"Four or five in the morning, depending."

"That's not a bad time to pull something though. Not too many extra people around."

"I guess. What were you planning to try?"

"I hadn't decided. Cops seem like kind of an obvious possibility."

"Ah hell," Hutton said dismally. "This whole bit is just idiotic."

Mercer sat down and hugged the Skorpion in his lap.

"Look, David. You don't have to do anything you don't want to do. There is no authority, remember? No authority, that's the whole point. If you don't feel like playing Simon Says, then you don't have to."

"It sure as hell looks like I do."

"Look. This isn't really the Mau Mau. You're already in the cell. Simon can't kick you out, you know too much. What's he going to do? He could skewer you with that hat pin, but he won't. He needs you. Or he can back down. It's as simple as that. We're all free agents. We could take these gizmos uptown and blow Simon into devilled ham if that's what we felt like doing."

"So why are you playing along?"

"I'll tell you why. When Simon stuck that goddamn hat pin through my shirt today it really kind of annoyed me."

"I have to say, you didn't really show it."

"Believe me, I felt it. I would have loved to break his neck right there, but that would have totalled the project. So I thought I'd just do the assignment. What I want, though, is to come up with something so gorgeous that Simon will get sick to his stomach and pass out from fear before he ever thinks of trying anything on me again."

"I hadn't thought of it quite that way." Hutton had relaxed and was even smiling a little. "You weren't ever in the army, were you?" he said.

"I went to college," Mercer said. "Sat it out."

"When I was in Nam, guys used to take ears off the dead Cong."

"Did you?"

"No. I saw enough, though. Simon asked us all for heads. What if I brought him a couple of ears?"

"Not bad at all," Mercer said. "That could be hard to top."

17
Simon Rohnstock (I)

AFTER HIS VISITORS had left him, Simon got up and began to pace at random through the five rooms of his apartment. The hat pin was still gripped in his right fist, but Simon was unaware of it. Eventually he walked off a part of his nervousness and came to a halt before the bay window in the living room. Below, the wind continued to ruffle the trees in the park, and there seemed to be a spatter of rain. Simon stood, a little stooped in the window, savoring his detachment from the weather.

Noticing the pin at last, Simon raised it to eye level and smiled at it in a friendly fashion, then stuck it back into the lining of his jacket, where he always carried it. His thoughts coalesced around the pin, becoming needle sharp. Simon caressed the pin through the fabric of his jacket, continuing to smile. He had been a little frightened by the episode which had just taken place in his apartment, more by his own riskily violent outburst than by Mercer's relatively insignificant challenge to his authority. Nevertheless, he had now decided that he was quite pleased with himself on the whole.

In the fall of 1982, Simon Rohnstock was thirty-six years old. He had been born at Lenox Hill Hospital, the first and only child of Paul and Isabel Rohnstock, in 1946. Paul Rohnstock was veritably rich beyond all dreams of avarice. His wealth was inherited, but he was shrewd enough to maintain and even increase it, with the help of a couple of stockbrokers, and minimal effort of his own. Rohnstock lived in a magnificent and elegantly appointed penthouse on Central Park West. His wife was an intelligent woman and also a notable beauty. A gentleman of cultivated leisure, Rohnstock occupied a part of his time with minor essays into philanthropy, and seemed to require no further vocation. He was an art collector of discernment, his taste running chiefly to German Expressionism. Rohnstock owned a very distinguished collection of such work, but Simon, as an adult, could not really recall any of the paintings, which had all been sold at auction following his father's premature death in 1962. Simon had not known his father well and did not often think of him, though in 1982 he was still living on a fraction of the annual income from the extremely substantial trust fund Rohnstock had created in his name.

Child of absolute privilege, Baby Simon disported himself at will on the rich carpets of his father's house. At evening he would convey by grunts and gestures his desire for Paul

Rohnstock to lift him up to one of the plate-glass windows which looked out from the apartment on every side. From each window, the baby could see the lights of the city fanning out in all directions to the horizon's limit. Simon, his mind so far unformed by the strictures of conscious thought, assumed that the chains of light were baubles already his own.

From 1946 to 1950, Simon and Paul Rohnstock seemed perfectly content with their distinctly easy lot in life. Isabel Rohnstock, however, was not. Always something of a hothouse flower, she found even the hothouse untenable at last. She was a woman of nervous disposition and prone to lengthy, apparently reasonless depressions. Isabel distrusted all psychiatric practitioners and refused to consult any, though Paul occasionally suggested that she do so.

In 1950, Isabel Rohnstock left her husband, abruptly and without warning, and flew to Paris. She took Simon with her, mainly out of her reflexive sense of the "Done Thing," for she was not especially attached to the child. Isabel had no clear destination in mind when she left New York. She spent a week in a Paris hotel and then went with Simon to Gstaad, a Swiss mountain resort, where she thought she remembered she had once been happy. In 1950, however, Isabel Rohnstock was not happy in Gstaad. For the next ten years she would pursue happiness on a winding trail from London to Paris to Vienna to Florence and back again, before settling more or less permanently in Paris, where she was not very happy either.

Simon was four years old in 1950 and scarcely aware of what had happened to him, if indeed any momentous change had occurred. Wherever Isabel chose to take him, Simon remained thoroughly insulated from his surroundings, wound up in a cocoon of money and luxury, distant from the world's hard edges as he had been in the penthouse on Central Park West, so absolutely removed from the city.

In 1950, while Simon Rohnstock wriggled and fretted in the cushioned seat of a New York-to-Paris airliner, Charles Mercer was celebrating his first birthday, with small ceremony, in a South Carolina town. David Hutton was three months old and living in New Jersey. Ruben Carrera and Larkin were as yet unborn.

18
Charles Mercer (I)

IN 1949, while Isabel Rohnstock was occupied with her third nervous breakdown in as many years, Charles Mercer was busy being born in Georgetown, South Carolina. The place of his birth was a small town on Winyah Bay, about ten miles from the ocean coast. The core of Georgetown was ancient and picturesque. Rows of stately ante-bellum houses, shaded by live oaks which dripped Spanish moss, succeeded each other all the way to the waterfront docks. Charles Mercer, however, was born into a newer and poorer section at the other edge of town. His father worked in the local paper mill, which most days covered the area with a sulphurous pall, an evil-smelling cloud which, with a land breeze, could reach as far as the seashore.

Charles Mercer was the second son of his parents. He had a brother, Dale Mercer by name, about eighteen months older than he. There were no more children. Shortly after the birth of Charles, his mother contracted uterine cancer, a disease which she made every effort to ignore. Her condition went undiagnosed until 1953, and she died of it in 1954.

Charles and his brother Dale were, as a result of their mother's death, allowed to grow up in circumstances of moderately benign neglect. They were irregularly slapped or cosseted by a series of black women, endowed with rich soft voices and hard hands, who sometimes came to cook or clean the house. Mercer senior paid his boys little mind. He usually came home late from the paper mill. Mr. Mercer would enter his house after nightfall, with an odor of brimstone clinging to his clothes, would eat whatever he could find in the refrigerator, or maybe the oven if one of the black women had been there that day, would drink three or four cans of beer while staring in the general direction of his black-and-white television set, and soon enough would fall asleep.

Almost entirely free from supervision, Charles and Dale ran at large through their town. They skipped school often, learned to fish with cane poles from the docks off Front Street, and sometimes shoplifted frozen dinners from the supermarket to supplement their diet, which tended to be meager. Dale Mercer, at fifteen, foreswore education altogether and went to work on the shrimp boats which put out of the Georgetown harbor. At thirteen and a half, Charles spent most of his days in an icehouse on the dock, heading shrimp and sorting them by size, though, unlike his brother, he still occasionally dropped into his school.

Long stints on the boats earned Dale Mercer enough money to buy an enormous, hearselike Chevrolet by the summer he turned sixteen. He and Charles repainted the car matte black and covered it with a dozen coats of Turtle Wax. The car extended their range to the resort towns of the coast, from Litchfield Beach and Murrells Inlet all the way to the huge amusement park at Myrtle Beach, thirty miles to the north. The brothers consumed their nights with endless driving along the seaboard, drinking in windowless roadside taverns, prowling the arcades and beaches in a generally futile attempt to pick up the soft daughters of the perennial summer people. At fourteen Charles Mercer learned to drive, urging the big car into its own cone of light, eating up the long flat stretches of coastal highway, with his brother passed out on Colt 45 in the seat beside him.

At fifteen Charles Mercer had all the growth he would ever get, which was not much. Already he was a chain smoker, favoring Lucky Strikes because of the nifty design of the pack. Following his brother's lead, Charles dropped out of school and started working on the boats, where he was picked on because of his small stature; bigger men pretended to confuse him with the shrimp. Hotheaded by nature, Charles raged within himself and soon learned to make up what he lacked in weight and reach with speed and anger, plus a home-designed sequence of elbow jabs and kicks. The teasing ended shortly before his sixteenth birthday, when Mercer inadvertently knocked one of his tormentors off a shrimp boat.

This incident terrified everyone involved in it, Charles himself not least of all. Like many old sailors, the man overboard could not swim; moreover, sharks often liked to follow shrimp boats to eat garbage and discarded fish. But the man managed to catch a rope thrown to him and was hauled back on the boat, blue in the face and spitting salt water, but alive and whole. Charles was immediately put ashore and threatened with permanent blacklisting, but he got himself reinstated by the next trip out. Picking on Charles Mercer ceased by general agreement; he was rechristened "Crazy Charlie" and left strictly alone. On his sixteenth birthday, Mercer went out and rewarded himself with a green tattoo. On the fingers of his right hand were stencilled the letters L O V E, on the left, H A T E.

Dale Mercer turned eighteen in 1965 and was promptly whisked off to boot camp and then to Vietnam. Nine days into his first combat tour, Dale put his foot in the wrong place and was transformed into a bloody mist by an antipersonnel mine of American make, popularly known as a Bouncing Betty. His remains were shipped home in a plastic-lined box, inextricably confused with quantities of mud and swamp grass not dissimilar to varieties found in the South Carolina marshes.

On September 18, 1965, Charles Mercer, half-choked by a tie he hadn't worn since he was twelve, stood beside his brother's grave in a Georgetown cemetery. A boy scout was trying to execute "Taps" on a bugle and making a pretty poor job of it. Charles Mercer wished to God the whole thing would get itself over with. In Boston that day, Simon Rohnstock was reading *Das Kapital* for a political science course he was taking at Harvard. David Hutton was playing eight ball against himself in the basement of his parents' home in West Orange. Larkin, age thirteen, was playing a section of Bartók over and over on the piano, trying to get it just right.

The night of September 20, 1965, was clear but moonless.

Mercer's shrimp boat circled off the shore of Litchfield Beach, well within sight of the summerhouse lights. Charles Mercer had remained on deck because he could not sleep. Constellations wheeled round and round above the boat, becoming suddenly unfamiliar. In the cargo hold, nameless cancroid monstrosities crawled among the shrimp, illuminated by greenish phosphorescence. Mercer, who had never been seasick, clutched the rail and threw up whatever he had eaten that day, and afterwards had a prolonged case of the dry heaves. He finally stopped gagging by an effort of will, sat down on the deck, and began to think.

The absurdity of his brother's death was not lost on him, but at that moment Mercer was more impressed by a salutary fear that the same thing might easily happen to him. He was sixteen and a high school dropout, and it turned out that he was just tall enough for the draft. Stumbling through his mind in search of some shelter, Mercer came upon a magical phrase which he knew could ward off the death angel: college deferment.

A brief conversation with his father, punctuated by a slap, informed Mercer that there was no money in the family budget for higher education. Inspired by terror, Mercer stopped shrimping, returned to high school, and hit the books, hard. Much to his own surprise he found he was good at studying, at least with the Grim Reaper looking over his shoulder he was. By the end of 1965 he had made up most of the time he had lost. In 1966 he took the college boards and shot out the top on the verbal section, though he did rather less well on the math. On April 1 of the following year, despite indifferent recommendations from his confused teachers, Mercer was awarded a scholarship to the University of Chicago.

19
David Hutton (I)

THE EARLY CHILDHOOD of David Hutton was not distinguished by extraordinary incident. Born in 1950, his parents' first child, Hutton grew up tranquilly enough in their suburban home in West Orange, New Jersey. He had a sister, four years his junior, whose name was Amy. His father worked as a middle-echelon administrator in one of the oil refineries which make either side of the New Jersey Turnpike such a wonder to behold, and made a fairly good living at it. The house was brick, and had three bedrooms, plus a rec-room in the basement with a pool table and a color TV. A plaster mold of the American Eagle hung over the front door.

In the fullness of time, David Hutton entered the public high school which served the Oranges. Though not a remarkable student, he managed to pass most of his work. Because he filled out early, becoming a large solid boy, he made the school's varsity football team as an offensive lineman during his sophomore year. In the games, David did a good deal of blocking for Peter Mathers, a junior halfback who was extremely quick on his feet and already something of a football star.

From 1965 to 1967, Peter Mathers and David Hutton were best friends. When Peter got his driver's license, the two began to double-date in the Matherses' family car. David was a trifle awkward and shy, but his social life benefitted considerably from Peter's greater poise and athletic notoriety. The double-dating continued after David got his own license and could share the driving. The most serious thing Hutton had to complain of was that he didn't yet have his own car.

On September 2, 1967, Peter and David were hanging around the parking lot of a New Jersey shopping mall. A friend had dropped them off at a record store there, and they were waiting to be picked up. Both boys were restless and perhaps a little depressed. School would recommence for David in about a week's time. Peter Mathers had graduated and would soon be leaving for Rutgers, where he had been offered a modest football scholarship. David, who, like Mercer, had a healthy fear of the draft, planned to spend his senior year working hard enough to get into some college or other. The dreariness of this prospect was compounded by the imminent departure of his friend.

Since their ride seemed to be late, the two boys began walking around the big parking lot, checking out different cars that appealed to them. David spotted a little green MG with the top down and both boys went over to look at it. The first thing David noticed was the keys dangling from the ignition. In an unaccustomed mood of daring, he suggested that they take the car for a quick joy ride. Peter, though a little dubious, finally agreed.

David drove. It was his first time behind the wheel of a real sports car and he wanted to see how fast it would go. When he hit seventy, about thirty miles over the posted speed limit, blue lights started flashing in the rearview mirror. David had intended to return the car in just a few minutes. Now he made a panic decision to try outrunning the police cruiser. He floored the MG; the speedometer quickly shot past ninety. Peter was screaming at him to stop but the wind noise was so loud in the open car that David couldn't even hear the siren.

Some time later he became aware that someone was trying to wake him up. He opened his eyes. A traffic policeman was prodding him gingerly. Hutton got to his feet and found himself standing on a steep grassy embankment. He was not visibly injured beyond a few cuts and bruises. The traffic cop directed his attention to the MG, which was upended on the far side of a slanting steel cable. David only shook his head. He couldn't recall ever seeing the car before. As was later discovered, he had sustained a mild concussion, with attendant amnesia, and he didn't immediately remember anything that had happened. The two cops, who were not much older than David, were honestly appalled by his wanton waste of life and property. When David went on refusing to see what he had done, one of them brought him Peter Mathers's head.

In less than a week, Hutton had recovered from his concussion, but he remained in a state of emotional shock. The Mathers family proved furiously vindictive and they pressed an alarming number of charges. In mid-September, 1967, David Hutton was convicted of grand larceny, reckless endangerment, and manslaughter. He was sentenced to ten years in state prison, then offered a suspension of the penalty by the presiding judge, provided that he joined the army immediately. Hutton accepted the deal. A better bargain could very possibly have been negotiated, but no one seemed to realize that. Hutton's family had been thrown into complete disarray by the incident, and he himself was still too numb to care.

On October 25, 1967, David Hutton was on a commercial airliner which had been modified for troop transport to Vietnam, bleary from forty consecutive sleepless hours, trying to find his assigned seat. In Chicago, Charles Mercer was cramming desperately for his first midterm exams. He was unaware that no one actually did all the assigned work, so he seriously believed he might lose his scholarship and be drafted after all. Larkin was still playing the piano; his legs were long enough to reach the pedals now, which made it more interesting. Simon Rohnstock had taken a year's leave of absence from Harvard and was pretending to study film at the Sorbonne. Ruben Carrera was standing on a box in order to look out the window of a one-room apartment on Clinton Street, in lower Manhattan. Owing more to luck and his own instincts than to any trouble taken about him by others, Carrera had recently achieved survival to the age of five.

20
Ruben Carrera (I)

THE FIRST PROBLEM Ruben Carrera was given to cope with, indeed a rather serious one, was the madness of his mother, Manuela, who so far as she ever understood had simply stepped into the world from sheer void, some time around 1947. Manuela knew less of her origins than the small amount Ruben would ever learn of his own. She was without family or close friends, and distinctly not bright; in fact, authorities were eventually to declare that she was severely retarded. During a short sojourn in a Catholic school, Manuela had not succeeded in learning much more than her own last name, along with its significant relationship to paychecks and government forms which she sometimes received.

In 1962, Manuela Carrera was living alone in a cubicle on Clinton Street. She was approximately fifteen years old and a rather pretty girl, if somewhat vacuous. She was very popular with several young bloods in her neighborhood, though not at all well liked by her female contemporaries. In the winter of 1962, Manuela began to put on weight with alarming speed. She didn't enjoy getting fat or understand it either, for she wasn't eating any more than usual. Manuela made no connection between her weight gain and certain activities which she and her male friends found very pleasant. But as she grew fatter, she noticed a sharp decline in the friendliness of the bloods. The women on Clinton Street, formerly aloof, now became overtly hostile.

Late in the winter of 1962, Manuela Carrera was fired from a Broadway sweatshop on the grounds, as she comprehended them, that she was just too overweight. Impoverished by the loss of her job, she began to get a little thinner at last, though nothing seemed to reduce her belly. Manuela also suffered frequent dizziness and shooting pains in her legs, and found it increasingly difficult to climb the three flights of stairs to her apartment. On a night toward the end of February, Manuela had a sudden sensation that her insides were falling apart. She staggered out into the hallway of her tenement, calling loudly for succor on God and a couple of saints whose names she recalled from the Catholic school. A neighbor woman looked out, deduced Manuela's predicament, and herded the girl back into her own apartment. There, working with reasonable efficiency and meanwhile shaking her head with disbelief, the neighbor hauled Ruben Carrera reluctantly into the world.

Because Manuela still barely understood where babies came from, she was unable to keep the figure she had so suddenly regained for long. From 1962 to 1967, her sudden weight gains continued to occur, at intervals of approximately ten months. And to Manuela's constant perplexity and dismay, her brood continued to multiply.

When Manuela had her weight under control, she sometimes worked as a sewing machine operator in one downtown sweatshop or another. She also drew welfare on the children, but often it never reached them. Manuela had never planned to be a mother and she made a remarkably careless one. During her slim periods, a large part of whatever money she had tended to slip through her fingers into those of her escorts. Manuela was also likely to be absent from Clinton Street for days at a time in the months when she was slender. Ruben Carrera, along with the five siblings he was eventually blessed with, lived on the intermittent charity of neighbors.

The apartment on Clinton Street was a small and unremarkable slum dwelling, consisting of one room. The landlord furnished a sink and a tiny refrigerator. The bathroom was in the hall. There was no stove in the apartment, but there was an electric hot plate. The radiator in the apartment generally did not work. Manuela owned a bed, a chair, and a mattress on which her progeny slept in a row.

Ruben Carrera, eldest son and man of his house, learned at the age of three to climb up to the hot plate and boil water.

The steam from the pot could sometimes make the room seem a little warmer. Ruben also discovered that a splash of scalding water, together with loud noises, served to discourage the rats which sometimes appeared from the tattered walls. At four he found his way out of the building and learned to shoplift from fruit stands and beg quarters. In this way he was able to keep eating and feed his brothers and sisters something when Manuela was absent. A precocious expert in dissimulation, Ruben knew how to persuade the welfare workers who infrequently came to call that all was well with him and his. For some reason, he feared a breakup of the family more than anything else.

Manuela produced her sixth inadvertent infant in 1967 and concluded that something must be done. For the first time in many years, she went to confession, where she confided her difficulties to a priest. The confessor first admonished her to obey the laws of God, and on further thought, explained to her the commandments which were especially pertinent to her case, allowing himself a rather more clinical analysis than was usual.

The formula worked to the extent that no more babies appeared. But, in a not entirely fortunate side effect, Manuela became a fanatic. Believing that more children would materialize if she flagged in her devotions for an instant, Manuela prayed constantly, went to confession weekly, and to mass every day. She acquired a white dress slightly reminiscent of the one in which she had made her first communion. This dress she lovingly washed and dried almost daily, in order to keep it fresh for the church, and she usually murmured prayers as she laundered it.

The conversion of Manuela did not much improve the condition of Ruben and the others. Population stabilization in the Clinton Street apartment was a definite step forward, but Manuela's religious mania was a step sideways at best. Though she held on to what money she had a little longer than in the past, her habit of muttering endless rosaries made her unemployable in the sweatshops, so there were no more paychecks. Also, Manuela's addiction to candles and novenas cut a sizeable hole in the welfare check. And she was no more attentive a parent than she had been before.

Manuela sustained her new faith through its first year, while her children hung on by the hardest. By the spring of 1968, Manuela had washed her white dress into a state of near transparency. Ruben Carrera was eating just slightly more regularly than before, owing to his mother's more frequent appearances in her home. Simon Rohnstock was trying to insinuate himself into the inner ring of the radical student group that was about to occupy the Sorbonne. David Hutton was clinging to the doors of a crashing helicopter, not far above the ground in Vietnam.

21
Simon Rohnstock (II)

FROM 1950 TO 1960, Simon Rohnstock floated around Europe in his mother's wake. Isabel Rohnstock, who possessed a cold beauty of bone which was slow to fade, busied herself with a lengthy succession of lovers, none of whom lasted very long. A generous settlement from her husband allowed her to support gigolos if she chose, to indulge most of her other whims, and to cross national borders with the graceful ease of a water spider. Isabel grew no closer to Simon during these years. The boy was raised by English nannies and French *au pairs,* and was reasonably well educated by various tutors. He became fluent in French and Italian, though German eluded him. Because of Isabel's penchant for abrupt and frequent relocation, Simon made no close friends of his own age.

When Simon was approaching thirteen, Isabel decided to begin formalizing his education. She removed herself to London and sent her son to an English boarding school to be whipped into shape. By 1960, Simon was sufficiently pulled together to be admitted to the Hotchkiss School, a venerable preparatory institution in Connecticut. Thus Simon returned to America for the first time in ten years. Isabel Rohnstock bought herself an apartment on the Left Bank in Paris. She curtailed her travel schedule, edited her list of gentleman friends, and set about becoming merely eccentric.

At Hotchkiss, Simon was neither very popular nor the opposite. He had already grown very tall, so that he went stooping through the halls of the school, wearing his obligatory skinny tie. Simon did quite well in his studies. He was an argumentative student, who often irritated his teachers by leading them into logical traps. Because of his height, Simon was encouraged to play basketball, but he was a little too clumsy to be very good at the game, which bored him in any case. With friends or acquaintances, Simon sneaked cigarettes in his dormitory bedroom, though he didn't much like cigarettes. Occasionally he spent a short awkward holiday with his father in New York. On longer breaks, Simon visited his mother in Paris.

In his senior year at Hotchkiss, Simon received a letter of acceptance from Harvard, the college of his choice. He went to Cambridge in the fall of 1964, began taking history courses, and, like many students of his generation, found himself involved in a naively passionate love affair with Marxism. Simon declared a major in political science and joined SDS. Civil rights and antiwar demonstrations didn't interest him much, however. He was becoming a political theoretician, and a very pedantic one. Simon read his way through great blocks of Marx and Engels, Lenin and Mao, and could quote from them all at such length that he bored the other student activists to tears.

At last Simon became enough discouraged by the poor reception his lectures received that he dropped out of SDS. In 1967, he also dropped out of the political science department and moved briefly to English, with a vague idea of becoming a student journalist. But it was too late for him to crack into any of the Harvard publications. Simon flirted for a while with painting, but he wasn't much good at that. Finally he conceived an interest in film, and the Harvard deans decided to allow him to pursue this interest at the Sorbonne, during what would have been his senior year. Simon packed a bag for France with film texts, political tomes, and an expensive 16-mm movie camera he barely knew how to use. He arrived in Paris in the fall of 1967, about eight months before the city exploded.

22
Charles Mercer (II)

MERCER ATTENDED his first college class, a broad survey of English literature led by a graduate student, in September 1967. Equipped with a new spiral notebook and a shiny Norton anthology, Mercer walked into the classroom. About fifteen other freshmen were already seated around a Formica table, waiting a little nervously for the TA to appear. Mercer sat down and folded his hands on top of his books. A girl in a green sweater pointed, whispered, and began to titter. In a moment the whole table was snickering softly over Mercer's tattooed fingers.

Mercer went pale with anger, as only a redhead can, but he took no action right away. In his dorm room that night, partially anesthetized by a half pint of vodka, Mercer picked up a razor blade and commenced the surgical removal of his tattoos. The cuts required were fairly deep and Mercer's desk was puddled with blood. His roommate, a pampered boy from Winnetka, walked in on this scene and fainted. Mercer, smiling with gritted teeth, shifted the razor and began the more clumsy task of cutting on his right hand with his left. Finished, he cleaned his desk top and sat through the night in front of it, rigid with pain and fulfilled pride. The cuts were still seeping a little when Mercer returned to his English class the next day. No one laughed or even ventured a smile.

There was a generous supply of hippies and war resisters at the University of Chicago, but Mercer did not join them. Nor did he have anything to do with the student riots at the Democratic Convention in 1968. Mercer, who tended toward conservatism by nature and upbringing, was uninterested in politics. His objection to the war in Vietnam was nonideological, was exclusively based on his wish to stay alive. Mercer kept his hair short and befriended others who shared his general inclinations.

By 1969, Mercer had become quite intimate with Frank Scotti, a native of Chicago, who drank expensive liquor, drove a Jaguar, and sold the best marijuana in the school. On weekends, Mercer and Scotti would get into the Jaguar and roar through Chicago from bar to bar. One night in the spring of 1970, police pulled the car over. Scotti, who had been driving, thoroughly flunked a field sobriety test, then resisted arrest with such vigor that the cops had to handcuff him to get him into the back of their car. Mercer remained quiet and unobstreperous throughout the struggle, asking just one reasonable question about bail. He was left in charge of the Jaguar, which he drove back to the university, thanking his lucky star that neither he nor Frank had been holding dope that night.

Mercer got back to campus at around one o'clock in the morning and began canvassing the dorms for bail money. By three A.M., he arrived at the downtown city jail, with two hundred dollars in small bills. Somewhat to Mercer's surprise, Frank Scotti was already at liberty. Still quite drunk, Scotti was wandering around the area of the front desk, flashing a V sign at the walls. The desk sergeant, bathed in sweat, was delivering an elaborate apology to two stubby Italian men in dark suits. These men, whose accents were very thick, addressed Scotti as Francesco. When Frank spotted Mercer, he threw his arms around him. He introduced Mercer to his Italian uncles as his best friend, brother in fact. The uncles beamed on Mercer, gold teeth shining in their smiles, and squeezed the muscles in his arms. Francesco Scotti said that he would never forget Mercer for coming to bail him out, not as long as he lived. Before they left the jail, in front of his two uncles and the cops, Francesco kissed Mercer on the mouth.

Charles Mercer graduated from the University of Chicago in the spring of 1971, with an honors degree in English and no plans. He had majored in English on the correct assumption that it would be impossible for him to fail the subject, but the degree did not prepare him for anything he much wanted to do. The prospect of law school did not greatly attract him, and grad school or teaching appealed to him even less. He was estranged from his father, had lost touch with him almost entirely, and had no desire to return to South Carolina.

In the summer of 1971, Mercer was hanging around in Chicago, watching his money run out, when Frank Scotti proposed to him that he go to work for the firm represented by his Italian uncles. Scotti told Mercer that he could make a lot of money quick by taking a trip to Colombia and returning with sundry white powders. Ever cautious, Mercer objected on grounds of illegality and other dangers. Scotti, recalling aloud the scene in the Chicago jail, assured him that his uncles could handle all matters of that sort. He, Francesco Scotti, would personally guarantee it. Mercer said he'd give it a try.

In the fall of 1971, Mercer completed a crash course in Spanish and flew to Bogotá, where he made contact with the local representatives of the Italian firm. He headed back for the states on a zigzag overland route, posing as a tourist and carrying about fifty thousand dollars worth of cocaine in a specially tailored vest. Mercer made it back to Chicago a few days before Thanksgiving, where he received a hero's welcome and more money than he'd ever seen before in one place at one time. That fall, Larkin received early notice of his acceptance at Juilliard. Simon Rohnstock began taking courses toward an advanced degree in psychology. Ruben Carrera had just been placed in his second foster home. David Hutton, then living in Hoboken, was waking up in the middle of almost every night, sweating and screaming from his horrible dreams.

23
David Hutton (II)

RIGHT FROM THE BEGINNING, David Hutton made a good soldier, in the sense that he was an effective and obedient automaton who threw himself with perfect willingness into the most pointless routines of his training. He was a model of discipline and was especially good with weapons, automatic weapons above all. Hutton really wanted to be mindless, and if drill, clean-up details, and calisthenics dulled his more unpleasant memories, machine-gun fire obliterated them altogether. Hutton's first priority was to forget Peter Mathers completely. In boot camp, this imperative took precedence over day passes and leave. During Hutton's first days in Vietnam, it was even more important to him than trying to stay alive.

Hutton was still a few weeks short of his eighteenth birthday when he was flown to Vietnam, but his record showed him to be one of the top three gunners in his training unit. He went in-country as a doorgunner on a helicopter team. Hutton manned an M-60 machine gun, which was mounted in the belly of a Huey gunship. Even from the jouncing helicopter, he was a better-than-average shot with the thing. His particular function was to pepper the ground with bullets when the Huey was making low maneuvers with its nose guns and rocket tubes out of position.

The light-fire team which Hutton and his chopper belonged to had several purposes: to knock out enemy mortars and artillery, to support ongoing surface operations, and to clear ground for new infantry advances. During the first few months he was in the bush, Hutton was in the comparatively enviable position of shooting fish in a barrel. He did most of his gunnery at long range, in a mood of near-total detachment. Sometimes, rarely, he had discernible human targets, but they were always unrecognizably small on the ground below. Hutton's Huey hadn't taken a direct hit since he started flying on it. Its immense firepower generally overwhelmed anything it was ever up against. David Hutton was several times commended for his expertise in returning whatever ground fire there was.

His luck broke during the spring of 1968 in the course of a fairly routine mission. Hutton's fire team was sweeping the jungle in what was supposed to be an area of Viet Cong concentration, preparatory to some sort of infantry movement. On the first few passes there was no return fire. As far as Hutton could tell, the most he was doing with his M-60 was chopping up leaves.

On the fourth or fifth pass, somebody opened up on the Huey with what Hutton's recently educated ears could identify as a fifty-caliber machine gun, which puts out a very large bullet indeed. Hutton automatically swiveled the M-60 straight down and began trying to shoot directly underneath his chopper. Fifty-caliber rounds were coming right up through the floor. The Huey tilted and Hutton lost control of his gun. He toppled over backwards and found that he was sliding around in small streams of blood. The crew chief had taken a round and appeared to be dead. Hutton crawled back to the door. The Huey had been in a low bank turn when it was hit and now the pilot was trying to climb. At about three hundred feet the motor knocked out and the chopper began to fall through a weird silence. Hutton got hold of the M-60 and started firing, though he had no visible target. He just wanted to put some sound back into the environment. The instant Hutton felt the chopper jar against the ground, he dove out the door in a paratrooper's roll.

Hutton didn't break anything or even lose consciousness, but the wind was knocked out of him and he couldn't get up. He was lying in a smear of mud. The only American he could see was the pilot, Earl Hendricks, a twenty-year-old from Georgia. Hutton was reasonably friendly with Hendricks and sometimes had a few beers with him back at the post. The pilot had his eyes open and seemed to be basically okay, but his legs were pinned in a cluster of wreckage from the helicopter. Elsewhere, the main body of the Huey was fitfully burning. Two VC, dressed in black trousers and American T-shirts, came softly out of the jungle. Hutton, still breathless and unable to move, found it all curiously reminiscent of the aftermath of his car wreck the year before.

The VC approached Hendricks and briefly inspected his legs. The first one to reach him made some remark in his own language, whisked out a knife, and slashed the pilot's throat, seemingly with complete disinterest. The second VC walked over to Hutton and trained a big US Army–issue .45 on him, holding the big pistol in both his small hands. Hutton stood up and carefully enunciated the Vietnamese phrase *"Chu hoi,"* meaning roughly, "I surrender." The first VC came over and tied his hands behind him with a piece of wire. At that point, the fire reached the Huey's fuel cell and the whole helicopter blew up. The two VC plunged facedown in the mud; Hutton remained standing. He was not hit. The VC popped onto their feet again and motioned for him to precede them into the undergrowth.

It had begun to drizzle and the terrain was slippery and difficult. Hutton stumbled often and once he fell. The pace was fast and whenever he faltered the second VC would prod him in the kidneys with the pistol's barrel, hitting hard enough to bruise. Hutton kept going. He was out of shock by now and beginning to be very afraid. The .45 seemed to be the only firearm the VC had between them but it was plenty as far as Hutton was concerned. They went on for about an hour, covering two or three klicks, Hutton guessed. He had no idea of their direction.

Urged on by the VC, Hutton blundered across a trail where three NVA infantrymen were dead. One gun lay near the bodies, a Kalashnikov AK-47. The first VC claimed the gun and began to confer quietly with his partner. Hutton experienced a flicker of hope. The dead NVA suggested that there might be American ground troops in the area already. But unfortunately the VC seemed to have reached the same conclusion. The first VC raised his new gun to his shoulder and aimed it at Hutton from a distance of about fifteen feet. A click woke Hutton to the fact that he was probably about to die. He opened his mouth to scream but there was no time. The Kalashnikov exploded when the VC pulled the trigger. It had lately become the practice of Green Berets and Lurps to mine Kalashnikov cartridges with C-4, a powerful plastic explosive, in retaliation for various booby traps which the Cong had been setting for them. Hutton didn't know about that, nor did he care. As soon as he saw the flash he was off and running. The surviving VC squeezed off a shot from the .45 that tagged him in the shoulder, but Hutton kept on scrambling. The VC apparently decided not to give chase, and Hutton had the good luck to be stampeding in the right direction. In about thirty more seconds he ran headlong into the point man of an advancing squad of Marines.

The slug that had hit Hutton was partially spent and did no permanent damage. Nevertheless, he was medevacked to Okinawa for treatment and a few days' R and R. He woke up his first day in the Okinawa hospital with a Purple Heart pinned to his pillow, but that didn't cheer him up much at all. Hutton was depressed, nervous, still badly frightened, and not even particularly happy to find himself still alive. He was obsessed with the death of Earl Hendricks and in spite of all efforts to convince him otherwise he believed that it was his fault.

When they let him out of the hospital, Hutton hit the dirt on the lawn out front and refused to get up. A couple of corpsmen finally peeled him off the ground and took him back inside. The doctor pronounced that Hutton had developed agoraphobia, a bad case of it too. That he would ever climb back in a helicopter seemed highly unlikely. In fact, Hutton could barely make it across a wide street, and he required heavy sedation simply to travel back to Vietnam aboard a passenger craft. He might have been shipped back to the bush as an infantryman, but he got lucky and was allowed to finish his tour in the rear.

24
Ruben Carrera (II)

IN THE SPRING of 1970, at about the same time that the friendship between Charles Mercer and Francesco Scotti was cemented outside the Chicago drunk tank, Ruben Carrera turned eight. During the previous three years, Manuela had remained fanatically devout. Ruben's life continued to be largely dependent on his own ingenuity.

On April 1, 1970, with the cold of winter finally broken for good, Ruben Carrera went out onto Clinton Street, loitered among the fruit and vegetable stands, and successfully pocketed three peaches, which he took back to the apartment. Manuela was out, but it seemed likely she would soon return, since she was boiling her laundry mixture on the hot plate, preparatory to washing her church dress one more time. Over the years, Manuela's washing solution had become quite formidable, consisting of scalding water, Clorox, and a large quantity of raw lye. The dress itself, reduced to a virtual rag by this time, lay waiting on Manuela's bed.

Back indoors, Ruben found a knife and halved each peach. His brothers and sisters, who were accustomed to this drill, fell out in steps-and-stairs formation, opening their mouths like hungry birds. Ruben awarded each of them a section of peach, proceeding in reverse order of birth. Then he sat down to eat his own half, still clinging to its pit, with his back against the wall.

Manuela came in to check her potion, which had begun to bubble and steam, as much from its high acid content as from the heat. Not quite satisfied, she waited at the window by the hot plate, whispering "Ave Maria," gazing emptily at a clothesline across the way. Ruben finished his peach and began tossing the pit up and down, the pit smacking wetly into his hand. Across the room, behind a hole in the wall above the bed, Ruben thought he saw a twitch of rodent movement. He threw the peach pit and missed. The pit bounced off the wall and rolled in a semicircle across Manuela's dress, leaving an indelible ocher stain. Manuela turned around and saw the damage. In the same smooth motion, like a discus thrower, she swept the pot from the hot plate and threw it at her eldest son.

It was April Fools' Day (also Larkin's sixteenth birthday, by sheer coincidence). Manuela screamed herself all the way into the street, tearing wildly at her clothing and actually ripping out big sections of her hair. Her demonstrations attracted two police cars, but it was another half hour before anyone found Ruben, who remained seated quietly against the wall. The left side of his face had been replaced by one raw third-degree burn, and his left eye was charred to a cinder. Deep in shock, Ruben felt little physical pain. Uppermost in his mind was the thought that his mother, whom he had loved in a way, was now lost to him forever, and that he would never see his brothers and sisters again.

Ruben Carrera was absolutely correct about both of those things. In the summer of 1970, a Legal Aid lawyer bought Manuela off her child-abuse charges, at the price of having her permanently institutionalized. It was a small sacrifice, because by the time Manuela came to trial she had regressed to the mental age of about two; clearly she would never be able to function in the outside world again. The other children were quickly dispersed among different foster families. Ruben, his face ineptly patched, came out of a charity hospital a couple of months after his family had already been scattered. He too was placed in a foster home, where his grisly scars won him little affection.

Later in life, when circumstances conspired to break him down so completely that he told the unadorned truth about everything else, Ruben Carrera would not tell the truth about what had happened to him on April 1, 1970. Instead, he would say that a fire had broken out in the apartment, and that his face had been burned in this fire. His mother had carried him out of the building, saving his life. Then she had returned for the other children, but had not come back. All six of them had died in the fire. Ruben Carrera would tell himself this story so often and so well that he actually believed it, wished that he too had been immolated with his lost family, wanted more than anything else to find and re-enter the burning building which he had falsified into his memory.

25

Simon Rohnstock (III)

WHEN SIMON ROHNSTOCK returned to Paris as a student, he stayed only a couple of weeks with his mother and then took lodgings in the Latin Quarter: a rather small and dreary single room. He could have easily lived more comfortably, luxuriously had he wished, for on his twenty-first birthday the income of his trust fund had come under his own control. On instinct, however, he camouflaged his wealth. The political sensibility half-formed in him at Harvard had been revivified by something in the atmosphere of Paris, 1967. So as not to compromise himself with the radicals, Simon spoke little of his background and visited his mother very seldom. He had no difficulty blending into the mass of Sorbonne students. Because of his fluency in the language, he could, when convenient, pass for French.

The winter of 1967 and the spring of 1968 initiated the second phase of Simon's revolutionary education. There was enough talk going on in the city to satisfy even him, and Simon found a better reception for his own rhetorical formulations in Paris than he had in Boston. Even en masse, the French students were more politically alert than their American counterparts: better read and better informed and seriously interested in theory. Simon perceived that the

Sorbonne students were or could become authentic revolutionaries. Unlike the Americans, the French radicals were
capable of accomplishing a seamless transition from rhet-
oric to action. Simon, whose film work had fallen by the way-
side by the spring of 1968, was easily carried along.

The third phase of Simon Rohnstock's education began on
May 10, 1968, in the second week of the student revolt. Simon had momentarily turned himself out of his tower of abstract thought and was standing behind a barricade made of
paving stones on the rue Gay-Lussac. The weather was fair,
balmy even, discounting the clouds of tear gas in the air. Simon, like most of the other demonstrators, was wearing a
large damp handkerchief around his neck, Wild West style,
which he could pull over his face when the gas drifted his
way. At the beginning of the day, enthusiasm and adrenaline
ran high.

May 10, sometimes referred to as "Black Friday," was the
first day that the French police made strong and serious moves
against the students. Simon was cut away from his barricade
and rather perfunctorily beaten up by a couple of CRS gen-
darmes with nightsticks. The same thing happened to about
three thousand other demonstrators that day. Along with
many of his *confrères,* Simon was instantly and permanently
radicalized by the event.

It was the first time he had suffered corporal punishment
of any kind, and predictably enough, he was more disturbed
by the humiliation than by the physical damage, which was
not very great. Simon was enough an American that he had
never suspected that any act of civil disobedience he might
undertake could be met with forceful repression. Many others shared the rude awakening, but Simon's reaction was
personal and peculiar. He decided that under no circumstances would anyone beat him again. It was at this point that
he bought the first hat pin and began to carry it in the lining
of his coat.

Simon thought of the hat pin as an ideal weapon for the
urban guerrilla he now conceived himself to be, nicely com-
bining relative innocence of appearance and ease of conceal-

ment with potentially lethal force. Its cool presence against his bruised rib cage comforted him hugely in the days following May 10, though he didn't have the slightest occasion to use it for several weeks. Immediately after Black Friday, the students found themselves riding a wave of public approval. Sensing danger, the government made a number of real concessions on Saturday the eleventh. The students, with the bit in their teeth, made light of the concessions and seized control of the Sorbonne on the thirteenth. Simon was among the occupying forces. Two days later, he was also a member of the group that made a sortie from the University, captured the Théâtre Odéon, and declared it the first beachhead of the cultural revolution.

Now Simon was back on relatively familiar theoretical ground. The main stage of the Odéon was given over to a twenty-four-hour marathon debate on all topics, and for about two weeks Simon distinguished himself in this forum. He had been reading some new books: Fanon, Marcuse, Kropotkin, Bakunin, et cetera, and he decided to start waving the black flag as opposed to the red. Simon preached anarchy with some real eloquence from the stage of the Odéon, but, as was ever his weakness, he didn't know when to stop. A dogmatic Marxist opponent, weary of Simon's discourse, resorted to the low expedient of digging into his past. In the last week of May, the Marxist disclosed to the crowded auditorium that Simon, so far from being a properly starved and oppressed student, was the son of a rich American bourgeois, was independently wealthy in his own right, and therefore must infallibly be a reactionary, if not a police agent or provocateur. Simon was disarmed by the attack and retreated from the podium in bewilderment.

Outside the Odéon, more pragmatic political events were proceeding on their merry way. During the first week of the Sorbonne occupation, the students had succeeded in attracting so much popular support that they had brought the city of Paris to a standstill. By May 21, the entire transportation industry was out on strike and there was no more gasoline in the city. Factory workers were also walking off the job. The

movement had spread to the provinces, where it was beginning to take on the aspect of a genuine popular revolution.

The unprecedented victories occasioned great euphoria
among the student left, but none of it lasted long. By the end
of May, at roughly the same time that the occupants of the
Odéon got bored with Simon Rohnstock, the factory workers
of France became collectively tired of their strikes, and began
to drift back to work, encouraged by a subtle carrot-and-stick
strategy which DeGaulle's government had devised. The
popularity of the students was rapidly declining and counter-
demonstrations had begun to take place.

Isolated now in the Sorbonne and the Odéon, the students
were plagued with the usual problems of disorganization and
internal dissent. They were also seriously inconvenienced by
intruders from a lower stratum of the proletariat: petty criminals, smalltime gangsters, and thugs of all description. These
new revolutionaries were devoid of principles or political
ideals, seemed utterly amoral, in fact. They were taking effective control away from the intellectual elite, and making
the whole revolution look bad.

By June 13, the rebellion looked as though it were going
to burn out altogether. The students in the Sorbonne, in a
last-ditch effort to restore their public image, conducted a
purge of their least desirable elements. Among those ejected
from the occupied buildings were about thirty men who called
themselves "Katangais." They had a loose paramilitary organization, and some of them claimed to have been foreign
mercenaries. Many of the Katangais seemed to have joined
the revolution mainly in order to avoid criminal warrants.
When they had been turned out of the Sorbonne, the Katangais took refuge in the Odéon.

Simon Rohnstock had remained in the occupied theater
into the first two weeks of June, partly because he couldn't
think of much else to do. His fall from oratorical glory had
been forgotten almost as swiftly as the glory itself, so that
Simon, his tongue unlatched again, had begun to pick up a
few new listeners in smaller discussions, far from center stage.
He was also getting a little something out of the free love

precept of the revolution, and in general not having too bad
a time of it. But the arrival of the Katangais rather frightened him. They were big and strong, sometimes armed, and
discourteous in the extreme. Simon was not much cheered
by the thought, which did occur to him, that the Katangais
were anarchists in the most elemental sense of the word. By
Friday, June 14, when a police cordon appeared around the
Odéon, Simon heartily wished he had already left.

When the police made their first offer of amnesty, Simon
was on the top floor of the theater, in a little attic which perhaps had once been a prop room, from which he could look
down and see the front steps. The police were declaring that
any students who left the building peaceably would not be
arrested or detained. They, the police, had only come for the
criminals who were hiding in the building. Simon didn't quite
believe that proposition, but he decided to go down. However, he couldn't get out of the room. A Katangai had appeared and was blocking the door.

This Katangai was almost as tall as Simon and significantly
heavier. He seemed in excellent physical condition, and was
wearing a heavy length of chain around his neck. Simon,
looking at the floor, tried to slip past him into the hall. The
Katangai pushed him quite roughly back into the room and
shut the door. He then demanded that Simon take off all his
clothes and turn them over to him. Quick.

Simon was embarrassed, also aghast. He realized that the
Katangai's plan was to escape from the building disguised as
a student. For some reason, Simon was thinking that if he
did exchange clothes with the Katangai, he would undoubt-
edly be taken for the other, be tried and punished for his
crimes. This scenario was of course completely irrational. No
one could ever have confused Simon with the Katangais, re-
gardless of what he was wearing. But Simon had no time to
detect the flaw in his reasoning. The Katangai had already
unslung the chain from his neck and was stating very plainly
that he wouldn't mind beating Simon to a pulp if that was
what he had to do to get his clothes. His mind going curiously blank, Simon produced the hat pin from his coat and

held it out before him, clasped in both hands, with the bead braced against the heel of one palm. The Katangai hesitated, then advanced. Simon let himself fall forward as though he were diving into a pool.

From Bakunin and Fanon, Simon had learned to accept extreme violence as a necessity, perhaps even a good, of the revolutionary struggle, but he had never imagined particular circumstances. Now, in the top-floor attic of the Odéon, the circumstance had become concrete. The Katangai stood propped in a corner by the door, inanimate as a broom or a mop. His eyes were still half-open. Looking at him, Simon understood that he had been very lucky to place the hat pin so neatly in his chest, just there, beneath the sternum. The pin had sunk in to its full length and only the bead at the end marked its presence. The bead rather resembled an ornament of some kind, possibly a tie tack, though the corpse was not wearing a tie.

There was no blood. Simon had stopped being afraid. Nor did remorse or even anxiety trouble him; he felt exactly nothing. His mind had reactivated and was running as steadily as a clock. Simon knew that he was perfectly safe. No one had seen him. The door had been shut. The hat pin he carried was his own secret. He had never told anyone about it. Therefore, the Katangai's death was certain to be ascribed to another Katangai, whenever the body was found. All Simon had to do was join the other students whom he could already see below filing docilely out between the columns of the theater.

That was all he did. Simon evacuated himself from the Odéon, in a perfectly orderly fashion, among a group of about 150 other students. He was not in the least way nervous. His dress and deportment conformed in every detail to those of the others. The police kept their promise and no students were detained, though a few Katangais were arrested. Simon walked away from the Odéon and lost himself in an ordinary Parisian crowd. The city had returned to normal. The May revolution was over. Simon Rohnstock's education was complete.

26
Charles Mercer (III)

IN THE SPRING of 1974, Larkin, then enrolled in the Rhode Island School of Design, looked over about a year's worth of black-and-white prints and decided he hated them all. He bought himself a set of oil pastels and began to draw on the prints, trying to make them a little better. That same spring, David Hutton was mired in a profound depression, whose monotony was sometimes relieved by acute anxiety attacks. Hutton was still living in Hoboken. His wife had recently left him. Charles Mercer was lying on the concrete floor of a small jail cell in Mexico. The floor was moldy and unpleasantly damp, but Mercer was too bruised and stiff to raise himself onto the cot in the corner. From where he was lying, Mercer could see into the open drain in the middle of the floor. Several species of queer bugs swarmed in and out of the drain. Their numbers were large. Mercer didn't know their names. They were foreign bugs. They bit.

From 1971 to 1974 Mercer had been doing quite well for himself. His partnership with Scotti and the uncles was prospering. Mercer was making money like a bandit. He had rented a plush Chicago apartment and bought a stereo system so elaborate he barely understood it himself. By 1973, Mercer owned a Porsche and was doing so well he could even pay the repair bills on it. He also had come as close to having all the cocaine he wanted as anyone ever does. Consequently, he had plenty of friends and girlfriends.

Mercer grew to enjoy the travelling life. He went to Bogotá about four times annually, and after the first year he became adept in the Spanish tongue. He learned how to amuse himself to perfection in Colombia and Panama and Mexico. By 1974 he considered himself an old hand at the drug-smuggling trade, practically an untouchable. That was the year his rented car was pulled over by a vanload of mustachioed *guardia* types, somewhere south of Mexico City. Mercer assumed he'd been stopped for some obscure traffic violation and got out of the car smiling and already telling some Spanish jokes as he reached for his wallet. He was a little startled to see a row of submachine guns pointed at him, and even more surprised that the police seemed to know precisely what he had and where he had hidden it.

During the next couple of weeks, the police proved themselves to be remarkably well informed about where Mercer had just come from and what he had been doing along the way. What they didn't know and wanted to find out was exactly where he was going and who would be waiting for him when he got there. Mercer, who expected some emissary from Scotti to turn up any minute, stood up to the questioning, in spite of strong pressures which were brought to bear on him. The Mexican methods of torture were not very imaginative, but they did hurt. Two basic methods were employed, with minor variations. In the first, the interrogators beat Mercer meticulously over every inch of his body. As the days went by, the rubber truncheons began to pile up new bruises on top of the old ones. The bruises on his bones hurt Mercer the worst. The second strategy involved the use of an electric cattle prod. Again, the interrogators took great care to leave no part of Mercer's surface area unattended. To break up this latter routine, the interrogators would sometimes pour water over Mercer's feet, or elsewhere on his body. This technique could sometimes bring hot sparks flying out of Mercer's skin.

Two weeks of that extorted just one sentence from Mercer: "I would like to speak with the American consul." By around the tenth day, the sentence had degenerated to the two words "American consul," half intelligibly muttered through bleeding lips. But Mercer told them nothing more. Then the questioning stopped. Mercer lay on the floor of his cell, literally unable to move, but full of a deep satisfaction nonetheless. He had kept his part of the bargain. He had not talked.

Five days later Mercer was able to get up and rattle his

cage, demanding better food, more water, soap and a towel and a razor (none of which he received), and could again articulate the complete sentence, "I want to see the American consul." The latter request was also ignored for about a month. Mercer fumed, then realized the jailors would wait till his bruises had healed. He was beginning to wonder about Scotti, but maybe no one in Chicago could find out where he was. Mercer himself wasn't quite sure where he was being held.

When someone from the consulate did appear, he wasn't particularly helpful. Mercer summarized the two weeks of torture. The diplomat remained unimpressed. Mercer inquired whether he'd be given a trial. The diplomat shrugged uneasily. He really couldn't say. The best he could offer was to send a telegram to someone in the States. Mercer drafted a message and sent it to a Chicago post-office box which Frank Scotti held under an assumed name.

He waited ten days, then started yelling for the consul again. The Mexican jail was an uncomfortable place. The food was of poor quality and roach ridden. Mercer had dysentery. There were biting insects in the bed and on the floor and in the air, and there was no cocaine whatsoever. Deprivation of cocaine made Mercer nervous and insomniac. It was three weeks before the diplomat returned. Yes, he had sent the telegram. No, there had been no answer. Yes, he would send another.

After one more month, Mercer repeated this process a third time, and also, without much hope, sent a telegram to his father. There was no response to either message. Mercer gave up sending telegrams and devoted himself to some long, hard thoughts.

It had already become clear to him that someone along the route from Bogotá had turned him in. That much was evident from the amount the police had known when they picked him up, and it wasn't all that surprising. Some people did crack under torture, or plea-bargained, or gave information for profit. Mercer knew it happened, though he hadn't thought it would happen to him. Well, he could be philosophical about that part. It was his bad luck. None of those people farther south had ever promised him much of anything.

Frank Scotti, on the other hand, had promised him quite a bit, and it was difficult for Mercer to believe that Scotti wasn't going to deliver. In order to believe it, he had to take a long step outside of himself and examine his role and position from a distance. Mercer saw that he had been what is known in the trade as a "mule." In the literal, animal incarnation, a mule is a pack animal, useful for its strength and endurance and a certain crude intelligence. But if a mule should break its leg, its usefulness is terminated. You shoot it. With this reflection, Mercer closed his own case.

He was never brought to any sort of trial. For the next four years, he was shuttled among different work camps and jails in central Mexico. He seldom knew exactly where he was. It was a difficult period during which bad things kept happening. Sometimes guards would come into Mercer's cell and beat jesus out of him for obscure reasons of their own. They might ask him questions during the beatings, often about things he had never done and knew nothing about. Or as often, there would be no questions, only the beating. Once or twice, despite his determined and desperate resistance, Mercer was raped by bigger, stronger prisoners. That was almost the worst thing that happened to him. But the very worst thing of all was the interminable, mind-boggling boredom. Mercer filled his time with fantasy, dreaming of whisky and women and dope, and soon enough got bored with them all. The only pleasure that never palled for him was imagining new and different ways to kill Frank Scotti.

In the summer of 1978, Mercer was turned out of his stinking hot jail cell and loaded onto a bus with some other American detainees. In Tijuana, with no explanation, his passport was returned to him. Within an hour, he and the others had been unceremoniously shunted across the border, back into the United States.

Mercer knew some people in San Diego who were loosely connected with some of his Chicago friends. These San Diego people were in the business of altering and selling hot cars. Mercer dropped into their garage when no one was there, achieving entry through a skylight, and left with a stack of loose cash and a freshly repainted Volvo, choosing the latter because it was not very conspicuous. It was Mercer's opinion that he was fully entitled to take these things, but he didn't hang around or leave a note. He left San Diego at once and drove without stopping till he passed out from exhaustion on the shoulder of a highway near the Mississippi Gulf Coast.

After that, Mercer slowed down for a leisurely tour of the southeastern seaboard. He swam and sunbathed. He drank beer and ate fish. Gradually he regained the weight he'd lost in Mexico and acclimated himself to freedom. By mid-August 1978, Mercer had drifted back into South Carolina.

There was no one he really knew left in Georgetown. Several of his contemporaries had been killed in Vietnam. The survivors had for the most part tunneled into premature marriage and the like. They didn't much interest Mercer, and they hardly remembered him. After all, he'd been gone for ten years. When Mercer went back to the house he'd grown up in, he learned that his father had died in 1974. That at least explained why his telegram hadn't been answered by so much as a "Go to hell."

Toward the end of August, Mercer floated into a liquor store he'd formerly patronized, on the coastal highway not far from Murrells Inlet. He knew the proprietor, one Tim Reston, a big moon-faced man, not very talkative. Reston didn't recognize Mercer at first. Mercer had aged, his tattoos were gone, and his nose had been broken in Mexico. But when Reston figured out who he was, he seemed mildly interested. He even offered Mercer a job, tending the store at night.

Mercer took the job. He stayed in Georgetown for about a year, selling whisky out of the highway store, then going back to his father's house to catch the late late show. Mercer was in a state of suspended animation, some kind of holding pattern. He remained solitary. The Mexican experience had left him feeling peculiarly underconfident about women, so he didn't pursue any. His only real company was Tim Reston, who didn't talk much and asked no questions at all.

Reston lived in a frame house at the edge of the salt marsh. He was a dedicated fisherman, and in the winter he hunted ducks. Mercer spent a good deal of time fishing with Reston. The older man taught him how to use his casting net, a white nylon spiderweb with a drawstring and weights at the edges. From Reston, Mercer learned to sling the net in a perfect circle, holding one of the weights in his mouth and releasing it just in time not to jerk out his front teeth. Mercer liked working with the net. It was a soothingly patternistic activity. He got so good at it that he caught more bait minnows than he and Reston could use.

Then, in the winter, Mercer learned to duck hunt. Reston took them down the narrow swamp channels in a flat-bottomed pirogue that barely ruffled the black water it passed over. Behind a mud bank spiked with marsh grass, they waited in silence, sometimes for hours. Afterward, at Reston's house, they ate duck dinners. Reston wasn't married, but he knew how to cook a duck.

Over Reston's mantelpiece hung an ancient and curious gun. One night Mercer took it down to look it over. It was a single-barreled affair and the bore was as big around as his wrist. Reston told him it was a punt gun. He said that before the game laws changed, he had gone out with the gun bolted to the bow of the pirogue and sometimes brought down as many as ten ducks with a shot. Listening to this anecdote, Mercer grew reflective. The gun surrounded itself with a number of interesting possibilities which were sprouting up in his mind.

In the late spring of 1979, Mercer told Reston that he had to leave South Carolina. Reston was disappointed. He was sorry to lose Mercer, especially at the beginning of the tourist season. Mercer insisted that he had to go, that he had some business. Then he asked Reston what he'd consider selling the punt gun for. Reston demurred. The gun was not much use. You couldn't get shells for it any more, for one thing. But when Mercer pressed him, Reston said he wouldn't take money for the gun. Mercer could have it as a parting gift.

On June 2, 1979, Mercer put the remains of his savings into his hip pocket, packed the punt gun and a new casting net in the trunk of the Volvo, and drove by the liquor store to shake hands with Tim Reston before he left town. Then he drove to Chicago, where he checked into a motel near the freeway. Mercer didn't visit any old friends. But by keeping his ear to the ground for a couple of days, he was able to ascertain that Frank Scotti's habits hadn't changed much during his absence.

On June 7, 1979, Mercer did two errands. He went to a uniform store and bought a peaked cap, and then went to a florist's and got a box of long-stemmed roses. Mercer spent that evening in his motel room, dismantling a half-dozen twelve-gauge shells with double-zero buckshot loads. Working with paper and glue, Mercer made the several little shells into one big shell, which fit snugly into the breech of the punt gun. He rounded out the load on the homemade shell with a generous handful of carpet tacks.

The next morning, Mercer put on his hat, checked out of the motel, and drove into downtown Chicago. He parked the car around the corner from an inconspicuous private social club. It was a warm day and the door was open when Mercer showed up with his florist's box. In the front room, three middle-aged men were playing cards around a green felted table. Mercer knocked on the door frame, stepped inside, and squinted down at a pink slip of paper he'd taped to the top of the box.

"Flowers for Frank Scotti," Mercer said.

One of the cardplayers called Scotti's name a little louder, without looking up. Scotti came out from behind a curtain at the rear of the room. When he was flush with the far edge of the card table, Mercer put his finger through a small hole he had cut in the side of the flower box and pulled the trigger of the punt gun. The explosion blew him back into the door frame and knocked him half unconscious. Otherwise, the result was almost exactly what he had expected.

27
David Hutton (III)

DAVID HUTTON completed his military service late in 1969. He flew to Hawaii and stayed there through New Year's Day, living frugally on accumulated pay. Hutton's agoraphobia had improved, though flying still frightened him badly. He was unsure of the future and nervous about going home. At the advent of the Christmas season, Hutton stalled his family with a fabricated story about an extension of his army duties. But in January 1970, he surrendered and went back to New Jersey.

The Oranges seemed simply to have shrunk. Hutton's house was smaller, its colors less bright. He had kept growing in the army, and was now a big man, over six feet tall, solid in body and bone. Hutton had to stoop beneath the low ceiling of the basement rec-room. He was nineteen. His high school friends, almost without exception, were off to their first year in college. By waiting till mid-January to come home, Hutton had cleanly missed them all.

Fifteen-year-old Amy, Hutton's little sister, had in a mild middle-class way become a hippy, peacenik, and war resister, and so had all her friends. Because his own former circle of acquaintance had been broken, Hutton courted his sister's company during the first months he was back. Amy didn't directly criticize him for going to war, but he began to sense that he made his sister uncomfortable, even embarrassed her. Clearly it wasn't at all hip to be a Vietnam vet. Then Hutton began to overhear whispers among the other longhaired teenagers. As he entered or left a room, often in his own house, he could just catch the epithets: "Murderer, baby killer."

So Hutton got angry. He hadn't gone to Vietnam because he enjoyed the thought of killing people. He'd been sent there in precisely the same manner that a person might be sent to prison. If he had killed, it was because under the circumstances it had been the proper thing to do. It was acutely unfair to blame him for it. But Hutton had no way to vent his spleen. If he flew into a rage at Amy's friends, that would only prove their point. Hutton decided it was time he got out of the house. He took a high-school-equivalency exam, which he passed without much difficulty or distinction either. By the fall of 1970, Hutton had got himself admitted to the Stevens Institute of Technology.

He rented an apartment a block off Washington Street in Hoboken, within walking distance of the school. Hutton was able to live fairly comfortably, with his G.I. benefits and a modest subsidy from his father. By the time he got to Hoboken, he had grown his hair out and bought a new wardrobe. He didn't have to tell anyone he had been a soldier. Hutton sleepwalked his way through classes at the institute. He had a vague intention of making himself into a mechanical engineer.

By 1972 Hutton was still somewhere between freshman and sophomore ranking. He hadn't been doing all that well at Stevens, but it didn't really seem to matter. Hutton was reasonably content. For about a year he had been dating and sleeping with Anne Paxton, a pale and prettyish blond girl, one year younger than he. Anne Paxton was from Franklin Park, New Jersey, and her upbringing seemed to have been similar to Hutton's in most particulars. She had come to college at Stevens in 1971. Hutton approached her under a few false pretenses; for instance, he never told her he had been in Vietnam. Anne Paxton was in some ways a programmed product of the sixties. She was a lukewarm war resister, and also considered herself to be something of a free spirit. But when she found out she was pregnant, Anne made an instantaneous reversion to type. Hutton married her a little hastily in the summer of 1972.

He didn't much mind getting married, for the security implicit in the arrangement attracted him. The wedding itself was a jolly affair, the two families were congenial, and there was a good party afterwards. Before Anne's pregnancy became very evident, she and Hutton were able to take a honeymoon at the Grand Canyon, driving there in a new car which her parents had given them as a wedding present. In the fall they returned to Hoboken and Hutton began to study in earnest. Anne would stay out of school, at least until the baby was born. Hutton was determined to get the engineering degree so he could find a decent-paying job.

The child arrived in January, only slightly "premature." It was a daughter, christened Margaret, and warmly received by both parents and grandparents. But in the spring of 1973, Hutton's relations with Anne began to deteriorate. With the baby there was no longer quite enough money, and there never seemed to be time for the two of them to relax or really talk. Both their nerves were frayed by twenty-four-hour child care. Hutton's school work suffered under the various pressures. At the end of the spring term, he was told he'd have to repeat the academic year.

For a couple of months in the fall of 1971, Hutton had been afflicted with excruciating nightmares. He normally did not remember these dreams in much detail, but they left him sweating and shaken. When Anne began spending her nights at his apartment, Hutton had stopped having the dreams. But in the winter of 1974, the nightmares began to recur, more vividly and much more memorably. Hutton had never committed atrocities in Vietnam, but, as he would later tell Mercer, he had known people who did, and he had sometimes witnessed the consequences. Asleep in his bed in Hoboken, Hutton began to commit gruesome cruelties himself: rape, murder, necrophilia, worse acts by far than anything Amy's friends could have accused him of. He would wake up from these dreams with his fingers curled in the trigger housing of an imaginary gun.

On March 18, 1974, while Mercer was being flogged around his cell by a trio of sweating Mexicans, David Hutton stalked through a dream jungle, angling toward a clearing where an American was trapped under some smoking wreckage. The American turned his head; it was Earl Hendricks. Earl smiled, relieved to see that it was only David. Hutton swatted Earl's head clean off with his Kabar combat knife. The head spun, rolled down an embankment off a New Jersey highway. When Hutton caught up with it, it wore Peter Mathers's face. Hutton drew the knife and cut off Peter's ears and nose. He scalped the head and skinned it, reducing it to bone. The bloody skull began to reproach him for what he was doing, using his little sister's voice, and somewhere he could hear a baby crying.

Hutton rolled out of bed and began scrambling in the corners of the room. Still asleep, he was looking frantically for his M-60. Somewhere in his dream he actually found the gun. Anne turned on the light and sat up in bed. Hutton was crouched on the floor in firing position. Anne asked him what the hell was wrong. Hutton woke partially up and began to chatter hysterically about Peter Mathers and Vietnam, blurring what he had actually done with some of the worst parts of his dream. All of this was news to Anne. As Hutton's vision cleared from sleep, he began to notice her face. His wife's expression read as plainly as print: "My God, I have married a monster." Hutton tried to wipe this expression away with a free sweep from the back of his open hand. Anne fell back into the headboard and began to cry. Hutton wasn't sorry. The truth was, he wanted to hit her again. In the next room the baby was crying, too. Hutton had a sudden and convincing hallucination in which he took his M-60 and machine-gunned his daughter into purée. Terrified, he ran out of the apartment.

Hutton spent the rest of that night on the bluff near Stevens Institute, staring out across the river at the New York City lights. By dawn he was very cold, but still unwilling to go back to the apartment. He could conceive an apology for what he had done, but not for what he had been thinking. When he finally went home around eleven A.M., Anne and the baby were gone. Hutton's first reaction was profound relief. A few weeks later he heard from Anne, who was in Reno by that time, preparing to serve him with the fastest divorce papers in the West.

The night he learned that Anne had filed for divorce, Hutton went to the Brass Rail, a Washington Street bar where they'd sometimes gone together, and got very drunk. Another Stevens student, an acquaintance of them both, asked how Anne was doing. Hutton hit him so hard he knocked out one of his teeth. Everyone else in the bar was appalled; Hutton, however, was proud of himself.

He dropped out of Stevens and got a job in the Maxwell House coffee plant. After the night in the Brass Rail, he discovered that he could block the memory of his dreams by drinking heavily before he went to sleep, but he often woke up in a condition of severe anxiety: sweating, heart pounding, and with a sensation that he was falling from an immense height. The falling delusion would often persist through Hutton's waking day. If it had not gone away by nightfall, he would suppress it with alcohol. Within six months he lost the Maxwell House job and went on unemployment. When that ran out, Hutton tried Stevens again, mainly to get his G.I. benefits back, but he lasted less than a semester. In 1976 he took another factory job, lost it, and went back on unemployment. Hutton spent a lot of his time in Lower Hoboken bars. He had become a quarrelsome drunk and a brawler, and he was still big and fit enough to win most of the fights he picked. Sane people did their best to avoid him.

Because of his general instability, Hutton got in frequent trouble over his child-support payments, which he often made late or not at all. A couple of times he was hauled into court. By 1978 he had begun to realize that if he didn't clean up his act somewhat he might end up in jail. Hutton thought he'd better try getting out of Hoboken. He took the New York Civil Service test and landed a job with the Sanitation Department. The job earned him enough to make his support payments, keep the courts off his back, and pay rent on the small apartment he'd found in Chelsea.

In the fall of 1978, Larkin was also living in New York. He was coming out the down side of a truly disastrous love affair, was drinking distinctly too much, and was only a few months away from his voluntary commitment to Bellevue.

Charles Mercer was in South Carolina, beginning to sketch a rough plan for his first murder. Simon Rohnstock had recently hung out his shingle as a practicing psychologist, though he hadn't attracted many clients yet. David Hutton was a full-time garbageman.

Things seemed to be slightly improving for Hutton in 1978. He was somewhat calmer, and had partially controlled his drinking. Because he didn't want to be a garbageman forever, he had enrolled in a couple of engineering courses at City College, and was doing better there than he had in his last months at Stevens. However, Hutton remained in a nearly continual low-grade depression. He still had anxiety attacks and the fear of falling also sometimes recurred. He fantasized constantly about guns. When he drank, he was prone to outbursts of unpremeditated violence.

In the spring of 1979, Hutton happened to notice an ad on the back page of the *Village Voice:*

> ANGRY? DEPRESSED? PROBLEMS WITH SELF CONTROL?
> If you suffer from free-floating anger and concomitant depression, you may qualify for a free, experimental clinic.

An address and phone number followed. Hutton's interest was piqued. He'd avoided similar programs offered by the VA because he wanted little to do with other vets. But this free clinic thing, no strings attached, looked like it might be worth looking into.

28
Ruben Carrera (III)

WITH HIS MOTHER permanently out of the picture, Ruben Carrera became a ward of the state. In late summer, 1970, a foster home was found for him, in a family on East 106th

Street, just off Fifth Avenue, in Spanish Harlem. Ruben, in social-worker parlance, "failed to make the adjustment." He ran away after only two weeks and went back to Clinton Street, trying to pick up the trail of his mother and the rest of his family. Ruben was eight years old. He lasted ten days on Clinton Street, begging and shoplifting food and sleeping in the hallways of his old tenement. Then the superintendent, a little reluctantly, called the welfare office and told them where Ruben was.

By running away, Ruben had turned himself into a problem case. He was detained in "protective custody" at the Spofford Juvenile Center, which is commonly recognized as a more vicious and brutal environment than many of New York's adult prisons. Ruben had committed no crime, but he was held at Spofford for over nine months because there was no place else for him to go. At length another foster family was found for him, this time in the Redhook section of Brooklyn. Ruben lasted in the new home for about three months. Shortly after Christmas, 1971, he again ran away and again returned to the Clinton Street area. He had become a little shrewder about street life and was able to elude the social workers who came to look for him for about five or six weeks. However, he had begun to steal more than the local commerce could bear. A neighborhood storekeeper turned him over to the police on shoplifting charges. Ruben, who badly wanted to avoid another hitch at Spofford, made demonstrations of repentance. His foster parents agreed to take him back. However, the juvenile judge who heard the shoplifting case sentenced Ruben to six months at Spofford anyway, so he gained little by his maneuver.

Ruben finished his second term at Spofford in August 1972, at around the same time that David Hutton returned to Hoboken from his honeymoon and Charles Mercer made his fourth trip to Colombia. For three wretched years, Ruben kept his promise not to run away from Redhook. His foster parents, a childless Hispanic couple in their middle years, were not unkind to him. But Ruben wanted Manuela back; he was committed to his blood kin. The foster parents, who knew just the bare minimum of Manuela's story, forbade her even as a topic of conversation. Ruben reacted by inventing an idyllic former life for himself, which he would sometimes detail in public. When his new parents grew weary of listening to his fantasies, they began to punish him for mentioning them.

During this period, Ruben was going to school and doing rather well at it. He had a noteworthy aptitude for mathematics and such natural-science courses as the school offered. But he was socially maladjusted. Outside the classroom, Ruben often seemed younger than his real age. His daydreams about his prior life contributed to that impression. The other children soon learned that they could drive Ruben into wild frenzies by questioning the tales he told about his past or by teasing him about his disfiguring scars. Ruben's lack of self-control in these respects made him permanently unpopular in his peer group, and also made him a perpetual discipline problem in his school.

In the summer of 1975, at the age of thirteen, Ruben ran away for the third time. On this occasion, he had planned his moves more carefully. He did not go back to Clinton Street, but instead went to an area farther uptown, not far from the open heroin markets along 13th Street at Avenue A. There, homelessness was so much the universal condition that Ruben's could pass completely unnoticed. He made a few very cautious forays into the Clinton Street area, trying to get some information about his family's whereabouts. Ruben never found out anything about his brothers and sisters, but he did finally learn that Manuela was being kept in a home for the retarded and for chronic mental patients, somewhere in the middle of Queens.

Ruben risked recapture in order to visit Manuela. To be allowed an interview, he had to identify himself as her son. No one took him into custody, however. Ruben entered a room where Manuela was pursuing a blue alphabet block around and around on the floor. When Ruben called her name, Manuela sat back on her haunches and looked at him. Then she picked up the block and began to chew on its corner pensively. The block was carved with the letter *D.* Manuela did not recognize Ruben.

At that point, Ruben might have returned to Redhook, but he was too much afraid of another season of juvenile detention. He went back to Alphabet Town, where he scraped out an existence of sorts by very petty thievery and rifling garbage cans. Winter came and Ruben began to freeze.

In the winter of 1976, Ruben Carrera met a group of three men in their early twenties who were professional burglars. They offered him a place to live, food, and some small payments if he would work for them. Ruben was slight and small even for his young age of thirteen, partially because of malnutrition, and he was able to slip over or around sloppily installed window guards in the richer parts of town. The night Ruben went on his first housebreaking run, he was nervous and seemed likely to choke. The leader of the gang decided to prop him up with a minute dose of heroin.

When the heroin hit Ruben's central nervous system, his fear was instantly gone, as if it had never existed. So were the assorted pains and traumas of his whole life up to that moment. Heroin brought Ruben a happiness he'd never imagined he would know, together with a sense of quasi-divine physical and mental powers, which inspired him with fierce joy. He carried out his part of the first robbery without stumbling even once, riding on the crest of his high. When he had passed the peak, Ruben immediately asked for more. By his fourteenth birthday, he easily qualified as an addict. By his fifteenth birthday, he was mainlining the drug.

Ruben couldn't have quit the burglary ring even if he had wanted to. He needed increasingly large amounts of money to support his habit, and since he bought heroin through the other burglars, they could manipulate him by controlling his source of supply. By the time he was sixteen, Ruben was being paid almost entirely in heroin. In the spring of 1978, he was arrested.

Luckily for him, he was not caught during a burglary. He was simply picked up in one of the unpredictable dragnets that the New York Narcotics Division periodically launches

on the Lower East Side. It was the most serious legal trouble
Ruben had yet been in, but there were a few things in his
favor. He had only been accused of a "victimless crime," he
had not been holding enough heroin to be charged as a dealer,
and he was still a juvenile. In the summer of 1978, Ruben's
court-appointed lawyer pled him guilty and got his sentence
probated by enrolling him in a behavioral drug-rehabilita-
tion program called Blossom Ranch Farm.

29
Simon Rohnstock (IV)

SIMON ROHNSTOCK returned to the States from France in
the summer of 1968. That fall, he went back to Harvard.
American student radicalism was somewhere just off the peak
that had been reached in France the year before, but Simon
no longer seemed to be interested. When he re-enrolled in
Harvard, he began to take psychology courses. In the spring
of 1969 he elected to remain at the university for another
year in order to complete a major in that subject. Simon
graduated with an honors degree in psychology in the spring
of 1970.

After taking his degree from Harvard, Simon moved back
to New York, where he used a small portion of his trust fund
income to rent the large apartment on Riverside Drive. He
was twenty-four, rich, intelligent, rather handsome in his
elongated way, and was incidentally an unconvicted murderer. Simon didn't know what to do next. His psychology
degree did not qualify him for clinical practice, and for the
moment he was uninterested in advanced studies in the field.
Of course, Simon didn't really have to do anything at all. If
he chose, he could remain a dilettante for the rest of his life.

For several years it looked as though Simon would do just

that. Rapidly he became known as a glamorous young man about town. Rather uncharacteristically, he traded on his aristocratic background, using it as a means of entry into some of the city's most privileged social circles. Simon became minor gossip-column material, a companion to celebrities, the unknown seen and photographed with the singer, the actress, the swinging politician. For the second time he made a stab at painting, converting a room of his apartment into a studio. He wasn't much better at it than he had been in college. However, he had become in a small way a patron of the arts, so gallerists were polite about his work, and he could be referred to as an artist on page 6 of the *Post*.

Simon became a cocaine addict at about the same time that Charles Mercer did. In fact, he sometimes snorted the identical toot that Mercer had muled out of Colombia, though usually it had been stepped on several times and its price much inflated by the time it reached New York. Unlimited cocaine maintained Simon in a very good humor until the spring of 1974. At that point, suffering from acute ennui and a collapsed septum, he retired from la dolce vita.

In the summer of 1974, Simon went to Switzerland to have his nose reconstructed and try to break his dependence on cocaine. Toward the latter end, he renewed his interest in politics, which so far in his own life had coincided with personal asceticism. Scanning the contemporary scene, Simon observed that the climate had significantly changed. The era of the mass movement was over, and something new had begun: a smaller-scale, secretive, and wildly violent *modus operandi*. Just over the border in Germany, Andreas Baader and Ulrike Meinhof were in detention for assorted crimes against the state. Simon went to the newspaper morgue and made a close study of their case, broadening his research to other similar groups. He was still in Switzerland when the Red Army Faction accomplished their successful kidnapping of Peter Lorenz, though he had nothing to do with that action. Following his nature, Simon was at that time looking for theoretical precedents, and in this way he came across the writings of Carlos Marighuella and Sergey Nechayev.

In the spring of 1975 Simon Rohnstock returned to New York from Switzerland, equipped with a rebuilt nose and a new vocation. He had been gone long enough that the New York jet set had altogether forgotten him, and Simon made no effort to freshen its memory. He cleaned out his studio and threw away his paints. Then, slowly and cautiously, using his old SDS contacts, Simon put a message on the wire. The purport of the message was that his capacious apartment might be used as a safe house for political fugitives.

Between 1975 and 1978, Simon sometimes played host to members of the Weather Underground and, a little later, the Black Liberation Army. Also, though less frequently, he sheltered a few European and Third World terrorists, whom he correctly believed could be useful to him in eventual arms transactions. But the United States was his real terrain and it was there that he most wanted to develop contacts.

Simon and the American underground did not much take to each other. The Weatherpeople and BLA personnel whom he periodically entertained tended to despise him as a weak-willed liberal fellow traveller, who lacked full commitment and took few real risks. They never completely trusted him and would not admit him to their planning sessions, though they were willing enough to use his apartment if their need was sufficiently great. Simon analyzed them by all the means in his power and decided that he could return their contempt. His occasional guests were amateurish, sometimes downright sloppy, and far too individualistic to be truly effective. They were always either blowing themselves up or turning themselves in.

Simon thought he knew the remedy. He began to design a cellular organization similar to the one Nechayev postulated in his *Catechism,* which later proved to be highly efficient with the assassination of Czar Alexander II. The ideal cell, Simon concluded, would be composed of a single omnipotent leader in charge of a small group of blindly devoted and obedient *mujahiddin.* It was these latter who were almost proverbially difficult to obtain, but by 1977 Simon thought he knew how to get some.

Not long after his return from Switzerland, Simon enrolled in a New School graduate program in clinical psychology. For someone of his intelligence and educational background, the academic demands of the program were almost absurdly easy. Simon chose the school with that feature in mind; he wanted to be licensed to practice as soon as possible. Nevertheless he applied himself to the work with great energy. Simon specialized in behavioral psychology, following the general path defined by Skinner and his colleagues. The idea that certain human responses could be as thoroughly programmed as the reactions of rats and pigeons intrigued him, and also seemed to adumbrate a practical utility for his overall plan. Simon was a screaming success at the New School and earned his degree in record time.

In 1978, Simon rented an office suite in a drab building on Fifth Avenue just below 14th Street. The suite consisted of a waiting room, a small consultation room, and a larger space which Simon planned to use for encounter groups and the like. With the aid of an answering machine and an intercom-buzzer system, Simon was able to serve as his own secretary. He set up shop as a behavioral therapist and began to build a modest practice. Simon helped people quit smoking and drinking, and also treated anorexia and a variety of phobias, all with fair results. By 1979, he had decided he was ready to advertise what clients would later casually refer to as the "anger clinic."

30
Charles Mercer (IV)

ON THE MORNING of June 8, 1979, Charles Mercer stood reeling in the entry of the Chicago social club, stunned from the shock wave and from hitting his head on the door frame.

The exploded flower box lay on the floor, smoldering at the edges. All that remained of the monstrous shotgun was the stock and trigger guard. The barrel had blown forward into the room in the form of shrapnel. Mercer felt an irrelevant twinge of regret for demolishing Tim Reston's nice antique gun. He owed his own survival to the fact that he'd been standing directly behind it. The rest of the room was wreckage. Scotti and two of the cardplayers had been turned into bouillon by the blast. Mercer couldn't even tell whose pieces were whose. However, one cardplayer was still alive, though leaking blood like a sieve.

"Kid," the cardplayer said. "What were the flowers for?"

"The funeral, naturally," Mercer said. "Sorry you had to be here." He walked unsteadily out of the club. A crowd of onlookers had gathered on the other side of the street.

"Somebody get help," Mercer called to them. Then he walked around the corner. Nobody interfered with him. Mercer got into the Volvo and began to drive. A loud ringing in his ears made it difficult for him to think. He drove in a straight line for about half a mile and then pulled into a parking lot. There he took his light suitcase out of the car and accepted a claim ticket from the attendant. Once out of sight of the lot, Mercer unloaded the ticket into a sewer grating. A few minutes later he hailed a cab and had himself driven to the bus station. Making his decision more or less at random, Mercer bought a ticket for New York.

The ringing noise subsided about three hours into the trip, but Mercer soon found himself nursing a horrible headache. At a rest stop along the way he bought an evening paper. The shooting, as late-breaking news, had made the third page. No survivors were listed. At the Port Authority, the following day, Mercer picked up another paper and saw that he'd touched off a minor gang war. One of the cardplayers must have been more important than he'd known. A reprisal shooting had already taken place in New York and the newspaper mob watchers anticipated more.

Mercer was a complete stranger to New York and he found the city not much to his taste. However, he thought he'd better stay there for a while. He certainly couldn't go back to Chicago and he had no confidence that he'd be safe in South Carolina either. He didn't much suppose that his part in the shooting was known to his old Chicago partners, but the third cardplayer could conceivably have recognized him, and might have lasted long enough to mumble a few words to somebody else. Then there were the police. Mercer had to assume that his trail would be followed as far as the Volvo. The car in turn could possibly be traced to San Diego, and it was also covered with his fingerprints. Mercer couldn't even recall if he'd been printed in Mexico. If he had, and if the crime computers were as omniscient as paranoia could make them seem, he might be looking forward to a federal warrant.

Mercer checked into a transients' hotel in the West 20s and started hiding. Then he developed a persecution complex, began dreaming of gangsters and FBI men. What had begun as well-reasoned caution progressed through several stages of paranoia and finally turned into a fugue state. By the time Mercer ran completely out of money and was evicted from the hotel for nonpayment, he no longer knew who he was or what he was doing in New York. He spent that winter in the city's soup kitchens and shelters, incessantly mumbling and muttering to himself.

One day in the spring of 1980, Charles Mercer took a nap on a bench in Madison Square Park, near the intersection of Fifth Avenue and Broadway. Sometime during his sleep, Mercer turned a mental corner and found himself shaking hands with that old friend, his identity. He woke up, almost himself again. He was hungry and more than a little irritated. He didn't yet know that nearly a year had passed, but he understood that he'd blown away a substantial amount of time. What now.

Pigeons clustered on the asphalt walks of the park, fluttering among patches of crumbs the strollers had dropped. Mercer regarded the pigeons. They were fat and rather overconfident, in Mercer's view. When he approached the pigeons, they didn't even bother to really fly away. The pigeons only hovered for a moment and then settled gently back to the pavement. Mercer thought they needed a serious shaking up. Not only that but he was very hungry and eager to get back in control. Mercer reached into his coat pocket and found his last possession, which had survived the winter because no one else could think of a reason to want it, the casting net.

On that same soft April day, Larkin was released from the Bellevue mental ward where he'd spent the previous eight months. He left the hospital on foot, no immediate destination in mind, and soon found himself walking into the north end of Madison Square Park. It seemed to have rained not so long ago. The air was fresh and the leaves were green and Larkin was pleased to be free again. Down a long diagonal pathway, Larkin saw Mercer's net burst into the air and soar. The net hung in suspension for a long moment, as if supported by the flashes of spring sunlight its white threads caught and retained.

When Larkin reached the net thrower, Mercer had already wrung the necks of two pigeons and was dropping them into his coat pocket. This coat was a hunting jacket he'd bought for excursions with Reston, and it had a huge game pouch in the back.

"Can you do that again?" Larkin said.

"I can," Mercer said. "And I'm going to." Mercer made another cast and this time caught three pigeons. Then he declared himself satisfied, but Larkin persuaded him to keep on throwing the net at nothing, just so he could watch it fly.

Later that evening, Mercer and Larkin found a place of seclusion, which was, however, still in the open air. Mercer dressed the pigeons and Larkin built a little fire out of garbage. They roasted the birds on a coat-hanger spit and found them passable fare. Larkin, who was comparatively solvent, contributed a stick of margarine and some soy sauce. After the repast, the two parted company, but Larkin was so enchanted with the whole episode that he gave Mercer his phone number.

*

During April 1980, Mercer put himself mostly back together again. Regarding much of the previous year his mind was a virtual blank. But he had recovered the rest of his past. Mercer decided he need no longer fear the Chicago gangsters or the law. Nevertheless he decided to remain in New York for a while. He felt a grudge against the city, which had plundered his memory and turned him adrift in its streets, and he wanted to get even with it somehow.

Through April, Mercer remained a vagabond. He panhandled a little, and went on netting pigeons, a mode of sustenance which he liked for its sheer madness. Sometime in May, Mercer found a job in a warehouse and took a room at the YMCA. At that point, he called Larkin and suggested a drink. The two became fairly friendly, tending to meet at different bars every ten days or two weeks. Larkin, two months out of the hospital, was drinking quite a bit already.

Mercer supposed that he was better off than he had been the preceding winter, but he was still discontent. His life was flat and seemed to lack savor. His mind began to turn back with tender nostalgia toward that moment in Chicago when he'd pulled the trigger. In retrospect it was not the revenge that charmed him, but rather the explosion itself. Mercer felt that he wanted to live that moment again in reality. He began to imagine new enemies and opponents. At night, in his austere YMCA single, he worked himself to peaks of undirected fury. In June of 1980, Mercer spotted Simon's ad.

When Mercer entered the anger clinic, David Hutton had already been attending it for a little over a year. He was a sort of senior member and was quite outspoken during the sessions. But it was Mercer who first intuited that there was a little more going on in the clinic than immediately met the eye. In the fall of 1980, Mercer requested a private interview with Simon and probed him on this point. Simon confided in him a little, though not much. He admitted that somewhere down the line, some patients might have special opportunities to "act out." Simon went on to give a profile of the certain type of patient he was referring to.

Mercer listened to this latter description with close attention and decided that it might fit Larkin, among others. Larkin often talked rather wildly when he was drinking, and Mercer thought that his conversation might be of some interest to Simon. He introduced the two in October 1980. Simon did indeed find Larkin intriguing, but Larkin declined to attend public meetings of the clinic after one trial appearance there. However, he did consent to meet with Simon privately, how often even Mercer didn't know. In December 1980, Simon advised Mercer that Larkin, while certainly a fascinating case in his own right, was not precisely in tune with the central aims of the clinic, at least, not for the present time. Simon was grateful for having met Larkin, however. He would, so to speak, put Larkin on hold.

By January 1981, Simon felt ready to move toward a second phase. He disclosed his plans in greater detail to Mercer, and, influenced to a degree by Mercer's recommendation, he also included David Hutton in the embryo formation of the cell. Charles Mercer, however, always retained a special status in the group, even when it reached full membership later in the year. Simon had been impressed strongly with his general acumen, and without making Mercer's role perfectly clear to the others, he appointed him a sort of lieutenant or second-in-command. Mercer was also the only member of the cell to derive any tangible benefit from his association with Simon. In 1982, Mercer was staying at the Riverside Drive apartment, in a bedroom that had once housed Simon's pet fugitives, and Simon was supporting him financially.

31
Ruben Carrera (IV)

IN THE SUMMER of 1978, Ruben Carrera was ferried out of the city to one of the several Blossom Ranch facilities in upstate New York. There were between 100 and 150 other clients at the center Ruben was delivered to, and all of them were under eighteen. Ruben entered the group still trembling slightly from the effects of withdrawal, though he had been detoxed before the transfer. Like most new arrivals in the program he was quite nervous about what was in store for him.

The Blossom Ranch center was administered from top to bottom by former addicts, most of whom had risen through the ranks of the program. There were two basic objectives to the therapy. The first was for the newly arrived client to discard his former, addicted personality as completely as a snake sheds its skin, though it was understood that for a human this process would be much more time-consuming and painful. Once tabula rasa had been achieved, the next goal was for the client to build a new personality whose essential characteristics derived from the ethics and principles of the program of treatment itself. This reconstructed personality, it was hoped, would become strong and self-sufficient enough to withstand the temptations of addiction once its possessor returned to the outside world.

Several means were employed to reach these two objectives. "Getting in touch with feelings" was of primary importance. A fundamental presumption of the program was that addiction always served to mask some unacknowledged canker at the heart and soul of the individual. In encounter groups that went on for torturous hours, these secret wounds would be subjected to full scrutiny of the public eye. The ethos of the group encouraged all its members to render complete account of all their most private guilts and terrors, and also of any resentments they might have developed against the others. Emotional displays of all kinds were strongly solicited. In the course of the daily group sessions, clients screamed themselves into near insensibility, raged and wept till they collapsed from exhaustion.

The program also made use of some classic behavior modification techniques, similar to those which Simon Rohnstock was studying at the New School. Positive reinforcement took the form of advancement in the program, toward eventual freedom. The greatest gifts were increases of independence and responsibility, and in the controlled circumstances of the center these had significant value. If negative reinforcement were deemed necessary, a client might be compelled to shave his head, or to spend a few days in strict silence while wearing sandwich boards which conveyed some such message as this:

> My name is Ruben Carrera and I can't deal with My Feelings. I can't deal with Others.
>
> Please Help Me.

Like most new Blossom Ranch residents, Ruben Carrera was habitually solitary and instinctively secretive. The climate of openness which the program fostered scared the wits out of him at first. The pressure of daily living was enormous and there was no relief from it except through the encounter groups and scream sessions. Privacy did not exist at Blossom Ranch. Of course, no drugs or alcohol were permitted, though cigarettes and coffee were available and were consumed in huge quantities. A special peculiarity of the program was that while it was coeducational, sexual contact between residents was strictly prohibited, and should it occur was grounds for dismissal from the program. Since most of the clients faced jail time if they failed at Blossom Ranch, this rule was taken very seriously. The black cloud of sexual tension thus created would burst into storm at every encounter session.

All of Ruben's defenses automatically went up when he arrived at Blossom Ranch. Nearly all of them were subsequently beaten down. Ruben endured constant questioning about his physical and emotional scars, and he could not respond to it with violence, as had previously been his habit. Three months into his residency, Ruben cracked and in a flood of shrieks and tears (surpassing Manuela's best performances) he vomited up the whole of his tormented inner life. Almost. Even at that moment of truth Ruben defended his last citadel and told his elaborate lie about the tenement fire he claimed had originally scarred him. Ruben told his story so vividly and so poignantly that many of the others in the group wept with him. His confession was taken at face value and Ruben was accepted into the Blossom Ranch "Family."

Many of the Blossom Ranch residents had never known another family, at least not a stable one. The group posited itself as the greatest good. And though from a distance the group might seem to be a monster with no head, Ruben was happy to surrender himself to it altogether. During the last half of his two-year term at Blossom Ranch, Ruben was a model of good behavior. He obeyed the rules and respected the ethics and frequently played a catalytic role in breaking down the initial resistance of newcomers.

The group rewarded Ruben by allowing him to pursue his education. He began to take high school courses, and his talent for the natural sciences bloomed. He was especially good at chemistry, and not long before he left the program the group permitted him to present a project at an upstate science fair.

In 1980, Ruben graduated from Blossom Ranch as one of the program's major successes. To all appearances he was a completely reformed character, and he looked likely to become an exemplary citizen of the "real world" he had reentered. While still in the program, Ruben had earned a high school diploma and he had been admitted to NYU, where he intended to study chemical engineering. Ruben was going to get a free dorm room from the school, and a job he'd found in a quickie photo lab made him completely self-supporting.

Ruben entered NYU in the fall of 1980, and for the first semester he worked hard and well and was happy enough. By the second semester he was in less good shape, though his academic work continued to go well and he had won a minor promotion at his job. Ruben missed the support system that Blossom Ranch had provided. In spite of all his recent training, Ruben could not easily "deal with others," and he often felt that he was still wearing a sign that said so. He had little in common with the other NYU students and found it impossible to make friends. This failure drove him to extremes of frustration which he had no way to relieve. The purgative outbursts of anger and emotion which had sustained him at

Blossom Ranch were obviously unacceptable in the general society.

In the spring of 1981, Ruben knew he was on the verge of serious trouble. He had begun to dwell lovingly on his memories of heroin, and he feared that he might "fall," that being the Blossom Ranch terminology for shooting dope again. He had also developed a new obsession: explosive compounds. During long hours spent in various chemical libraries, Ruben became an armchair expert on this subject. In March 1981, he slipped into the lab over a holiday weekend and managed to synthesize a variant of nitroglycerin. Ruben badly wanted to throw it against the wall to make sure it would really blow. It required all the will power he had left to dismantle the little bomb he had made.

Then Ruben knew he had reached his breaking point. Blossom Ranch had taught him to seek help when he needed it. But to return to Blossom Ranch for assistance would be a crippling admission of defeat. These thoughts were chasing each other's tails through Ruben's mind when he first saw Simon's ad.

Ruben's job made him a few minutes late to his first session of the anger clinic. Someone buzzed him into the office and he tiptoed into Simon's group room. Simon had already begun a little introductory talk for the benefit of the novices. He paced in the center of a ring of chairs, speaking with an urgent intensity, gesticulating with long fingers. Seven or eight others were attending to his speech, among them Charles Mercer and David Hutton. When Ruben sidled in, Simon was in midsentence:

". . . for you to cope with this anger, this rage. But this society instructs you to repress your anger. To turn it inward. In effect, to attack yourself. But is it right or reasonable to be ordered to attack yourself? I suggest to you that it is not. Don't you think that whoever or whatever gives you such an order is really the thing that must be attacked?"

Ruben found a seat and composed himself in time to register this last question. Silently, but with complete conviction, he answered, *yes, yes, yes.*

32
Simon Rohnstock (V)

IN THE WINTER of 1981, Simon took his material in hand
and began to mold it toward its final form. The anger clinic
had proved even more successful than he'd originally hoped.
Simon himself held separate sessions three times a week, and
had developed a group of about thirty dedicated patients.
Since the fall of 1980 he'd allowed Mercer and Hutton to
lead their own groups, and between them they had raised the
total membership to fifty or more. Of course, these fifty-odd
people composed too unwieldy a mass to be incorporated into
the finely tuned organization Simon envisioned. But Simon
was carefully indoctrinating them all with his own hybrid
psycho-political dogma, and they made a good pool for more
specialized recruiting.

In 1981, Simon had two such recruits under his personal
control. David Hutton was probably the man of whom Simon
felt most certain. In private sessions, Simon had dissected his
personality and found it much to his liking. He had been able
to control Hutton's anxiety syndrome and in so doing he had
transferred Hutton's dependency to himself. Simon believed
that he could channel Hutton's violent impulses in whatever
direction he chose, and he understood that Hutton's expertise with firearms would be extremely useful to the cell. On
the debit side, Hutton was indecisive, incipiently alcoholic,
and Simon feared he might balk in a crisis. However, some
of these same qualities made him very easy to manipulate.
David Hutton came close indeed to Simon's conception of
the ideal revolutionary foot soldier.

Charles Mercer's case was different and rather more com-
plicated. To begin with, Mercer was far less tractable than
Hutton, cagier, and less willing to part with personal secrets.
In his analytic sessions with Simon, Mercer resisted interro-

gation. Simon knew much less about his past than he did about Hutton's. He did know of his dope-smuggling career and something of his jail time in Mexico. But Mercer never told him anything about the killing of Frank Scotti. He also tried to force Simon to trade information evenly, point for point, which was certainly not a norm of therapy or of Simon's private plans. Every conversation with Mercer was a sort of fencing match, but Simon rather enjoyed that. He appreciated Mercer's leadership abilities and general shrewdness. The advice Mercer offered was usually sound. Simon had not at first intended to share the least authority with other members of the cell, but after studying Mercer he decided to relax that rule. The chief drawback to Mercer, in Simon's view, was the chance that he could break out into serious insubordination. However, through 1980 and 1981 Simon was able to control him without his appearing to notice or resent it, and he was helpful in enhancing Simon's power over the others. Simon knew that Mercer was a somewhat risky proposition, but he thought the risk was worth it.

Larkin . . . Larkin was the most peculiar and least predictable of all the people Simon seriously considered recruiting into the cell. He would not attend group sessions and seemed unimpressed with Simon's new doctrines, which were working so well on the others. And yet for a time he was very interested in talking to Simon. Larkin did not seem to have any fund of repressed anger for Simon to draw on, or if he did, it was anger so weirdly transformed that it was unrecognizable. Simon could elicit very little of Larkin's past history. Larkin preferred to talk about people he had known as opposed to himself. If he did make reference to his own past, he did so anecdotally and tended to eliminate himself from each anecdote early on. And much of what he said was sheerly incredible. Simon was unable to learn *anything* very concrete about Larkin, who was oddly adroit at sliding away from questions. He did not know that Larkin had been a mental patient at Bellevue and had no idea that he was a diagnosed epileptic. Simon came to his own conclusion that Larkin was psychotic, though he couldn't narrow the diagnosis any further. He finally decided that Larkin was too unstable to be admitted into the cell.

However ... Simon couldn't dismiss Larkin altogether. Larkin had some potential virtues for Simon's purposes and plans. Larkin seemed to care absolutely nothing for his own well-being. Self-preservation, as far as could be determined, was a matter of complete indifference to him. This phenomenon of Larkin's character was doubtless pathological, but Simon felt that it could somehow be turned to account. Under certain circumstances and if the spirit moved him, Larkin might be brought to do truly mad things. He might accept missions which no one else would willingly undertake, and where it would be foolhardy to risk a stabler man. In the summer of 1982, Simon found an opportunity to test this theory, and it proved correct beyond his greatest hopes.

But it was Ruben Carrera, not Larkin, who completed the cell's core membership. Carrera turned out to be a quick and easy convert. Simon was able to pick up the reins which controlled him where the Blossom Ranch people had dropped them. On the other hand, Blossom Ranch had also taught Carrera how to manipulate a group without obviously seeming to do so. And Simon was astute enough to realize that Carrera's account of his childhood was covering something up, though he didn't think it much mattered. Carrera was more open than Mercer and easier to manage, and he was more confident than Hutton. And his knowledge of explosives was literally priceless. Simon knew that with Carrera in the cell he would be able to achieve great things. Nevertheless he was taken aback when Carrera first told him how easy it would be to build a simple fission bomb.

33
Mau Mau

WHEN RUBEN CARRERA left Riverside Drive on November 2, 1982, he went directly to a uniform outlet, where he bought an orange reflective jacket of the type worn by construction and road workers. Then he took a train down to West Fourth Street and walked over to his dorm at NYU. Once there, he dragged a chest from under his bed and opened it to see what kind of supplies he had on hand.

Carrera would have preferred to manufacture his own explosive, but he knew that time pressure made that method unsure. In the chest he already had a substantial quantity of plastique, a high-yield explosive which Simon had somehow obtained for him, and also a big bundle of fuse. Unfortunately there were no blasting caps, but Carrera thought he could get around that. For the rest of the afternoon, Carrera worked daintily with the plastique and fuses. He was going to try a method commonly called "lacing." First he looped a length of fuse and thickened it into a heavy knot. Then, cautiously and delicately, he molded plastique around the knot. The end result was a large blob of plastique with a couple of inches of double fuse protruding from it. Carrera continued working until he had laced four such lumps of plastique.

By then it was four P.M. and he was sweating a little from the extreme concentration required to lace the explosive effectively without blowing up his dormitory. Carrera packed the prepared charges away in his chest and went down to Canal Street, where he bought a jumbo radio (broken), six D cells to fit it, two rolls of wire (one insulated and the other not), and a light switch. Back in his room, Carrera broke the battery pack out of the radio and connected it to the light switch. He made a coil from the uninsulated wire, connected it to the battery pack, flipped the switch, and timed the period it took the coil to glow red-hot. That established, he disconnected the whole apparatus. He made three more coils and cut some lengths of insulated wire. These he put into a knapsack, along with the laced plastique and the other supplies, except for the batteries, which he dropped into the pocket of his coat. When he had done all that, Carrera felt sleepy. Already it was dark outside. Carrera set his alarm for three A.M. and lay down to take a nap.

He slept soundly but when the alarm went off he was instantly alert. Carrera got up, found the knapsack in the dark, and left his room quietly. In the hallway of the building he picked up some scraps of plywood he had noticed there earlier. Then he took the A train to Fulton Street.

As he had anticipated, the platform was empty when he got off. Carrera put on his reflective vest and strolled to the concrete booth at the far end. Some ambiguous pipes ran up the wall of the booth through the ceiling, and as he had hoped there was enough space along the pipes for him to push two ends of his insulated wire through. Carrera fixed the wires in place with a piece of tape, jumped down to the tracks, and walked into the tunnel, spooling out wire behind him.

Somewhere up the tunnel he found a switch on the uptown A track. He knelt, lit the flashlight he had brought, and began to pack the plastique on either side of the rails at the juncture. When he had finished he wedged a piece of plywood over each charge and began connecting his open wire coils to the fuses.

At that point he heard voices back toward the platform. Carrera looked back. There was a crew of track workers on the platform, and one of them seemed to be calling to him. Carrera stood up, displaying his orange vest, and made a vague gesture with his flashlight. The track crew went away down the platform and disappeared up one of the stairways. In a cold sweat, Carrera finished wiring the fuses. He connected the loaded battery pack and quickly left the station.

Ruben Carrera spent the next two or three hours in Battery Park, watching the day break over the bay. He was the only one watching this view. At seven A.M., Carrera returned to the Fulton Street station and went down to the J train platform. The station was crowded with incoming passengers, but not many people were waiting for trains. Carrera found his two wires in the floor at the end of the platform and hooked up the light switch. The wait was not really a long one, though it seemed so to him. When he heard the echo of an A train approaching below, he flipped the switch. The explosion was muffled by the thick walls and floors, but Carrera could hear it distinctly, and as soon as he did, he jerked the switch free of the wires and put it in his pocket. Providentially, a J train was pulling in at that very moment. Carrera got on it along with a few other passengers, none of whom seemed to have noticed anything untoward. The train was packed and Carrera could barely wedge his way in. The doors stayed open for an agonizing time, but at last they closed and the train ground slowly out of the station.

On his way uptown from Hutton's Chelsea apartment, Charles Mercer stopped in a sporting-goods store and bought a short hatchet. When he got back to the Riverside Drive apartment, it was midafternoon and Simon had gone out. Mercer went into his bedroom, put on his hunting jacket, and placed the Skorpion in the game pouch. For the next two or three hours he worked on drawing the gun, unfolding the stock, and changing clips. He practiced the sequence until he had it down to about fifteen seconds.

At six P.M., Mercer went into the kitchen and made himself a tunafish omelette, which he ate in front of the TV news. For the next several hours he watched television, changing channels frequently. Once he got up to wash his dishes and open himself a single beer. Simon had still not returned by midnight. Mercer put the Skorpion and the hatchet into his hunting jacket, left the apartment, and walked leisurely across Central Park. He rather hoped that someone would try to molest him, but no one did.

Mercer got on the uptown 2, a train sometimes called the "Beast," and rode it into one of the worse sections of the

Bronx, where he got off. He was wearing a watch cap which partially disguised his race, and none of the natives bothered him. The streets were quite empty in any case.

For about forty-five minutes, Mercer ambled in a widening circle around the subway stop. At last he saw a two-man patrol car pulled into the curb on the next block. Mercer approached the car from behind. He could see that the passenger-side window was open, and both officers were in the car, apparently eating pastries. When Mercer was parallel to the open window he whipped out the machine gun and squirted a clip across the front seat, changed clips with lightning speed and blew the second one into the car. Remembering Hutton's caveat about wasting ammunition, Mercer decided to let it go at that.

Once Mercer had left his apartment, David Hutton decided to disregard the other's advice and have another drink. During the afternoon of November 2, Hutton had several drinks. By seven P.M., when he had to go to work, he had finished the bourbon and most of the beer and he was plastered. One of his coworkers remarked that he looked sort of sick. In fact Hutton did feel queasy, and while handling some unpleasantly fishy garbage outside a Brooklyn restaurant, he threw up.

Hutton clocked out sick at around ten P.M. and took a train back to Chelsea. On his way back to his apartment, he stopped for another pint of bourbon. He drank about half of this when he got home, and passed out on the couch. His sleep was troubled with worse nightmares than he'd had for months, though he slept heavily.

When he woke up, it was already the afternoon of the third and time was running out. Hutton had a horrible hangover. He took aspirin and drank a couple of eggs beaten in beer. Though he was able to keep this down, Hutton called his supervisor and said that he still had the flu and could not work that night. After making the call he went back to bed and slept for several more hours.

Hutton woke up for the second time around eight P.M.,

feeling fit for another drink, though when he had one, it seemed to have little effect. He paced the small apartment, and for a few minutes occupied himself by returning the guns to the stash hole behind the couch, excepting one Sten and clips for it. During the next hour or so, Hutton mopped up the remains of the bourbon. He did not feel drunk, but somewhat calmer. At around nine-thirty he armed himself with the Kabar knife he'd kept from the army and the Sten, which he was able to conceal beneath the loose field jacket he wore.

Hutton got on the Broadway local, headed uptown. He had conceived no plan and during the trip he thought of none. The random rage which often visited him when he drank was conspicuously absent now. Somewhere in Harlem he got off the train and crossed to the downtown track. Riding back toward Chelsea, he began seriously to consider Mercer's suggestion that it wasn't really necessary for him to carry out an action. Perhaps he would just go home. But when the train stopped at 23rd Street, he did not get off.

At Canal Street, Hutton noticed a solitary transit cop waiting on the platform. The head of the train, where Hutton was sitting, pulled well past the cop, who presumably got onto a rear car. Hutton made a deal with himself. He would get out at the next stop. *If* the cop also got off, and *if* there was no one else around, Hutton would make a move. Otherwise he would call it a night.

As the train slowed down in the station, Hutton took out a ski mask he'd thought to bring along and rolled it up on the top of his head. The doors opened and he stepped out. The cop was alone on the platform. Hutton's stomach knotted, but he kept his bargain. He pulled the mask over his face, brought the Sten to his shoulder, and screamed.

The cop froze upon seeing the gun. As it happened, he was a Chinese cop. His features disclosed no obvious reaction, which somehow made it easier for Hutton to begin carrying out what he had vaguely contemplated. Hutton instructed the cop to handcuff himself and when he had done so, Hutton began backing him toward the door of a disused restroom down the platform.

The cop's black eyes were locked on the holes of Hutton's mask. As ordered, he retreated slowly, hands locked before him, toward the restroom door. Hutton remained about six feet distant from him, with the Sten at full auto. When the cop reached the door he dove through it, gaining a few seconds of cover. Hutton followed quickly, now realizing he'd forgotten to secure the cop's side arm. When he got into the bathroom, the cop had managed to reach the gun with his fingertips but Hutton was in time to kick it away. He retrieved the pistol and hit the cop over the temple with it, striking lightly so as not to kill. The cop slid down the wall to a sitting position on the watery floor. Hutton exhaled deeply. The moment of action had relaxed him; indeed he felt as though he had passed into some trancelike state, well beyond the uneasiness that had paralyzed him for the last two days. Hutton propped the Sten against the wall and drew the Kabar knife. Smoothly and calmly, he enacted one of his nastier dreams.

On the morning of November 4, David Hutton called Charles Mercer and suggested they meet for a drink at the Dublin House before going to Simon's. Mercer agreed, and he duly showed up at the bar a little after three P.M. He got a draft beer and went to the back. Hutton had already taken a seat in a booth. He was drinking neat whisky with a beer chaser. Mercer noted that he looked a little pale.

"You okay?" Mercer said. "You look a little shaky."

"Touch of flu," Hutton said. "No problem, really."

"Did you decide to do it?"

"I did it," Hutton said.

Mercer sipped his beer and made no comment.

"You?" Hutton said.

"Man, I have got the original stuff," Mercer said, "Right in Simon's own freezer."

"What stuff?"

Mercer smiled. "Wait and see."

"You don't think he's already found it?"

"Who, Simon? He eats out. He won't even put ice in a drink, because he likes to keep his metabolism at flat zero. I really don't know why he bothers to own a refrigerator, tell you the truth."

"If you say so," Hutton said. "What do you think Ruben did?"

"I'm pretty sure he blew up the Fulton Street subway. Didn't you see any papers?"

"No."

"Front page yesterday. I imagine it was him. We'll be finding out soon enough, anyway."

"Simon'll love that."

"Sure," Mercer said. "Better drink up, David. He wants us there a half hour early so we don't blow the meet with Larkin."

At the corner of 79th Street and Broadway, Mercer and Hutton were accosted by a wino.

"Spare a quarter?" the wino said.

"I don't got," Mercer said.

"A dime. Anything." The wino stepped across Mercer's path and fell into him, grasping the lapel of the hunting jacket with both hands. He was an old man, bearded and snaggle-toothed, and his breath was foul. Mercer hit him sharply in the chest with the heel of his hand, pushing him back a few steps. The old man flashed into a cone of flame. Mercer and Hutton fell back into a doorway, to shield themselves from the sudden wave of heat. A skeletal form appeared in the pyre, black on orange. Then, in a matter of seconds, there was nothing. Except for a smear of greasy ashes on the sidewalk.

"Jesus," Hutton said. "How did you *do* that?"

"I didn't," Mercer said. "I had nothing to do with it. Let's get the hell out of here."

Carrera had arrived ahead of the others and was again sitting in the window seat. Simon was in the armchair beneath the Warhol print of Mao. Mercer and Hutton took places on the couch. They had decided between them that it would be as well not to mention the curious burning they'd witnessed.

"Well," Mercer said. "Do we show our hands? I say Ruben goes first since he's the youngest."

Carrera came forward and presented an envelope of clippings from the *Times* and *Post*. He had made the front page of both papers. Simon opened the envelope and began reading selections aloud, his eyebrows arched in approval. Carrera had had some spectacular good fortune. By chance he had derailed the uptown train into an oncoming downtown train, and the collision had killed upwards of a hundred people. It was one of the worst subway disasters in history. The track was expected to be out of service for weeks. Sabotage was much suspected, but the police had released no information.

Simon concluded his reading and returned the clippings to Carrera.

"You'd better burn these," he said. "What did you do about traces, by the way?"

"I wore gloves in the subway," Carrera said. "Everything I used was Canal Street secondhand and I junked it when I was done. Everything else is blown up except for a few feet of wire, maybe."

"Very good," Simon said. "Were you armed?"

"I don't like guns," Carrera said.

"You'd better learn to like them. What if you'd been interrupted? Go with David and do some gun drill. Today."

Carrera shifted position in the window seat, turning his scarred side to the room. There was an uneasy silence.

"Well, there's no need to sulk, Ruben," Simon said. "We just don't want to lose you, that's all. But we're all very proud of you, I'm sure. In fact, we might even want to claim this . . . It'll have to be discussed. Who's next?"

Mercer jerked a thumb at Hutton. Hutton pulled a plastic sandwich bag from his field jacket and shook two yellowish ears onto the coffee table in front of him. Simon bent forward to inspect them, without much sign of surprise.

"Those are real cop ears," Hutton said. "Fresh ones."

"Ah," Simon said. "One of your little fantasies, I see, David. How does it feel?"

"Okay."

"How did you deal with the body?"

"What body? I didn't kill him, I just took the ears."

"Your reasons?"

"General demoralization of the police force," Hutton said, as if by rote.

"All right," Simon said. "Not too subtle, but effective, I suppose. Get rid of those ears. Charles?"

Mercer left the room and returned with a cardboard box, which he set on the floor. He opened the box and folded the mouth of a black plastic bag down over the flaps. From the bag he removed two human heads, one brunette and the other with sandy hair. Mercer arranged the heads on the coffee table so that they were facing Simon. No one spoke aloud, though Carrera turned back from the window and Hutton sucked in his breath.

"You want heads, you got heads," Mercer said quietly. "What do you say, Simon? Will you hit or sit?"

Simon did not reply. After a long moment, Mercer reached back into the box and got out two police caps with badges, which he fitted carefully onto each head.

"I brought their little hats along, see," Mercer said. "For verification, and like that."

Simon, still leaning forward, was rapt in his contemplation of the two heads. Clearly, both were frozen solid. The eyes, though open, were glazed with ice crystals, and the brows and facial hair were stiff with frost. Yet Simon felt that one or the other of the heads might open its mouth and speak to him, though what it might say was beyond his imagining. But he knew he had opened a door into a world in which such things could happen.

"I'll hit, of course," Simon said, at last. "We'll all hit, won't we. There's no more turning back."

34
Madison Square

A RANK OF UNDIVIDED benches ran in a gentle curve along the south side of Madison Square, facing into the park. That afternoon, sunset cast its colors through the leafless trees, soft reds and golds intersticed among the shadows of branches on the paved walkway, like panes of stained glass. A file of pigeons processed solemnly along the walk. One deviated from its path and cocked its head sideways at the benches, fixing Larkin with its round black eye.

The pigeon waited. Larkin reached into a wadded sack beside him, which held half of a cinnamon doughnut, his only meal of that day. He rolled some crumbs between his forefinger and thumb and flicked them toward the bird. The other pigeons turned and formed a circle, pecking. Larkin threw more crumbs.

Near him on the bench lay a tattered copy of the previous day's *Post*. Its banner referred to the Fulton Street catastrophe. The secondary headline read: 2 COPS AXED IN BRONX. A wind rose sharply from the east, turning the pages of the newspaper. The center sheet lifted and sailed over the backs of the benches toward Fifth Avenue, was followed by another and another. The pigeons raised their heads and flew. Larkin went on studying the pavement, where the shadowed branches were tossing and the amber hues of evening pooled and ran together.

At about four-thirty P.M. on November 4, Simon dismissed Hutton and Carrera and took a cab downtown. Mercer accompanied him. Simon wanted him along in case Larkin did not appear in the park. Mercer might be able to recall or intuit another meeting place. During the cab ride Simon was silent and pensive, though not because he was still stunned by the spectacle of the heads, as Mercer happily assumed. The objections Hutton and Carrera had raised to Larkin had disturbed Simon more than he'd shown, and he was beginning to feel anxious.

They disembarked from the cab at the north end of the park. Simon paid. He and Mercer walked a diagonal path to the center of the park and looked about themselves. A young woman in a sweatsuit was exercising an Irish setter; the red dog ran from tree to tree. A couple of loose-joint types were standing around despondently. There were no customers; the day was too cold.

"He's not here," Simon said, glancing at his watch.

"Wait a second," Mercer's attention was caught by the papers flying from the bench at the lower end of the park. Near the blowing sheets a dim figure sat, shrouded in a full-length overcoat. Mercer pointed.

"I think that's him."

Simon followed him down through the park. He did not think that the man on the bench much resembled Larkin. His posture was not quite the same and the glasses he wore made him look abnormally benign.

"It's him, all right," Mercer said.

"He looks different, somehow," Simon said. They had reached the curved south pathway, but the man on the bench did not look up. However, it was indubitably Larkin.

"Stay here," Simon said, waving Mercer back.

"What?"

"I want to talk to him alone. Just wait for me. Or go get a coffee somewhere."

Mercer shrugged and took a seat on a bench across the path, hunching with his hands in his pockets against the cold. Simon walked to the bench where Larkin was sitting, brushed the newspaper away and sat down. Larkin did not seem aware of his presence, though Simon was only a foot away. The glasses radically altered his appearance. Simon found both these things mildly unnerving.

"Well, well, my friend," he said, attempting geniality.

"Am I your friend?" Larkin did not turn.

Simon examined his profile, trying to subdue his irritation. Larkin always had the knack of putting him at an instant disadvantage, often using the methods he himself preferred.

"Touchy, aren't we?" Simon said.

"Not particularly. Did you have anything special to say to me, or did you just want to chat?"

"Tell me where you were on Tuesday."

"No."

"Why didn't you come to the meeting?"

"Because I don't like going to meetings. And some people are looking for me. Maybe police. I'm sure you wouldn't want me to bring them up there."

"What for?"

"It's not related."

"It could be important."

"You don't need to know."

Simon followed Larkin's glance to the walk in front of the bench, where the paper continued to unfurl in the wind.

"When will it be?" Larkin said.

"Times Square, you mean?"

"What else?"

"I'm not sure now," Simon said. "When we called on Tuesday, I thought very soon. But the situation has changed. Maybe a few months more, even. Ruben isn't quite ready. I can't make the schedule definite.

"Then you're wasting my time, aren't you. What did you bring me here for?"

"I told you, the situation changed these last two days. I decided to do some development first. Haven't you read the papers?"

"What, do you want to be congratulated?"

Simon fell silent. He sensed he'd lost another point. A match flashed across the way. Mercer had lit a cigarette. Larkin had buried his hands deep in his coat pockets. It almost seemed to Simon as if he had no arms.

"You look different," Simon said. "I hardly recognized you at first."

"I believe I mentioned some people are looking for me."

A single pigeon walked the path, its neck feathers ruffled by the wind. Simon said nothing. He was getting cold.

"If we don't have anything to say to each other, we might as well say goodbye," Larkin said. "I think it's a poor risk to be meeting at all now."

"I feel it's important that we stay in touch. You didn't make contact for more than a month. You haven't been answering the phone. What if you were to disappear?"

"I won't disappear. And I'm sure you can find out if I'm in the city or not without actually seeing my face. I'll send you post cards if you like."

"What, you're not staying in Brooklyn anymore?"

"I don't think it's safe. I've told you three times now, people are looking for me. But if you need to reach me you can leave a message on the machine."

"You'll get it?"

"I can pick it up by remote."

"Who's looking for you, Larkin? Why are they looking?"

"Like I said, you don't need to know."

"Larkin," Simon said, slipping into his therapeutic couch-side manner. "Tell me what's wrong."

"Why do you want to get to know me, Simon? There isn't any point."

Mercer flipped his cigarette away. The butt rolled toward Fifth Avenue, trailing sparks. The solitary pigeon had approached Larkin's feet. Larkin reached into the bag and fed it crumbs. Then he returned his hand to his pocket.

"You might as well get going, Simon. I tell you, it's dangerous for us to be together now."

"I'll worry about the danger. You don't have to think about it."

"I'm not worried. I'm just making observations at random, since you insist on staying here and we have nothing of importance to discuss."

"Larkin, to tell you the truth, I'm a little concerned. Maybe you'll fail us, maybe you'll back out. You say yourself you're without commitment. Why should I trust you?"

"Why should you trust anyone? We've been through this before. I thought you were happy to have someone who didn't care. Or else you could use one of your own people. But I'll tell you something new. Someone in your position can only trust someone who's capable of anything."

"That's not terribly encouraging."

"Did you come down here to be reassured? Why yes, I believe you did. I might be a little disappointed in you, Simon, if I cared enough."

Simon sighed.

"Let me be candid with you, Larkin. I don't know very much about you, and maybe it's better that way. As you suggest. But I have to depend on you, just the same. I'd feel a bit easier if I knew your motives."

"I can't very well tell you my motives, since I don't understand them myself. But you don't have to worry. I'll go through with it."

Larkin scattered another handful of crumbs beside his shoes. The pigeon pecked its way closer. Simon closed his eyes and pressed his fingertips lightly on the lids.

"How can anyone act without motives?" he said.

"Have you never heard of *stillness?*"

"Stillness?"

"Never mind. I didn't say I had no motives, only that I don't know what they are. Or want to know. Awareness has never been all that conducive to action, right? I've heard you say that yourself."

"Maybe you're right. But you don't think much of our idea, do you? I don't quite see why you don't just go and kill anyone. Snipe from a rooftop."

"I may end up doing that, if you keep on annoying me with trivial questions. Hasn't that occurred to you? But I'm not doing that, I'm helping you instead because you're going to expand the chaos. You'll do more than I could do alone."

"Chaos isn't our objective."

"You'll get it anyway. But you'd be better off not listening to me. I don't especially want to interfere with your principles."

"Tell me, Larkin, what do you really think of our program?"

"I don't think about it. Do you really want an answer to that?"

"Yes, I think I do."

"All right, then. I believe that you and whoever the ones behind you might be are people of great cunning. But your cunning will be wasted, and you will not succeed. Subtlety is wasted on what you're going to start. You'll never be able to control it in the end. You tell me something, Simon. Is there really anybody behind you at all?"

"Why are you helping us then, if that's the way you feel?"

Larkin smiled. He was still looking only at the pigeon at his feet.

"I'm just a humble servant of the apocalypse. I've had the visions and seen the signs. Don't *you* read the papers? And since we last met, I've even seen one person marked with the sign of the Beast. Sorry you asked yet?"

"You're insane, Larkin."

"You've always thought that anyway. It's supposed to be to your advantage. And it doesn't really matter. You think I'm working for you and I think you're working for me. It'll have the same result. You don't have to worry. I'll do what you want."

"But you do have a motive, Larkin. You just told me what it is."

"Did I? But perhaps I've just been lying, perhaps I'm more cunning than you. I think we'd better not talk anymore."

"I suppose I agree," Simon said. "Do one thing for me, though. I want you to call in once a week. I'd rather not depend only on your machine."

"All right," Larkin said. "Try to be quiet when you get up, if you don't mind. I don't want to frighten the pigeon."

Simon did rise softly, obedient against his own will. Mercer also stood up from his seat across the path and began to move toward Larkin. Simon caught him by the elbow.

"Leave him alone. He's in a tricky mood."

Mercer was annoyed. He had badly wanted to quiz Larkin about the sudden burning of the old man, for it seemed to him that Larkin had once mentioned something of the kind. However, Mercer let Simon guide him toward the north end of the park. Once he looked back. Larkin was still sitting on the bench, apparently motionless, though he had taken his hands out of his pockets. The pigeon had flown to his left fist and was pecking at something in his other hand.

Part III

The Desert

Save me, thought the Consul vaguely, as the boy suddenly went out for change, *suelteme*, help; but maybe the scorpion, not wanting to be saved, had stung itself to death.

> *Malcolm Lowry,*
> *Under the Volcano*

Let them that think hell is a metaphor look at me.

> *Andrew Lytle,*
> *The Velvet Horn*

35
The Diabolist

A LEAN LITTLE MAN, all bone and gristle, yellowish eyes, head rudely shaven, mustache curved into a pointed beard, crept muttering away from Bellevue Hospital. He hated the very sight of the place. Everything was white, down to the people and their clothing, the noncolor from which he involuntarily cringed. They had stolen his child, his altar, his sacrifice. The diabolist hurried toward the warm darkness of his shelter in Hell's Kitchen. It was the first day of November, but he did not know or care, having by will and his secret rites placed himself beyond the constraints of time and the calendar.

Stealthily the diabolist entered his home. The windows were blacked out thoroughly as though for war. There was no light whatsoever and the room was as hot as the inside of a pig's stomach. The diabolist lay on the floor, sweating, listening to the rasp of his own breathing. He discovered that he was afraid. In the hospital he had contrived to overhear a conversation between two blue policemen and a nurse clothed all in the horrible dead white, and had learned little to comfort him. He was a hunted man and his enemies seemed strong. His sanctuary was no longer safe. Soon the police would occupy it.

So he would make best use of what time he had left. The diabolist got up and stripped off his clothing. By touch in the darkness he found talismans of his belief. There was an ointment which he rubbed on the insides of his arms and legs and between his fingers and toes. With the salve burning and stinging his skin he mixed a preparation of rum and herbs in a dented metal cup. Then he found matches and lit two black candles on a low table at the narrowest end of the room.

From the center of the floor he regarded the charcoal drawing on the wall. A goat's head inscribed in an inverted pentangle, horns up, ears and beard dangling down. The pentagram in its turn inscribed in a circle composed of the arcane lettering. The image of Baphomet. The diabolist drained his cup, approached the wall, and rang a gong standing between the candles. He fell back into an attitude of worship and in the declining echo of the bell invoked the names of the four chief princes of darkness —

> . . . Satan . . .
> . . . Belial . . .
> . . . Lucifer . . .
> . . . Leviathan . . .

(Next, a host of lesser demons . . .)

> . . . Abbadon . . .
> . . . Adramolech . . .

(All formerly respected gods of the ancient worlds . . .)

> . . . Dagon . . .
> . . . Damballah . . .
> . . . Demogorgon . . .

The salve burnt in on his body and the potion outward, struggling to meet and mingle with one another. The diabolist's body was glazed over with sweat —

> . . . Mania . . .
> . . . Marduk . . .
> . . . Melek Taus . . .

(List reaching back into the whole world's history, great and small demons, possessed or dispossessed . . .)

> . . . Perun . . .
> . . . Stribog . . .
> . . . Volkh . . .

(. . . whose idols the Christianized Prince Vladimir tumbled down the hillside from the city of Kiev a thousand years before. Liberating them all into universal night thereby.)

The diabolist vibrated with passion. Locked muscles strained against his skin. He trembled with his efforts —

. . . Yaotzin . . .
. . . Yen lo Wang . . .
. . . Zorya . . .

These was all the names he knew. The diabolist swung without pause into an incantation meant to protect him from the oppressors who hemmed him in, to bring down destruction and vengeance on each of his enemies —

Noroni bajihie pasahasa Oiada! das tarinuta mireca ol tahila dodasa tolahame caosago homida: das berinu orocahe quare: Micame! Bial! Oiad: aisaro tox das ivame aai Balatima. Zodacare od Zodameranu! Od cicale Qaa! Zodoreje lape zondiredo Noco Mada, hoathahe Saitan!

At his climax he fell unstrung and facedown on the floor, then limply rolled over onto his back. The diabolist was wholly drained and dampness pooled off his body onto the floorboards. Would there be a visitant, this time? Batlike shades fluttered on the walls, cast there by the candlelight, and the diabolist could hear a housefly buzzing at the corners of the room. The fly hovered before the candles, blanketing the room with its winged and multilegged shadow. Baal, latterly known as Beelzebub, lord of the flies. The insect landed on the diabolist's inner thigh and began to explore and feed on the stickiness there.

Master . . .
My servant . . .
What must I do? They will turn me out of the temple.
Do not weaken. Success is your proof.
I need the boy again.
Perhaps not yet. You will find others.
They have robbed me.
Punish them for it, then.
I was afraid at the hospital.

*You need not return there. The thief is not at the hospital. It is another. You
overheard his name today.*
Larkin?
Yes.
Master, how will I find him?
Search among the homeless.
And then?
Punish the thieves. Punish them all. Bring me more blood. And carrion.
Master?

The fly rose from his body, sated. The diabolist sat up and
scanned the room but the fly had vanished. Wearily he approached the table, bowed to the image, rang the gong in
conclusion, and extinguished the candles. Again by touch he
found his clothing and hastily dressed, though he was weak-
ened by his fit of ecstasy and puzzled to interpret the dictums
of Baal. The diabolist gathered such of his accoutrements as
were portable and left the room. Perhaps it did not matter if
he fully understood. *Among the homeless . . .* He could follow
the fly's last counsel by going where victims were easily found
and unlikely to be missed. The diabolist reached the street
and plunged into the anonymous darkness of the outer world.

36
Larkin Changes His Shape

LARKIN REMAINED seated on the park bench, waiting for
nightfall. The pigeon kept its perch on his right fist and Larkin fed it more cinnamon crumbs from the bag, though after
a time his arm wearied from supporting the small weight of
the bird. When there were no more crumbs, the pigeon
hopped to Larkin's shoulder, then to his head. Shifting its
feet in Larkin's hair, the bird plotted a course and at last flew
to roost with others in a nearby tree.

Then it was fully dark. Larkin reached to his left ankle and drew a knife from a sheath fastened to the inside of his calf. The handle of the knife was wound with soft black leather. Its blade was about five inches long and spade shaped, unusually broad at the base. Larkin felt both edges with his thumb. The knife was satisfactorily sharp. With the point he ripped the outside of his right pants leg from the ankle to the knee. Then he placed the edge of the knife against his exposed shin and scraped downward, repeating the procedure two or three times. The cut he made was not terribly deep but it was wide and raw. Larkin dirtied his hand on the pavement and soiled the surface of his new wound.

A little blood ran from the cut over his ankle and into his shoe. Larkin sat up and leaned his back into the rails of the bench. The stinging of his abraded skin made his eyes run and he blinked to clear them. Then, with the knife's point, he made a short slash along his left cheekbone. Again his eyes began to tear, the salt burning in the shallow cut. Larkin closed his eyes and rested. After a moment he cleaned the knife on the lining of his coat and replaced it in the ankle sheath.

Larkin stood up. The park floated lightly all around him in the faint radiance of its pole lamps. Larkin was dizzy. Except for part of the cinnamon doughnut, he had not eaten since leaving Little Russia that morning. When the walkway began to angle up toward him, Larkin took off his glasses and put them in his pocket. The pavement smacked him on the right side of his face. Larkin smiled. He got up and fell again, and again did nothing to break his fall. This time he lay for longer, with a brassy taste of blood in the left corner of his mouth. He was still smiling and his head was clearer. Larkin rose and left the park.

He picked up Broadway beside the Flatiron Building and began to walk downtown. The collar of his coat was turned up on the back of his neck and he stooped and stumbled as he went along. Other passersby made generous semicircles around him. Larkin's ripped pants leg flapped open and shut, covering and disclosing the red scrape on his leg.

Larkin reached Union Square and circled the park to the

east. He waited for a traffic light at the corner of 14th Street, looking idly into a plate-glass shop window there. Framed in the window was the figure of an ordinary drunk or derelict, posture broken, cut and bruised about the face and body, indistinguishable from a thousand others in the city and entirely unworthy of note. Larkin smiled again and bowed in the direction of the glass; the reflection nodded its approval.

37

Hours of the Dead (I)

". . .AND THE SUCKER just burnt right *up*. Nobody even *near* him. Just . . . *blooey. Everything* gone. Ain't that right, Two Tone?"

" 'At's right, all right."

"The sucker was *gone*. One second. Never saw anything like it. Not my whole life long. The *clothes* was gone. The *body* was gone. The *bones* was gone. No more Hairy Hal. Not even a smell. Ain't that right, Two Tone?"

" 'At's right."

Larkin heard with half an ear. He laid his cigarette on the edge of the small pool table and studied a shot on the fifteen ball. Deciding on the side pocket, he stroked the cue lightly. The fifteen started for the pocket but at the last moment turned away on a rough spot in the felt. Larkin straightened up and collected his cigarette.

"Not enough," he said. "Take it away, Aztec."

Aztec Sam smiled through heavy lips and bent over the table. His left eye was already shut with a bruise so he didn't have to bother closing it. Long greasy hair fell around his face and dragged on the dirty felt. Aztec sent the cue ball toward the eight, lipped on the edge of a far corner pocket. The black ball went in and the white one followed it.

Larkin stretched out his palm.

"Hard luck," he said. "That'll be a dollar."

"What you talking? Didn't I sink the eight? You saw me sink the eight, I won."

"You scratched, Aztec," Larkin said. "Scratch on the eight, it means you lose. Everybody knows that. Nobody argues about it. Just pay me."

Aztec Sam came quickly around the corner of the pool table and swung at Larkin's head. Larkin sidestepped but caught the punch on his upper arm anyway. He dropped back and raised his hands. Aztec tried to close, heavy shoulders working under his oily coat. Larkin slipped around a support pole in the middle of the room. Aztec slugged the pole under the nail where the rack from the pool table was hanging. He drew his hand away and examined his knuckles, eyes dulling. Then he turned away from the pole, forgetting Larkin, and wandered slowly out the door.

Larkin propped his stick against the pole and glanced around the room. Rusty was nodding off behind the bar. Two Tone and Docker sat at the table near the juke box, with a quart bottle of beer between them. Both were big black men, though aged. It was said that Docker had once been a longshoreman. Two Tone had great pink patches on his face and hands, thus his name. Beyond the plate-glass window it appeared to be raining. Wet footprints were spotted among the cigarette butts and other detritus on the floor.

Nobody seemed interested in pool and Larkin drifted away from the table, sipping beer from a longneck bottle. A pale and pitifully emaciated man sat cross-legged in a chair by the window, with his head lolling. Larkin thought from the looks of him he might be dead. At a table in the opposite corner sat a man in a frayed black suit and a black fedora, which he hadn't bothered to take off. Larkin claimed his coat from another chair and went to join him.

"Dutch," he said, sitting down. The man in black lifted his hat from silvery hair, then replaced it.

"Young stuff," he said. "Where you been?"

"Trying to be respectable," Larkin said.

"Looks like it didn't work."

"No."

"Boy, you better hurry up and get your street smarts back. Aztec about to had you back there."

"Didn't see you come in."

"I was here. Saw the whole thing. Wish I'd missed it. You looked like garbage out there, young stuff."

"What is this, the Garden? You don't want me to hit old Aztec. He's just drunk."

"You better not let him hit you. Slip that punch, boy. Stand out of the way." Dutch lifted his arms and demonstrated.

"Did you ever say you were a boxer, Dutch?"

"Don't know if I did or not. It's been about forty years. I was a young man, younger than you I bet."

"Were you any good?"

"Not much." Dutch pushed his hat up to scratch the side of his head. "I was on a carnival circuit. Just before the war. Five southern states. Shared the bill with a ape. Anybody fool enough could fight with the ape. Ape whipped everybody. He got top billing. I was second. Featherweight."

"How'd you do?"

"I reckon I whipped a few."

"If you got hit much you don't show it."

In fact Dutch's face showed no scar tissue and his features were clear and sharp. In spite of his age, speculated to be around seventy, he looked saner and in better shape than anyone else in the bar, Larkin included. His clothes were neat and his back straight and there was some dignity about him.

"I was quick," Dutch said. "Didn't like to get hit, not that most people do. Hardly ever did." Dutch looked over Larkin's shoulder toward the rainy street. "Then I had me a bout with the state champion."

"What state?"

"I forget. First round he walked over and hit me bang in the mouth. Knocked my teeth right down my throat and they came out the other end the next day."

"But you have teeth, though," Larkin said.

Dutch clicked his tongue and spat a mass of bridgework

into the palm of his hand. His face collapsed around his empty mouth as though into a sinkhole. After a moment he replaced the bridge and became himself again.

"These ain't my teeth," he said. "Dentist made 'em."

"So what did you do?"

"I give up boxing. After I woke up, that is. Then the Army got me. What was all that between you and Aztec?"

"Ah. He's always kind of quarrelsome, you know. He scratched on the eight ball and didn't want to pay."

"Probably didn't have the money."

"That's what I thought. I wasn't going to hit him over it, anyway."

"Don't stand flat-footed, then."

"He'll pay me when he's sober."

"Cold day in hell when Aztec is sober and got money at one and the same time."

"You think he's really an Aztec?"

"Get off it, young stuff. The Aztecs been all over with for thousands of years. I think he's a greaser from Mexico, is what I think."

"Let me buy you a drink, Dutch."

"You don't need to."

"I know I don't. You'll buy me one."

"I guess I could use a beer."

Larkin clanked his empty bottle on the counter, rousing the bartender from his reptilian lethargy. Rusty got up, creaking to his height of six feet plus. He was a big-boned man, though his flesh seemed shrunken, with red-mottled scaling skin and rheumy eyes and huge arthritic fingers.

"Two," Larkin said. Waiting, he rolled the empty longneck back and forth between his palms. The lower part of the mirror behind the bar was blocked with a ragged line of bottles. Rusty went to the far end of the counter and rummaged in a tin ice chest beneath it. Past him and beyond the toilet cubicle was an unlit storage area which held some fractured chairs and tables, broken pool sticks, all or part of a small motorcycle, and against the far wall an old upright piano with the harp exposed.

Rusty returned trailing a Miller longneck in each hand. He opened the bottles, letting the caps drop on the floor, and slid them across the moist Formica. Larkin paid. A few more people had come into the bar. Estrellita, ancient lady of the evening, fumbled at the juke box. Some men had also entered to sit at the crooked tables scattered randomly around the floor. A younger man in a ripped leather jacket leaned intently into one of the pay phones between the bar and the window.

Larkin went back to Dutch's table and passed a beer to the old man. They clicked their bottles at the bottom and drank.

"Obliged," Dutch said.

"Don't mention it."

"Some schnapps?"

"Would I turn you down?"

From the pocket of his suit coat Dutch produced a lime-green object which resembled an egg cup and set it on the table. Larkin looked into it. There was a bubble of glass or plastic at the bottom but he could see nothing under it. Dutch filled the cup with a clear liquid from a flat unlabelled bottle, which he hid away quickly in his coat. Larkin examined the cup again. Floating on the liquor's surface was the image of a naked Oriental woman, plump and leering. Larkin laughed.

"Where'd you get that?"

"I'll never tell. Drink up, boy."

Larkin picked up the cup and tossed it off. The raw liquor sliced at his throat. He blinked once and drank from his beer bottle.

"Hot stuff, Dutch. Make it yourself?"

"Nah. It's bottled and bonded."

Dutch poured a shot for himself, then Larkin accepted another drink. He could now feel familiar boiling surges in the center of his chest.

"What's the news, Dutch?"

"Since when?"

"Since recent, I guess."

"Well." Dutch rubbed the knife edge of his nose with wrinkled fingers. "There's been a killing."

"When?" Larkin bent his head in attention.

"Three nights back, I think. Nasty little job. A garrote, piano wire or some such. And then the body was carved up, they say. Little signs and numbers cut in."

Larkin's head snapped erect.

"What kind of little signs?"

"Couldn't tell you. I didn't see it. Hairy Hal found him. He was the one that said."

"How's the feeling about it?"

"Not so bad. Nobody knew the guy, the dead guy. Say he'd just tramped in from Florida a few days before. Maybe somebody followed him up here. If it was somebody known, then people would worry. Or if it happens again."

"Like San Francisco."

"Touch wood when you say that, boy."

Larkin rapped the table leg and got up to go for more beer. Out past the window it was raining harder but in spite of that a group of men moved among the cars stopped at the intersection, cleaning windshields and begging for change. Inside, Estrellita had taken off her pea coat and was engaged in a shuffling dance with Two Tone in the middle of the floor.

> Heaven knows . . .
> 'S not the way it should be . . .
> Heaven knows . . .
> 'S not the way it could be . . .
> Don't you know . . .

Two Tone and Estrellita embraced like bears. Estrellita wore a pink tank top, and on her stringy shoulder was a tattoo of a bumblebee. They danced a circle around the prone form of a grizzled man who had slipped asleep from his chair to the floor. Larkin took two beers to the table and had another drink of schnapps.

"Hairy Hal been around today?" he said.

Dutch began to laugh.

"You could ask Two Tone. Or Docker."

"Oh yeah," Larkin said. "I forgot. What was all that? I didn't quite catch it."

"They *say*," Dutch went on laughing, "they *say*, that old Hal just burnt up for no reason at all this afternoon on the Upper West Side."

"Really," Larkin said. "Let me get some schnapps."

"Those old men got a bad case of the D.T.'s, I think," Dutch said, wiping his eyes. "Next time Hal walks in here, they going to feel real foolish." Dutch glanced over at Two Tone and Estrellita, who still swayed and clung together, though the song had stopped. Docker, smiling, beat time from his seat near the juke box. "They so full of it I don't see how they can breathe."

"What if it's true?" Larkin said.

"How could it be true, boy, when it don't make no sense?"

"But what if it is?"

"Well . . ." Dutch stopped laughing. "Be a bad way to go, I guess."

"Think so? Maybe not so bad."

"What's on your mind, young stuff?"

Larkin took a pair of grease pencils out of his coat pocket and began to draw on the table top, upside down so that Dutch could read the picture. In black he outlined a snarling mouth with conical teeth and slitted beast's nostrils above it. Within the mouth he sketched in red some human figures dancing among triangles of flame. As an afterthought he drew two catlike eyes above the mouth and filled in the pupils with red.

"That's ugly," Dutch said, grown serious.

"If you say so. I guess it is."

"Get rid of it."

Larkin nodded. He dampened his fingertips in a ring left by his beer bottle and wiped the picture away.

38
Stillness

LARKIN LEFT THE BAR when it closed at four, quite drunk but walking evenly nonetheless. He and Dutch had finished the bottle of schnapps and the old man had gone home much earlier, returning to his room in an SRO hotel nearby. Afterward Larkin had resumed playing pool. He felt that he must have done well, though he could not remember the games, for there was a sheaf of ragged dollar bills in his pants pocket which had not been there before.

It had grown colder and the rain had turned to sleet. Larkin walked down the Bowery with ice forming and melting on his coat collar and bare head. All the missions were closed for the night and he could see some few derelicts who had failed to find shelter curled up in doorways on either side of the street. Larkin walked downtown a few blocks and turned off to the left.

Midway along the street he'd chosen were three vacant buildings, blasted and windowless. Larkin inspected them from the sidewalk opposite. The one to the far left had been unsealed in places and there was light within it. Larkin withdrew into a doorway and studied the traffic around the lit shell, concluding at last that it was for the moment a shooting parlor and best left alone. The other two shells were dark and seemed to be tightly shut up with sheets of tin at ground level, but Larkin, who was beginning to shiver in spite of the schnapps, crossed the street to examine the seals more closely.

One of the tin sheets on the building at the right had been bent up in a triangle from the bottom. Larkin dropped to his knees and crawled into the dark aperture. Halfway in he groped across what felt much like a pair of legs. An incoherent rattle of protest came out of the darkness from points unknown. Larkin could see nothing. He tried to proceed, but someone began to kick him about the head and hands. Larkin backed painfully out onto the sidewalk and sat on his heels, looking up.

Sleet continued to whirl down in spirals from the invisible sky. Just above Larkin there was an iron railing curved around the lower half of a second-story sash window. Larkin stood up and stretched for the rail but it was not quite within his reach. He found a foothold in the masonry of the wall, snatched the bottom of the ironwork, and began hauling himself up hand over hand. For a moment he teetered on the top of the railing, then lost his balance and fell forward against the window, breaking out the wooden sashes. Larkin rolled through the opening and landed heavily on the floor beyond. The window had been glassless and he was unhurt, though the cuts he had inflicted on himself in the park earlier that day stung him afresh. He lay silently for a moment, listening for any response to the crash of his entry, but there was none.

Larkin sat up and lit a match. The room he was in had once been rather grand. It was not especially large but the ceiling was high and covered with elaborate moldings. Other moldings of some dark wood ran along the walls, and in one corner there was even a fireplace, though it was choked with rubbish. A door dangled from one hinge at the far end of the room, half open onto oblivion. Shreds of a rich floral papering drooped from all four walls, whose lathe and plaster was everywhere perforated with large holes. The match burned down to Larkin's fingers and he dropped it.

He got up and walked cautiously around the room, letting his eyes adjust to the faint light from outside. The floor seemed reasonably sound, beneath the layers of crumbled plaster fallen from the ceiling. Larkin peered through the inner doorway but he could discern nothing beyond it so he turned away. There was another window in the wall facing the street, besides the one through which he had come in. Larkin approached it and sat cross-legged on the floor beneath the sill, looking out. Just past the window stood the scraggly ruin of what once had been intended for a tree, and otherwise there was nothing in view. Every so often there came the muffled hiss of a car passing over the wet pavement outside.

Seated before the window, Larkin shut his eyes and thought of *stillness,* remembering the precepts of certain early saints whom he admired. To drain his mind of conscious thought had of late become surprisingly easy for him, and yet the practice brought him little peace or comfort. Rather it was during just such states that demons were most likely to appear to him, and not as images or thoughts but as concrete entities seemingly independent of his own mind or will.

"Safeguard the way of stillness," wrote Evagrios the Solitary, but the way itself often seemed distinctly unsafe to Larkin. Smiling slightly with his eyes still closed, Larkin recalled another text, words of Hesychios the Priest: "Let your model for stillness of the heart be the man who holds a mirror into which he looks. Then you will see both good and evil imprinted on your heart."

Acceptable, Larkin thought, rocking his upper body gently from the hips, but most puzzling just the same. His own mirror was no window upon Eden but instead reflected a constant desire for something that curiously resembled the flames of Hell. Perhaps his heart was not properly guarded. Drunkenness, all the desert fathers agreed, was incompatible with *watchfulness* (another inarguable proposition in its literal terms). And stillness was impossible without that watchful attention, but Larkin required drink to palliate his reluctant commerce with the demons . . . certainly his heart felt heavy within him, beating in a clock's monotone, and he was unable to raise it up.

Now on the inside of his eyelids appeared the shape of a black spider, neatly outlined in its details, with the red hourglass on its underside that marked it as deadly. Another demon had broken through, though in an unaccustomed form. Larkin opened his eyes to confirm the visitation, and yes, the spider was still there, suspended between two branches of the tree, though it was smaller.

Or possibly it was not a demon after all . . . Larkin watched the spider; he could now make out the fine strands of the web that spanned the branches. The spider moved to the edge of its web and waited there without moving. On his eyelids the insect had seemed monstrously large but now it was reduced to the proper scale of the rest of the world around it. And Larkin remembered how John of Karpathos had made the spider an image of stillness, for its silence, its perfect detachment, its patience in waiting for whatever God's providence cast into its web. Hesychios wrote, "The spider hunts small flies, but you will continually slay 'the children of Babylon' if during your struggle you are as still in your soul as is the spider." It occurred to Larkin that perhaps that was what he had meant himself when he carelessly broached the topic to Simon earlier in the day (was it that same day? he was no longer certain), without clearly understanding the tendency of his own thought. Yet the image itself seemed a paradox, for was it not true that the spider could be rapacious and bloodthirsty and exceedingly cruel? The matter required a concentration which Larkin could no longer supply. The loud beating of his heart had been taken up in his groin and wrists and temples and the noise of it overpowered his mind. Larkin fell asleep to the sensation that he was drowning in the rush of his own blood.

39
The Strangler

THROUGHOUT THE FALL the murders continued. The Bowery Strangler, as the *Post* soon titled him, attached new victims to his score on the average of one per week. Coroners' reports always indicated the cause of death as either simple and straightforward strangulation, or, less frequently, severance of the jugular vein. The strangler's weapon of choice, evidently, was some sort of wire garrote. Invariably

he altered the corpses, carving unfamiliar diagrams or lettering on the chest or back or belly. Conventional mutilation,
decapitation and castration and the like, seemed not to interest the strangler. Except for the knife-point manglings, he
left his bodies intact.

The diabolist killed his way through the end of fall and into
the dead of winter, and yet remained unsated, as did the
various devils whose edicts he desired to obey. Despite the
terror his efforts had occasioned there was never any short-
age of new prospects. On any given night some portion of
the Bowery's population would be too drunk, too careless, or
too helpless to get itself indoors. Interrupting sleeps so reck-
lessly profound that death could scarce be told from them,
the diabolist brought real death along the street. But the
gnawing appetite which had first moved him on that path
was unassuaged and nothing that he did could satisfy it.

No one had seen him; no one knew his face. He might well
have lived among the derelicts he slew, for he looked no
madder than any of them, and the survivors, after the first
few weeks, suspected each other in any case. But the diabolist
held himself apart. Part of the daylight hours he spent in
sleep; in afternoon and evening he lurked in the lower end
of Loisaida, sufficiently far removed from his killing ground.
He plundered the pockets of the men he killed and often
found enough to sustain him till his next murder. Panhan-
dling seemed more profitable than he would have at first
supposed. Then again, his material requirements were slight.
The diabolist's lean being was maintained by his hatred and
the inward and outward compulsion to go on killing more.

Nightly, most often between the hours of four and six A.M.
the diabolist returned to stalk the Bowery and adjacent streets.
By then all bars were closed by law, and always for some there
would be no further shelter until they reopened again the
next day. Most nights the diabolist simply prowled, recon-
noitering the hideouts and habits of future prey. For six or
seven days he'd study victims; then, when his urges coincided
with the omens he could read, he'd strike.

*

At four A.M. on January 12, Two Tone and Aztec Sam were hustled out of a bar at the corner of Grand Street, where they'd spent the better part of the evening. They were the last two patrons in the place and the bartender was weary and bored. Aztec went out sullenly but without significant protest. Two Tone had to be pushed, and once out the door he tried to rush back in, pleading with the bartender to let him sleep on the floor. Without especial malice the bartender hit him lightly on the chest with a short steel rod he was carrying. Two Tone fell over backward on the sidewalk. The bartender ran the rod through the inside door handles and secured it with padlocks and chain. Then he moved back through the dim interior, turning out the greenish lights one by one. Two Tone got up groaning and began to hammer on the double doors.

"Killer," he cried. "You leavin' us out here to die." The bartender looked back once dispassionately, then vanished through a door at the rear of the main room. Two Tone went on shouting and pounding on the doors; his eyes ran with alcoholic tears.

"Shut up, Two Tone," Aztec said. "Keep that up you'll only spend the night in jail."

Two Tone turned around and leaned his back against the locked doors, panting.

"Better than the street," he said. "Been five, six days. He get somebody tonight. I know it in my bones."

Two Tone was trembling, not only from the cold though it was bitter. Aztec stood rigid as a carving, his long hair whipped about his face in the hard northeast wind.

"Scared of the strangler?" Aztec said. One corner of his mouth lifted in a kind of mocking smile.

"Ain't you?" Two Tone paused and breathed loudly. "Aztec, you got money for a flop?"

"Nope," Aztec said. "Not even close. Strangler going to get you sure, Two Tone."

Two Tone shuddered. Aztec stepped forward and shook him by one shoulder.

"Snap out of it," he said. "Just two, three hours till day-

light. You can make it. We can go up Prince Street, get out
of the wind."

"Prince Street," Two Tone said. His eyes grew round and
white. "Why, he kilt one there not two weeks ago."

"Maybe he won't come back to the same place," Aztec said.
"One of us could stay up to watch. You come on if you're
coming."

Aztec began trudging up the Bowery. After a moment Two
Tone pushed himself off the doors and began to weave along
behind him. Aztec turned the corner of Prince Street and
entered a ragged doorway. He walked directly to a large tin
trash can in the center of the ruined foyer and began to stir
its contents with a stick. Two Tone came up behind him and
stopped.

"Nobody here," Aztec said.

"No foolin'. He kilt Mudcat here two weeks ago."

Aztec hawked and spat on the floor.

"He won't come back. Ain't got nobody in the same place
yet. Look here, we can have a fire."

Aztec lit a twist of paper and dropped it into the garbage
can. Something toward the bottom began to flare. Aztec scavenged more fuel from the littered floor and added it to the
can. He took a bottle of Thunderbird from his coat pocket
and drank, then offered it to Two Tone.

"Better get you some," he said. "Stop that shaking." In spite
of the windbreak it was very cold in the shell. Two Tone
accepted the wine with some surprise; it was unlike Aztec to
share his liquor. The two men sat down against the warming
metal of the can. Intermittent tremors ran up and down Two
Tone's spine. The bottle passed between them several times.
Flame lept inside the garbage can, throwing curious shadows
on the ceiling. Two Tone began to yawn.

"You could get some sleep," Aztec said. "I can stay up awhile,
keep an eye out."

"Well, all right," Two Tone said. "You wake me up, now,
you get sleepy." He curled embryonically around the rear
side of the can, opening his coat to let the metal warm his
chest. As he began to drift, the ugly notion crossed his mind

that Aztec himself might be the strangler. Two Tone imagined gruesome human sacrifices, on the peaks of Indian pyr-
amids thousands of years old. Nevertheless he was soon asleep
and fitfully dreaming.

Aztec sat with his back against the burning can and his legs
stretched out before him. When he heard Two Tone begin
to snore he took a longish cigarette butt out of his shirt pocket
and lit it. He had another drink of wine and found it was
hitting him a little harder than he'd expected. The cigarette,
burning against his knuckles, roused him from a doze. Aztec
flipped it over his shoulder into the can and crashed into a
heavy sleep.

Two Tone awoke when the can turned over, spilling the fire
out across the floor. In the light of the scattered embers he
could see Aztec's shoulder's heaving, his arms flapping in long
coat sleeves like the wings of a clumsy bird. In the center of
Aztec's back hunched what looked like an ugly little ape. The
ape tugged at two ends of cord or wire which somehow
emerged from Aztec's hair, and meanwhile gibbered in some
senseless tongue. Aztec bucked for a minute or more, struggling to throw his rider, and at last lay still.

Two Tone was away behind the spilled can and its light.
He thought the ape thing could not see him, but he dared
not move or breathe. Fear centered in a knot below his navel,
like a tumor only surgery might remove. He wanted to close
his eyes but was not able. The thing, which he now reluctantly concluded was a man, flipped Aztec's twitching body
over and with a few strokes of a straightedged razor slashed
away the clothing from his upper trunk. The strangler bent
over the body, cutting into the chest with small deft motions,
maintaining a steady chant which Two Tone could not com-
prehend. But often in the chant recurred a word, a name,
with which he was quite familiar: Larkin, Larkin, Larkin. Two
Tone fainted dead away.

Spent and weary, the diabolist rose at length from the corpse
of Aztec Sam. He wandered in a slow ellipse around the foyer,

trailing the straight razor from his fingertips. By chance he happened on the prostrate form of Two Tone, but he felt no interest in his presence there. The single death had sated him; for the moment he lacked appetite for more. But the twelve sacrifices he'd so far accomplished had brought him little satisfaction and he felt cheated or deserted by his gods. It was Larkin, only Larkin, whom he wanted to destroy, and despite his most dedicated searches he'd been unable to find him so far.

40
Hours of the Dead (II)

ON THE EVENING of January 13 Larkin sat at a rear corner table in the Houston Street bar, leafing through the final edition of the *Post*. The banner read: END OF THE WORLD SIEGE: EIGHT DEAD. In Memphis a group of seven cultists led by one Lindberg Sanders had captured and eventually killed a policeman because Sanders had told them that the police represented Antichrist. Sanders also believed that Armageddon was soon to occur. He had habitually refused to drink water because he interpreted Scripture as forbidding that practice. Police had stormed the house after hearing these words on electronic eavesdropping equipment: "The devil is dead." It seemed to Larkin that Sanders and all of his followers had been killed in the ensuing fire fight, but the story was not perfectly clear on that point.

Inside, the paper reported a three-million-dollar award to Otto Pampellone in his suit against US Trucking. One of the company's vehicles had struck him on the street, permanently injuring his tastebuds. Mrs. Pampellone won a separate judgment of thirty thousand dollars because her husband's "kissing sensation" had also been damaged beyond repair.

Stage magician Doug Henning informed an interviewer that "the real secret of magic is psychological."

Christina Onassis was reported to have left a Swiss weight salon sixteen pounds heavier than when she entered it.

A two-column item on page 5 was headed: SHC ON UP- SWING. The story discussed the novel phenomenon of spontaneous human combustion, which had thoroughly baffled all doctors and scientists confronted with it. SHC, characterized by the instantaneous and apparently causeless burning of human individuals, was definitely on the rise. Twenty-three incidents had been reported in the New York area since the fall of 1982, with slightly smaller figures coming in from such points as L.A., Chicago, and Miami. Experts were unwilling to speculate as to how many SHC episodes might have gone unreported. No rational explanation of SHC had been forwarded as yet, though cranks were blaming everything from nuclear power plants to the deterioration of the ozone layer. A burn-ward specialist who preferred not to be named described the difficulty of studying the problem: "The burnings take place very rapidly in uncontrolled circumstances. Afterward, there is little material remaining for tests." The specialist noted further that while SHC had hardly reached epidemic proportions, the dramatic increase over the past several months was cause for real concern.

Larkin groped under the table for the necks of several bottles which protruded from a small white garbage bag, which was packed with ice. He rotated each of the bottles through the ice bag, meanwhile turning pages of the paper with his other hand.

Twenty-two-year-old Andrew Brooks of North Babylon, Long Island, had been charged with the murder of his two-year-old son. Brooks had been punishing the boy for taking a bottle away from his younger sister Sarah. Police officials stated that Brooks "admitted he beat the child twenty times during the day"; subsequently he strangled him.

After a robbery of a New England sporting-goods store the only item found missing was a poster of Elite model Carol Alt. The poster depicted Ms. Alt dressed in Sport Obermeyer skiwear.

Two recent immigrants from the Soviet Union were arrested as suspects in the murder of a thirteen-year-old girl from Queens.

Filmmaker Kenneth Anger, author of *Hollywood Babylon,* scheduled a benefit soirée for himself, his purpose being to recover losses sustained in a Halloween burglary of his apartment.

An elderly man suffered a fatal heart attack while driving past the St. Peter's Medical Center in New Brunswick, New Jersey. His car crashed through the hospital's emergency room, injuring fourteen people.

French actress Isabelle Huppert stated as follows: "It's over. I refuse to be associated with illness, prostitution, death, and immaturity. I need to be wanted by the whole world."

Larkin turned back to the front of the paper and began to tear out the SHC article. While he was occupied with that, Dutch entered the bar quietly and took a seat at his table.

"What you reading, young stuff," the old man said. Larkin glanced up, pushed the torn section of newsprint across the table. Dutch leaned back, tilting the paper toward the light. Larkin reached under the table and twisted the bottles through the ice.

"Strange business," Dutch said. He shoved the scrap of paper back to Larkin, who folded it into a pocket without comment.

"Docs ain't got no answer," Dutch said reflectively. "What you know about this, young stuff?"

"Anybody's guess." Larkin shrugged. "It's just one of life's little mysteries."

"Little, he says." Dutch snorted. "Well . . . the only one we known so far is Hairy Hal. You don't reckon it could be drinking does it, do you?"

"I doubt it," Larkin said. "It happens to all kinds."

"What, then?"

"Evil thoughts, maybe. That could be it. Sickness of the soul."

Dutch laughed.

"It's not getting many of us, anyway," he said. "What we got to worry about is the strangler."

"Do you worry about the strangler, Dutch?"

"No," Dutch said, though his smile was uneasy. "Not for me. Strangler gets people asleep on the street. I got my room to sleep in."

"We're about due for another one though," Larkin said automatically.

"So we are. Bad luck to talk about it."

Goose flesh pricked the back of Larkin's neck. Like others in the area he found the strangler unnerving to mention or contemplate and yet the subject drew him. At times he felt that were the strangler a specific omen the message might be personally addressed to him, though he did not like to think about that either. Involuntarily Larkin indulged in a silent catalogue of the eleven victims whose names he so far knew, and sensed that Dutch was doing the same, though neither spoke aloud.

"Could you use a beer?" Dutch said.

"Not yet."

"How's that?" Dutch said, surprised.

Larkin pointed under the table. Dutch's eyes fell on the bag of bottles and widened. "What's that for, young stuff? You in the money?"

"New Year's Eve," Larkin said.

"You missed that, boy. It was two weeks ago."

"Russian New Year. It's a different calendar. Everything's a few days later." Dutch made to object again but then did not.

"What's in that bag, exactly?"

"Vodka. Good vodka. Can't drink it till midnight though."

"Vodka. Well, now. If you say it's Russian New Year, then I guess that's what it is."

"It's not so long to midnight anyway," Larkin said.

It was true. The hands of the clock above the bar stood at quarter to twelve. Larkin glanced around the room. The bar was more crowded than usual. The deep freeze of the preceding night had given way to a cold heavy rain which still continued, driving the derelicts off the street. Most of the customers were drenched and even the inside of the bar was liquid; water reached depths of an inch or better in var-

ious depressions on the floor. Two men Larkin didn't recognize circled the pool table, their shoes squelching. At her
preferred table under the front window, Estrellita was locked
in conversation with another, less vivacious crone. All the tables and chairs were full to capacity and people who had found
no seats rested on their feet like sleeping livestock. Some few
lay on the floor. Nearest Larkin's corner table a man sprawled
across the pocked linoleum, one hand trailing through a pool
of slush. Larkin noted the graveyard pallor of the hand, then
that its owner had no hair, not even eyebrows. The whole of
his skin was a cavefish white.

"Who's that?" Larkin said.

Dutch looked down.

"That's Worm. Just old Worm."

"What makes his skin that way?"

"The tunnels."

Larkin dispatched a look of inquiry.

"Just the tunnels, you know," Dutch said.

"No, I don't."

"Steam tunnels down under Times Square. Underneath
the subway. That's where he lives, old Worm. Or did. There
were a lot of them. They only come out at night, see. That's
why they get so pale."

"Oh," Larkin said. "I didn't hear about this."

"Well. There's a million tunnels under Times Square, nobody knows how many, how deep. Unless maybe Worm. They
got steam pipes in them. So it's warm down there. Hot, I
should say. There's pipes down there you can cook on. That's
what they do. They live down there. Nice if it's what you
like."

"Were you ever down there?"

"Me? I couldn't even tell you where to find the hole. I like
a little daylight, young stuff. And Worm is a weird guy. Not
sociable. Don't like to talk."

"Are they all like that?"

"Can't tell them apart. I call them all Worm. They don't
use names amongst themselves, I don't think."

Dutch looked down pensively at the twisted and skeletal
body of Worm. With the toe of his shoe he pushed the man's

hand out of the puddle. Worm stirred and mumbled but did not open his eyes.

"They don't like people. Other people. A lot of them never come out. They store things. Eat bugs. I don't know. But it's all over now. Right, Worm?"

Dutch had raised his voice. Worm turned over onto his back.

"Nyaah," he said, half snoring.

"Why'd they come out?" Larkin said.

"Couldn't say for sure. But they don't like interference. Don't like people to know where they are. I remember, a few years back, there was a lot of them under Grand Central. Newspapers found out and started sending guys down there. The worms all left. They didn't like that. Next place they showed up was Times Square."

"So what happened there?"   .

"Couldn't tell you. Worm could but I doubt he will. Something happened. Late summer or early fall. Something bad down there. They don't mention what. Everybody left. Worm don't like to talk about it. Do you, Worm?"

"Last fall. That's very interesting, Dutch," Larkin said. "I'd like to talk to him about it."

"Don't think he knows how to talk very well. Do you know how to talk, Worm?"

"Nyaah," Worm said.

"He's not going to make it up here, old Worm. Can't hack it. Too cold, too much air. Look at him, he's a fish out of water. You don't like the outside, do you, Worm?"

"Nyaah," Worm said.

"You miss your bugs, don't you, Worm? Crunchy little bugs?"

"Nyaah ah ah," Worm said.

"Not very outgoing, is Worm."

The hands of the clock were joined at midnight. Larkin began to stack bottles from the bag onto the table, hundred proof Stolichnaya in fifths. Freezing water and crushed ice spilled over his shoes. Dutch studied the line of bottles with quiet respect. Larkin stood up and shouted:

"Ladies and gentlemen, according to the true calendar of the true religion of the true church of the one and only God, the nineteen hundred and eighty-third year since the death of our Lord has just begun and in honor of this event I invite you all to drink with me."

Larkin sat back down. The murmuring and muttering throughout the bar declined into silence as people began to notice the bottles and move toward the table where they stood. Larkin took up the first bottle, so cold his fingers stuck to the glass, and opened it. He turned the bottle up to his mouth and held it bubbling there a long moment before he set it down. Larkin pulled back his lips in a mad grin and passed the bottle to Dutch, who inclined his head and drank.

Larkin reached to the floor, snatched Worm by his collar and pulled him to an upright position beside his own chair against the wall. Worm's pallid mouth hung slackly open; his eyes opened also and rolled. Larkin opened a second bottle and poured into Worm's mouth until the clear liquid ran over. Worm gasped and swallowed. Dutch smiled.

"Stuff will keep him from freezing tonight anyway. Won't it, Worm?"

Larkin drank and laughed wildly, his eyes bright. He slapped the bottle into Worm's limp hand and closed the fingers over it. Larkin unscrewed the cap from another bottle. The table was surrounded now and hands reached toward the vodka from all sides. Larkin sensed that the room was already beginning to whirl and he raised one hand in admonition.

"Under the special circumstances we'll dispense with formal toasts," he said. "But ladies and gentlemen, no shoving, please. There will be plenty for all. Rusty," Larkin called, "Bring some glasses." And Larkin's raised hand shot out to right a bottle that had toppled to its side.

Rusty came forward and gloomily began to distribute shot glasses.

"I should charge you rent on these, kid," he said. "You never bought that booze in here."

"Take it in trade," Larkin said, indicating the bottles. Rusty poured himself a drink but still did not seem pleased. A loud sound like a deranged elephant trumpeting distracted him, however, and with many of the others standing around the table, Rusty turned toward the door. A path cleared and Larkin could see who had just come in: a short skinny man in a gray pinstriped suit a couple of sizes too big for him. He stood in the open doorway, legs bent slightly at the knee, pointing a straight horn, which Larkin knew to be a soprano saxophone, in the direction of the ceiling. Larkin smiled; the horn player's appearance oddly warmed him. Dutch had stuck his fingers in his ears.

"Jesus," Dutch said. "I thought he was never coming back. Hoped so."

"You know him?" Larkin said.

"More's the pity. It's Porco. He's stone crazy. And a bum. The worst bum in the city. Not to mention that godawful noise."

"Doesn't look so much like a bum, look at that suit. It looks new," Larkin said. "And those shoes." In fact the stranger wore a glowing pair of wing tips, polished to a military shine.

"I believe you're right," Dutch said. "Ventilators on the toes of them, as I live and breathe. Porco looks to have come up in the world. As I recall, he used to run with gangsters. Maybe he killed somebody."

Porco's cheeks deflated. He removed the horn from his mouth and flourished it over his head.

"Drinks!" he said. "Drinks for the house. Everybody. On me. The prodigal son returns." Rusty had approached him and something passed between their hands.

"Introduce me, would you?" Larkin said. "I used to be a musician."

"I told you he's stone crazy. He's even worse than you."

"I'd like to talk to him."

"You'd like to talk to some odd ones tonight, wouldn't you? But I guess if he's talking he at least can't play that thing. Hey. Porco. Over here a minute."

Porco came over to the table and held out a hand, which Dutch loathingly took.

"This is our young stuff, Larkin he's called," Dutch said. "He wanted to meet you, don't ask me why."

"Have a drink," Larkin said. "I like your playing."

"Sweet Jesus, Lord, I am hallucinating again. No one has ever liked my playing. Not in this bar anyway."

"Really I like it," Larkin said. Porco smiled. One of his incisors was gold. Skin hung in loose folds around his mouth. His eyes were hooded with little wrinkles. Brown, gray-flecked hair crept away up his skull.

"I guess I have to believe you," he said. "Do you play?"

"Used to," Larkin said. "Piano."

"Ah. But did you know that there is a piano right here in this very spot? Over there behind the shall we say piss hole?"

"It's been a long time," Larkin said. "And the piano is under a ton of garbage. Besides I think it doesn't work."

"But maybe it does work. Or maybe some of it works. We owe it to ourselves to check it out at least. Come on."

Larkin stood up, swayed and caught himself. He followed Porco around the corner of the bar, past the toilet cubicle to the enormous pile of rubbish beneath which parts of the old upright could be seen. Porco began to shift boxes and bits of broken furniture.

"Look at that," he said. "This piano is mounted on a motorcycle." Larkin saw that Porco had indeed unearthed a small Yamaha trail bike.

"Or no," Porco said. "Looks like the motorcycle comes separate." He balanced the bike and shoved it away toward the main room; it rolled a few feet and crashed into the bar.

"Hey," Rusty said, but Porco had turned back to the piano. Estrellita detached herself from another group and straddled the motorcycle, rocking her bony hips against the seat.

"Here we go," Porco said. The piano was cleared and looked intact, though a few of its keys were permanently depressed. Porco brushed the harp with the back of a fingernail. A low chord shimmered and sustained.

"The damper's gone, see," Larkin said doubtfully. But Porco had already brought him a chair.

"That will make it more interesting. Sit down there and play something. Anything you like."

Larkin fell into the chair. He stretched his hands out over
the keyboard, let them hover a moment and finally dropped
them. The piano crashed into discord at once but Larkin
doggedly began to play. As he had expected, the instrument
was in no kind of tune and without a damper all the notes
ran together into perfect nonsense. All the same Larkin found
the exercise of playing rather pleasant. Presently, in a cracked
voice, he began to sing.

> The little man walked up and down,
> to find an eating place in town.
> He read the menu through and through
> to see what fifteen cents could do.
>
> One Meat Ball
> One Meat Ball
> Well, he could afford but
> One
> Meat
> Ball.

Larkin became aware that he had saxophone accompaniment. He vamped through another verse and chorus, softly
as he could, wishing that the damper worked. Porco seemed
unconcerned. He finished his solo and nodded to Larkin,
who felt unequal to a break and began to sing again.

> He told the waiter near at hand
> The simple dinner he had planned.
> The guests were startled, one and all
> to hear that waiter loudly call —
>
> One Meat Ball
> One Meat Ball
> Well, this here gent wants
> One
> Meat
> Ball.

It seemed to Larkin that others in the bar had taken up
the chorus so he ran through it once more. At the end of the
second chorus the motorcycle suddenly roared into life and
Estrellita, a look of puzzlement on her face, began to ride in
teetering circles around the bar. Porco was laughing. The
noise leapt to incredible levels but Larkin sang against it anyway.

The little man felt very bad,
for one meat ball was all he had.
And in his dreams he hears that call —
"You gets no bread with one meat ball."

One Meat Ball
One Meat Ball
You gets no bread with
One
Meat
Ball.

Larkin slumped over the keys, then raised himself to drink from another bottle of vodka that had somehow appeared at his elbow. Rusty was serving drinks to all without restraint or payment, winking occasionally at Porco, who continued to play against the grinding of the motorcycle. Estrellita was now at the head of something like a conga line. Most of the people in the bar had locked on behind her and she was leading them all with the bike. Every so often she crashed into a wall, dragging the others after her.

"Do you know a conga?" Porco said.

"No."

"Play something else, then."

Larkin began hammering on the piano with his right hand. He was half-turned in his seat so that he could look into the rest of the bar and his left hand held the vodka bottle, from which he frequently drank. Everyone seemed to have joined the conga line except for Rusty and Dutch and Worm, and some still seemed to be attempting the chorus of "One Meat Ball," though the accompaniment had shifted to another key. Dutch and Rusty were stationed behind the counter, perhaps for their own protection. Worm remained propped on the wall where Larkin had left him. He still had his bottle and somehow the motorcycle had not yet run over him.

Estrellita drove the motorcycle around the pool table and turned right past the toilet. She rode around the rear of the piano, crushing old crates and sticks of furniture, grinning up at Porco, squinting at Larkin with one eye. The snake line completed its circuit of the piano, some dancers still chanting "One meat ball, one meat ball." Swept up in a curious wave of euphoria, Larkin began to laugh. He turned farther around to watch the snake line as Estrellita led it back into the main area of the bar.

The outer door opened with a rush of cold and damp and Two Tone stumbled in through it. By now Larkin was seeing double in any case but he still thought Two Tone looked peculiar in his own right. His whole face seemed to have faded toward the color of the lighter patches on his skin and he appeared generally shaken. Several people in the snake line hailed him but Two Tone seemed uninterested in the game. He slipped behind the counter and began to whisper urgently into Dutch's ear, supporting himself on the old man's shoulder.

There was news and it was bad, Larkin was convinced. Don't think about it, he instructed himself, and mechanically lifted the bottle and finished it off, closing his eyes. The motorcycle coughed and rattled into a silence heavy as a shroud. Without noticing, Larkin had let his hand slip from the piano; Porco had also lowered his horn. Larkin opened his eyes. The snake line had broken up and its members wandered about aimlessly, like shock victims after an accident. Some had clustered around Two Tone and Dutch, who were both staring hard at Larkin.

An unsettling stare. Larkin passed a hand before his face to avert it but the gesture had no effect. He stood up; a cold bulb of vodka rolled in his belly. Larkin began walking toward the door.

"Wait a minute, kid."

Porco was calling him. Larkin ignored it. He concentrated on his steps, on keeping his head level. But when he came abreast of Dutch he had to turn and look at him. The old man leaned on the counter, hands folded around the brim of his black hat, gray eyes boring into Larkin. Larkin stopped and waited but Dutch said nothing at all.

"The morning is wiser than the evening," Larkin finally said, recalling a proverb or some old tale. Dutch made no response and his expression did not change. The message had arrived. *Don't think about it.* Larkin walked out of the door.

"Wait a minute, kid."

Larkin was on the street and suddenly drunk beyond belief. It had stopped raining and the air was clear and colder. The bulb of vodka in the center of his body had become animate and was dictating to him. *Walk,* the vodka said. Larkin was in the middle of Houston Street. *No,* he told himself, *I don't want to be going uptown.* But he was trapped in headlights like a rabbit. A car screeched and swerved behind him and Larkin ran across the street. Here there was a vacant lot surrounded by a storm fence which in one place had been partly beaten down. Larkin began to walk across the low spot, the chain links flexing under his feet. As he was about to step into the lot the fence rebounded and flipped him over. Larkin rolled through a syrupy puddle, tangling himself in a small bush. He heard or imagined a more distant voice: "Wait a minute, will you?" The lot streamed with bright moonlight, or possibly it was only a street light somewhere. Larkin dragged himself toward a brick wall at the upper end of the lot. There was an old car hood propped against the wall and beneath it a strip of cardboard which was relatively dry. Larkin poked his head back out from under the hood to admire the moonlight, or streetlight. Hard shadows from the undergrowth were patterned all over the wet ground. Larkin, unreasonably happy, experienced a feeling similar to love. *At last, that's all there is,* he thought as he passed out. *Only these little dancing shadows. That's all.*

41
Larkin Picks Up His Messages

MORNING CAME like a stone breaking. Larkin propped himself up on his elbows and peered out from under the car hood. The tracked mud in the lot had frozen during the night and the bushes and weeds were coated with a light layer of ice. Larkin sat up with difficulty. Someone else was lying across his lower back. Larkin's head felt like concrete; only a small area above his left eye seemed at all sentient and that part was vibrating with pain. Rising, he knocked his shoulders into the hood and pushed it over, away from the wall.

The other man seemed to be Porco, but much the worse for wear. The cuffs of the horn player's suit were tattered and his shoes were scuffed and scored with gashes around the ventilated toes. Porco's eyes creased open, squinting into Larkin's, and he began to shift himself.

"Oh lord, kid," he said, "I think I'm paralyzed. Look, I can't bend my left arm. I must have frozen . . . Where's my horn? Goddammit, WHERE'S MY HORN?"

Porco sat up flailing. It was true that his left arm was rigid as a plank.

"Wait a second," Larkin said, catching his sleeve. He reached inside the cuff and carefully withdrew the tube of the little saxophone.

"Ah," Porco said. "That's a relief. I forgot I put it there."

He pulled the horn up into his lap and began to caress the stops. Larkin pressed his forehead against the cold bricks and rolled it back and forth.

"Touch of a hangover?" Porco said. "You should drink a lot of fluids. Alcoholic fluids work fastest, though I find it's a short-term effect."

Larkin reversed himself on the stodgy cardboard and leaned back into the wall, eyes slitted.

"You screwed up your suit," he said.

"True. I could always get another one. Except I think I gave all my money to Rusty. You don't happen to have any loose change, do you?"

"I think not. I think I spent my last on that vodka."

"Ah. Well, it was a good party. Up to a point." Porco peered along a shaft of sunlight. "You haven't got a watch?"

"No."

"I was supposed to be somewhere this afternoon I think. Looks like it's still morning though."

"Maybe if we went back to the bar Rusty would let us borrow a beer."

"You know, I sort of doubt that, kid. Public opinion kind of turned against you after you walked out."

Larkin sighed.

"What happened?"

"I forget exactly. There were some people who seemed to think you'd been consorting with the devil, if I didn't make that up. Nobody seemed to have too much to say for you, I remember that. Except for me. People were kind of aggravated about something. After you bought them all that vodka, too. Ingrates."

"Is that what happened to your suit?"

"It didn't fit so well anyway." Porco shrugged. "You were playing all right till you stopped paying attention."

"It's been a long time," Larkin said wearily. "Besides, I was classical. How'd you end up here?"

"I followed you till you fell out. Then I went back to the bar. Got a little unpopular there so I came back here to check you out. I was worried you were going to freeze. Couldn't wake you up. So I stayed."

"Thanks."

"Well, I was also worried that I was going to freeze." Porco rummaged in an inside pocket and pulled out a pair of printed tickets which he held out to Larkin.

"Take these. I've got a date next week. You can come for free."

"All right." Larkin took the tickets. "If there is a next week."

Porco regarded him narrowly. "Have you really been consorting with the devil, kid?"

"Not on purpose," Larkin said. "But —"

"No, don't tell me. I've had my dose of that. I'm too old. I have a rehearsal. See you later, I hope. Best of luck." Porco got up with surprising alacrity and was gone.

Larkin rubbed his temples. "You too," he said. He drew himself to his feet and walked a block east, then turned down on Forsyth Street. He entered a bodega at the corner of Broome and shoplifted a quart of Tropicana so clumsily that the owner noticed and chased him for two blocks. Larkin finally lost him by dodging through a construction site at the bottom of Forsyth. He walked slowly into Chinatown, drinking the orange juice.

At an East Broadway corner Larkin tossed the carton away and entered a small restaurant. The place was crowded with Chinese and the smell of food made his stomach turn over. He went down a short hall at the rear behind the drinks cooler and bolted himself into a tiny bathroom, where he ran cold water over his wrists, head propped on the mirror. Afterward he felt a little less groggy. He ripped a stitch on his coat lining and pulled out two halves of a black plastic casing, a nest of circuits, and a couple of small batteries. Using a nail file on the screws, Larkin reassembled the device. When he had done this he pressed a button on the side and the gadget twittered like a bird. Larkin nodded to himself, and dropped it into a side pocket. On top of the mirror frame there was a long butt from a Pall Mall straight which he snatched up and lit.

On an empty table at the outer end of the hall some loose change had been left for a tip. Larkin palmed a dime and ducked back to a pay phone beside the bathroom door. He inserted the dime and dialed a number; after one ring his own taped voice began to speak. Larkin placed the remote box over the phone's transmitter and pressed the button. There was a hiss of rewinding tape. Larkin studied the lengthening ash on the Pall Mall butt.

Click.

"Larkin, it's Thursday. January thirteenth. This is Anton Leveaux. I need you up here, ASAP. With cameras. Nothing to do with that other business. Just another job, I swear it. As soon as you can."

Beep.

"Larkin. It's Charles. Are you getting these messages? I keep calling . . . Look, call me back nights between six and eight. Simon's usually out. I want to talk about these burnings." Mercer's voice paused. "I hope you're going to erase this tape, at least."

Larkin dropped the nub of cigarette on the floor and ran his shoe sole over the sparks. His mouth was dry.

Beep.

". . . Clare . . ."

A woman's voice. Larkin blinked and before his eyes appeared an oft-recurring dream.

". . . It's Karin . . ."

A dream in which nothing at all happened. Larkin's eyes fell shut. Karin lay sidelong on a hardwood floor, propped on one elbow, her long legs drawn up under her. She wore a midlength one-piece dress, simply cut, deep blue. Folds of it curling around her calves, a scallop cut in the fabric just below her collarbone. The fine-boned face inclined a little toward his own. Her long rich hair ran down her arm and broke like falling water on the floor.

". . . I really need to talk to you . . ."

But most discomforting were her eyes, the look that drew him down and in. Larkin floated will-lessly toward the image, feather-light. Amnesia with a touch of vertigo.

". . . see you . . ."

"Not now," Larkin said aloud. He pressed the reset button and hung up.

42
Larkin Goes Back to Brooklyn

LARKIN WALKED the platform on the Bowery J-line stop, shivering a bit from the subterranean chill. He was alone on the platform. A loud invisible dripping somewhere in the station oppressed him. Larkin was low-spirited and there was a buzzing humming noise around the corners of his mind, like an untuned radio or an indistinguishable conversation in some distant room.

At last the hum was briefly smothered by the roar of an approaching train. Larkin got on. The car he'd entered was empty. Essex Street, the bridge, Marcy Avenue, where he did not get off this time. He waited for the next stop along Broadway to disembark. Going down the stairs he peered anxiously at both sides of the sidewalk below but he saw no face he recognized nor did any stranger appear to be waiting for him.

Still he did not go directly home. Larkin circled past the local branch of the Brooklyn Library to Lee Avenue and walked slowly down toward Louise Sobel Park. Hasidic mothers steered their strollers well away from him, no doubt because of his crazed and battered appearance, Larkin thought, or perhaps he had begun to talk out loud to himself again. The incoherent distant hum had recommenced, and he could not stop himself from snapping his head to and fro, trying to isolate a voice. Larkin walked by the concrete park and crept toward Bedford Avenue. An excess of caution, he was nearly sure, but he deeply feared some unknown thing.

Bedford and Broadway; nothing seemed amiss. Larkin scanned the street for trouble signs but there was not so much as an unfamiliar car. Salsa music shook the little bodega he was standing near, momentarily scattering the voices, which had grown stronger during his walk, though no more comprehensible. Across the street a window hung half open in Larkin's loft, but he recalled he'd left it that way himself. He darted across Broadway and let himself in his front door.

All clear in the stairwell. The usual metallic grinding issued from the die cutters' half-open doors. Larkin mounted to the top landing and started back against the wall. The inverted pentangle had been scratched out at knife point in the paint of his door, a drooling goat's head crudely sketched within it.

"We've got you now!" One of the voices had suddenly come clear. From the corner of his eye Larkin saw a dingy little man or gnome, dressed in loose dull clothing, hovering down at the bottom of the stairs, but when he turned to look directly the figure had disappeared. The voices also had abruptly ceased. Larkin breathed. He drew his own knife from its ankle sheath and began to chip at the door, but it was too much labor to efface the diagram completely and finally he simply etched the Russian cross on top of its remains.

Someone had also been chiselling at his lock but apparently with no success. Larkin's key still worked. He slipped his knife into his sleeve and shoved the door open. There was no answering sound nor any reaction. Larkin peered around the doorjamb; the loft seemed vacant. He rushed the darkroom door and jerked it open. As of its own volition the knife had jumped back into his hand but there was no one in the darkroom. Larkin sighed and sheathed his knife.

There was a faint odor of decay in the loft but it had no definite source, seeming rather to be general to all of the motionless air. Something he'd left in the refrigerator Larkin supposed, but still he was nervous of lingering there long. Quickly he moved to the south end of the loft and gathered cameras and lenses from their hiding places, packing them into the green bag. In his haste he dropped a lens cap, which rolled in a wide curve along the floor and fetched up against the tiles beneath the stove. Larkin stooped to pick it up. A silvery object underneath the stove was winking up at him.

A can of Bumble Bee tuna fish, standing on its edge. Near it Larkin could also discern a little jumble of bones and tiger-striped fur. He knelt and looked closer. The cats. He had completely forgotten all about the cats. But now it was quite simple to deduce what must have occurred. Dwango had beat it out the open window, walked the ledge and vanished down the fire escape. The kitten, with its crippled leg, wouldn't have been up to the trip. Larkin didn't like to consider how long the kitten might have rolled the sealed can over the floor, before creeping under the heatless stove to die. He touched the surface of the stove and the cold of it bit his finger. Larkin rocked back onto his heels, lowered his head to his knees, choking on utterly unexpected tears. He had not known so slight a lapse of his attention could be fatal.

43
Bellevue

"YOU LOOK LIKE unholy hell, Larkin," Dr. Leveaux was saying. "On a cracker." Larkin scarcely heard him. The muttering voices had resurfaced, though once again he could not make out any words, and they were distracting him badly.

"What's wrong with you?"

"I went to a New Year party," Larkin mumbled.

"What?"

"Russian New Year."

They had come to a door at the end of the hall. A pair of uniformed security guards frowned at them from either side of it. There was a placard strung to the door handles which read: ENTRY BY PASS ONLY.

"All right," Leveaux said. "I have to warn you, Larkin, we don't know what this is. It's beginning to look like an epidemic, but I've got no idea how it's communicated. All I can tell you is we've had patients for about six weeks and none of the hospital staff seems to have come down with the thing."

"I don't care," Larkin said. Leveaux presented a laminated badge to the two guards, who let them pass.

The first patient, a middle-aged man, sat in a partially cranked up bed. His face and arms were covered with small blood blisters, under an inch in diameter for the most part. While Larkin set up and began to take pictures, the man sucked greedily at an outsized cup of water. When he had finished it he threw up into a kidney-shaped bowl which was balanced on his chest and asked for more. Leveaux refilled the cup from a tap on the wall and he and Larkin left the room. At the next four beds they visited the situation was much the same.

"Okay," Leveaux said. "Let's try the second stage." In the

next room there was a black woman in her twenties who looked absolutely normal. Larkin glanced at Leveaux perplexedly but the doctor motioned for him to begin photographing. The young woman was restless and while Larkin took pictures, she repeatedly asked the doctor to set her release date. Leveaux assured her as often that it would be best for her to remain where she was.

"She looked fine," Larkin said, when they had left the room.

"They tend to go into remission after the first few days. But she doesn't have to worry, she'll get worse in a couple of weeks. I wanted the pictures, who knows what they might show. This is the shotgun approach."

"No difference to me," Larkin said.

"Now for the criticals," Leveaux said, opening another door. The woman inside was wholly bald and seemed prematurely aged. There were traces of blood on her pillow slip. She was either asleep or under sedation and she did not awaken during the photographing, despite the lights.

"How many of these people do you have?" Larkin said, out in the hall again.

"Fifty-two or -three. If none of them died today."

"I'm almost out of film."

"One more?"

Larkin nodded. Leveaux opened another door. Inside was a swiftly balding man who also seemed to Larkin to be asleep. But Leveaux went quickly to him and searched for a pulse in his wrist, then held a finger under his nose.

"Dead," he said heavily. "We lost another one." Larkin rewound his camera.

Larkin sat in Leveaux's desk chair. Leveaux was making an effort to pace but the office was really too small for that.

"You don't look well," Leveaux said. "You don't look right to me at all. I think you're headed for serious trouble, Larkin. I wish you'd come in for treatment."

"I'm better off than those people upstairs," Larkin said. "Don't you think?"

"Maybe. Maybe so." Leveaux sat on the edge of his bookcase. "It does look bad up there, I'll give you that."

"Worse than SHC?"

Leveaux smiled weakly. "At least there's something to examine," he said. "Not that we're getting anywhere with it. But with SHC there's not really a treatment problem anyway." Leveaux laughed shortly. "For this we don't know what to do. It's insane. There's no precedent and no real treatment either."

"Are they all dying?"

"No. Some of them pull through. But that's no credit to us, I don't think. All we do is let them sit there. And run tests on them."

A thin reedy voice detached itself from the general grumbling in Larkin's ears.

Ask him where they all come from, the voice said. *Ask him where they live.*

"Where are they coming from?" Larkin said.

"Times Square. All of them live around there or work in the area. Usually out in the open. A lot of pushcart people and street hustlers . . . it's not affecting commuters. Funny you should ask that, Larkin, it's almost the only correlation we've found."

It's radiation sickness, the reedy voice said. *Tell him it's radiation sickness. Go on, TELL HIM.*

"Radiation sickness," Larkin said.

"What?"

"It could be radiation sickness."

Leveaux took a ballpoint from his pocket and sucked on the tip, staring at Larkin over the shaft of it. Then he pulled a manual from a shelf behind his knee, opened it, and began to read. After a minute or more he looked up again.

"You know, you actually could be right," Leveaux said. "It really does seem to fit the symptoms. There's just one problem, though."

"What's that?"

"It takes very high-level radiation to get these effects. You just wouldn't be getting that kind of thing in the middle of Manhattan. It doesn't make any sense."

"A lot of things don't make any sense," Larkin said. "It looks like that kind of year."

44
Larkin Calls Simon

LARKIN WENT into a phone booth on First Avenue and dialed a number. When Simon's well-polished voice answered he opened without prologue.

"You're a fool, Simon. Either you or Ruben."

"What are you talking about?"

"I got called up to Bellevue today. They've got a whole ward full of people with radiation sickness. And all of them come from Times Square. The stuff is leaking, Simon. Ruben screwed up the seals."

"Larkin, *shut up!*" Simon was shouting. "Don't say this to me on the telephone."

"Why worry, Simon? The cat's already out of the bag."

"You weren't supposed — What makes you think it's there? It's not there, Larkin. Like I told you, we stored it upstate."

Larkin laughed.

"I think it's there the same way the doctors at Bellevue are going to think it's there. And the newspapers and the police and the FBI. Because half the people in Times Square are falling down dead with radiation —"

"Don't say those words, Larkin. Try to remember the phone."

"Then why don't you stop saying my name so many times? If you're so worried about it."

There was no answer. Larkin listened to the humming of the line. He could hear no suspicious irregularity but he hardly knew if that were grounds for reassurance.

"I don't think you're tapped," Larkin said at last. "I wouldn't worry so much about the phone if I were you. I'd be worrying about the leak. What are you going to do about it? You'd better do something. Soon."

"What I'm going to do," Simon said aimlessly. "What am I going to do."

Larkin looked through the scratched glass of the phone booth at the hospital across the street. On the phone he could hear small disturbances in Simon's breathing.

"My dime is going to run out," Larkin said.

"All right," Simon said, his voice suddenly cool and brisk. "We just go right ahead with it, that's all."

Larkin's nervous system revolted from the control of his mind. His heart began to pound and his mouth grew papery and dry.

"Now?" he said.

"Now."

"Is it ready? I thought Ruben was having some problems."

"He'll just have to get it ready," Simon said. His poise seemed completely restored. "If not, we'll use one of the fallback methods. No need for so much finesse in this kind of project, don't you agree?"

"Yes," Larkin said. "How soon?"

"Four or five days," Simon said cheerfully. "Definitely within the week. I'll check with Ruben and let you know. Make sure you stay in touch, Larkin. Call in every day from now on."

"Yes," Larkin said. He might have added something more, but the pay phone clicked and cut him off.

45
Karin

LARKIN JOINED A LINE in front of the checkroom at Penn Station. When he reached the counter the attendant stared at him with some disbelief, but the ticket Larkin presented was valid. The attendant carried it to the back and in a moment had returned with Larkin's black shoulder bag.

With the bag in his left hand Larkin went down the stairs and along a concrete corridor toward the washroom. The hall was lit with greenish fluorescent light and halfway along it stood a shaggy black man, blowing listlessly into a harmonica. He looked up briefly as Larkin passed but did not ask for money.

In the bathroom Larkin propped his bag against the base of a sink and pulled a wrapped bar of soap and a razor from the top of it. He washed his face and shaved carefully, then dried his things and put them back in the bag. In a toilet stall he removed his torn clothes and put on clean ones. He zipped the old clothing back into the bag and tried brushing the worst of the dirt off his coat before he put it back on. Larkin left the washroom and went down another subterranean tunnel to the Seventh Avenue subway. After a five- or ten-minute wait he boarded an express train uptown.

At 96th Street he got off and began to walk up Broadway. After a couple of blocks he turned off to the left and went to the corner of West End Avenue, where he entered a small doorway. Standing in the tiny foyer he noticed that the inner door latch looked broken, but he rang the buzzer instead of trying the door. Larkin spoke his name into the microphone on the buzzer plate and went into the building. He climbed a tight stairway and knocked on a wooden door at its second turning.

Karin hung herself around his neck. They were of a height, and Larkin found himself with his chin on her shoulder, looking into the small apartment, which was clean and neat as a jewel. This excess of tidiness suggested to Larkin that Karin was entering a new phase or terminating an old one. With a small effort he lifted her a little off her feet and set her down inside the door, which he closed behind him.

"Well," Larkin said.

"It's been a long time."

"So it has."

"I didn't know you were coming. I thought you might call."

"I was in the neighborhood," Larkin lied. "What's going on? With you."

"Oh, just things. You know."

"What kind of things?"

"Do you want some tea?"

"Sure."

Larkin set his shoulder bag on the floor with a clank and followed Karin into the small kitchen cubicle. Unlike the rest of the apartment the kitchen was a disaster area. Fetid pots and plates piled upward out of the sink. By some feat of dexterity Karin had induced water to flow into a copper kettle which she was now placing on the stove. Karin wore loose trousers and a V-necked cashmere sweater. She lit a match and stretched out her arm toward the gas burner. Of itself Larkin's right hand rose toward the bare white patch of shoulder disclosed between the sweater and the falling column of her hair. Larkin arrested his hand and jailed it in his pants pocket.

Then they were drinking tea, sitting side by side on Karin's small striped sofa. Larkin raised his cup from a coaster on the polished wooden table before him, tasted it, and put it carefully back. Jasmine.

"Have you got cigarettes?" Karin said. Larkin produced a box of Marlboros and flipped open the lid. Karin took one. Larkin managed to light it without looking at her. He had another sip of tea and lit a cigarette himself, blowing smoke toward a tiny raised fireplace which was lined with blue Dutch tile.

"So," he said. "You called."

"Yes," Karin said. But she did not elaborate on her reasons.

In a surprisingly short time Larkin found he had finished his cigarette and stubbed it out in an ashtray to his left. Karin had put the side of her thumb in her mouth and was gnawing at the cuticle. Reflexively Larkin pulled her hand away and toward himself and spread the fingers; all the tips were raw.

"You're eating yourself again, I see."

Nimbly Karin slipped her fingers under his wrists and drew both his hands up to the tops of her knees, which she had tucked up under her chin. With a tattered fingernail she traced the scars on the backs of Larkin's hands.

"Once in a while is different," Larkin said.

Karin looked at him intently. Larkin dropped his eyes. The sleeves of Karin's sweater were pushed high on her arms and at her elbows he could see two quarter-sized bruises which rather resembled thumbprints. Inside her left forearm there was also a healing cut. Larkin glanced up at her face again but it was unmarked. *She'd leave him if he hit her in the face,* he thought. *He's too smart for that, at least.* Abruptly he twisted her arms over. There were more fresh bruises on the other side.

"Ouch," Karin said. "You're hurting." Larkin let her go and leaned back on his own side of the couch.

"So how's Henry," he said.

"Well . . . we had a fight."

"So I see."

"I provoke him."

"I'd be the first to admit you can be provoking," Larkin said. "But you're not supposed to beat on girls."

He stood up and circled the two chairs on the other side of the table. He scanned the bookcase on the wall by the door, then turned to the other side of the table. He scanned the bookcase on the wall by the door, then turned to the other side of the room and approached a small curio cabinet in the corner. The cabinet was adorned with minute old photographs of Karin's family, dried flowers, and the like. There were also a number of eggshells which Karin had painted herself. Larkin picked one of these up and studied the intricate filigree. He controlled a brief impulse to smash it and put it delicately back on the shelf among the others.

"I think we're getting engaged," Karin said.

"You and me?"

"Me and Henry."

"Congratulations," Larkin said. He came back to the couch and sat heavily down. He lit another cigarette, leaving the box on the table for Karin.

"Was that what you wanted to talk about?" he said.

"No . . . It's since I called. We had a fight. But we made up. Now it's better."

"And later it'll be worse."

"Don't say that." Karin took Larkin's hands again and made him look at her. Larkin felt his mind begin to twirl. He was soberer than he had been in some time but he was not feeling very lucid. The worst of his hangover had dissipated during the afternoon at the hospital. Now, however, he felt uncontrollably dizzy.

"I've been having dreams about you," Karin said.

"Please don't tell me about them."

Larkin got up and walked through an open archway into Karin's bedroom. On the rear wall, up a pair of steps, was a glass door letting onto a balcony, which overlooked an enclosed garden. Larkin opened the door. Ivy climbed the walls of the garden. At the center of the paths among the flower beds there was a stone birdbath on a pedestal. He did *not think* about the presence of Karin behind him.

"It's cold," Karin said. Larkin closed the door and leaned back against it, looking at her through the arch.

"Are you happy about it?" he said, gently as he could manage.

"I think I am."

"THEN GET YOUR THUMB OUT OF YOUR MOUTH FOR CHRIST'S SAKE."

Karin cringed. Larkin rocked his head slowly against a cool pane of the door. There was a passport-sized picture of Henry stuck in the frame of Karin's mirror on the opposite wall. He was a bland, inoffensive looking man, a lawyer. Larkin had never met him. But Karin's taste in escorts was notoriously perverse. Larkin turned around and stared out through the door.

"Sorry," he muttered. Some drab winter bird had settled in the ivy of the garden wall. Karin's fingers slipped into his belt loops, over his hips. Larkin turned, breaking her grip. Standing on the steps made him a little taller.

"Why do you have to get married to a psychopathic lawyer?" he said.

Karin looked up at him.

"But I'm a nice psychopath," Larkin said. "I don't hit you."

Now Karin was tugging a little petulantly at his belt loops in the front, unbalancing him slightly.

"You'll make me fall," Larkin said, teetering on the steps. He put out his hands to steady himself, bracing back against her shoulders. But his elbows loosened and began to bend.

"What can I do?" Larkin said, half audibly. He smiled a little, slipping into her, naturally as water poured in water.

Larkin woke suddenly in a mad terror. There was a sucking darkness in the room and he could see nothing. Whatever dream had alarmed him had passed unremembered, but he felt as though he were pressed down under a heavy pane of glass. His hands were itching and he wanted to scratch them, but one was tangled up in Karin's hair and he did not want to wake her.

Somewhere in the room a clock was ticking and Larkin calmed himself by listening to the small regularity of the sound. His eyes adjusted enough to make out the dim shape of the window just beside the bed and his sense of oppression lifted somewhat. Cautiously he detached his hand from Karin's hair and drew it up to his chest. Larkin drifted back into a doze.

He was swinging wildly at a glass wall or door. Gratifyingly raw shocks travelled from his fists to his shoulders. Beyond the wall Karin was rapt in some brown study. Larkin could not discern whether she was alone or in company, but she remained unaware of him until the glass began to splinter. Larkin shot both hands together through the shattering pane, slicing them nastily to the bone. The barrier was gone, but he had no further wish to cross the threshold. Instead he carefully pounded the remaining shards of glass into powder, working methodically around the edges of the frame. Droplets of his own blood whirred around his head. When there was no more glass, Larkin stopped and inspected his mangled hands, amazed and entranced by the utter lack of pain. He had expected to feel this, but there was nothing.

Karin had risen and was facing him, tottering on the edge of
a faint. Larkin recalled her horror of blood. He had not meant
to frighten her, and he began to say this, but somehow was
unable to speak. Larkin put his hands behind his back to hide
the wounds, and at the same moment he erupted back into
the waking world.

Now there was light at the window beside the bed. It had
been no dream, Larkin understood, but a denied memory.
The thing had happened; the scars proved it so. It was also
true that there had been no pain, only a maddening itch much
later when the stitches were in and Larkin was on a locked
ward at Bellevue, studying forgetfulness of his berserk jealousy of Karin and the failure of his love for her. In this he
had succeeded so absolutely that he could not even recall if
Karin had actually been present at the time when he had
chosen to beat down the glass wall.

There was a sharp draft from under the sash of the window, cooling the panic sweat on Larkin's body. He sank back
down to his pillow, congratulating himself on the relative
success of his decision to forget. From his present position
he could see only the chalky sky, with an airplane now trac-
ing a silent vector across it. Larkin raised his hands before
him. The scars had flushed to a rich red, but he presumed
that was only from the cold. Perhaps it would have been better if he had not come here. Certainly it was better not to
remember and to feel nothing. *But nothing is nothing.* Larkin
sat up. *And all that is nothing.* A swallow flashed almost imper-
ceptibly across the window, and Larkin noticed that drops of
rain were collecting on the glass. Soundlessly he slipped out
of the bed.

In the other room he dressed quickly and quietly. Done,
he glanced back into the bedroom. Karin had rolled partly
into the space he'd occupied, but she was still deeply asleep.
Larkin smiled, numbed his mind with an effort, and left the
apartment. Before shutting the door, he loosened the locking screw of the cylinder with his nail file.

Outside it was raining gently. Larkin walked slowly up to

Broadway and stopped on the corner. His demons had been wholly silent during the time he'd spent with Karin, but curiously he found he rather missed the voices and looked forward to their return. Back down the street he saw veils of the light rain falling successively one behind another, closing like curtains along the path he'd taken.

46
Hours of the Dead (III)

UNDER THE WINDOW at the far end of the bar, Estrellita, the little star, sat doubled over her table with her nose just bumping the edge of her wine glass. She snored a little and mumbled a fragmentary description of her old recurring dream, in which an enormous Silver Shadow, long as the block, pulls up to her beat at Houston Street and Second Avenue; a liveried chauffeur jumps out, wraps Estrellita in a silver-fox cape to protect her from the angry needles of winter, then ushers her into the car's sunshaded rear compartment. There a beautiful man of Latin complexion extends to her a glass of the very finest port wine, which Estrellita accepts with regal courtesy, and he engages her in the very best of conversation while the car flows smoothly as perfumed oil uptown toward the building he owns on Central Park West. And Estrellita is handed out of the car and into the building by the chauffeur, the doorman, and at last a butler, all of whom treat her with the most delicate respect.

Estrellita stirred at the table, her actual being somewhat disturbed by the dream in which she shoots to the roof in a fast elevator, where the beautiful man excuses himself with a bow and a smile, giving her into the care of five Japanese maidens in white kimonos. Estrellita is escorted into what she takes to be a Turkish bath by the maidens, who spend what

seems to be a day and a night planing away at the old scars
and fresh sores of Estrellita's twenty-odd years on the street,
during which time every feature of her face and body has
been respectively beaten or slashed by cops or pimps or, every
so often, a truly crazy trick. But the best efforts of the Japanese maidens do not take any part of this away, except for
the dirt, so that when Estrellita arises from her baths and
salves and unguents, she is only cleaner, not transformed.

But the Japanese girls clothe her in a fine evening dress
and conduct her to a room where a splendid repast is waiting, beginning with every last one of Estrellita's favorite dishes
recalled from her childhood in Cuba and proceeding to the
unimaginable mysteries of French cuisine, and the beautiful
man is there also, though he does not eat or drink. Instead
he entertains Estrellita with an elegant discourse highly com-
plimentary to her, until she is sated, and she eats long and
heartily, though she is wondering all the while what kind of
payoff can possibly be in it for him.

Now, when the meal is finished and Estrellita has had her
brandy, the beautiful man brings her into another room at
the top of the building, or perhaps of the world, where a
crystal dome serves as walls and roof, and all around the
room the lights of the city are spread out like a carpet for
Estrellita's feet, while the stars of the sky appear to be looking in at her from the top. And Estrellita is so taken aback
by this splendor that it is some time before she notices
that in the center of the room is a huge white bed shaped like
an egg.

Ah, thinks Estrellita, from the bottomless resources of twenty
years spent in the close vicinity of Delancey Street, *so it's just
the same old gruesome dance after all, and this man is just simply the
biggest fool yet, with his looks and a place like this, to want an old
shoe like me.* And she gets out of her dress with a whore's
rapidity, not thinking any more about it. But when she is
lying on her back with her knees drawn up, and the beautiful
man has removed his own garments, she sees that he is as
hairless and sexless as a mannequin up at Macy's, and he tells
her, in the marvelously poetic diction which seems always
at his command, that he has brought her here for the

single purpose of adoring and wondering at her terrible humanity . . .

Larkin came in and banged the door. Estrellita raised her head for a moment at the sound.

"You rotten filthy sonofabitch," she said, adding Spanish words to the effect that Larkin should return at once to the ninth circle of hell, whence it was obvious to all sensible people he had originally come. Then she dropped her face back on her arms and was instantly back asleep.

"Rusty," Larkin said. "Will you let me have a beer?" In the shadows at the back end of the counter the bartender might have stirred a hair. It was somberly quiet and Larkin's voice echoed on itself.

"A lot of money got spent that night, after all," he said. "For pity's sake?"

Rusty reached into the cooler near him and simply rolled an unopened bottle across the bar. Larkin popped the cap off on the edge of the counter and turned around. So early in the morning there was little trade and the house lights were turned off, except for the neon beer signs. Dull rain-drenched daylight seeped in through the grimy windows. Besides Estrellita there were just two patrons in the bar. Worm sat against the wall in more or less the same position Larkin had last seen him in. And at his accustomed corner table, staring vacantly before him, there was also Dutch.

Larkin approached the table, his heart failing him, and sat down. Dutch turned his head to face him with a chilly absence of expression.

"Wait," Larkin said. "I didn't know. I still don't know. Try to believe me. I *can't* know. I've lost the knack. I've got no memory for things. I taught myself to lose it and now . . . now I couldn't get it back if I wanted to. I can't connect things any more. The skills are gone. I've run out of logic. But memory, logic, it's just like your appendix, Dutch. It's vestigial, there's no more use for it . . . in these times, these last days. I . . . do you know what I've been doing the last five years? I've been *killing time*. Literally. Eliminating it. Murdering it. Making it go away . . . And now it's really gone. *There is no more time.* And nothing happens for reasons."

Larkin paused for breath. Dutch made as if to speak.

"Wait," Larkin said, raising one hand. "You have to under-stand this. I never wanted to do evil. But I've been trying to . . . to skin myself. Like those old pictures, Dutch, where there's a door, with a little doorknob, here in your chest. You can open it and see the heart, the lungs, the viscera, healthy or decayed, it doesn't matter, all the parts of the body which the mind invented anyway. And behind it there's a mirrored room with a small fire burning, incense or offal, I don't know. Even the mind can't get into that room, because the mind also was invented by the soul. But there are visitors there.

"Wait," Larkin said. "Do you know that the devil is real? There are angels too, I believe it, but it's been so long since one has come to me. But demons visit me nightly, day and night, and more and more these past few days. They're whis-pering to me, nasty hissing voices, telling me terrible things. That I've failed in my tests and tasks, and that the devil owns me now. That the killings going on are all my fault, and other things as well. That now you hate me, Dutch, when there was love and friendship between us.

"Wait," Larkin said. "It's only temptation, after all. Once there was a desert saint who suffered a serpent to twine around his feet for hours without interrupting his prayer. Trust me, I've lived with demons and I know their ways. They'll stop at nothing to corrupt our souls. And resisting them . . . is like being torn by beasts. But God looks down and laughs at our simplicity. Laughter of kindness, I mean, not mockery. Be-cause, truly, there is nothing to fear. Though it is also true that this world is soon going to be burned with fire. But after . . . after we have passed through the pain of death, we will all climb Mount Zion."

Larkin bowed his head. Dutch cleared his throat.

"Why should I have to listen to this?" he said. "I don't care how crazy you are. But I do believe that the devil is real. You've *made* me believe it. You brought him down here. You invited him. *And now he's killing us off one by one.*"

Larkin spread his fingers on the table.

"What can I do?" he said.

"I don't know," Dutch said. "But I hope to God you think of something."

Larkin rubbed his eyes.

"All right," he said. "What about this? Every night I sleep in a shell on Stanton Street. It's right by a shooting gallery, no trouble to find. I'll be there tonight and every night. I'm available to be killed at any time."

Larkin stood up.

"You can pass the word," he said, "to anyone who might be interested." Larkin left the bar quickly, leaving behind the beer he had not tasted.

47
Flowers

NOW NOTHING REMAINED to him but to kill the time left until darkness, but that was the whole of the day. Larkin wandered westward from the bar, drifting into Soho. Since he had washed and changed the night before he did not seem much out of place, but he was scarcely aware of his surroundings or of anyone's regard.

The drizzle had broken for the moment and it was growing colder. Above the rooftops clouds were parting over faded sections of blue sky. Larkin walked to West Broadway and for no special reason turned downtown. By now the shops were open and there was traffic on the street. Larkin passed a dull-colored van parked with one wheel on the curb and was struck by a twinge of recognition. He stopped a moment and looked back. It was not only an Aardvark Florists van but even the very one he used to drive, and he still had the ignition key in his pocket.

Larkin jounced over the broken pavement of the West Side Highway in the stolen (or borrowed) van. Reaching the elevated section of the highway, he picked up speed. Below and to the left the Hudson River spread glassily out toward the bluffs of the western bank. Larkin shot around a turn and pointed the van at the distant shape of the George Washington Bridge. The verve of the van's motion raised his spirits, but he knew he was driving too fast. He slowed the truck and pulled off the highway in the 90s. On West End Avenue, around the corner from Karin's building, he parked.

By this time Karin would be at work, so he assumed. Larkin padded to the entry door and pushed in past the faulty latch. Outside the apartment he paused to listen but the small sounds he could hear seemed to come from other floors. Larkin slipped the point of his nail file into the lock and twisted counterclockwise. The cylinder resisted for a moment and then, more smoothly, began to turn. Larkin removed it from the lock plate and opened the door with his finger.

Karin had indeed gone out and all was quiet within. The two rooms had been tidied, the bed made, even the sink cleared out. Larkin replaced the cylinder in the door for appearance's sake and pounded back down the stairs. He reached the street and opened the rear doors of the van. Inside it was wall-to-wall flowers, flowers of every kind.

It took Larkin over an hour to deliver all the flowers to Karin's apartment. There were enough and to spare to fill the place and overflow it. Larkin loaded tables and windowsills with tulips, buried the bed in red and white roses, carpeted the floor with day lilies. He wreathed the walls and furniture with flowers whose names he did not even know. The rooms were finally reeling with a confusion of colors and conflicting scents. A little dizzied by it, Larkin tightened the cylinder and locked the catch on leaving.

Outside, he glanced at the van and decided to abandon it where it was parked. Larkin strolled toward Riverside Drive, for the moment reasonably well content. He had managed to pass some time. He had done away with the hours of morning.

48
The Voices

. . .youreafoolamadmanaknaveyouredrunkderangeddeludedyourein-
saneyouresickyoureasicksickman . . .

The voices had come back and Larkin found them most
unwelcome. They distracted him so seriously that he found
it difficult to walk. By some triumph of internal ingenuity he
had contrived to combine a state of paralytic depression with
another of acute prickling anxiety. The voices buzzed on.
Larkin clutched at his hair and ears; he wagged his head back
and forth like a dog. Involuntarily his tongue kept curling
backwards, trying to climb down his throat. *Maybe it's rabies
you've got,* a voice said. Larkin laughed loudly at the suggestion.

Oh no, it's not rabies, a crisper voice said. Larkin noted a
tone similar to that of Dr. Leveaux. *You've got a big fit coming
on, my little friend. A great big slobbering fit. It could be today, it
could be tomorrow, but it's coming, sure as death. Can't you tell?
Don't you know? Haven't you felt this way before?*

"NO GOD DAMN IT!" Larkin shouted. "It can't be that. I
don't have time. I've got too many things to do." Someone
tapped him on the back and Larkin spun around, hands raised
to strike, but no one was there, after all, and no one had
really touched him. "I am not insane," Larkin told himself
carefully. "I am standing on the corner of Broadway and 75th
Street in New York City in the United States of America." A
fissure opened in the pavement before him, clapped shut,
and opened again. Smoke rose out of the crack. Hell's mouth
yawning.

jump, a voice whispered, *go on, jumpjumpjumpjumpjumpjump.*
Larkin dove toward the chasm. Too late he understood the
trick and threw out an arm to break his fall. He had flung

himself onto a subway grating. His sleeve was torn and his arm was scraped and he had banged his elbow. Larkin pulled himself up on a utility pole and sat against it, with his legs stretched out across the grate.

"Stop fooling me," he whispered. He arched his back and bent his neck in such a way that the top of his head pressed against the pole behind him. From this position, Larkin screamed.

"GIVE ME A *TRUE* SIGN!"

A startled pedestrian flipped a dime in his direction. The coin landed on its edge and began to roll toward the grating. Larkin observed its progress, wondering if it would fall into the grating and farther, to melt in everlasting fire. At the edge of the grating, however, the dime wobbled and fell over. Heads. *Iwintailsyoulose.* The coin glimmered. The profiled face of Roosevelt opened its mouth and began to speak. *Pick me up, stupid,* Roosevelt said.

Larkin picked up the dime and put it in his mouth, underneath his tongue. The dime was very cold and had rather an acid flavor. Larkin became rational. He planned.

With perfect care and precision Larkin inserted his mouth-warmed dime into the pay phone slot. Dial tone. Larkin punched in his own number and raised the remote box to the mouthpiece, performing these operations much in the manner of a sane and healthy person not possessed by devils. The tape rewound briefly and began to play.

"Hey, Larkin." It was Arkady's voice. A mildly amused tone. "Something funny is happening. The boy started talking. Tommy. Remember him?"

"Uh huh," Larkin said.

"But the funny thing is, he only says one word. And you know what that word is? It's *your name.*"

"Weird," Larkin said.

"Maybe you'd like to hear him do it. Maybe he might say it into the phone for you."

A new and unfamiliar voice, not especially childish:

"Larkin? Larkin?" Then, affirmatively, "Larkin."

"Hello, kid," Larkin said. "I hope you're doing well out there."

Arkady's voice resumed. "I don't know if that's all he knows," he said neutrally. "But that's all he ever says."

49
The Devils

BY NIGHTFALL Larkin was back in the Stanton Street shell, freezing. He reached for his shoulder bag, which he had somehow managed to retain throughout the madness of the day, and searched in it for a sweater. Instead his hand closed on something wriggling and alive. Larkin recoiled. A tiny naked homunculus crawled out of the bag. It had pointed ears and a curled tail like a pig's.

"Lovely to see you again," the demon piped.

"I wish I could say the same," Larkin said.

"How can you be *so rude?*" the demon said, its voice mincing and effeminate.

"This is what I get for a demon," Larkin said. "A lousy little faggot with a curly tail."

"I'm not good enough for you, is that it?" the demon said. "No? Our poppet wants a grand romantic devil? Horns and hooves and breathing fire? You can't bear reality, child. That's what your problem is."

"Ah, shut up," Larkin said. "Don't talk to me about reality. I made you up, you know. You're a figment. A bad dream."

"Am I now? Am I now?" The demon's voice squeaked with outrage. "Maybe I just am. I'll grant you that, I will. But what then? What about your precious God and your precious little saints?"

Larkin's fist struck down like a hammer on the gnome but

it was gone. Never, never, had he been quite quick enough . . . Once again he felt the cold. Larkin raised his hand and opened it, flexing the fingers. It felt as if he might have pulled a tendon, smashing the floor so hard. Larkin felt his weariness. Truly, he was tired to the bone. He closed his eyes, slipped over onto his side. There was not so much farther to walk after all. He was near to warmth and light, and before him he could see naked men and women dancing in firelight. Larkin yearned toward them, hastening along the road. Ahead, just beyond those white columns, there was shelter, in the heart of the fire. And even the road was warming his feet and curving up behind him, helping him, hurrying him down . . . At the colonnade Larkin paused to admire the perfection of the architecture. Each column was elegantly tapered to a fine point, in one direction or the other, up or down. Like stalactites and stalagmites . . . or like teeth. Larkin stared farther into the maw and saw that the naked revelers were in fact writhing in unspeakable anguish, were screaming without sound. And behind him, what he had taken for a road was curling up and cresting like a wave, that enormous dragon's tongue now about to flick him down the long burning gullet, in among the others . . .

"That's ugly."

It was his own voice speaking. Larkin stood in a corner of the wrecked room. A dreary little man in shabby brown crouched by the door.

"You drew the picture," this man said.

"Oh, it's you," Larkin said, sapped of all will. "You're supposed to be the noonday demon. Who let you out at night?"

"It was you who wanted to stop time. Remember?"

rememberrememberrememberrememberrememberrememberremem-
ber

Larkin swayed, mind caught in a black vortical swirl.

"I'm still here," the demon said.

Larkin opened his eyes. The words were true.

"All right, then," he said. "You're still here."

"So. What have you got to offer me?" The demon of despondency paced the crumbled plaster on the floor. "Cup of coffee? Cup of tea? Buy me a drink? Haven't you at least got a cracker?" The demon rubbed his head, which was bald and shiny, abnormally narrow and long.

"Ah, you're a sad case," the demon said, turning his back on Larkin, facing the dark opening of the door letting into the hall. "Pathetic, I should say. What have you ever done for anyone? You can't even do anything for yourself. You and your ratty little . . . *pictures.* That you can't even finish. They're a botched job. Like you, just like you. You're not put together right, Larkin. You're just not."

The demon whipped around and grinned at him.

"Can't say anything, can you? I couldn't either, if I were in your place. I'd sympathize, if you weren't so contemptible. Look what a mess you've made of your life. Look how you've ruined love."

"You're hurting," Larkin said, turning away toward the window.

"That's what I'm for," the demon said. "You know that much, at least."

"Are you finished?" Larkin said. "It's been a long day. I'd like to get some sleep."

"Would you? So would I. But we don't sleep, you know. I'm not quite finished with you yet. Do you know the worst thing, the most despicable thing about you? It's that in spite of all this . . . this charming little cesspool of vice and error you've contrived to live in, you still believe that you have a *great soul.* Don't you? Don't you? Don't even try to deny it. You have the gall, the audacity, to imagine that God is so intimately concerned with you, so interested in your miserable little sins. You want to be one of the Great Sinners. And you think that will endear you to him, more than common people's virtues could. Why, your sins don't even interest *me,* when I'm the one who profits by them. They disgust me, Larkin, really they do. And just to make that perfectly clear, I'd like to show you one right now."

Reluctantly Larkin faced the demon, who was spreading, tearing the air between his hands. Out of the space thus opened there issued forth a ghastly stench. There on the floor, beside a spilled, fire-blackened trash can, lay an oblong bundle of rags which seemed to be the source of the bad smell. Large black flies whined in circles around it, dropping occasionally to feed. Larkin was hypnotized by the drone of the flies, bidden to approach the bundle. Touching the rags he felt a contour of bone. Larkin turned the bundle over. The body was decayed, drooling putrescence, but the face on the far side of the almost severed neck was recognizably that of Aztec Sam. The flies settled over the face to shroud it, buzzing with a damned, insentient concentration.

"I never wanted this," Larkin said.

"It's not what you want that makes you fat," the demon said, sidling through the door. "It's what you get."

Larkin shivered by the broken window, which was set low enough that he could look out over the sill from his squatting position on the floor. He could not tell if his trembling came from the cold or from his simple misery. Not for a long time had Larkin felt quite so bleakly wretched as this. He sensed the late departure of his demons almost as a loss, for they had left him with no company in the sour sealed bubble of his mind.

Outside the window the twisted tree shuddered, perhaps from the wind . . . but there was a pattern to it; the motion seemed an echo of some movement in the house below. Larkin listened. Behind him the door groaned loudly on its hinges, moved by a sudden draft. It occurred to Larkin that he had never passed through this doorway. He always came and went by way of the window . . . and what there might be beyond the darkness of the door, Larkin had no idea. A hall, a stair no doubt, more rooms like this one.

But surely those were footsteps he heard out past the door. Footsteps mounting the stairs, creaking . . . Larkin strained his ears, but the noise had stopped. An illusion. Or another demon, though usually they arrived in silence. This last thought made Larkin nauseous. He could not bear another demon after all, not this night. Larkin dropped his forehead to the windowsill, concentrating on the banishment of the ascending steps, which had recommenced. *There's no one home,* Larkin's mind said to itself. *Just go away.*

The steps had stopped. Larkin raised his head and something cold and narrow dropped around his neck and closed there. He opened his mouth but he could not even move the air, much less speak or shout. He raised his fingers to his neck and curiously touched the tightening wire, which was already cutting into his flesh there on the left side. It came to Larkin with an odd detached clarity that he was being murdered. He flailed his arms behind him and touched nothing. However, he realized that on the right side of his neck the garrote was caught on his coat collar . . . Larkin put his finger into the small gap, tugged, and was rewarded with a breath. He somersaulted forward, landing on his back, spine bruised by something on the floor.

Instantly the wire retightened. The strangler knelt over him in a horrid parody of a lover's pose, shouting loudly in some glottal language Larkin intuited to be the first original tongue of the devil. Larkin understood that he was dying. His life opened before him like a flower, kaleidoscoped and whirled, his past rushing up to the present. *I understand it,* Larkin inwardly remarked, rapt in the intellect's irrelevant pleasure at knowing anything at all, as the hurrying sequence reached the *now,* this moment, where Larkin lay on a splintered floor, a stranger killing him. *Live,* an inner voice urged, no demon this time but a kind advisor. *Bend your knee. Draw up your leg.* Obeying, Larkin touched the handle of his knife.

However, he had no more strength. A pattern of golden motes danced on his eyes, alluring him, seducing him toward sleep. *Live,* the voice insisted. Irritably Larkin jerked the knife from its sheath and with the same awkward motion up into the strangler's groin. The blade met some resistance and escaped him. Larkin's hand dropped weakly to the floor and groped through chunks of powder, searching for the knife, not finding it. The hand surrendered and turned over, fingers curling toward the position of rigor mortis. Warm liquid flowed and filled its palm. The strangler gave a little grunt, surprised or maybe disappointed, and fell over on his side.

Larkin rolled over and crawled on his belly a little distance away. He lay with his arms stretched out before him, breathing the breath of life.

A general gasp went round the bar when Larkin entered it; he was a sight to inspire fear. Blood soaked his clothing and one hand was stained to the wrist with it. Larkin himself was bleeding from the neck, where the garrote still hung, wires crossed, the wooden handles knocking on his collarbone, as he stepped or stumbled forward.

"I killed the devil," Larkin said, falling toward the floor. He knew *what was happening* . . . the gut wrenching scream already building out of his diaphragm. And yet already he knew none of this. Wild happiness suffused him as the floor rushed toward his face. Bees hovered over a golden field with a rich delirious hum. The rising floor became a sheet of the finest, whitest vellum, torn from the very skin of the Lamb, and the bees sucked sweetness from the inscription written there . . .

"No one can love God consciously in his heart unless he has first feared Him with all his heart. Through the action of fear the soul is purified and, as it were, made malleable to the action of love."

From the historiated letter *O* in the last word of the text the child Tommy stepped as from a door. The boy's face was welcoming and wise, his voice so gentle that Larkin desired to weep at the sound of it.

"The world is a gift," the child said, raising two crooked fingers of his right hand. "Accept it."

It was Dutch who grasped the situation and could act. He reached Larkin almost before he hit the floor, knelt beside him, shouting for more help. Dutch tore off his belt and stuffed it into Larkin's mouth, preserving him from biting off his tongue. Two Tone and Estrellita helped the old man hold Larkin down, for the five or ten minutes it took the convulsions to subside.

Then Larkin stopped his thrashing and his head lolled back.

Dutch removed the belt. He and Two Tone lifted Larkin, supporting him with his arms over their shoulders, and half carried, half dragged him down the block and up the stairs of the old man's hotel. There, moving clumsily in the matchbox room, they put Larkin into Dutch's narrow bed. That done, Two Tone shrugged and left without a word.

Dutch sat out the watches of the night in the single chair beside the bed, smoking and sipping schnapps straight from the bottle. Dawn had blued the windows before Larkin stirred and woke.

"It's not over," Larkin said.

"Hush," Dutch said, dropping a hand on Larkin's forehead. "You done all right."

"It's not finished," Larkin said.

"All right," Dutch said equably, "maybe it's not. Like Angelo Dundee said to Roberto Duran, 'This thing ain't over till it's over, boy.' "

"I'm not finished yet," Larkin said, falling easily back to sleep.

Part IV

Ground Zero

I may not live but another five minutes, but it will be five minutes on my terms.

George Jackson,
Soledad Brother

50
The Bomb

FOR HALF A YEAR the mind of Ruben Carrera had whirled with images, diagrams, designs, his coalescing plans for the bomb. He had discovered much in a short time, had possibly driven himself to learn too quickly. That part of his intelligence which ran as meticulously as a clock, respectful of the slow laws of chemistry and physics, reproached him for his careless speed. In another mental chamber, a chained demon raved for even greater haste.

Now he was very close, on the verge of a workable design. The raw material, the eight-plus kilograms of plutonium nitrate, had over the course of long nervous weeks been properly dried to crystals. Crystals which were ever present to Carrera's mind's eye, waking or sleeping, as an icon or an emblem of destiny. Against Simon's orders and his own best judgment, Carrera went often and unnecessarily to the hiding place, to caress the twelve lead-lined caskets which kept the crystals safely apart from themselves. It was his persistent fantasy that from their separate cells the crystals consciously yearned to commingle with each other, that they glowed secretly with longing and love. Within that fantasy his own part was simply to perform a marriage ceremony, to wed the crystals in their final, ultimate union.

Critical mass.

But it had to be done right. Carrera's task was to build a device which would bring the material to the proper density at the proper speed for a truly luxurious reaction. The most likely method was implosion. Given the limitations of Carrera's technical resources, that was effectively the only method. He had experimented with models, had improved on his earliest versions. Simon had been harrying him, more and more vigorously of late. But that part had ceased to matter to Carrera. The real pressure of obligation was intrinsic to the work itself. The work, the design, the reaction, had become a ritual mystery, in which he was compelled to perfect himself.

With the ritual perfected, Carrera would win transfiguration. He was contemplating an infinitesimal particle of time, a tenth of a millionth of one second, perhaps, in which much would happen: *The heart of the material reaches a temperature comparable to the inside of a star. The fireball erupts from the bowels of the earth, utterly consuming everything at its center and sending out shock waves which flatten everything else within the radius of a mile or more. A barely perceptible pause, and the dark river meets itself over what was formerly a city.*

Carrera's being reached out toward that moment with all the intensity of faith. If tempted to doubt his purpose or his hope of success, he comforted himself with the thought of his role as mere agent. He believed this: that the incomprehensible forces latent in matter innately possess a desire for release. That the universe is ever prepared to accomplish its own unmaking. That a thread dangles from the fabric of the world which if anyone were to grasp it would unravel the whole. *But this is what we all know.*

51
Void

WHEN HIS CONNECTION with Larkin was broken on January 14, Simon inadvertently replaced the telephone receiver on the table, instead of on the hook. He sat for a long moment with his fingers curved around the instrument. The sudden burst of beeps came in due course, but Simon was slow to respond to it. He picked up the receiver and held it before his face, regarding it without real recognition, with a queer, unjustified sense of its complete unreality. At length he set it back on the hook where it belonged.

Silence ensued. Simon reconnected with his immediate future; there was much to do and to manage. Contact Mercer, Hutton and Carrera . . . no, first it would be better to pick the exact day. Because of the plane tickets. But he would have to speak to Ruben before the day could be decided. But the time pressure! If Larkin had told the truth, the risks were now very great, and though Larkin was a wizard of evasion, Simon had never caught him in an outright lie. He found that he had picked up the phone again and it was talking to him.

"If you would like to make a call, please hang up and dial again . . ."

Irritably Simon hung up. But again he found himself pointlessly entranced by the objective presence of the telephone, its color, form, solidity. Where would it be in a week or ten days' time? Nowhere, along with the entire apartment, the building, the block. All as planned. But Simon felt displeasure, alarm even, as he considered the imminent non-entity of the walls and floors which contained him. With equal discontent he noticed that his hand was trembling slightly, as though the surface on which it lay did not provide it with sufficient support.

Then Simon forced himself to master his disorientation. He would proceed with the program; certainly, this was a poor time to hesitate and falter. The city's plunge into nothingness was, after all, his own desire, and in another sense it was none of his concern. By the time — Simon found himself evasive about naming the event even in thought — at any rate, when the thing had been accomplished he would be far away. He would be in Berlin or Paris or Geneva, but only as a way station en route to some place closer to the heart of the real action . . . Syria, Libya, somewhere. It didn't much matter.

With the great, unparalleled achievement behind him, he would be welcome anywhere. Sought after, even. At last he would have perfect credibility, indeed, a reputation which no one could hope to rival, would be a prince among . . . among what? Somehow Simon had lost track of the later moves in the game. It did not matter. Of course, there would be variations, many different potential lines of play. All of them favorable. What was important now was to execute the plan of the hour quickly, efficiently, mindlessly even — that might actually be an asset. No use in projections, not for the moment. Simon stood up.

But immediately he stumbled and almost fell, as if the floor had receded, dropped away under his feet. Simon had to grasp the edge of the table to regain his balance. There was a pressure of darkness rising under his eyes; also, he was distinctly afraid. Simon stood leaning over the table. It was nothing but the perfectly ordinary dizziness which often came over him when he stood up so suddenly. And one of his legs had simply gone to sleep, but now sensation was returning to it. Simon stamped his feet to restore his circulation. Carefully he pushed back away from the table, and straightened up. The room retained its form and solidity.

He walked down the hall to the room which Mercer occupied. Through the door he could hear a radio playing dimly. Some country-and-western tune. Simon was mildly annoyed by Mercer's choice of music, and paradoxically by the fact that he could not quite make out the words of the song. Lightly he knocked on the door.

"Coming."

The radio stopped. A dragging sound of footsteps and Mercer opened the door. A freshly lit cigarette hung from the corner of his mouth. Stale smoke was layered to the ceiling in the room behind him. Despite such evidence, Simon rather doubted that he and Mercer were truly occupying the same space. He felt that if he reached out to touch the other man, nothing would prove to be there. But where would Mercer be, in that case, and what would be there in his place? Simon lifted his hand, prepared to test his intuition.

"Are you feeling okay?" Mercer said.

"Of course," Simon said reflexively, with panic swelling in him. If he went on in this manner, he would lose all authority. Unthinkable. Activity, action, was all that he needed. That would clear his head. Simon composed himself and began telling Mercer what he had to do.

52
The Plan

ON THE EVENING of January 15, Charles Mercer parked a recently rented Chrysler on the block in Chelsea where David Hutton lived. Mercer locked the car and crossed the street to the entry of Hutton's building, where he rang the buzzer.

"I'm coming down," Hutton's voice said, through a crackle of static.

"Let me up first," Mercer said. "It's me."

He found Hutton waiting by the elevator.

"I've got to go to work," Hutton said. He was dressed in the rank green coveralls.

"No, you don't."

"Oh, yes I do," Hutton said peevishly. "Simon doesn't pay my rent, like."

"But your landlord's not long for this world," Mercer said, with a faint crooked smile. "And your boss is bound for glory. So you don't have to go to work. No one cares."

Hutton looked at him without comprehension.

"Tee minus two and counting," Mercer said. "The balloon goes up tomorrow night."

Back in his apartment Hutton poured two drinks and for once Mercer did not decline. They sat with glasses of bourbon on the low black couch.

"Looks like your plants have croaked off altogether," Mercer said.

"Yeah. I guess."

"Maybe they knew what was going to go down. You talk to your plants, David? Doubt they'd want to hear anything we've got to say at this point."

Ice rattled in Hutton's glass.

"No need to get shaky," Mercer said. "We'll be out of range in plenty of time." He took an envelope out of his pocket and handed it to Hutton, who inspected the contents. A one-way plane ticket to Los Angeles, for the evening of the sixteenth.

"What's the idea?" Hutton said.

"The idea would seem to be that we don't want to be in New York tomorrow night. Since there might not be any New York for us to be in."

"L.A. I was stationed up the coast from there once, for a little while. Fort Ord."

"Yeah," Mercer said. "Maybe you can think of somebody you could visit." He passed Hutton another envelope, a thicker one.

"Jesus," Hutton said. "This is a lot of lettuce. Where'd you get it from?"

"Simon, more or less."

"Simon?"

"Let me tell you all about my interesting day." Mercer lit a cigarette, still talking. "See, first Simon gets this phone call yesterday afternoon. And whatever it is, it freaks him out. He's trying to cover it, but I can tell something's up. But he won't tell me what. All he tells me is go out and rent this car and buy these plane tickets for different places and so forth. Do this and do that. Then he hands me this credit card in some John Doe name. To pay for everything with."

"So how does this get you cash?"

"Well. Since Simon didn't mention any expense account, and time seems to be getting kind of short, I drew out the credit line on the card once I got done being the errand boy. I just gave you half of that."

"What about Ruben?"

"What about him? Let him look after himself."

"Simon won't like it you drew that money."

"Listen. *I don't care what Simon likes.* Simon would sell either one of us down the river for a dime and you'd better get that through your head quick, because if you don't, you could be gone, David, any time at all these next two days."

"Two days."

"Well, call it thirty-six hours."

"What's going on? Why didn't we get a briefing? I can't figure what's going on."

"Listen, you know perfectly well what's going on. Simon didn't tell me anything either. But I'm making an educated guess we're going to blow up the city of New York with a plutonium bomb sometime around when those tickets are for."

Hutton coughed; an amber trickle of his drink ran from the corner of his mouth.

"What's the problem, David? This is no news. You've known about it all along."

"I know I have," Hutton said, wiping his mouth on his sleeve. "I know, but it's different now. It makes me feel funny to think about it."

"Understatement of the year," Mercer said. "In fact, let's have another drink."

"I mean," Hutton said, when he came back with the glasses, "doesn't this seem kind of sudden to you? Like the last I heard, Ruben was still working on his goddamn gadgets. And besides. I thought we'd get told something, before we got to this point. I thought we'd be hearing a little more about the main plan."

"Well, you could look at it this way," Mercer said. "We're lucky. Think about all those people we've been bringing along through the clinic. They don't know nothing from nothing. They're just going to get blown to the moon."

"Yeah. What, we're just letting them go?"

"Looks that way. Simon must have decided they weren't worth it."

"Or the International."

"Right, Simon or the International."

"I just wish we knew a little more."

"Sure," Mercer said. "But so far it's rule-book procedure. We're in the cell. Simon's the leader of the cell. He's the only contact point. That's the way you're supposed to do it. What I don't like is the idea that if something breaks, the leader maybe gets away and the followers maybe don't."

"But Simon's got a plan. We've got these tickets."

"Sure, Simon's got a plan and we don't know what it is. I also have a plan, and I do know what it is. I kind of like mine better, so far."

"So what is it?"

"Let's think about Simon's for a minute first. Simon says, Ruben should go to Mazatlán, so I bought him a ticket for there. Simon goes to Zurich. To contact the International, so he says, which I guess means he's going to alert all the big-shot terrorists to turn on their TVs and watch the US news. You're supposed to go to Dallas, and I'm supposed to go to Chicago, but we're not doing that, see."

"No. See what?"

"Think about it. Simon's getting out of the country. So's Ruben. We're not. I wonder why? Maybe it's so if Simon needs a goat, he can feed us to the CIA. I mean, if this does go down, the government is going to be very annoyed. I don't think anybody needs to know where we are. Not Simon, not anybody. You follow me so far?"

"I guess. Where'll you go?"

Mercer laughed.

"Zurich. I booked the same flight as Simon."

"He'll freak out."

"Let him. What can he do? I've got a ticket and a bale of cash. He'll just have to grin and bear it. Either he'll let me go with him or I'll go anyway. I want to find out what he's up to."

"Reasonable."

"Glad you think so. I hope you appreciate I'm taking a little chance on you here. You're not going to say anything to Simon, are you?"

"No."

"Good. Because if you give him as much as a cross-eyed look, I'll shoot you in the back. Don't think I won't." Mercer stood up. "Come on. We've got things to do."

"Like what?"

"Like hump all the guns up to Times Square. Simon wants security. Let's get on it."

Mercer pulled his end of the couch away from the wall. Hutton knelt and began to unseal the cache. When he had opened the lid, he paused and looked up.

"Charlie?"

"Yeah?"

"Why are you even going along this far? If you don't trust Simon. Why not get out now?"

"I don't know," Mercer said. "Good question. Curiosity, I think."

"Killed the cat," Hutton grunted, pulling guns out of the wall.

"Sure," Mercer said. "Satisfaction brought it back."

The car loaded, Mercer and Hutton started up Seventh Avenue. Traffic was heavy and their progress was slow. Mercer turned off to the west in search of a less congested street.

"Will it work?" Hutton said.

"Will what work?"

"The bomb."

"Sure, it should work. I mean, Simon and Ruben try to make it into some tremendous high-tech mystery, but really it's fairly simple. All you have to do is get enough stuff glommed together somehow and you've got your explosion."

"Except you go up with it."

"True. That's what's making all the delay. Ruben's been building a detonator."

"Which might not work."

"That's why we've got Larkin."

"You know, nobody ever told me exactly what he's supposed to do."

"Oh," Mercer said. "Well, now. First he tries it with Ruben's detonator. If that doesn't work, he picks up the pieces and just . . . piles them all on top of each other. And hits them with a hammer or something, I don't know."

"You mean —"

"Right. Larkin the human, ah, I'm not sure what you'd really call it."

"That . . . that is *completely* crazy."

"Well," Mercer said equably, making a smooth turn onto Eleventh Avenue, "it was his own idea."

53
The Boiler

FAR BELOW the Times Square subway, well beneath the utility tunnels still in use, beyond a maze of disused passages, there was an abandoned cast-iron boiler, sunk into a floor. The boiler was eight feet deep and twelve feet in diameter. About three feet of its corroded surface stuck up out of the floor, and on top there was a two-foot hatch, secured with heavy clamps, through which someone might enter it. Whatever foundation had supported the big tank had eroded, so that the boiler tilted at an angle, but it was reasonably stable at the spot where it had settled.

Inside, Simon and Ruben Carrera labored against the slant of the floor. They wore full-body safety suits, which made them look rather like astronauts or divers. Each suit's material was heavy, and additionally weighed down by the metal helmet and the small airtank attached to the back. Inside the suits Simon and Carrera moved awkwardly. They could communicate by gesture alone.

It was hideously hot inside the boiler, and the suits made the heat more intolerable. Inside his helmet, Simon was nearly blinded by the sweat perpetually running over his eyes. Also, the heat made it very difficult for him to concentrate. But then Simon, for once, was not in charge. It was Carrera who gave the instructions now, indicating his wishes with motions of his clumsily gloved hand. Simon responded lethargically, almost in slow motion. His body and mind seemed to be gradually shutting down, component by component. A sour clammy pool of sweat was gathering in his boots. His vision was clouded by dark patches which seemed to spiral over his eyes.

Carrera knelt on the floor at the middle of the boiler, his gloved fingers slowly manipulating a spherical metal gadget somewhat larger than a medicine ball. The inner part of the sphere was composed of wedges which fit together like sections of an orange. The wedges were made of aluminum. The outer shell which contained them was steel. Carrera crooked his finger at a wooden crate against the wall of the boiler. Sluggishly Simon opened this box and removed some sticks of dynamite. Carrera began to fit these into pockets between the steel shell and the wedges.

For the moment there seemed nothing for Simon to do. He leaned against the wall, then slid down to a sitting position on the edge of the case of dynamite. Spreading out from the case in a circle around the wall were the twelve smaller boxes which held the plutonium and which, if Larkin had it straight, were leaking. Simon contemplated the boxes dimly, through the fogged glass visor of his helmet.

"God but it's hot down here," Hutton was saying. "I'd forgotten how hot it was."

He and Mercer were dragging two heavy duffel bags full of guns along a passageway. A barrel-sized pipe, drooling scalding water, ran along one side of the tunnel, and the two men pressed against the opposite wall to avoid it. Mercer was in the lead, carrying a flashlight which he aimed down the tunnel with his right hand.

"It's not much farther," Mercer said.

"But it won't be any cooler when we get there," Hutton said.

"True."

Mercer had stopped; before him there was a star-shaped hole in the floor. He aimed the flashlight into it, then nodded to himself. "This way." Mercer lowered himself into the cavity. Hutton passed both duffel bags to him and dropped down after them.

"Ouch."

"Got to bend your knees when you do that."

The new passage went off at an angle to the one above, curving gently to the right. As Mercer and Hutton followed it the curve became more pronounced, finally tightening into a claustrophobic spiral. Always just before them was a wall. Then the tunnel opened into a wide, rectangular area, with three more passages coming off the corners. Mercer crossed this space and entered the tunnel directly opposite. After thirty feet or so he had come into a small square room. Mercer stopped. The cone of his flashlight swept across the exposed section of the boiler.

"Here we go," Mercer said. He crouched over the duffel bag he'd been carrying, took out the Skorpion machine gun, and fit a clip into it.

"What's that for?" Hutton said.

"You never know," Mercer muttered. With the gun tucked into his armpit he walked to the boiler and began kicking the side of it with the toe of his shoe. Clang and echo blended in the little room. After a minute the clamps on the hatch began to squeal and Mercer stopped kicking. The hatch opened and a space-suited figure emerged ponderously and sat with its legs dangling into the opening. The suit paused a moment, then swung its legs up and refastened the hatch. The suit removed its helmet. Simon was inside.

"How goes it?" Mercer said, stepping back a bit.

Simon's neck craned, frail-looking inside the huge round collar of the suit. "All right," Simon said. "On schedule, or close." Mercer had left the flashlight tilted on the duffel bag, and it illuminated Simon's jawline from below; his face was barely visible. Simon removed one of his gloves and wiped at his face and hair.

"We could use some help in there," he said. "Charles . . ."

Simon stopped to breathe, his head sunk in his hand. "David. David, stay up here and cover the tunnels. Charles, you come back down with me and help Ruben."

"Sure," Mercer said. "Where's my space suit?"

"There's only two," Simon said.

"Forget it," Mercer said, lifting the machine gun one-handed and silently unfolding the stock. "No way."

"What?" Simon said, as though he really had not heard. "What did you say?"

"I said," Mercer enunciated carefully, "I'm not going down there without protection."

"You'll do what I tell you," Simon rapped out.

"No." The word was punctuated with a click. Simon looked toward Mercer, assisting the turn of his head with his hand. The light was poor but Simon could see the machine gun raised in his direction; everything looked to be in working order. Simon began to whistle an irritating little theme from Jacques Brel. After a few seconds the tune collapsed into a monotonic nasal hum, then to a mere exhalation. Simon drew another breath.

"Very well," he said. "We'll work in shifts."

Mercer lowered the gun a hair.

"Guard detail," Simon said slowly, "and work detail. You and David both keep watch. Stay in earshot, please." Simon replaced his glove and helmet and lowered himself painfully back into the boiler.

Carrera had taken off his suit. Simon made a gesture of dismay. Carrera's mouth moved soundlessly. By reflex, Simon lifted off his own helmet in order to hear what he was saying.

"I can't work in that thing," Carrera said. "I have to have my fingers. This is the tricky part."

"But you'll get radiation sickness," Simon said.

"There can't be all that much exposure," Carrera said. "I don't understand how there could be anything wrong with the seals in the first place."

Simon considered. He was unable to focus on the point that Carrera had to be absolutely wrong, because the bone-racking heat made his proposition seem so rational and right. Simon undid the fastening of his own suit and stripped it off. He did not feel much cooler, but it was good to be relieved of the weight.

"We'll have to put them on again when we open the boxes," he said. "We have to do that at least."

"Yes," Carrera said impatiently. "When we get to that. Get me some of those caps. Careful."

On the floor beside the dynamite crate Simon found a carton full of blasting caps. He began to pass them to Carrera, who took each one and delicately crimped it over the end of a dynamite stick. Done with that, he began connecting the leads from the caps to a battery-powered alarm clock which was taped to the outside of the steel shell. Simon sat back on his heels.

"How is it?" Simon said.

"Good. Nothing much to do after this but put the payload into the wedges."

"Will it be all right?" Simon said. "Is it going to work?"

"I think so," Carrera said. "I don't see why it wouldn't."

"That was just a little hairy," Hutton said, when Simon had descended back into the boiler.

"Maybe. But I'm not going to mess around with that stuff in my bare skin, thank you. Not if Simon and Ruben won't."

"Simon seemed kind of out of it."

"Could be the heat."

"Yeah. It's terrible."

"What now?" Mercer said.

"Guard duty."

"Who would ever come down here? Let's go try and find some air." Mercer picked up the flashlight and led the way into another tunnel.

"Where we going?" Hutton said.

"I think there was an air shaft down this way." Mercer walked steadily on, sweat pouring into the corners of his eyes. Hutton's breathing was ragged behind him. After about a hundred yards the passage intersected with another. Mercer stopped. To his left he heard a rustling. He jerked the light around and the beam fell on a troop of large gray rats. The rats stared back at him, unafraid, eyes shining red from the reflection.

"Ugh," Hutton said, coming up behind him. Mercer said nothing. He turned off to the right.

"You think they'd come after us?" Hutton said.

"We ought to be equal to a few rats with all this firepower."

"Gives me the creeps just the same. I hope there's nothing worse down here."

"Shut up, why don't you," Mercer said. "Don't you feel a breeze?"

In fact there was a faint movement of air in the tunnel ahead of them. The two walked on. After a few more yards the tunnel made a sharp turn to the right and dead-ended into a vertical shaft. Mercer aimed the flashlight up. Ladder rungs were driven into the curved wall, receding toward infinity. Mercer switched off the lamp. Far above, a patch of grayish daylight shone like a star.

"Load it and it's ready to go," Carrera mumbled. He was sitting in a pool of sweat against the wall of the boiler.

"We'll need the suits for that," Simon said groggily.

Carrera's response seemed slow in coming. "We need a break," he finally said. Unsteadily, he got up.

"All right," Simon said. He adjusted a stepladder under the hatch, climbed up and opened it.

"David? Charles?"

Only the echo returned.

"God damn it," Simon said.

"What's the problem?" Carrera said from below.

"They've wandered off somewhere." Simon dragged himself out of the hatch and Carrera came up after him.

"So we have to wait," Carrera said.

"No. I'll stay. You go on and take a breather." Simon took the second Sten from the duffel bag and leaned against the boiler, cradling the gun in both arms.

"Are you sure?" Carrera said.

Simon laughed inanely. "I'm getting used to it," he said. "You go on. Take the flashlight."

Carrera stared at him.

"I don't know," he said. "The air's not good down here."

"But people lived down here," Simon said, giggling a bit.

"Not this far down they didn't," Carrera said. "All right. I won't be long. You'd better have a suck on the oxygen tank though, if you feel dizzy."

Carrera walked into the outer room where the other tunnels began.

"Ruben," Simon called, "take a gun."

Carrera sighed but obediently turned back and picked up the Beretta from one of the bags. Then he moved away down a far tunnel, the one by which Mercer and Hutton had come. Simon watched the light bobbing off around the bend and allowed his eyes to close. He did feel giddy. The air was bad. Simon rocked the Sten in his arms, back and forth, crooning aloud.

"Take a gun, pick up a gun, bring along your little gun . . ."

Unnerved at the sound of this, Simon silenced himself. His temples were throbbing, perhaps from the heat. Darkness whispered all around him.

Hutton had taken off his shirt and was mopping his face and trunk with it. He had brought a Sten along with him and now it stood propped against a ladder rung. Mercer sat on the floor of the shaft, with the flashlight between his feet, shining down the tunnel they had come from.

"It's like hell down here," Hutton said.

"Yeah. Hard to believe that people could live here."

"I know. God they were weird looking."

"I'd rather have the rats," Mercer said.

"I'm glad they're gone." Hutton sat down, his drenched shirt twisted and draped over his shoulders. Mercer lit a cigarette. Smoke coiled greasily up the shaft.

"Wonder if anybody'll see that up top?" Hutton said.

"Doubt it."

"How long you think we'll be down here?"

"No idea," Mercer said.

"How long you think it's been already?"

"I don't know," Mercer said. "It's hard to say."

More time passed unmeasured. Hutton had begun to snore. Mercer's eyes were heavy. He turned out the light and leaned back into the wall. The scrap of daylight up above was fading into black.

Carrera lifted himself through the jagged hole into the upper passage. Though he would have preferred to reach a higher, cooler level, he lacked the energy to go on. He sat cross-legged on the floor with the Beretta resting in his lap. The flashlight rolled out of his numbing fingers and twirled away to one side. Dully, Carrera looked along the beam. About ten feet away from him, in a nest of pipes, was a pallet made of cardboard and newspaper, with a few empty cans scattered around it. One of the tunnel people must have slept there, before Carrera and the others had driven them all away.

Then the air here must be reasonably safe. Carrera relaxed, giving way to his exhaustion, smiling a little. In spite of his extreme fatigue, he was more confident now than before. Drowsing, Carrera recalled Simon's doubting questions with a royal contempt. The bomb was fine. It was a perfect bomb. It was going to work like a dream.

54
Larkin Makes a Deal

MORNING, JANUARY 16. Larkin stood on the sidewalk opposite the row of shells where for the last few months he had lived, if you cared to call it living. He was braced with four raw eggs that Dutch had beaten for him in a cup, and his mind was lit with clear post-epileptic tranquillity. Hand in pocket, Larkin pricked his thumb on the tricorner folds of a five- and a ten-dollar bill Dutch had loaned him without inquiry.

Across the way it was still as death. Larkin waited. It was very early. Strangely, the otherwise silent street resounded with birdsong, though he could see no birds. The twisted tree shivered before the window frame that had lately served Larkin as a door. For the first time it occurred to him that the corpse of the strangler would almost certainly still be there. But the building presented a perfectly neutral face, no hint of any spirit power working either good or ill.

A young Latino came out of the empty doorframe of the shooting gallery and crossed the street toward Larkin on jellied legs. He stopped in front of Larkin, cocked his head, said something unintelligible, and held out his palm. Larkin remained still, eyes front, noting privately that the young man, boy really, wore only a denim jacket and no shirt against the cold. The boy swung at him without preface; Larkin drew his head back fractionally and avoided the blow. The boy walked off muttering. In the doorway of the shooting gallery a black man in pea coat and watch cap had appeared. He scanned the street in both directions, eyes flicking over Larkin with a reptilian lack of interest. A purely physical thrill ran through Larkin's nervous system, bound in the general direction of his hypothalamus. At other fairly unmemorable low points of the past, he had done this sort of thing before. Larkin crossed the street.

"A C-and-D."

The man in the pea coat said nothing. His hat was pulled down to his eyebrows. He did not move his head, but his eyes tracked sideways to cover Larkin. Both hands in coat pockets. Larkin raised his own left hand to his waist, letting a green corner of cash peep out of the top of his fist.

"Nothing for you here," the man said. Somehow he had contrived to speak without moving his mouth at all.

"Sure?" Larkin said. He opened his hand, let the triangle of bills lie on his open palm, numbers legible. The man blinked in slow motion. Larkin flipped his hand over, letting the money fall on the top step.

"Keep it then, I can't use it," he said, turning away, taking a pace or two down the block toward the Bowery. Something bounced lightly off a spot between his shoulder blades. Larkin swung round. The man in the pea coat had disappeared. In the litter on the pavement before him lay two small mint-green envelopes of a suitable size for holding something like eyeglass screws. Larkin stooped and picked them up.

Halfway to Houston Street he stopped cold, chilled by recognition of an oversight. He walked unwillingly back to the line of shells, and, allowing no time for hesitation, he scaled the ironwork and flopped in through the window. Once in, he looked back out. The branches of the tree, he noted with mild disbelief, were studded with tight new buds, bitter, hard and promising. *Let me see what I want to see,* Larkin thought, chiefly addressing his superstitions. When he turned from the window his eye fell first on his own flat-black shoulder bag, intact and improbably still there.

Larkin thumbed it up to his left shoulder, the strap fitting comfortably into the groove there. His hand fell over the zipped outer pocket, palpated, identified reassuring forms. Larkin was ready to go.

But the room was oddly bright and ordinary with daylight. Corners which had sheltered devils the night before now held only plaster dust. The only thing in the least respect unusual was the body positioned just left of center on the floor, head cocked back on a stiffened neck, one leg drawn up and the other straight. Fanned out on the floor around the lower body was a near-black, sticky-looking substance which resembled roofing tar. Larkin's clinician's camera eye paused on a cut inside the body's left thigh, which he could presume had severed the big artery running there.

Setting down his bag, Larkin went to the dead man and squatted on the floor beside him. The corpse was rigid, vacant, and to Larkin without significance of any kind. A man of under-average height and almost pitiably thin, he lay with his arms flung out behind him, fingers curled to grasp some object that was gone. His pointed goatee thrust at the ceiling; the ridge of his thinning hair ran back onto the floor. His eyes were open but clouded over with a dull bluish mist, as though he might have suddenly gone blind. Whatever energy could have moved him had drained away with his blood and life through the gash in his leg and left no trace of itself behind.

Looking curiously into the corpse's milky eyes, Larkin found he could not remember why on the previous night it had seemed so vitally important that he should live and this man die. The thought came to him unattended by any distress of conscience; it was only a failure of recollection, irritating as an almost-remembered task or name. Cautiously Larkin reached and pressed down on the dead man's palm, and the whole body rocked a little, inevitably connected to itself. Then he remembered the things he had to do, difficult and demanding things, some of them perhaps impossible.

Still squatting, he pivoted on his heels to face the window. A drab brown bird had landed on the tree and it too turned round, sending a little tremor down a branch. Larkin took the two green packets out of his pocket and shook the two different powders into one. Then he divided the mixture, rolling up the second envelope to save. The bird bounced on the limb, head flicking from angle to angle, studying Larkin's movements. Larkin flexed the first envelope, bringing a line of powder to its mouth along the crease, and got it up his nose with two hard sniffs. He stood up. There was no immediate effect. Larkin got his bag and started for the window. The bird saw his approach and flew.

55
Worm

LARKIN TWITCHED his way up the Bowery to Houston Street and banged into the dim shades of the bar. No one was there but Rusty, who sat on a revolving stool before the counter, swinging gently back and forth in a doze.

"Where's Worm?" Larkin said, a little loudly and abruptly. Rusty raised his head and squinted at the light of the open door.

"Don't know'm," Rusty said.

"Yes, you do," Larkin said. "The one from the tunnels, the one that's white all over. He was here the other night. Sleeping on the floor."

Rusty swung a semicircle on his stool, displaying the emptiness of the bar with his huge knobby hand outstretched, and shrugged. Larkin slammed out and came to a halt in the street. A piece missing from his plan so early quite dismayed him, and his nerves were already a bit raw from the cocaine, which also made him grind his numbing teeth. Cocaine demanded movement. Larkin lunged around the corner toward Second Avenue, with some half-formed intention of quartering the neighborhood.

Different casualties of the previous night were strewn in doorways down the block, but none that he was looking for. Larkin turned down Chrystie Street and walked a block, two blocks. Above Delancey Street another derelict lay sandwiched between a water spigot and the wall. His form was mostly covered up with rags, but Larkin knew the fishy pallor of his trailing hand. He pounced on Worm and snatched him up. The sewer fish hung light and boneless in his hands. Larkin shook him.

"Wake up," he said. "Wake up wake up." Worm's head bobbled loosely on his neck; his eyes opened and closed at random like a mechanical doll's eyes. Worm began to burble what might have been sheer nonsense or words of an unknown tongue. Larkin locked his hands behind the other's head, holding it steady.

"Talk English," Larkin said. "Talk sense. You have to take me in the tunnels." Worm's eyes came clear with terror.

"*No,*" he said, quite distinctly. He ducked out of Larkin's hands, but Larkin caught him by the shoulders and raised him up again.

"I've got to get down there," Larkin said. "Just show me how to get in."

Worm slipped away with an eel's alacrity; Larkin snatched the clothes around his neck and pinned him to the wall, then dropped his own head down as if to butt. Something hot and roaring burst underneath his sternum and sent mindless jet surges of energy all through him. It was the second part of the mix kicking in, the heroin. It would be there for a while. Larkin looked Worm over and with chemically induced ruthlessness he slapped him twice on each side of his face. Two black hookers standing on the corner turned to point and giggle.

"Bust him another'n," one said. Larkin bounced Worm off the wall, not too hard but hard enough.

"Take me to the tunnels," he said. "This is very important for me and for both of us." Worm's eyes darted then fell dull and hopeless.

"D train," Worm said, speaking clearly once again.

Larkin rode uptown with one hand locked around Worm's upper arm, the arm so thin that his fingers met his thumb. Worm slumped to the other side, keeping as much distance from Larkin as the circumstances admitted.

"Don't go there," Worm said, and kept on saying it over and over. "You don't want to go. Not nice."

"Why not?" Larkin said. "What's not nice about it?" Worm wriggled and squinched his eyes.

"Bad people," he said. "Bad people came. Sickness. Guns."

"I just want to make the bad people go away," Larkin said.

"Can't," Worm said. "They're stronger."

At 42nd Street they got off and Worm led the way to the crosstown shuttle track, still in Larkin's grip. They walked to the western end of the platform, where Worm sidled onto a concrete ledge that continued down the tunnel, a few feet above the tracks. Because the ledge was too narrow for them to walk side by side, Larkin had to release Worm's arm, but he kept close behind, well within snatching range.

Larkin thought they must be almost under Broadway when he saw the lights of a westbound train approaching. Worm jumped down off the ledge onto the tracks. Maybe a suicide bid, Larkin thought, but he followed anyway, lifting his legs high to clear the electrified third rail. A pair of rats broke for cover toward a fissure in the far wall and Worm went after them into it. Reaching the opening, Larkin saw it was an open service door. It was unlit on the other side but he could hear Worm clattering down a steel ladder and he pursued. At the bottom Worm broke and ran down the passageway into thorough darkness. Larkin chased him, running effortlessly on cresting waves of heroin. He caught Worm by the back of his collar and pulled him up short.

Worm bent double, panting so hard he seemed to sob. Larkin let him rest, staring at the solid dark and seeing nothing at all. He had completely lost his sense of direction during the chase. Worm began to breathe more easily and Larkin felt him straighten up.

"Show me where the bad people are," Larkin said. Worm gasped and pulled away, getting nowhere.

"I'm sorry," Larkin said, pulling him back. "Just put me on the way."

Worm began to march down the tunnel, stooping, his arms clutched over the front of his body as if his stomach hurt. Larkin followed, still holding him with one hand, cupping his bag with the other. The ceiling was apparently getting lower; soon Larkin also had to stoop. From changes in the air flow he could guess that they were passing other openings to the left and right but these were perfectly invisible. Ahead of him, Worm snuffled like a dog.

Larkin had to assume that Worm could see in the dark, or else he operated by sense of smell or sonar, for somehow he was making decisions, turning onto new passageways, sorting out the maze. At last the two of them dropped through a shallow hole to another level. Here it was very hot. They sat where they had fallen, backs to the wall. Worm tried to rise and Larkin got up with him, still clinging to his shirt. Worm moved forward. The passage became narrower and much lower so that both of them had to bend to their knees. Larkin was reaching over Worm's entire back to keep his grip on the collar. Worm held his hands up under him; Larkin felt his elbows bobbing as he fumbled at something on his abdomen.

Then Larkin was holding an empty shirt. He rose and tried to run, but immediately smashed his head into the ceiling. Rubbing the lump and gritting his teeth, he made what haste he could, keeping his head ducked down. He could hear Worm scuttling off ahead; the man could evidently go on all fours as quickly as a rat. The ceiling lowered further. Larkin was forced to crawl on the floor. Then the tunnel narrowed enough to catch his bag and he had to back up and go on pushing the bag in front of him. He could no longer hear anything ahead.

The bag popped out into a wider, higher space and Larkin followed it. He stood up, arms outstretched like a sleep-walker, and instantly burned his fingers on something damp and scalding. Larkin sucked the burned spots quietly. To the right he thought he heard an echo of someone running and he set off after it.

Larkin ran in the total dark, the bag flopping and pounding his left side. In spite of the drug he was beginning to flag. Occasionally he lurched and scorched some part of himself against the huge boiling pipe on the wall. The sound of his own movement drowned out any other noise, and he had no confidence that Worm was still ahead of him, but he kept on.

Then, amazingly, he *saw* him: an arachnid figure whirling its limbs before a shocking burst of light. Worm windmilled his arms, turned back, flinched from Larkin, and darted to one side. Larkin caught up and followed him into a side passage. But after some little distance, he sensed the tunnel had branched. Larkin felt his way along the walls and made out three different openings. No sound came from any of them. It would have been an idea to bring a flashlight, Larkin realized. Without one, he just might consider himself lost. Then again, someone seemed to have a light down here. Larkin began to grope his way slowly back toward where he thought it had been.

56
Times Square (I)

CARRERA WOKE UP with no sense of the time. The flashlight beam spread out on the floor in front of him seemed to have yellowed, but he could not be sure of that. He had not meant to sleep at all. There were slow footsteps coming down the tunnel. It must be Simon; he'd left Simon alone for much too long. Except the sound was coming from the wrong direction. Carrera jumped up, clutching the Beretta across his chest, then aiming it down the tunnel.

A pair of feet came into the farthest weak reach of the beam of light and stopped there. Carrera looked at the shoes and did not recognize them.

"Who's there?" he called. "Stay where you are." *Are-are-are* his own voice came bouncing back.

"It's only me." The voice came from just above the shoes, vaguely familiar but so masked with echo that Carrera could not be sure of its identity.

"Don't move," Carrera said. With the Beretta's stock clamped in his armpit, he bent and picked up the flashlight and played it down the tunnel. There was the maniac, Larkin, idiotically dressed for cold surface weather, wearing his heavy black bum's overcoat and carrying, of all ridiculous things, a whole suitcase on a shoulder strap. The coat was so baggy and out-sized that Larkin seemed to have no arms, and the sleeves of it completely covered up his hands, which troubled Carrera for some reason not quite clear to him. Great balls of sweat burst out of Larkin's head at the hairline and rolled all over his face. Larkin took a few slow steps forward.

"*Stop that,*" Carrera yelled. "Stop moving. Don't move any more."

"It's just me," Larkin said reasonably. "Just Larkin. That light hurts my eyes a little."

"You shouldn't be here yet," Carrera said. "How did you get here anyway? You're not supposed to be — will you *stand still?*"

Larkin had begun to walk again; he was not much more than twenty feet away.

"What do I have to do?" Carrera said. "Do I have to shoot you? You can believe it, I've got a gun." Left-handed he turned the flashlight down over the barrel of the Beretta.

"Oh," Larkin said. "So you do."

Under the flashlight Larkin could see the machine gun crouched in Carrera's armpit like some angry little animal. He dropped his left hand, hidden in its sleeve, over the side pocket of his bag and began to open the zipper, quarter inch by quarter inch so as to make no noise. At the same time he tried a few more steps forward. Carrera jerked the gun up; gun and flashlight clanked together. Larkin froze. Carrera set the flashlight carefully on the top of the hot pipe and returned his hand to the front grip of his gun. The light was in Larkin's eyes again and he squinted. The short time he'd spent here underground had made him quite unused to light. He forced his hand down in the bag, blind fingers circling, searching, and began to move forward again.

"One more step and I shoot you, Larkin," Carrera said. "I swear to God I will."

"Okay," Larkin said. "But why? I only came to help."

"I don't need your help," Carrera said. "I don't want it. I never asked for you, Larkin. I'd rather you were gone."

Carrera came a little forward so that the light shone on him, too. The scar on the side of his face was a twisted knot of shadow; shadow hooded his eyes as well.

"Don't you need me, Ruben?" Larkin said. "Who else would blow the bomb?" His coat fluttered, as though he'd meant to spread his hands and changed his mind about it.

"*I'll blow the bomb with the detonator,*" Carrera hissed. "Who says it won't work? Who? You? You just want a way to die. Don't you want me to shoot you?"

"No," Larkin said. "Not quite yet."

Carrera came a little closer. *Closer, closer,* Larkin thought; the distance between them was now about ten feet.

"I think I should shoot you," Carrera said. "I really feel like I ought to shoot you."

"Simon might not like that," Larkin said.

"Why?" Carrera said. "Why would he care? I built the bomb, not you. I built it."

"Of course," Larkin said. "Of course you did. Everybody knows that, Ruben. I'm just . . . a *part* of the bomb."

"You're unnecessary," Carrera said. Larkin studied the machine gun, rock-steady in his hands.

"Maybe you're right," Larkin said, "but Simon might not think so."

Carrera hesitated. "Simon didn't say you were coming now, either. I think you're up to something, Larkin. Give me one good reason why you came down here today."

"I don't know," Larkin said. "April fool?" The Beretta wavered slightly to one side and Larkin dropped to his right knee and began squeezing the trigger of the Browning automatic he'd taken from the truck driver in Virginia, shooting through the fabric of the bag and rotating the whole bag on the pivot of his raised left hip as he overbalanced and began to fall backward. Carrera jerked the machine gun against his shoulder once, twice, but it did not seem to fire, and then the gun jumped out of Carrera's arms, which went on jerking in spasms on nothing as he too fell. Larkin drew his left hand with the gun in it out of the bag and disengaged it from the strap. He crawled over to where Carrera lay on his back, still breathing with a horrid vacuous sucking sound from the wounds in his chest.

"My God, but you're bleeding," Larkin said out loud and delivered a mercy shot through Carrera's temples, closing his eyes so as not to see the effect of it, and pulled the trigger again, but the clip was empty. Larkin threw the gun away and began to gag, propped on his elbows, eyes shut tight; this was not nausea but a knot in his chest strangling him and Larkin was laughing and starting to cry, too. He had killed three men but virtually failed to notice the first two of them;

with the strangler it had all taken place in the dark and the truck driver had just crumpled neatly over Larkin's knife blade like something being folded away for future use. Nothing like this, not like murdering Ruben so dreadfully, Ruben whom he'd known, if not much liked, and who'd had practically no life to take, which somehow seemed to make it all the worse. Larkin's fingers dug deep into the meat of his face, trying to squeeze out tears but none would come, only dry sobs and the animal groaning he could hear now above the gunshots ringing in his ears.

Larkin sat back and pounded his chest to start his breathing. The flashlight was still balanced on the pipe and he could see the Beretta machine gun lying where Ruben had flung it on the floor. Larkin got up and took the flashlight, winced at the heat of it and set it down. Now he could feel how hot he was, he was suffocating, and he took off his overcoat and then his shirt too. There was a thick smell of gunpowder in the tunnel that would not dissipate. Larkin shone the flashlight down the passage past Carrera's body, and noticed the jagged hole in the floor. When he pointed the light down in the hole he could see what looked like boot tracks in the sludge on the floor of the lower level, some sort of trail for him to follow, the only one he had.

Larkin went back for the machine gun and jumped down the hole with it, landing clumsily and bruising his heels. He started along the passage with the light trained on the footprints. The metal of the machine gun warmed to his bare skin, the weight and shape of it awkward in the crook of his right elbow where it rested. "Lord Jesus Christ have mercy on me a sinner," Larkin said aloud, and laughed bitterly at the sound of it; a fine thing to be saying as you crept underground toward hell, he thought, killing various people along your way. But he kept on saying the prayer silently as he walked, feeling the words of it with his tongue, for it did seem some comfort. His own steps made a sucking noise that recalled the sound of Ruben's dying breath, and that made Larkin stop and sob again.

57
Times Square (II)

MERCER DREAMED that he was dead, decayed, and stripped to bone; his skeleton rattled against a wall, but with a sound like metal . . . He came awake with Hutton shaking him.

"Hey," Mercer put out his hands on Hutton's wrists. He leaned back and looked up the shaft; there was light again above.

"Good Lord, we must have slept through the whole night."

"Shut up," Hutton said in a low whisper. "Talk quiet."

"What is it?"

"Shots." Hutton knelt at the mouth of the tunnel with his Sten thrust out before him. His voice barely disturbed the air. Mercer moved nearer so he could hear him.

"Can't believe it didn't wake you up," Hutton said.

"So maybe Ruben and Simon shot a rat."

"Uh uh," Hutton said. "I wish. It wasn't any of our pieces, though."

"You can tell?"

"I was in the Army, don't forget. I know what guns sound like."

"Echoes and things down here, you could make a mistake."

"Maybe," Hutton said. "Maybe not. This was single shots. What we got's automatic. I heard four, five, one after the other. Then one a little later. I'd swear it was a handgun. We don't have any handguns."

Mercer blinked, recalling his dream uneasily. What if it were premonitory? He was not especially superstitious, as a rule. But the situation was weird. Mercer felt for the Skorpion and picked it up.

"Okay," he said. "Okay, you scared me. What do you think we should do?"

"Recon," Hutton said. "Either that or sit and wait."

"Let's recon, then."

"Check." Hutton got up and began tiptoeing down the passage. Mercer got the flashlight and followed.

"Shut that light," Hutton said.

"What for?"

"So whatever's up there can't see it. I'd like to see them first if there's a way to work it out."

The two of them padded along in the dark. Mercer remembered this tunnel had been straight, but now that he could not see it, it seemed to curve. Hutton stopped suddenly and Mercer ran into his back.

"This place reminds me of a goddamn crab trap," Mercer said irritably.

"Ssh," Hutton said. "Listen."

A long, low moaning came down the tunnel, seemingly from just ahead of them.

"God, it must be a ghost," Mercer said. Goose flesh pricked on his arms.

"Ssh," Hutton said. The moan came again and ended in a rattling choking sound. Hutton turned around and whispered low in Mercer's ear. "It sounds like someone *crying,* for Christ's sake."

Larkin's state of mind was not the best. He had traced the line of footprints to the big rectangular room, where they doubled, crisscrossed, and became confused. One set of tracks detached from the jumble and went off to the left, and for no special reason he had followed these. But he was troubled about what might happen when he got to wherever they led. The painkilling properties of the heroin were on the wane and a backlash vacuum of depression sucked eagerly at Larkin's head and heart. Whenever he thought of Ruben, he lost control of his faculties, had to set down the gun and flashlight to gnash his teeth and wail out loud before he could go on.

The keening sound disintegrated into hoarse and heavy breathing.

"That's not a ghost," Hutton said. "That's somebody."

"Better have a look-see."

"Yeah."

They inched a little farther down the tunnel in the dark. Then Hutton stopped again.

"I think we're near the corner," he whispered. "Wait a second. Look."

Mercer stared, straining his eyes to the limit. The corner was there. On the wall of the side passage he saw very faint, fragmented light, trapped in beads of water on the wall. Hutton touched his arm, drew him to the turning, and hissed into his ear again.

"Got the light?"

Mercer nodded.

"Okay," Hutton said. "We're going around this corner. Together. I'm the gunner. As soon as we make the turn, you hit the light. Got it?"

Mercer nodded again, his ear bobbing against Hutton's face.

"All right," Hutton said. *"Go."* They swung around the corner in unison, Mercer punching the button on the flashlight, and as he heard Hutton flick a switch on the Sten, he tried to bring the Skorpion up to his shoulder with his right hand unassisted. In the wavering beam of the flashlight he saw a figure jumping up from the floor twenty or thirty feet back; it was Larkin, bare chested and grimy, eyes red as the tunnel rats' eyes, and with his own machine gun at the ready.

"Get back," Hutton was shouting, and Mercer, unsure if he or Larkin was being addressed, felt himself freezing under Larkin's flashlight, his body unable to follow a decision; then without knowing how he had moved, he was back around the corner, shoulder to shoulder with Hutton, both of them panting against the wall.

"I don't think I like this," Mercer said.

"You and me both."

"What the hell you think's going on?"

"Couldn't tell you. He's got our Beretta, that's one thing."

"You're sure it's ours?"

"Ours or one just like it."

"You left it in the bags, didn't you? Maybe he just came along and picked it up."

"Yeah. Or Simon might have given it to him."

"So everything could be okay," Mercer said.

"It could be," Hutton said. "But what about those shots I heard?"

"I killed Ruben," Larkin said. "I don't want to have to kill you."

Larkin switched off his flashlight and crawled silently toward the end of the tunnel. He could see the elliptical shape the others' light cast on the rear wall of their passage. Close to the turn, he rose to a squatting position and edged up to the corner, where he laid his head against the wall.

"I'm right here," Larkin said softly. "Why don't we talk?"

Mercer and Hutton jumped out of their skins.

"That —" Hutton silenced Mercer with a hand over his mouth.

"You've got to talk low," he whispered in his ear. "He can hear us."

"That tears it," Mercer mumbled. "No Ruben, no bomb."

"What do you think he did it for?"

"How would I know? He's crazy, like you always said."

Turning toward the corner, Hutton noticed an inch of Larkin's gun barrel protruding past the wall. He prodded Mercer.

"Look at that."

"Jesus. You think he knows how to shoot that thing?"

"Don't know. I think we better assume he does."

"Yeah," Mercer said. Then, raising his voice to normal speaking tones, "Larkin. You there?"

"I'm here." The voice was alarmingly close.

"What did you want to talk about?" Mercer said. "What have you been doing?"

"I shot Ruben," Larkin said. "I didn't want to. He said he was going to shoot me."

"Where's Simon?" Mercer said.

"I don't know. I didn't see him."

"This is all screwed up," Hutton whispered.

"This is all screwed up, Larkin," Mercer said. "What do you want us to do?"

"I think —" Larkin hesitated. "I think I want you both to go away. So I don't have to kill you. I always liked you, really. Ever since we met. I don't have anything against you."

"Likewise," Mercer said. "How about if we kill you?"

"I don't think so," Larkin said, as though he were weighing this suggestion carefully, objectively. "There's a few more things I need to do. Besides, why would you want to?"

"Well," Mercer said. "You did shoot Ruben."

"You never liked him, though," Larkin said. "That wouldn't be a reason."

"What are you up to?" Mercer said. "Why are you doing all this?"

"I'd rather not say."

"Sweet Jesus," Mercer said. "Now he's being coy."

"I never wanted to kill anybody," Larkin explained. "I know I did it, but I really never wanted to. Things just kept turning out that way."

"The hell with it," Mercer whispered. "Screw him and his conscience, I'm shooting the little sonofabitch right now." He picked up the Skorpion. Hutton caught his arm.

"Don't even think about it," he whispered. "You ever shoot a machine gun into a corner? There'll be rounds flying around here like a hailstorm. If anybody pulls a trigger, we're all gonna get hit with it."

"Interesting," Mercer said. "You probably should tell Larkin that."

Hutton told him.

"Oh," Larkin said.

"Now what?" Mercer said.

"You could both just go away," Larkin said. "You could go somewhere and live a long time instead of getting shot down here in this hole."

"This is true," Mercer said. "What do you say, David?"

"What about the International?" Hutton said. "They'll execute us if we drop out now."

"There isn't any International," Larkin said. "Simon's been putting you on."

"I don't believe that," Hutton said.

"Why not?" Mercer said. "It would be just like him."

"It would be, wouldn't it?" Larkin said.

"I don't see the International down here now anyway," Mercer said, glancing again at the nose of Larkin's machine gun.

"Sufficient unto the day is the evil thereof," Larkin said.

"Now he's quoting the Scriptures," Mercer said with a wondering laugh. "Well, how about it, David?"

"I guess," Hutton said.

"Hear that, Larkin?" Mercer said. "We accept the offer. Congratulations. You win."

"Good," Larkin said. "I'll let you come out past me if you put down your guns."

"I think not, thanks all the same," Mercer said. "There's a way out this way."

"Good," Larkin said. "That's nice to know."

Mercer and Hutton climbed up the ladder toward the top of the shaft. They had abandoned the flashlight but they still carried the guns in slings made of their shirts. The patch of daylight was broadening up above them.

"What about Simon?" Hutton grunted from below. "Shouldn't we have done something about him?"

"Simon's dead," Mercer said, without premeditation, but he was suddenly convinced his words were true.

58
Times Square (III)

CLOSING HIS EYES, Larkin deepened the darkness around him, felt his heart rising and falling like a tide. Fatigue brought sharp fleeting images across the backs of his eyelids; then he was looking into the heart of a lush green tree, bursting with white cross-shaped flowers and alive with birds, gay and richly colored, singing with a single voice he knew to be intelligent,

compassionate even, though the sense of it passed his understanding. Gazing farther into the tree he saw its contorted
skeleton of branches and recognized it for the blighted plant
that had trembled outside the window of the shell all winter
long . . . Larkin opened his eyes with a jerk and the imageless
underground night returned. He still had to sort things out
with Simon, and that might turn out to be difficult. Larkin
found the second envelope in his pocket and did up the rest
of his dope.

Addled by noxious underground gases, Simon was hallucinating too. He felt himself small and helpless, lifted up by
stronger hands in the midst of the air above the night city,
the gemstone lights patterned out below him like a carpet.
Then as though it really were fabric, the tissue of lights bil-
lowed slowly up, wavered and wound into a single strand, a
chain of real jewels, he saw now, on his mother's aging wrin-
kling neck. Simon emerged from this daze with his mind made
incoherent by a sharp unfamiliar sense of loss, of error,
thinking confusedly that he needed oxygen. Far away he heard
the sound of gunfire, five, six shots together, a pause, and
then one more. Simon pushed himself off the edge of the
boiler and lurched through the short passage into the large
rectangular room where he stopped and peered uselessly into
the dark, the Sten held out rigid in his hands.
    Nothing visited his senses. Simon, his head clearer now,
cursed Mercer and Hutton for their negligence again, and
decided it would be better not to leave the boiler unattended,
though waiting was a chore inimical to him. He went back to
the boiler and climbed into the hatch. If he sat on the top of
the stepladder, he could raise his head and shoulders out
and brace the gun securely on the tank. But the oxygen, he
really ought to go down and draw a clean breath, as Ruben
had advised. However, he was afraid to risk being trapped in
the boiler by some enemy coming from above.
    Simon remained where he was, reeling a little every few
minutes and recovering himself when his shoulders brushed
the edges of the hatch. A noise in the next room brought his

full attention back. There was someone there. He could see a dim ring of light floating back and forth across the doorway, pointed at the floor. "David," Simon said to himself, "Charles, Ruben," but he did not dare call the names aloud; it might be someone else, a stranger. The light crossed the doorway one more time and vanished. Simon heard steps going away down another passage. When this noise ceased, in spite of his tension and dawning fear, he began to drift again.

"It's over," Larkin said, training his light on Simon, who slumped in the mouth of the big rust-spotted tank. Simon's eyes popped open and then contracted with anger; he squeezed off a short unaimed burst from the Sten which missed Larkin by a foot and went crashing off into the room beyond. Larkin dove to one side, dropping the flashlight, which spun off in the other direction and went out. Fetching up against a wall, he found himself pointlessly trying to remember just what the appearance of the boiler reminded him of; it had something to do with that dried blood color . . . then he had it: Moloch, the iron-god idol, and also an actual furnace into which living humans were thrown.

Fully alert now, Simon raged. He could not tell where Larkin was, and the last flashlight was down at the bottom of the boiler, out of his reach. It occurred to him that he might spray the entire area with machine-gun fire — but then, with an even deeper sinking feeling, he realized that the extra clips and ammunition had been left in bags somewhere on the floor outside the boiler, useless to him now. Disorganization, amateurism, Simon reproached himself disgustedly; the position was poor, though he thought it likely that Larkin would be unarmed. Still, the circumstances seemed to call for diplomacy.

"Larkin," Simon said in his sweetest tone. "Sorry, you startled me, I must have been dozing. You shouldn't have just come in that way with no warning. I didn't mean to shoot."

No answer.

"I'm glad you've come," Simon said, nearly convinced by his own unction. "We're almost ready for you now."

Again no answer.

"Are you ready?" Simon said. "Are you prepared?"

"No," Larkin said. "Simon. Would you consider giving this all up?"

Simon shifted the Sten in the direction of the unseen voice, but he could not be sure. He wondered suddenly how Larkin had ever found this place, though it scarcely mattered now.

"Why give it up?" Simon said, controlling his voice with an effort. "Why now? When it's what we've all been working for."

"You won't be able to finish it anyway," Larkin said. Now his voice seemed to come from a completely different direction. Simon moved the gun again, uncertainly. "I shot Ruben," Larkin said.

"Why?" Simon said. "Why did you do that? You told me you were sure."

"I changed my mind," Larkin said. "It was always a possibility."

Simon still could not get a fix on the voice. It had to be some quirk of the acoustics in the room.

"What about David?" Simon said. "What about Charles?"

"I talked them out of it," Larkin said. "They're gone."

"I'll see you dead for this, Larkin," Simon shouted, losing all control. "You're a walking corpse. I'll turn you over to the Inter —"

"Is there really any International?" Larkin said. "Hasn't it always been just you?"

"God damn you," Simon said. "God damn you to hell." He pulled the trigger on the Sten and released it quickly, hearing bullets clattering off the walls in the midst of a ricochet whine. He knew at least half the clip was gone.

"I hope you're dead, Larkin," Simon said. "I hope to God I killed you. But if you're not — Ruben finished. I'm going to set it off, right now. I'm going to, you'll see if I don't. I'm doing it. You'll never stop me now."

*

Larkin was not dead or even hurt and the fresh rush of heroin kept him from being properly terrified by the machine-gun blast, which had come closer this second time. There was a click from the inside of the boiler and he could see a pale column of light rising from the hatch, which Simon had left open when he went down. Larkin crept cautiously to the edge of the boiler, with the Beretta tucked under one arm, and peered down into the interior.

What immediately caught his eye was the large steel ball that stood in the middle of the floor like a disassembled fruit. Simon bent over it, pouring crystalline powder from several small boxes into pie-shaped wedges of its interior. But it was the bomb itself, not Simon's activity, that fascinated Larkin; he believed in it, and the belief was numbing. The world tilted, dislocating Larkin from his body so that he felt as he might feel if he were on the brink of a seizure, though he was not. He was at the verge of an outer void. *There was no more time.*

Larkin hopped up on the edge of the hatch, ringing metal. Simon snatched up the Sten and aimed it. Larkin jumped into the boiler without thinking. The shock of his landing dislodged the tank from its uneasy resting place and it fell down onto its side and rolled. Larkin slid backward along the curved wall, seeing Simon lose his balance and drop the Sten, which came sliding toward Larkin and ended up behind his back somehow as the boiler made a complete revolution, the flashlight, the boxes, and the bomb skittering up the sides of it, and finally stopped. Simon got up to his knees and pulled what appeared to be a foot-long hat pin from the inside of his shirt and came toward Larkin with an unpleasant fixed smile. Larkin propped himself up on his elbows and lifted the Beretta, which he had managed to hang on to. He had cracked both elbows falling and so had pins and needles in his hands.

"Stop," Larkin said, working a numb finger into the trigger housing, but Simon came on, eyes glassy. Larkin pulled the trigger, to no result, jerked it again, still nothing happened. The boiler shifted again and Simon fell, landing heavily on the side of his face. He lost the hat pin and retrieved it while Larkin fumbled frantically at the unfamiliar knobs and switches on the side of the little machine gun, pulling back hard and constantly on the trigger at the same time. *This is ridiculous,* he was thinking, not believing the gun would not work, then believing it thoroughly as the hat pin's point, his whole focus of attention now, came very near and then drew back. Simon had reared back on his heels, grinning now, the pin in both hands pointed down, Larkin thinking he ought to move, dodge, but not having time to try. The trigger gave way and the machine gun jumped and chattered in his hands like a dog lunging at a leash. The overpowering racket in the boiler made Larkin imagine himself inside the clanging bells of hell; then the gun leapt out of his hands altogether and disappeared in the sudden dark. Larkin lay quiet as the ringing in his ears subsided, he did not know how long. There was no further sound or movement. He thrust out a hand and found the flashlight quite by chance; when he pushed the switch, the light came on. Larkin scraped his finger back along the ridged tube of the flashlight, making a grating noise. After all that, it was unbearably frustrating to him that he found himself still alive.

59
The News

TIMES SQUARE NUKE PLOT BLOWN ran the headline occupying the entire front page of the *New York Post* final edition of January 16. By the next morning all the New York papers were running headlines similar in content, if not style, and wire services had put the story on every front page nationwide. It ran for a week or a little longer, mainly sustained by tangential expert opinions and partisan or political commentary. Antinukers took to the streets in significant force, calling for the immediate shutdown of all breeder reactors. In Congress there was talk of new antiterrorist statutes, which ultimately came to nothing. In San Diego a psychic made the AP spike with a prophecy that there were still bombs germinating under most major US cities, and that the radiation from them was responsible for current outbreaks of SHC.

During the course of the first week, the bomb plot story crawled toward the back pages; at the end of ten days, it was dead. Doomsday in the abstract had limited audience appeal, and after the second day there was little specific information to add. The basic known facts were few and fairly simple: on the afternoon of January 16, each and every New York City police precinct had received one or more anonymous phone calls to the effect that if officers entered a certain maintenance shaft located along the Eighth Avenue IND line near 44th Street, they would find explosives, guns, dead bodies, and other items of professional interest to them. The first few calls were disregarded, but once all the calls had been connected, officials decided to investigate the tip. They also decided to honor the quirky suggestion made by the caller that whoever went down the shaft should wear protection against radiation.

A seven-man SWAT team, awkwardly garbed in safety suits, was finally dispatched. At the bottom of the shaft, team members found a trail marked out for them with shreds of wood and clothing, a few dynamite sticks, and assorted bits of automatic weapons. The trail ran into a maze of tunnels and then forked. In one direction it led to the body of a male Hispanic, estimated twenty-one years of age, dead of gunshot wounds. In the other direction the trail ended at an outsized water tank which held the body of a male Caucasian, estimated thirty-five years of age, also dead of gunshot wounds. Also in the tank were a large timed explosive device powered by dynamite, which appeared to be disarmed, and several boxes, some of them spilled, which proved to contain a significant quantity of plutonium 239.

Autopsy and investigation of the two corpses did not bring much more to light. The Hispanic, identified as Ruben Carrera, had died of three wounds in the chest and one in the head, inflicted by 9-mm parabellum rounds fired from a Browning automatic handgun found on the scene. At the time of his death, Carrera was enrolled at NYU, but he seemed to have had no friends there, and no acquaintances who could comment on his character, beyond the fact that he was quiet and solitary. Carrera's rap sheet was relatively undistinguished. He had a juvenile record of assorted petty crimes, and had been convicted of heroin possession, one count, in 1978. Since then Carrera had been clean. He had no known political associations; his motive for joining a terrorist group was not apparent.

The second man had been shot some twenty-five times at close range with rounds fired from a Beretta submachine gun which was found by the SWAT team at the base of the maintenance shaft. After some delay occasioned by the poor condition of the cadaver, he was identified as Simon Rohnstock, a wealthy painter of small reputation who had, in the early seventies, been quite prominent on the New York social scene. Friends from that period expressed extreme surprise that Rohnstock would be involved in something like a bomb plot; however, none of them had heard from him in years and most were under the impression that he lived abroad. Inquiry into Rohnstock's more recent background turned up the fact that he had been a practicing psychologist for the past few years. But interviews with recent patients did not reveal any significant clues. The patients testified that Rohnstock had helped them control habits, phobias, anxiety, and irritability by way of unexceptional behavioral technique. Most were satisfied with the treatment they had received; all were much startled to learn of the strange end to which Dr. Rohnstock had come. Simon Rohnstock had no police record. A number of theoretical Marxist tracts were found in his Upper West Side apartment, but Rohnstock, like Ruben Carrera, had never been active in politics, at least not since his college days, and he seemed an even less likely candidate for involvement in a terrorist organization.

As for the plutonium 239, markers on the packing material allowed it to be traced back to an unsolved truck hijacking which had occurred outside of Roanoke, Virginia, in the summer of 1982. The plutonium found in the boiler, however, was only a fraction of the original shipment. Investigators combed the entire network of tunnels beneath Times Square in search of the remainder, but they did not find it.

Reconstruction of the events leading up to the January 16 underground shootout was problematic. The New York SWAT team had obscured many of the more subtle traces with their own activity, to the irritation of the FBI and CIA personnel who were soon called in. Analysis of what traces remained seemed to indicate that two or perhaps three persons other than Carrera and Rohnstock had been involved. A spokesman for the investigators presumed that there had been "internal dissension culminating in aggravated violence." But the identity and whereabouts of the third, fourth, and possible fifth parties to the episode remained unknown.

The expert consensus regarding the bomb itself was that it very likely would have worked.

Dr. Anton Leveaux did not ordinarily spend much time on the newspapers. But beginning on January 16, he bought and examined them all in close detail. By the seventeenth, higher-ups at Bellevue were notifying police and the newspapers of the now-explicit relationship between the Times Square bomb plot and the outbreak of what had been definitely diagnosed as radiation sickness in that area. Other city hospitals were following suit. Leveaux, as the first person to put forward the radiation sickness theory, was asked for an interview by several journals; however, he chose to decline.

He read the bomb plot stories with sharp interest, but on the seventeenth his attention was distracted to a much smaller back-page item: the body of Hector Morales had been discovered, on follow-up of another anonymous tip, in a vacant building east of the Bowery a few blocks below Houston Street. Morales had been sought for a couple of months on child-abuse charges; he was suspected of having tortured his son, whose exact age and first name were not on record. The caller had not told police to seek Morales in the shell; instead they were advised that they would find the corpse of the "Bowery Strangler." Concerning this claim, police spokesmen had no definite conclusion.

Leveaux pored over his papers; though there seemed to be absolutely no connection between the big story and the little one, he believed that Larkin might well supply one. The doctor chewed up a whole pocketful of ballpoints as he pondered what to do, and finally decided to do nothing, or almost nothing. He began dialing Larkin's number a few times every day, but Larkin never answered the phone, and he never responded to messages.

Part V

The Ark

Faith is the power which permits us to believe what we know to be untrue.

Werner Herzog,
English subtitle to *Nosferatu*

60
Felice

". . . AND TO RECAP the hour's lead story, authorities now say that the nuclear-fission-type explosive device found late yesterday in a utility tunnel near Times Square would most probably have been effective . . ."

Mr. Zeraschev's hand glided over the surface of the radio and turned it off. He had heard the story many times already and did not particularly believe it in any case; the news generally lied, he thought, either outright or by implication. The bomb plot would not have interested him much even if he had believed it. He was as prepared to be blown up overnight as he was for anything else, and forewarning of such a prospect would not have caused him undue concern. Mr. Zeraschev thumbed the dial of the radio, without, however, turning it back on. He was aware of faint inanimate noises issuing from the four floors of his house, a brownstone in the Park Slope section of Brooklyn, which had been a bordello some fifty years before.

The cat ran over his feet to the left. Mr. Zeraschev turned his head in the direction of the movement, merely from habit; he was so nearly blind that he could not see the cat or anything else, could just barely tell the difference between light and darkness. The cat was now grumbling over its bowl in the kitchen, a fat sulky creature, left here by his daughter when she went to the convent. Mr. Zeraschev got up and went into the kitchen, not needing to feel his way. His mem-

ory was excellent and he was sensitive to infinitesimal movements of the air which would usually warn him of anything
in his path. By such means he was still able to shop and take
the subway back and forth from work, disdaining even to
carry a stick. Mr. Zeraschev fed the cat a handful of dry meal
and turned to the stove to heat the coffee he'd left there that
morning. Returning from the kitchen with his cup, he inadvertently trod on the cat's tail. The cat yowled.

"Glutton," Mr. Zeraschev said, misinterpreting the situation. "You eat too much, all you think about is food." Now
he was unsure quite where he was. With his free hand extended he took a step forward and touched the whale-shaped
mass of books and magazines and unanswered correspon-
dence which covered the entire surface of the long dinner
table at which he usually sat. Reoriented, Mr. Zeraschev made
his way back to the chair at the head of the table and sat
down. His right hand had fallen on the radio, but he did not
turn it on. The front window, two rooms away, appeared to
him as a formless blob of light dulling at the edges; soon it
would be dark. He could hear the cat softly retreating into
the farther reaches of the house. Mr. Zeraschev raised his
hand from the radio. If it was dark, then soon Felice would
come.

In fact he could hear her now, moving back and forth along
the third-floor hallway where she preferred to walk, light feet
in slippers or mules scuffing the boards of the floor. Now a
creak of a step announced the beginning of her descent of
the stairs. Hearing a rustle of cloth, Mr. Zeraschev tried to
picture what she might be wearing; a long skirt, possibly, a
loose robe or a peignoir . . . he thought he could hear something fluttering down the steps in her wake. Preceded by a
current of the rose-petal scent she tended to wear too much
of, Felice came into the room.

"It's so cold," she said, a tremble in her tone. "I feel lonely."

"Well, what do you want me to do about it?" Mr. Zeraschev
said. He was often made cross by Felice's relentless self-pity.

"It's always so dark here," Felice whined. "You could turn
on the lights."

"Why should I?" Mr. Zeraschev said. "What good would that do me? Besides, it's expensive. You don't pay the bills here, you know."

Felice shuddered, audibly it seemed. She had the capability of making it seem a little colder in whatever room she entered.

"You want them on, you turn them on," Mr. Zeraschev said.

"You know I can't." Then, archly, "I don't think you're very nice."

"Well, nobody asked you to kill yourself, did they?" Mr. Zeraschev said. "You dig your bed, you lie in it."

The ghost, Felice, told different stories of her origin, none of them especially reliable in Mr. Zeraschev's opinion. He knew from other sources that she had been a prostitute, years before when the house itself had been a brothel, and had died there, by either violence or accident. She had killed herself by jumping down the stairwell, or possibly she had been pushed, by an enemy or a lover or just some faceless patron of the brothel. Her own versions varied on this point. Once buried, however, she had returned to the house in spirit, to walk with loud invisible footsteps along the third-floor hall, approaching the stairway again and again. That was depressing for the customers. The brothel shut down and the building was sold to a succession of ordinary householders, all of whom vacated fairly quickly because of the ghost's ceaseless presence.

Moving into the house with his wife, a son, and a daughter, Mr. Zeraschev had had no such qualms. What if the house were a little haunted? It was also, for just that reason, very cheap. Being Russian, he and his family already lived on a different calendar from other people, and could manage small dislocations in space as well as in time. Besides, this ghost seemed harmless, a mild and inoffensive lost soul, and for years she made no great disturbance, merely walking the halls at night, quieter and less bothersome than the corporeal occupants of the house, as Mr. Zeraschev sometimes thought.

Only lately, after the death of Mr. Zeraschev's wife and the departure of his children, had she begun to speak.

"I never killed myself," Felice said. "I was murdered. *Murdered,*" she repeated, with delicious melodrama.

"Umph," Mr. Zeraschev said. "So what's your story today?"

"It was jealousy that did it," Felice said. "Jealousy and spite. Though why shouldn't she be jealous, the ugly old thing?"

"That's a new one," Mr. Zeraschev said, grasping that a female assailant was now being implied. "You're saying it was one of the other whores, are you?"

"Whores indeed," Felice sniffed.

Mr. Zeraschev sensed her drawing herself up. How tall was she? he wondered for the ninety-ninth time. What did she look like?

"This was a class establishment," Felice went on. "French. They called us mademoiselles."

"French in a pig's ear," Mr. Zeraschev said. "Bet you a quarter you're from Brooklyn, right up the block."

"You don't understand," Felice said. "No one understands."

"Who could understand all the tales you tell? All those stories and never the same one twice."

"You're not sympathetic," Felice said. "I wish your son was here."

"He was here twenty years and you never paid any attention," Mr. Zeraschev said. "He's a bum, anyway. He threw up his education and went off to become a fool somewhere. He won't be coming back."

"I'm going away then," Felice said. "You certainly don't want me."

"Don't go," Mr. Zeraschev said. "Stay a minute."

Felice, who had been moving away, stopped. Mr. Zeraschev thought he heard her garments shimmering on her.

"Tell me what you look like," he said.

"I've already told you. At least a dozen times."

"So do it again."

"Well," Felice said. "*Mignonne.* That's what they used to call me, *mignonne.*"

"Sounds like a piece of steak," Mr. Zeraschev said, shifting restlessly in his seat. "What else?"

"A beautiful bone structure," Felice said unselfconsciously. "A heart-shaped face, fair skin, would bruise at a touch, blue eyes. And everyone always said my hair was lovely. Like lace almost, and fine, but a lot of it, with a natural wave. It comes past my waist when I take it down. I could sit on it, if I wanted to."

"Come a little closer," Mr. Zeraschev said.

"I'm delicate," Felice said. "Just ninety pounds and the smallest hands and feet you ever saw, just like a China-woman. But I've got a perfect body. That's what she said when she hired me here. Though she didn't say anything at first. Just sat there and stared."

Mr. Zeraschev was also staring but he could see nothing but the dark; even the aureole at the window was gone completely. He did think Felice had come a bit nearer, judging from the sound of her voice.

"Don't you wish you could see it?" Felice said. "I wish you could. There's no one to appreciate it, not any more."

"Well, I can't, you know," Mr. Zeraschev said. He leaned forward, sliding his hand out along the edge of the table.

"No, you can't, can you," Felice said absently.

"You could let me touch you," Mr. Zeraschev said. "I see with my fingers, now."

"Naughty, naughty," Felice said. "That's what they all say."

She was so close now that Mr. Zeraschev believed he could feel the temperature of her body, and he snatched with his extended hand at the place where he thought it had to be. The movement almost overbalanced him and he sat back, grasping only a handful of air.

"For shame," Felice said, now from somewhere near the door. "And you an old man, too. Maybe I'll come back when you've learned how to treat a lady."

Mr. Zeraschev could hear her creaking up the stairs.

"Well you're an old woman, then," he shouted suddenly. *"You've been hanging around here fifty years, you're probably older than I am."* There was no reply. Mr. Zeraschev subsided. He had never done either better or worse with Felice. There was

nothing lost; she would return the next night or the one after, to play the same or a similar scene. Besides, she was probably ugly, he thought; the unreliable ghost might lie about her looks as well as anything else. Probably her real name was Myra or Ethel, something plain like that. French in a pig's ear, Mr. Zeraschev grunted to himself. Though she did have a pretty voice. It frequently occurred to him that Felice might not be visible to anyone.

61
Pushkin Park

IT WAS WEIRDLY WARM for January 16, Arkady thought, or January 2, depending on which calendar you happened to be using. The day dawned with an unlikely balm of spring, and Arkady got up and opened windows. He found an egg-shell on the corner of the sink, which Tommy had saved for the garden. That meant the boy had eaten and was out, probably in the thicket at the lower end of the back yard, where he spent hours each day, doing what, Arkady didn't know. Arkady broke off the end of a loaf of bread and buttered it and went with a cup of coffee to sit on the back steps.

The weather was truly strange, and Arkady, still half asleep, began to rehearse his last conversation with Larkin, which he hadn't really thought of much before Tommy had begun repeating his name the day before. Larkin had remarked on the oddity of the weather, and Arkady had answered with something that made Larkin give him a funny look, but what was it he had said? Arkady couldn't remember; the vodka they'd drunk later had blown it all away; he could just dimly recall that Larkin had been rambling about the desert saints, which was not so unusual. Then in the morning, Larkin had called him Batiushka, a term of respect or affection one might address to a spiritual elder, but they'd both been hung over and irritable, and Larkin had not meant the epithet kindly, though in the end they'd parted well.

Or had they? Arkady would freely admit that he was unqualified to be Larkin's elder; perhaps they were both equally in need of one. The church warned of the dangers latent in the recorded ecstasies of the saints, saying that a careless study of such things could even corrupt an unprepared or unformed spirit. And Larkin had said he had been courting demons, Arkady suddenly remembered, with a near-physical prick of anxiety that made him shift on the steps. Or maybe they'd been courting him. It *was* dangerous to delve too deeply into the soul, Arkady could believe it, but how risky it might turn out to be for Larkin he didn't know and there was no one he could ask.

But the day was good, Arkady concluded, forgetting Larkin easily for the moment, chewing the last nub of the bread; it was an extraordinarily fine day. A section of brush was trembling at the end of the yard. The boy was moving around there, no doubt; he'd made a den in the thicket that a fox might have been proud of. Arkady saw himself at four or five years old running naked through tall grass higher than his head, in the secure midst of that old world that had surrounded him until the magic circle was broken for everyone and the Orthodox went into diaspora as surely as the Jews, a world that was still permanently built into the back side of his brain. He saw his grandfather standing on the porch steps, a sky full of rose-colored twilight arching over the whole house behind him, calling him, "Arkasha, Arkasha," to come back inside. His grandfather who had killed a man and undone his entire life in repentance for it and invented a new life in which he could still call the child Arkady into supper, from the steps of a house in New Jersey he'd always call a dacha. Larkin had always loved his grandfather's story, and why? Because he'd killed for the love of God, you might say, and it was just that sort of paradox that would draw Larkin, Arkady realized, like new leaves appearing on the trees in midwinter, which he could see before him now. And now, with perfect clarity, Arkady did remember his own response to Larkin's comment on the weather.

"Maybe it's the end of the world, who knows?"

By late afternoon Arkady was in Pushkin Park. For most of the day he'd been walking around the area with eighty pounds of video equipment strapped to his back, and though he'd run three hours of tape he still wasn't sure what he had. He'd done shots of the Communist-leaning church and the Czarist church and shots of the cemetery they shared. He'd shot the old community buildings and some long pans over the lake. Now he was setting up the camera in the shadow of the half-length bronze of Pushkin, which stared straight out toward the rear of the church, ignoring a drab stretch of state highway which was also in view.

Camera rolling, Arkady picked up a cassette recorder and began to improvise narration.

"After the Don Cossacks and the Kalmuks had come, there was a feeling among the Russian factory workers in favor of building a cooperative community, a *mir*, on this spot. But at first they couldn't do that. Why not? Because they didn't have the money, that's why not.

"Then the KGB arrived. They put up the money to buy this land, who knows why they did it. Maybe they thought they could start a revolution here. Or maybe they just thought that it would be a nice place for spies to spend their summer vacation. Who knows what went on in their minds . . . this might be the worst narration I ever recorded," Arkady said, and turned the cassette machine off.

Then he shut off the camera and slung the deck over his shoulder. He picked up the camera and tripod together under one arm and went up the short slope behind the statue and into the tight embrasure of cedars behind it. The trees lining the passage scraped at his shoulders and the gear as he went through. At the other end he emerged into a wide shimmering field. The angle of the sun was such that the blades of grass seemed to be lit from below. At the far edge of the field there was a pylon dedicated to the Russian-American World War dead, and Arkady could see Tommy's small distant figure wandering away from it. He put the tripod down and spread its legs completely flat.

With the lower edge of the lens brushing along the grass, Arkady panned slowly to the right. The image curved and slipped along the edge of the tiny built-in monitor; Tommy was zigzagging back and forth deep in the frame, and every so often he stooped and picked something up. Arkady felt behind him for the cassette recorder and began speaking again, reciting a fragment of a tale his mother had often read to him.

"The peasant began singing a song and heard two voices. He stopped and asked his wife: 'Was it you who accompanied me in a thin voice?' 'What is the matter with you? I wouldn't think of singing a note!' 'Then who was it?' 'I don't know,' the woman said, 'but sing again, and I will listen.' He sang again, and although he alone sang, two voices could be heard. He stopped and said: 'Is it you, Misery, who are singing with me?' Misery answered: 'Aye, master, I am singing with you.' 'Well, Misery, let us walk together.' 'We shall, master. I will never desert you now.' "

Arkady went on with the story. In the end, after much torment, the peasant lured Misery to a ditch and buried him there. Arkady switched off the tape recorder and then the video deck.

"That's a good story," Tommy said. The boy had slipped up behind him while he'd been looking into the camera.

"Yes," Arkady said. "I think it might work. We'll go back now, the light's going." He unscrewed the camera from the tripod and packed it in its case and stood up.

"Wait a minute," he said. "You can talk."

"Of course, I can talk," the boy said.

"Well, why didn't you before, then?"

"Didn't have anything to say."

Arkady considered this.

"I guess you must have really liked that story quite a bit."

"Just practice," the boy said. "Larkin's in trouble. You'd better go look for him."

*

By late evening it was still uncannily warm and Arkady stood in the twilight out in the back yard, over a little fire he'd built. He was cutting slices off an eggplant and roasting them over the flames with the knife and then eating them directly from the knife point, consuming each slice with one snap of his jaws. Arkady was in a bad temper; he didn't want to go back to the city, but it appeared that he had no choice. He could worm no further explanation out of the boy, who had remained obstinately silent since the afternoon, so that Arkady was beginning to wonder if he could possibly have imagined their entire conversation.

He roasted the last section of eggplant until it blackened and dripped, and then sat down on the ground, gnawing the flesh away from the stem. Above him the stars grew stronger against the fading sky and in a nearby tree a mockingbird trilled a song his mother had sung before she died. Arkady did not want to leave this place; it was a sanctuary, presided over by his mother's soul, whose presence was remembered even by the birds. He wondered how long a mockingbird might live, whether this one might have learned its song from another. Dropping the eggplant stem in the fire, he lay on his back, and in the deepening darkness he pictured the dead souls rising softly from the cemetery and fanning out to circle the houses and the church, a ring of spirits linking hands to ward off evil. In the outer world there was no such shelter from confusion and there he too might wander and lose himself, as Larkin had most probably done. He did not seriously doubt that the boy's intuition was correct.

But why should he be responsible for Larkin, when he himself was equally in need of a guide, an elder, a *starets*? Briefly Arkady considered consulting a priest over this matter, but knew at once that he would not. It occurred to him that perhaps he and Larkin were both lost in some ambiguous zone between faith and nothingness, dabblers, dilettantes, Arkady thought with sudden self-disgust. Larkin would be closer to the edge, driven there by his apocalyptic obsessions or fantasies, armed only with fragments of a theology he might very well have misunderstood. Arkady would go back to the city and look for him because no one else was going to do it, probably no one else would know how to start. He rolled over onto his stomach, then lifted himself to his hands and knees, remaining for a moment in that posture, like a bear. It was better to have the decision made, at least. He stood up and tramped the fire out, then walked back toward the house.

Tommy was sitting propped against the wall on the third bed, but he did not look up when Arkady entered the room. Arkady sat down on another bed and switched on the big color monitor that stood on the floor. He chose a tape from the day's shooting at random and popped it into the deck. A band of noise rolled over the screen, and then the room was illuminated by the shot he'd taken in the field.

"Okay," Arkady said, contemplating the image. "We're going tomorrow."

"Good," the boy said. "It's the right thing to do."

"You don't talk much like a little kid, you know that?"

"I'm not a little kid," the boy said. "I'm thirteen. I'm small for my age, that's all."

"Well, you don't have to get all prickly about it," Arkady said. "You don't speak for yourself, then people tend to make assumptions."

The boy did not answer that. Arkady leaned forward toward the screen. "Look at that," he said. "There's a strawberry there, I don't believe it."

"You can believe it," the boy said. "I ate it. It was good."

62
Arkady Goes to Brooklyn

BY THE NEXT DAY the boy had fallen mute again and Arkady, determined not to care, addressed him no remark. Arkady spent the better part of the day stalling the departure, first by sleeping till almost noon and then by making a long elaborate procedure of closing up the house. He boarded several windows and shut off the water and electricity and spent two hours crawling underneath the house to inspect pipe joints and the wiring. After that, he moved on to the car, took the simpler bits of the engine apart and cleaned them. Then, finally, he packed the trunk with the video gear and a few loose clothes on top, and summoned the boy with a snap of his fingers.

They got into the car in silence. Arkady pulled into the road and headed for the Garden State Parkway. Every so often he glanced over at the boy, whose gaze was fixed on the double-sided icon replica which swung from the rearview mirror. By the time they reached the freeway it was nearly dark.

"What about some more talking practice, Tommy?" Arkady said. "We could have a conversation, get us through this drive."

"Quit calling me Tommy," the boy snapped. "My name's Gabriel. Gabriel Morales."

"How should I know that?"

"Sorry," the boy said, after a pause. Then, "You could tell another one of those stories."

So Arkady commenced the story of Tsarevitch Ivan and his quest. It was a long tale, beginning and ending, as Arkady recalled, with Ivan's search for the Firebird. But he soon became lost in the tale, which was extremely long and crowded with redundant detail. The car was in Staten Island, coming up on the Verrazano Bridge, before Arkady had brought the story to some sort of close.

"That's not as good as the other one," the boy said.

"Maybe not," Arkady said. "It's been a long time since I thought about those stories."

"The other one was better," Gabriel said. "Misery. I liked that."

"You should know," Arkady said, wishing at once that he hadn't.

"No, it wasn't so bad," the boy said. "Not like you might think. Anyway, I was used to it."

"You got used to that? It must have hurt. A lot."

"Being scared was worse," the boy said simply. "But I wasn't scared anymore after a while."

"Why not?"

The car was climbing the ramp to the Verrazano. Arkady had to stop and pay a toll before he drove on. Gabriel had spread his hands about a foot apart.

"Every time my father . . . every time I got burned I'd see this thing in the dark. Like a line. It was always yellow. It started down low with the burning and then it just went up and up. But before the burning, there wasn't even the line. There was just nothing."

"You speak good English," Arkady said. "Correct and everything." Gabriel shrugged.

"I went to school till I was twelve," he said. "I did okay."

"What made you stop talking?"

"When I saw the line. Because I was afraid it wouldn't be true."

The car swept over the top span of the bridge. It was now completely dark. Arkady glanced down at another plastic icon affixed to the dashboard and then looked back at the roadway.

"It is true, though. You're good. Larkin's good."

"No, we're not," Arkady said. "We're all mixed up."

"You try," Gabriel said. "That's something."

"I hope it is."

"My father tried to be bad," Gabriel said.

"I'd say he did a good job of that."

"That way you know where you are, though," Gabriel said. "But everything's real. All of it. Even the paths in the bushes, they're on the line. I see other things, too. Most of the time they're true."

"Did you see Larkin? Lately?"

Gabriel hesitated.

"I saw him in a dream two nights ago. He was hurt but he wasn't dying. There was a lot of light where he was. I think he might have seen me too."

"Was that when you started saying his name?"

"No. I just had a feeling then."

"Do you know where he is now?"

"I can't tell. I know he's been in a dark place," Gabriel said, "but I can't see him."

Arkady dropped into silence, coming down off the bridge onto the BQE, wondering if the boy was prescient, visionary, or merely insane. He knew precedents for all three options, but tended to lean toward the first two; time might or might not tell which one was correct, and Arkady decided to forget about it for the moment. Back in Brooklyn again, he could feel little tingles coming toward him from the city. The return was not as bad as he'd expected, so far.

"What's the Firebird?" Gabriel said.

"I don't really know," Arkady said. "Just something for people to go look for, I think."

Arkady parked above Sixth Avenue and with Gabriel he walked a long avenue block down the steep slope of his street. His own block was lined with a solid rank of four-story brownstones on one side; on the other there was the rear of a school with a fenced-in playground facing the sidewalk. In the middle of the block Arkady mounted a stairway, found his key and let himself into the vestibule. He flicked the light switch there but apparently the bulb was gone. Turning toward the light of the street, he found the key to the second door and entered the hall. Gabriel followed him softly in. Reaching for another switch, Arkady tripped over something that crashed.

"Who's there?" Mr. Zeraschev called from the rear of the house. "Get out, whoever you are."

"It's me, Arkady," Arkady called. "I came back." The second light was also dead and the hallway seemed to be impassable. Arkady fumbled toward a pair of double glass doors to his left, opened them, and went into the front room. In the vague light from the window he could see a mountain range of plunder, including three couches standing on their legs, two more upended, a grand piano, an electric organ, several ancient televisions, and a number of odd-shaped tables and cabinets piled high with smaller unidentifiable items. The floor was not visible. High on the opposite wall hung a stuffed head of a moose wearing sunglasses and a tie. Arkady bowed to the moose and began to pick his way carefully through the room. Finally he reached another pair of glass doors which let him into the dining room and kitchen.

This time the light came on. The room was ell-shaped, with the kitchen in the far end of the ell, and not so cluttered as the other. Most of the dining room was taken up by a big wooden table covered from end to end with mail and books and paper. Arkady saw that his father had carved out a clearing at the far end of the table, which contained his radios, a cassette recorder, a clock that talked, and just now the remains of his supper: some chicken bones, Arkady noticed, and nubs of carrots and potatoes. In the uncurtained window in back of his father's chair Arkady could see his own reflection.

"Not too many of the lights seem to work anymore," Arkady said. "I guess you haven't been using them."

Mr. Zeraschev sat in his chair behind the table, palms beside his plate, with the foursquare rigidity of a carved Egyptian king. His hair was very white and thick. He seemed to be staring right through Arkady, though his eyes were wrinkled almost shut.

"So you came back," Mr. Zeraschev said, "did you?"

"I came back," Arkady said.

"Did you bring back the apples?"

"No."

"Did you bring the day-old bread?"

"No."

"Aah," Mr. Zeraschev said. "YOU'RE A BUM! WHAD-DID YOU GO TO THE COUNTRY FOR?"

"I WENT THERE TO LIVE THERE!" Arkady screamed. "WHAT ELSE?"

"WHADDID YOU COME BACK FOR THEN?"

"To look for Larkin," Arkady said, lowering his voice. "Remember him?"

"Sure I remember him," Mr. Zeraschev said. "He's a bum too."

"Maybe so," Arkady said. "He didn't happen to call up here, did he?"

"No, he didn't." Mr. Zeraschev shifted his head from side to side. "You've got somebody with you."

Arkady discovered that he did not want to explain about Tommy, or Gabriel rather. Supposing that he could. He gave the boy a little push on the shoulder and he tiptoed out of the room.

"What makes you think that?" Arkady said.

"I can feel it."

"So maybe it's the ghost."

"No, it's not the ghost. It's somebody alive. And he's not very big. I don't care. He'd better not rob the house, that's all."

"Everything's broken," Arkady said. "What could he really take?"

Gabriel climbed three flights of stairs in the sheer dark and the last one brought him into a small square room with windows on all sides, a sort of cupola at the very top of the house. Here there was illumination from outside, and going to a window he could look out over the roofs and lights of Brooklyn to the black band of the river. After a moment he turned back toward the room. There was a small bed, a sink, a sewing table, and a little cabinet against one wall. Gabriel went to the cabinet and opened one of the drawers. It was divided into tiny thumbnail-sized compartments which were all empty.

Gabriel closed the drawer and looked up into the mirror above the cabinet. It had been a long time, a year perhaps, since he had looked at himself. In the dim light his eyes appeared as perfectly black and glossy ovals, and against them he could see the golden line hooking upward, ascending and ascending.

"You're going to live a long time," Gabriel said to his reflection. "You'll be a wise man before you're through."

There came a minute sound from the floor below and Gabriel went to the banister and looked down. A woman stood on the third-floor landing, peering gloomily into the stairwell. She wore a blue dressing gown with Chinese embroidery and her blond hair ran over her shoulders like a shawl.

"Hey," Gabriel called to her, "you live here too?"

The woman looked up but did not answer.

"Oh," Gabriel said. "You're dead. You're dead, aren't you?"

Arkady had begun to dig through the paper on the table.

"The mail's been piling up, I see."

"You think I'm going to answer it?" Mr. Zeraschev said.

"I guess you're not."

"So what are you going to do? Move back in? You're going to get a job, maybe? Pay some rent?"

"No," Arkady said. "Not right now. I'm going to stay somewhere else. I just thought I'd come see you. See how you are."

"Here I am."

"There you are."

"So maybe you could move back in," Mr. Zeraschev said. "You could fix some things."

"I'm sure."

"The bathroom upstairs is busted," Mr. Zeraschev said. "That's one thing."

"Wait a minute," Arkady said, cocking his head toward the stairwell. "I think somebody's talking."

"Maybe it's the ghost."

"Oh," Arkady said. "The ghost talks now?"

"You're really pretty," Gabriel said. "You really are."

"You're sweet," Felice told him. "Hardly anyone says that anymore."

Arkady picked up the cassette recorder from beside his father's plate and switched it to record.

"This is the voice of your son speaking," he said. "You can call me at 216-0033, if you want to call me, that is."

"Maybe I'll call," Mr. Zeraschev said. "You could come for dinner."

"Sure," Arkady said. "I could fix the bathroom too, maybe. Tommy? Gabriel?" he called. "We're going now."

"So you do have someone with you."

"Just a little kid. He can't hurt anything."

"Where'd you ever get a little kid from?"

"I think I adopted him."

"Nobody'd let you do that, you're not responsible."

"Nobody's been complaining so far," Arkady said. "I'll see you later." Because he still didn't want to talk about Gabriel, he went out to wait for the boy in the hall.

Mr. Zeraschev sat still, poised and listening; he heard every movement the boy made coming down the stairs. Gabriel entered the room and walked very slowly and quietly to the corner of the table where the old man sat, his blind face bent down on him.

"So?" Mr. Zeraschev said.

"She says she looks like what she told you she does," Gabriel said. "She wanted you to know that."

63
Arkady Eats Meat

"Visitors," Arkady said, looking at the designs scratched on Larkin's door. "Not very nice ones either, maybe. Your father have any friends would draw this kind of picture?"

"He used to," Gabriel said. "Not the last couple of years, though."

"Hm," Arkady said. "Well, the cross is on top. Looks like Larkin was here later, maybe. We'll go in."

It was cold inside the loft. Arkady walked to the Broadway side and shut the open window, then turned back to survey the open space.

"I don't think anyone's been here," he said. "Not for quite a while."

"No," Gabriel said. He was kneeling beside the stove. "Look. One of the cats is dead."

"You better build a fire," Arkady said. "Otherwise we'll freeze to death in here."

"I wouldn't have thought he'd leave the cat," Gabriel said.

Arkady opened the darkroom, looked in it, and came back out into the kitchen. Everything was dusty. Arkady looked into the refrigerator.

"Some interesting molds he's growing here." He came back into the main area of the loft and walked slowly along the wall where Larkin's half-done prints were hanging, inspecting them and stroking his beard. Passing along the work tables, he completed another circuit of the loft.

"Well, the answering machine is blinking its little brain out," he said, coming back toward the stove. "Seems like the camera stuff is gone."

Gabriel crouched in front of the open stove door, staring into the building flames. Arkady sat down beside him and held out his hands toward the heat.

"It gets a little warmer here anyway," he said. "Hey. What is it?" Gabriel had begun to cry silently, tears rolling out of his wide open eyes.

"The cat," he said. "The kitten."

"Do you think Larkin's dead too?"

"No."

"Well, don't stop then," Arkady said, dropping a hand on the boy's shoulder. "It's probably good for you."

Arkady had himself taught Larkin how to disappear, and in the course of a long day spent fruitlessly looking for him, he began to think Larkin might have learned the lesson too well. He started with the bus and train stations, remembering the old method, which he and Larkin had both resorted to from time to time, of sleeping in pay toilets with feet propped up on the latch. But though he did find several practitioners of the trick, none of them seemed to be Larkin.

From the stations Arkady worked his way downtown, passing through the likelier parks along the way. He looked closely at every vagrant and even at the bag ladies, recalling Larkin's queer aptitude for making himself unfamiliar. But he could draw no twitch of recognition from any of the strangers that he met.

By the time he reached the Bowery it was dark, and Arkady had blisters and shinsplints and he hated the city. At a bar on the corner of Houston Street he stopped and bought a beer, mainly for the privilege of sitting down with it. When he was halfway down the drink, an old man in a black suit and fedora appeared at the edge of his table.

"Don't I know you?" Dutch said.

"You might," Arkady said, looking up at him blearily. "I think I'm too tired to tell."

"Friend of Larkin's?"

"Yes," Arkady said. "You don't happen to know where he is, do you?"

"Nope. Ain't seen him in two or three days. Been looking for him, though."

"That's funny," Arkady said. "So have I. You're doing better than me, though. I haven't seen him in two or three months."

"He's been coming in here pretty regular," Dutch said. "You want I should give him a message?"

"Just tell him to stop by home," Arkady said, and he got up and left.

At other bars along the street there was no one that had heard of Larkin and by the time Arkady reached Chinatown he was more discouraged than before. It was not an inviting prospect to spend many more days like this one. On Canal Street he bought a newspaper and got into the subway. The *Post* was still running the bomb plot story under the head, SEARCH FOR NUKERS GOES ON. It was the first Arkady had heard of it, for he read no papers in Little Russia. He skimmed the story with slight attention; at most it seemed a suitable background for the madness of his own day. Then, on a back page, he saw the notation of the death and discovery of Hector Morales.

*

Walking back across Broadway toward Larkin's building, Arkady passed a vaguely familiar face hovering above a gray three-piece suit. He knew the features, he was sure, but something was wrong with the context. Arkady stopped and called.

"Hey."

The Sparrow turned round and walked back to where Arkady stood.

"I thought that might be you," he said.

"Didn't recognize you in the suit."

"I don't recognize myself sometimes."

"What are you doing?"

"Interview," the Sparrow said shortly. "I thought you were in Jersey."

"I came back last night," Arkady said. "I've been trying to find Larkin."

"He's not home?"

"No."

"I haven't seen him in a couple of months," the Sparrow said. "I call up now and then but all I ever get's the machine."

"Right," Arkady said. "I've been doing that too. He did tell me the last time I saw him he was going on one of those weird journeys to the other side of the wall."

"Oh."

"I've been beating the bushes all day," Arkady said. "But I didn't find anything. Only there was an old man in a bar that said he'd seen him a few days ago. That was it. You might let me know if you hear anything."

"Sure," the Sparrow said. "Where are you?"

"His place, for now."

"Convenient."

"It is," Arkady said. "Stop by."

"Been reading the papers?"

"Just today."

"Interesting idea," the Sparrow said. "Sometimes I think it might be a good idea."

"Ah," Arkady said. "Larkin was running on about something like that the last time I saw him."

"You think?"

"Not really," Arkady said. "That would be pushing it."

"What's cooking?" Arkady said, entering the loft. There was a thick smell of pepper and bay leaf in the air.

"Bean soup," Gabriel said. "I found some dry black beans."

"Good," Arkady said. "Phone ring?"

"Social Services called."

"Really?" Arkady said. "What did they want?"

"Me."

Arkady stood over the stove eating bean soup out of a bowl.

"What are they planning to do about it?" he said.

"Send somebody. Tomorrow or the next day. Maybe I should try to go back to New Jersey."

"No, don't worry," Arkady said. "I won't let them get you. Did you talk to them?"

"It just went on the tape."

"Good," Arkady said. "Well done." He returned to the kitchen and refilled his bowl. "What was your father's first name?"

"Hector," Gabriel said.

"Oh," Arkady said. "He made the paper. I'm afraid he's dead."

"I thought he might be," Gabriel said.

Arkady looked at him narrowly but the boy seemed undisturbed, not even surprised at this news. "You thought right, then," Arkady said.

"Did you find out anything else today?" Gabriel said.

"Not really. I found myself a pair of sore feet, that's all." Arkady sat down on one of Larkin's straight chairs, holding a spoonful of soup reflectively in his mouth.

"This could use something," he said. "I'm not sure what."

"There wasn't any meat around," Gabriel said. "We used to make it with chorizo."

"But I don't eat meat," Arkady said. He put the bowl on the floor. "Maybe I should eat a little though. With social workers coming around, and everything like that."

*

Nightmares revolved through Arkady's sleep, with Larkin's dim image passing constantly through them all, sometimes benevolent, sometimes the reverse. He awoke too early, cold and stiff and quite uneasy. Gabriel still slept. Arkady got coffee and listened to the whole of Larkin's message tape, with the volume turned down so as not to awaken the boy. There was no real clue to Larkin's current whereabouts. The tape ended with some social worker's bureaucratic whine, and Arkady crossly shut it off. He did not want to spend another day combing the city, but what else was there to do? He found his coat and went quietly out of the loft and down the stairs.

Ten minutes later he stood in the center of a North Seventh Street meat market, surrounded by flesh in every edible permutation: beef, pork, chicken, lamb, turkey, hamburger, salami, knockwurst . . . no fish, though. Also, on a steel track fixed to the ceiling, there hung several whole sheep, eviscerated but not yet skinned. Arkady selected the fattest of these and lifted it off its hook.

"That's not ready to go yet," said the white-aproned man at the cash register.

"It's ready enough for me," Arkady said.

"If you say so," the butcher said. "It'll cost you." He named a figure. Arkady set down the carcass, which slumped chilly against his leg, and took a checkbook from his coat.

"We don't take checks," the butcher said.

"But from me you'll take a check," Arkady said. He smiled very broadly, eyes vanishing into slits, white teeth emerging from his beard. "Can't you see what a good customer I'm going to be?"

Arkady walked back down Bedford Avenue with the sheep slung across his shoulders, his arms clamped down over its legs. The few people abroad in the streets so early stopped to stare after him as he passed. When he reached Larkin's building he carried the carcass directly to the roof and dropped it there, then returned to the street. There he found an oil drum doing duty as a garbage can and dumped it out and carried it upstairs.

Gabriel was awakened by the noise of the hacksaw. Arkady was cutting the oil drum vertically in half.

"What are you doing?" Gabriel said. "I thought you went to look for Larkin again."

"I was going to," Arkady said, making the final cut, "but I changed my mind." He picked up the two halves of the drum and left the loft. Gabriel dressed and followed him up to the roof. Arkady had put the two sections of drum together like a trough and was laying a fire along the bottom of it. As Gabriel watched, he turned to the sheep and began to skin it.

"What are you doing?" Gabriel said again.

"I'm going to cook this sheep," Arkady said. "Then I'm going to eat it. You can have some, if you want."

"Oh," Gabriel said. "Do you need anything?"

"Yes," Arkady said. "I do, as a matter of fact. Why don't you run out to the store and pick up about ten heads of garlic."

When the boy returned, the sheep was flayed and Arkady had quartered it. Without speaking he began to peel garlic cloves and push them into shallow incisions he made in the meat with the point of his knife, topping them off with handfuls of coarse salt. As he prepared each section he laid it across the drum above the fire. Fat dripped and a rich plume of smoke began to rise.

"You're drawing a crowd," Gabriel said. He had gone to the edge of the roof and was peering over. Arkady also went to look. A crowd of Hispanic people had indeed begun to gather, in a semicircle spreading into Broadway, and were staring up at the roof. A few began to catcall when they saw Arkady, who waved at them dismissively and turned away.

"I hope the Fire Department doesn't come," Gabriel said. He was feeling the tar beside the oil drum, which had got warm and sticky.

"I wouldn't worry," Arkady said. "It can't be any hotter than the sun." He squatted over the sheepskin and began to scrape it with the knife.

"We'll make a sheepskin coat," he explained. "Or maybe a little blanket."

For the next few hours he rotated the joints of meat over

the fire, as Gabriel sat quietly and watched. The smell of meat and garlic became overwhelming. Arkady turned the sheepskin fleece side down and began setting the meat out on top of it.

"Eat," he said. "Eat. Let's have some shashlik." He handed the knife to Gabriel and sat down.

Gabriel cut a slice from one of the shoulders and began to eat it, holding the meat at his fingertips. "It's good," he said.

"Of course," Arkady said. "I don't know why I didn't think of it sooner." He picked up a leg as if it were a chicken wing and bit into it hugely. Within a few minutes he was flinging away the bone. Gabriel sat back from the fire, eyes goggling. Arkady removed his coat, his shirt, and his shoes. There was a thick pelt of black hair all over his upper body, which even covered his arms and back. He picked up a shoulder and began to gnaw.

"Aren't you cold?" Gabriel said.

"No," Arkady said, with a little juice running from the corner of his mouth. "Meat warms the blood."

"I don't believe it," Gabriel said somewhat later. Bones were scattered all over the roof around Arkady, who sat in lotus position with his belly expanding over his knees. "You ate a whole sheep."

"Except the head," Arkady said agreeably. "It's good for you. Changes the metabolism."

"I bet," Gabriel said. "What does it do to you?"

"It makes me fierce," Arkady said. He beat his chest and roared, then began to laugh quite merrily.

"Mr. Larkin? Clarence Larkin?" A voice was calling up from the street. Arkady's face became instantly grave. He got up with some effort and went to the edge of the roof. The crowd that had collected earlier was still in place, and in the center of the ring, before the entrance door, stood a balding man in a blue suit, holding a clipboard.

"Oh, look at that," Arkady said. "What do we have here but a fuzzy-headed little social worker with a clipboard. Trying to locate himself on the map of the universe." He came back to the middle of the roof and picked up the roasted sheep's head.

"What are you going to do?" Gabriel said.

"I'm going to give him this sheep's head."

"You think you should do that?"

"Why not?" Arkady said. "It's got eyes, it's got brains. It's a delicacy. I was going to have it for dessert." He put the sheep's head under one arm and padded barefoot down the stairs.

"Clarence Larkin?" the man in the blue suit said. "Are you Clarence Larkin?"

Arkady walked out on the doorstep. When the social worker looked up from his clipboard, they were nose to nose.

"NO!" Arkady bellowed. "I'M NOT LARKIN! WERE YOU LOOKING FOR LARKIN?"

"Well, yes, I was," the social worker said, backing up several steps onto the sidewalk. Arkady advanced, teeth gleaming, face smeared with lamb tallow, ursine hair bristling all over his body.

"BUT THAT'S WONDERFUL!" Arkady roared. "I WAS LOOKING FOR HIM TOO! YOU FIND HIM, YOU BE SURE AND LET ME KNOW, OKAY?"

The social worker retreated into the street, looking nervously over his shoulder at the crowd which watched and waited, silent now. Arkady followed. Out from behind his back came the sheep's head.

"Actually," the social worker said. "Actually, I was looking for a child."

"WELL YOU WON'T ACTUALLY FIND ONE HERE!" Arkady screamed. "IS THIS A PLACE FOR CHILDREN? THERE ARE NO CHILDREN HERE!"

People in the crowd had begun to clap and stamp their feet.

"No," the social worker said, backpedalling farther. "I suppose not."

"YOU SUPPOSE CORRECTLY!" Arkady shouted, his diaphragm slamming back and forth like a gigantic bellows. "WE DON'T WANT YOU TO THINK YOU CAME OUT

HERE FOR NOTHING THOUGH! HAVE THIS!" Arkady presented the sheep's head with both hands. "GO ON! TAKE IT! ENJOY IT!"

The social worker broke through the crowd and ran for his car. Once behind the wheel, he glanced back once in utter disbelief before he popped his clutch and drove away. Arkady fell to his knees, dropping the sheep's head on the pavement. He wanted to laugh but had no breath to spare for it. The crowd continued to stamp and clap. Arkady knelt, gasping, looking down at the sheep's head with its thick lolling tongue. After a moment he picked it up and went back into the building.

64
The Firebird

THROUGHOUT THE AFTERNOON and evening Arkady lay on his back beside the stove, with his head turned to one side, watching the windows go dark. Every so often Gabriel came over to feed the fire. The sheep's head reposed in front of the stove door, but Arkady showed no interest in it whatsoever.

Some little while after darkness had fallen a soft knock came on the door.

"Get that, would you?" Arkady said. "I don't think I can get up."

Gabriel opened the door and the Sparrow sidled in. Arkady turned his head the other way and noted that he had changed back to his accustomed loose brown garments. There was a brown paper sack hanging from one of the Sparrow's hands.

"You'd better introduce yourselves," Arkady said. "I'm not quite up to it."

"I'm Gabriel."

"The Sparrow," the Sparrow said. He went into the kitchen and got a glass, came back and sat down at one of the work tables. He poured a greenish fluid from the sack into the glass and put the sack down on the table.

"What's that," Arkady said.

"Pernod."

"I thought people put water in that."

"So I hear," the Sparrow said. He drank the glass down and held the sack with the bottle in it toward Arkady.

"I don't think so," Arkady said. "I've been overindulging."

The Sparrow glanced briefly at the sheep's head.

"What's the occasion?"

"It's a feast day. Theophany."

"A minor feast."

"Well, I had a major one," Arkady said, groaning. "Maybe I should have gone to church instead. Maybe I should pray. Find me a Bible, somebody. We'll read the text for the day."

Gabriel discovered a Bible in a stack of paper beneath one of the tables and fetched it to Arkady, who held it over his head like a tent as he searched for the passage.

" 'I therefore so run, not as uncertainly,' " he read aloud; " 'so fight I, not as one that beateth the air:

" 'But I keep under my body, and bring it into subjection: lest that by any means, when I have preached to others, I myself should be a castaway.' " He closed the Bible and set it down beside him, away from the stove.

"I think I came across that one too late," Arkady said. "My body won't be under subjection for the rest of the week." He closed his eyes and sighed.

The Sparrow smoked a cigarette and drank another glass of Pernod more slowly. Then he strolled over to Larkin's radio and began to try to tune in a distant jazz station in Newark. There was a click of a key in the lock and Larkin walked into the room.

"*Christos voskres,*" Larkin said. Arkady sat up suddenly and clutched his stomach.

"You're quite a bit early," he said. "It's Theophany, not Easter."

"I haven't been paying attention," Larkin said.

"Well," Arkady said. *"Voistinu voskres,* then. I'd been looking for you."

"It's a popular pastime," Larkin said. "Don't ask me why. The people who found me so far haven't liked it very much." He went into the kitchen and drank a large quantity of water directly from the tap. Then he came back into the center of the loft and stood looking uncertainly down at the floor. After a moment he took off his coat. The Sparrow lifted the bottle of Pernod out of the sack and showed it to him. Larkin shook his head. There were small red blisters broken out all over his face.

"You don't have smallpox, do you?" the Sparrow said.

"I've got radiation sickness," Larkin said. "I was in that Times Square thing."

"Oh," the Sparrow said, brightening with interest. "How was that?"

"Well, it wasn't the end of the world, after all," Larkin said. "It was only the end of me."

"Are you going to be okay?" Arkady said.

"I'm going to die," Larkin said with finality. "It evens out, though. I just got through killing a lot of other people. I can't complain."

Larkin sat down abruptly on the floor and dragged his fingertips across the boards. He looked over at the sheep's head, then at Arkady. "Dutch told me you were looking," he said. "So I thought I'd drop in."

"Dutch?"

"From the bar," Larkin said. He looked up at Gabriel, who had walked a little way toward him and stopped.

"I killed your father," Larkin said. "Maybe you already know that."

"I knew," Gabriel said. "I saw it."

"Yes," Larkin said. "I could tell you were there. It changed things . . . I owe you something." He looked up questioningly at the boy.

"I don't know," Gabriel said. "I don't really see you now. You're here, but you're not here."

"I'm not staying, you mean." Larkin dropped his chin to his collarbone.

"I don't think you have to be afraid," Gabriel said.

"I'm not," Larkin said. He raised his head and then stood up. "Come out, everybody," he said. "Come up to the roof, and I'll show you something."

"Like what?" Arkady said.

"Something different," Larkin said. "Something I learned from my life."

Larkin stood in his shirt-sleeves at the western edge of the roof, his back to the others, who waited in a row near the door to the stairwell, the boy in the middle. He was looking out over the river toward the walls and the lights of the city. His sleeves fluttered a little in a gathering wind.

The wind grew stronger and began to whistle. Larkin turned suddenly and walked toward the middle of the roof. He kicked some bones aside and remained standing in a crude circle defined by the bones, with his feet set apart as if he were prepared to receive a heavy weight. The wind rose further and Larkin's body trembled. He stretched out his arms and then brought them forward, palms out toward the others. Larkin smiled.

Gabriel darted forward, but Arkady caught his arm and held him back. Larkin ripped his left sleeve to the shoulder. A tendril of blue flame ran backward up his bare arm, training like a vine around the limb. When it reached his shoulder, it flared to sudden orange all across his chest. Fresh columns of fire rose from Larkin's ankles up his legs. Larkin was burning, burning at last. Great wings of flame sprang from his shoulders and folded over his face. Larkin was still smiling. Through the fire, in spite of the fire, he could see that the others had all joined hands. Larkin summoned the last remainder of his will and exploded like a falling star.

*

—*Brooklyn, 1979–1984.*

*

At the beginning of the centuries God used the mountains as nails to fix the Earth; and washed Earth's face with the water of Ocean. Then he placed Earth on the back of a bull, the bull on a fish, and the fish on the air. But on what rested the air? On nothing. But nothing is nothing — and all that is nothing. Admire then, the works of the Lord, though he himself considers them as nothing.

Farid ud-Din Attar,
The Conference of the Birds